LOVE AND DEATH IN
A PERFECT WORLD

Sharon!
Thank you so much
for celebrating with us
+ for cheering me on.
I treasure your friendship
+ love you dearly.
May 2015 bring you
all good Things. (Hope you
enjoy The book!)
Love, Barbara

BARBARA GERBER

LOVE AND DEATH IN
A PERFECT WORLD

Terra Nova Books

SANTA FE, NEW MEXICO

Terra Nova Books

Published by Terra Nova Books, Santa Fe, New Mexico.
www.TerraNovaBooks.com

ISBN 978-1-938288-46-3

For my family, both far and near

Acknowledgments

When I conceived of this novel in 2007, I had no idea what it would entail nor the degree to which I would need to rely on the generosity and expertise of others to bring it to fruition. I am fortunate beyond measure to have tremendously talented people in my life who were willing to hash out, read, and edit the many drafts of this book. Marty Gerber, Sandra Vail, Joel Dinerstein, and Sheri Sinclair—I am forever in your debt.

I am deeply grateful to my husband, Scott, for all he has done behind the scenes to launch this book, and for his abiding love; to my children, Nick and Maggie, for being wonderful people who give me faith in the future; and to the many extraordinary family members and friends who have buoyed me with their constant love and enthusiasm. May I someday return the favor.

I would like to thank Susan McMeans for her insight, Julie Cameron for her book *The Artist's Way*, and singer-songwriter Greg Brown for his infinitely inspiring music.

I would also like to thank Mark Hopko, Twentynine Palms Historical Society, the National Park Service at Joshua Tree National Park, and Twentynine Palms High School for providing some of the information in this book.

Contents

February, 1998

Prologue

ROSEMARY FRETTED IN THE TOMATO SAUCE AISLE. EACH CAN and jar presented a host of decisions to be made, but if she spent too much time shopping, Dylan would fall asleep in the car and his afternoon nap would be ruined. Then she'd be bitchy when Liam came home, and the happy shiny family time she hoped to create with this meal would be destroyed.

"Ma-ma, Ma-ma," Dylan sang, seated in the grocery cart.

"Dy-lan, Dy-lan," she sang back.

Making the sauce fresh from organic Romas would be the healthiest, but then she'd have to blanch and purée the tomatoes and cook them for hours, which would only work if Dylan took a long nap.

"Cawot!"

"Are you enjoying your carrot?"

The roasted tomatoes made the tastiest sauce, but they weren't organic, and the pesticides could give Dylan all kinds of cancer.

"Mama eat cawot?"

"Yummy carrot," she said, pretending to nibble on it.

The organic Italian tomatoes also made a good sauce, but they were packed in chemical-leaching lined cans that could give Dylan man boobs.

"Cawot!" Dylan dropped the carrot.

"Bye-bye, carrot," Rosemary said cheerily, kicking it under a shelf.

"Cawot," Dylan whimpered.

The glass jar was perfectly inert, but it was the heaviest, so it required the most fuel to get to market. A pot of sauce shouldn't have such a hefty carbon footprint.

"Cracker time!" she sang, reaching into the cart and opening a box of graham crackers.

"Cwacka," Dylan said, tucking in to his new snack.

The Everyday Savings tomatoes were packed in cans without that dreadful lining, but unlined cans could leach lead into the food. What if Dylan developed learning disabilities because of it?

"Cwacka."

And they were most certainly picked by exploited migrant workers.

"Mama kiss."

"Kiss kiss," Rosemary said, bending toward Dylan so he could smear her cheek with spit and cracker crumbs.

But they were by far the cheapest. How much should a pot of spaghetti cost, anyway?

Dylan started to stand up in the seat.

"No, Dylan, we're sitting now," she said, pushing his legs back through the chrome openings.

She and Liam had just paid for a new timing belt and brakes for the landscaping truck, so she'd have to charge these groceries. How much interest would they ultimately pay on this pot of spaghetti?

"Up!" Dylan shouted, turning to stand again.

"No." She held him in place.

Should she be practical, like her mother, and buy the Everyday Savings brand? Or should she resolutely uphold her principles, like her friend Lara, and buy the organic?

"Up!"

"No up."

She'd already chosen the organic pasta, but not the whole-wheat because that slop tasted like spackle. But shouldn't she be raising Dylan to prefer whole-grain foods?

Dylan scrambled to his feet, teetering.

"Dylan!" she barked, scooping him up and settling him on her hip.

Liam would expect meatballs, too, which would cost another five dollars for organic ground beef, or seven, if she bought the locally raised.

Dylan smacked his heels into her butt and upper thighs. When she held his right leg still, he kicked harder with his left.

But should she even buy beef? The protein was good for Dylan, but raising cattle took so much water and resources, and all those farting cows released more methane into the atmosphere every day.

"Bouncey!" Dylan demanded, pushing upward in her arms.

Rosemary bounced him on her hip as she studied the sodium content on the labels. Too much salt could strain a child's kidneys.

"Big bouncey!" Dylan squealed, meaning he wanted her to toss him and catch him.

"No big bouncey in the store." She glanced at her watch. Nearly one p.m., dangerously close to naptime.

"Big bouncey!" he shouted.

"No, Dylan. We're shopping."

"Sketti!" he yelped, pointing at the pasta shelves.

"Yes, we're having spaghetti tonight."

And when was the last time Liam cooked? Even on the weekends, it was always up to her to put on the dinnertime show.

"Sketti! Sketti!"

Liam had come to expect it, but he had no idea how much effort it took, how delicate the timing was with a toddler.

"I go down," Dylan announced, curling his torso toward the floor.

"No, no down," Rosemary said, catching him at the waist.

But she knew they couldn't afford this kind of food anyway.

"Down, Mama, down," Dylan moaned, slithering down her leg.

And why should she always spend her precious free time cooking?

"Down!"

Dylan's feet hit the floor, but Rosemary quickly clutched his overall straps.

"No, Mama!" he wailed. She put him back in the cart, grabbed a jar of Prego, and raced toward the checkout. Sobbing, he shrieked, "No, Mama! No, Mama!" as she filled her cloth bags, swiped her credit card, extracted him from the grocery cart, and wrestled him into the car seat.

But he quieted as she drove through the parking lot, which sent her into a panic.

"Dylan!" she shouted. "Remember the three little piggies?" When he looked at her with glazed eyes, she opened the windows to let the cold winter air rush in and shouted even louder.

"Dylan! Remember the piggies? What sound does the piggy make? Make the piggy sound for Mama! I'll huff and I'll puff. . . ," she began, but it was no use. He was asleep once she hit the highway, a constellation of cracker globs crusted on his tear-stained cheeks.

A familiar dread gripped Rosemary as she drove the twelve miles home from Santa Fe to Cielo Vista. She knew she could forget about thinning the bulbs in her front garden, reading a chapter of that Margaret Laurence novel she'd just begun, or even trying to salvage dinner. These twenty minutes would be her only Dylan-free time that day.

But no, she shouldn't think so negatively. It was up to her to create the life she wanted. "We are going to have a beautiful afternoon," she said aloud, envisioning Dylan's smiling face, his joyful laugh.

He woke when the car stopped in the driveway. She considered cruising around the neighborhood for an hour to keep him asleep—she'd done it before—but there wasn't much gas in the

Camry, and she couldn't handle the environmental guilt that driving-naps produced.

"My son and I are harmonious beings," she proclaimed as she slid the key out of the ignition.

Dylan jerked awake, looked around in terror, and began to whimper.

"Hey, sweetie," she cooed.

He stared at her wide-eyed.

"Did you have a dream? Don't worry, baby boy. Everything's OK. Come, sweet one. Let's go inside."

But everything was not OK, no matter how clearly she visualized and affirmed it. He fussed through the soothing music and the chamomile tea. He tossed his tiny tools when she tried to work in the garden. He climbed all over her as she lay on the rug pretending to sleep. When Liam called at 5 o'clock, the time when he should have been walking through the door, she was spent.

"Remember that I'm going to the optimist today," he said.

Goddamn it, when would he realize his little word switches hadn't been funny for years?

"You have an optometrist appointment today?"

"Yeah, remember I told you?"

"No."

"Why don't you write things down?"

"Because I always have a baby in my arms."

"And then I have to run an errand."

"For what?"

"I need to rent a rototiller for the Sanchez job."

"No, you can't. We have an outstanding balance with the rental place."

"Well why haven't we paid it?"

"Because we had to fix the truck! Remember that cool eight hundred bucks?"

"Goddamn."

"Yeah, I know."

"Well, I'll figure something out."

"Maybe they'll take Dylan as a trade."

"Ro, cut it out."

"He napped for exactly twenty minutes today."

"Sorry to hear it."

"Yeah, me too. Tell the optimist I say hi."

"What's for dinner?"

"Crap."

"OK, see you later."

Rosemary tried to amuse Dylan as she assembled a salad and set the table, but by 6 p.m. his whining had escalated into wails and she gave up. The day was beyond salvaging. She slipped the well-worn "Frog and Toad" tape into the VCR and watched in wonder and disgust as he calmed down and smiled for the first time in hours. She had devoted every waking moment to this kid all day—every day for the past seventeen months, actually—but evidently that wasn't enough. And here she was again in her crappy living room with the crappy furniture, waiting for Liam to come home so she could look at him also in wonder and disgust and debate whether or not he was a crappy husband. Another day gone by, and for what? She was young yet—just twenty-eight—and she clearly was no good at this. She had expected—and affirmed!—something quite different for her life. So what had gone wrong?

She thought of the Toyota in the driveway and the Visa card in her wallet that still had plenty of available credit. Maybe it was time to cut her losses.

CHAPTER 1 | SEPTEMBER, 1982

Twentynine Palms, California

ROSEMARY SABIN LAY SLEEPLESS IN BED ON THE NIGHT OF her thirteenth birthday. There was so much to think about, so much to worry over. This mental debrief, more overwrought and breathless than usual, was after her party at the Luckie Park pool, after the pizza and cake, after her brother had been nice to her for a change, after her mother had fooled everyone into thinking she was normal, and after her dad had managed to hide his disappointment that her favorite gift was a pair of beaded flip flops and not the fish tank he'd surprised her with.

As the Santa Ana winds lashed the house, she replayed the party in her mind, an afternoon of buzzing, glittering sensual delight. There was the swimming, with the boys vying to carry the girls on their shoulders one minute and grabbing at their legs underwater the next. There was the giggling with the girls, the dizzying, bright desert sun, and the whooshing feeling of cool quiet when she plunged to the bottom of the deep end. But most importantly there was that kiss. Jimmy Werner's saliva tasted like popcorn and he'd mashed his lips savagely against hers, but it was still a kiss. And it had unleashed a longing deep in her pelvis that stirred every time she relived those moments.

Too agitated for sleep, she removed her nightgown, turned on the bedside lamp, and stared at herself in the full-length mirror. There they were—those boobs. She was not yet curvaceous, not yet regular in what her mother called "the monthlies," but it was all about the boobs, it seemed. They'd grown up out of nowhere last spring. She'd hated them at first—they were pointy and made lying on her stomach uncomfortable. But those early-growth boobs, sprouting round and full when most of the other girls were still flat-chested, had been her ticket into the new world she now struggled to navigate. And now that she was in, she resolved never to go back. She remembered her twelfth birthday, when she had managed to scare up just one friend, Sheila, to come over for her birthday dinner of spareribs, mashed potatoes, and cole slaw. But this year there were three boys and five girls at her party, and they were all popular kids. No, there would be no turning back.

She slipped her nightgown back on and looked into the new fish tank. Rainbow tetras and zebra danios flit among the plastic plants, moving together in tiny schools. A cory poked among the green and blue gravel. A freshwater shrimp—she'd already named him Shylock—stood against the brilliant background picture of a coral reef like an extra on a movie set. Did he know he was in a tank? Or did he think this tank was the world? She'd begged for a fish tank in sixth grade, after Sheila had bred tadpoles for the science fair. But now—well, the tank was nice, but it was just there. Or rather, here. In this place. And she was tired of this place.

The world was elsewhere, she had recently discovered. The world was at school, at the handball courts, at the stores, at friends' houses—the places where others confirmed that you existed. The world was the people who told you who to like and what to want. She used to feel safe at home, but now she felt safe out there. At home you could drift, dissipate. At home, if you weren't careful, you could morph into something unrecognizable to the people in the world, the people you needed so badly, and then where would you be? The world had moved, and she had moved with it.

As she watched the shrimp step delicately over a ceramic deep-sea diver, she recalled with a vague shame her former self, her old inconsequential, forgettable self. Back then she would say whatever came into her head with no regard for what others would think. She would blithely tell her peers that she loved spinach, that she wanted to be a marine biologist, that her dad was her best friend. She wore sweat pants to school, paid no attention to her hair, and read books at lunch. She showed genuine interest in her schoolwork and teachers openly praised her. It was horrible.

Well, actually, it was fine until the boys who had been her friends started fawning over horrible girls. It all started with Joseph, with whom she had spent hundreds of summer days swimming and riding bikes. Last winter, instead of playing four square with Rosemary at recess, he began hovering around that awful Amanda Tildon, with her blue eyeliner and Billy Idol T-shirts. Seemingly overnight, wearing his brother's ratty jeans and clutching a portable cassette player, Joseph was too cool to even look at Rosemary, much less spend time with her. And the same thing happened with Carlo. They used to play chess at lunch with Mr. Dreyfus, but now Carlo hung around a cluster of stupid girls who did nothing but yell "Shut up!" and punch him whenever he said some nonsensical thing.

But at the end of sixth grade, everything changed. She recalled the moment precisely: She was helping her favorite teacher, Miss Othmar, decorate the gym for the sixth-grade dance. Standing on a ladder with a roll of orange streamers in her hand, she'd had to reach up to tape the crinkly paper to the wall. Her loose cotton blouse moved with her, and suddenly Matt Straub was standing beneath her, leaning on the ladder and looking up as if she were a saint performing a miracle. That night in the gym, as she drank Cokes and watched people dance to REO Speedwagon, Matt found a hundred reasons to be near her, and suddenly the engine of her popularity roared to life.

She eased the bedroom door open and slipped into the living room. The house was silent except for the refrigerator's hum and the wind buffeting the house from the east. Knick-knacks on the front windowsill stood in garish silhouette against the moonlit night. Rosemary unlatched the front door and crept outside, instinctively closing her eyes against the windborne grit. The desert night was cold, but when the Santa Anas gusted warm, it was like pouring a cup of hot tea into a gallon of iced, creating a swirling of dry heat and chill that was pleasantly disorienting.

When the blast of air abated, she gazed up at the black sky and found Orion. Miss Othmar had told her that although he was "The Hunter" to the Greeks, many different cultures had attached stories to the constellation. The story of the Yokuts, one of California's native tribes, had something to do with the footprints of the god of the flea people, who was chasing after his wives. They'd left him because he made them itch.

See? That was exactly what she needed to quit doing, quoting her teachers and being such a hopeless dweeb.

As the hot Mojave air gusted again, Rosemary yanked her nightgown up to her neck and let the wind rush against her tender skin. With her eyes squeezed shut and her feet fixed like a backyard swing set in Qwikrete, she stood firm against the power of the wind. No, there would be no screw-ups, no turning back to stupid, lonely Rosemary. Like the good-service pledge at her favorite local diner, she resolved to do Whatever It Takes.

CHAPTER 2 | MARCH, 1985

Morongo Valley, California

ROSEMARY CUPPED HER HANDS AROUND THE BLUE PLASTIC bong, pressed her lips to the smoke-filled tube, and inhaled deeply. A rush of harsh, damp smoke filled her lungs, and she immediately expelled it, coughing loudly and doubling over on the mounded soil along Amboy Road.

"Hey, babe," Pete said laughing. He ran his fingers through her long, wavy hair. "Pick up your lung, babe. It's not polite to leave your organs all over the place."

Rosemary laughed and concentrated on not coughing. At sixteen, she was getting a little better at it. She took a small hit and held the smoke in for a few moments, feeling the familiar whoosh in her brain as the pot began to do its work. She exhaled slowly and passed the water pipe to Alejandra.

"Rosa Maria," Alejandra said, lowering her mouth to the bong. "You're a freak."

Clumps of teens, shivering in the spring night, dotted the earthen berms along Amboy Road, south of Route 66 and just north of Twentynine Palms, the gateway to Joshua Tree National Monument. The fact that climbers came from around the world to sling ropes and pound caribiners into JT's massive outcroppings of granite and gneiss thoroughly mystified Rosemary. The park, down there past a few dull houses and miles of dried up salt lake beds, seemed to her just another slab of desert like the one she lived on every brown, scratchy day.

Twentynine Palms, a town with fourteen thousand souls and one traffic light, lay deep in the Mojave Desert, parked atop a bed of arid soil that could support little more than cactus and scrubby trees. Buffeted by hot, gritty winds, rich in sun and poor in water, the town had a way of seeming illusory to Rosemary, a fact confirmed by the signs out by the chloride plant that read DRIFTING SAND. It seemed to her that if the entire populace took a vacation at the same time, the town would granulate and blow away into the desert wind without a sound.

Rosemary, Pete, Alejandra, and Omar, zipped into hooded sweatshirts and denim jackets, had already gathered a heap of rocks. They planned to spell out in stones the name of Pete's band, Flavor Pack, on the dirt embankments that lined the highway. The earthen berms, low ridges of soil originally mounded for erosion control, were stone-studded with messages written by generations of bored teen-agers. Many of these messages were cryptic—some thoroughly indecipherable—but most were clear to anyone who could read at 75 MPH: Class of '81. Joey and Berta 4ever. Disco sucks. Shoot the hippies. Fuck the Marines. Eat shit Owen." Miles and miles of messages written with stones pressed into soil. To write new messages, you just collected stones from old, forgotten messages.

"See?" Rosemary said as they gathered the stones. "Even the graffiti in this town erodes away."

Kids had hung out along that stretch of highway forever, although Rosemary's dad, a sheriff's deputy, had warned her repeatedly to steer clear of it. "It's what the loser kids do," he'd said. "You are not a loser kid." Of course, Deputy Sabin didn't know everything. All the kids hung out on Amboy Road, except maybe a few who didn't have access to cars, or the lucky fewer who could hang out in the comfort of their own tract homes because their parents were cool enough to pretend they didn't smell pot smoke. But really, all the kids hung there, just in different areas, and all careful to stick with their assigned group and acceptable means of intoxication. The jocks pounded Coors or Bud cans, drama students passed around gallon bottles of Almaden Red, hippie throwbacks had their Ziploc baggies of Mexican weed, computer geeks carried flasks of cheap vodka, wannabees drank wine coolers, and the occasional wild man or bearded artist might have a tattered piece of waxed paper folded around a cluster of magic mushrooms that looked like dog turds.

Rosemary had made her debut on the berms just a few months earlier with her bitchy friend Bernadette. It seemed like a lifetime ago, and she remembered clearly how awkward those first nights were. You had to be seen there, and you had to be perceived as having a good time. So they would sit and drink their wine coolers and laugh loudly at their own unfunny comments. They kept up a constant vigilance, their heads rotating like sonar pulses, gathering data on which kids from Twenty-nine Palms High School were present that night, who they were with, and whether they seemed to be having a better time than Rosemary and Bernadette.

But Rosemary had observed that a choice few—fish who could swim in all seas—managed to bypass the strict groupings. They might wander up and down the highway, happening onto berms as they chose and talking with whoever looked or sounded interesting.

Rosemary had seen Pete Dean, a senior, do that fish-in-all-seas thing many times. He would carry a guitar and sometimes stop to sing songs. Amazingly, some kids would know the words and sing along, even getting emotionally worked up at certain parts. This would baffle Rosemary, who could barely think of anything to say to the other tenth-grade wannabees shivering on the berms. She would steal glances at her watch, try not to think about how badly she needed to pee, and look forward to going home so she could lie to her parents about where she had been.

But one night Pete sauntered up to Rosemary and said, "Hey, what's up?" His dark hair fell perfectly to his shoulders, framing his unshaven face. A string of wooden beads ringed his neck and his green eyes seemed to radiate a deep knowing. Suddenly in the presence of a kingfish, Rosemary stammered, "Nothing." He nodded and wandered away. Rosemary looked after him, a warm quickening spreading through her chest.

"Yo, Ro," Bernadette said, shoving her shoulder into Rosemary's. "He just said hello 'cause he thinks you're pretty, not 'cause you're cool."

"I know!" Rosemary shot back, suddenly mortified.

"Yeah, right," Bernadette responded sullenly, sliding a tissue from under her jacket sleeve to blow her nose for the umpteenth time that night.

"Why don't you take medicine for that?" Rosemary snapped.

"I told you, brainless," Bernadette shot back. "Allergy meds make me drowsy."

Suddenly exasperated, Rosemary stepped away from Bernadette and tried to follow Pete with her eyes.

"Oh, please," Bernadette said, wiping her nose on her sleeve. "Give it up."

But the visitations continued, and soon Rosemary grew to expect them. Pete's attention, however, required a personal overhaul. She quit returning Bernadette's phone calls and avoided her at school—she was so uncool. She started paying attention to her brother Deet's album collection, studying the lyrics so she could sing along to the Bob Dylan and Grateful Dead songs Pete played. She even read liner notes so she could drop an occasional name. "Oh yeah, Russ Kunkel played drums on that track," she'd say, and Pete would nod approvingly.

Rosemary learned to never talk about school. Even putting down a teacher was not cool—better to pretend none of it even existed. She bought tight jeans and a short jacket. She quit buying wine coolers and learned to always carry gum, eye drops, and a Coke bottle full of water to stave off cotton mouth.

Soon she learned how to be a girlfriend, too, which really wasn't that difficult if you knew how to watch and listen. She learned to be agreeable, to go with the flow. Being mellow was of utmost importance—never be a buzzkill, and when you have a complaint or an original thought, release it slowly, like a leak from an air mattress.

She soon adopted this way of being around her parents. She mastered the art of the nonchalant response and even began to spend more time in the living room, knowing that to be secretive or sullen would invite her parents' scrutiny. But while her friends seemed to always be fighting with their parents, she found that Mark and Martina just became increasingly irrelevant to her. She had a soft spot in her heart for her dad, who really could be cool sometimes, but her mom was so bland and dry, like a slice of Wonder bread left out on the counter for too long. Often in her stoned musings she would wonder how a person could become so very small and boxed in, so automatic in her responses, so invisible.

Being Pete's girlfriend opened up many doors for Rosemary, beyond the sweet elixir of popularity. She was surprised to learn that even if you did things only because you couldn't come up with a reason not to, those actions could yield interesting results. Like the night she pretended to be sleeping at Alejandra's house but really stayed out all night at Indian Canyons with Pete—who knew the desert was so beautiful at sunrise? And the night she, Pete, and a car full of friends drove down to Salton Sea and dared each other to swim in that salty sink of a "lake"—who knew she could feel so free?

But there was one night that turned out to matter a whole lot. It began as a lark like all the others, but soon became a sort of bellwether. An acquaintance of Pete's, a drummer everyone called Grace Dog, had convinced them to go to a drumming circle out in the desert somewhere off the road to Searchlight, Nevada. "It's just a bunch of crazy people banging on drums in the desert—pure joy," was how he described it.

Grace Dog, at twenty-one, had a full beard and a job in the town library. "You have no idea how cool a library really is," he maintained. "All sorts of folks come in to research stuff you wouldn't believe." Grace Dog never drank, claiming that alcohol was poison, but he always had something to smoke. So they drove out there, listening to Grace Dog explain how public libraries were the last bastions of freedom in the U.S. and how the time was coming when the civil liberties of Americans would be drastically curtailed.

"Mark my words," he said ominously, "there are dark days ahead." Pete turned to Rosemary and rolled his eyes as Grace Dog rambled on about Benjamin Franklin and John Locke and why he was so careful to drive the speed limit. "Trust me, you do not want to get into the system, man," he explained. "You just stay under all their radar. What I wish is that my parents never got me a social security number. Man, I wish I could be out, totally out, of all this crap." When Grace Dog launched into a rant about how the government's decision to drop the Gold Standard was the beginning of the end, Pete mouthed, "I'm sorry" to Rosemary and stared out the window like a sullen child.

As soon as they stepped out of the car, they heard the drums, distant but insistent, like a gathering storm. As she collected her jacket and water bottle, Grace Dog pressed something into her hand, like a grandmother slipping ice cream money to a child.

"Don't chew it too much," he said. "Swallow it fast and chase it with water."

"What is this?" Rosemary asked, straining to see the dry, scratchy lump in the waning light.

"It's magic!" Grace Dog answered. "But just a tiny piece— just enough to hear the drums in a new way." Rosemary quickly chewed the tiny mushroom stem and chased it with water.

"I'll pass," Pete said, handing his piece back to Grace Dog. Rosemary panicked. Why didn't Pete want to take the mushroom? Should she have declined too? Was something wrong? She searched his face for a clue.

"I'm just not in the mood," he said with a shrug.

"That's cool," Grace Dog replied and popped Pete's piece into his mouth as well.

They followed the sound through the cool, still night for about a half-mile to a small circular clearing ringed by rock. Rosemary was astounded to find about thirty people there, each with a drum of some kind or a shaker full of beads or something to scrape on something else to make a sound that chased the rhythm. In the center was a fire, blazing under the black sky, and in its light were faces—faces that smiled and faces with their eyes closed and faces that stared into the fire, entranced. To her surprise, when Grace Dog plunked a drum in front of her, she joined in. And she stayed there for hours, drumming, drumming, drumming. Sometimes she fit herself into the rhythm going 'round and sometimes she pioneered a new one. Sometimes she drummed quietly within a pattern and sometimes she pounded loudly. Pete drifted in and out of the circle and eventually she stopped noticing him. Finally he nudged her, reminding her of her curfew, and they all walked silently back to Grace Dog's car.

But nothing was the same. The smooth ridge of a rivet on her denim jacket was so very smooth. The feel of Sprite against her lips was so intriguing that she forgot to swallow. The sound of fighter jets overhead, common in a town so close to a Marine training base, was jarring, almost frightening. She longed to lie down on the ground and sleep there in the desert, still hearing the drums, still smelling the fire, but she got into the car and they drove back to Twentynine Palms.

When they reached the house, she appraised it with a critical eye. It looked so small, so limited. Was this the sum total of her parents' lives? Was this all her dad worked for?

Pete kissed her lightly and said, "Sweet dreams."

After she closed the car door, Grace Dog reached through the open window, clasped her hands, and looked into her eyes. "Awesome to spend time with you, Rosie," he said.

"Thank you," she replied, holding his gaze for several seconds. Then she made her way to the front door.

❧　❧　❧

Martina heard the car pull up in front of the house just as a new skit began on "The Carol Burnett Show." It was one of those funny-sad installments of "The Family," with Carol Burnett as Eunice, Betty White as her snarling sister, and Vicki Lawrence as their angry, perpetually dissatisfied mother. These skits always made Martina wonder how different her life might have been had her brother not died at twenty-three and her mother at forty-two. Evidently the world was full of husbands who barely tolerated their mothers-in-law, of sibling rivalries that were never put to rest, and of women who struggled for years to keep everyone happy. But these issues had simply passed her by. Her own in-laws were rarely around, and she had no extended family of her own.

But it was hard enough being a parent to her own children, two teenagers who had somehow written her off years earlier though they all still lived in the same house and spoke politely to each other. How had they slipped away so quickly? One day she was the center of their worlds and the next they were smiling through lies and making plans that did not include her. It was like those old black-and-white movies in biology class— one moment the cell was whole unto itself, and the next it was divided and divided and divided again. The cells were related to each other, but separate, and no one seemed to mind—except Martina. Her husband, Mark, told her to be patient, that it was a natural phase in the life of a family, but it made her worried and sad. What if she died young, before they all came to their senses? It all seemed so unnecessary, this elaborate dance of separateness. She believed she should be able to transform the relationships, to find just the right thing to say to have everyone let down their guard and be truly together again. But those perfect words never came.

A car door slammed, a sound different from a van door sliding shut, which meant that her daughter was not getting out of her boyfriend's vehicle. She would never know who Rosemary had spent the evening with, nor what she had done that night. The girl routinely lied, even when she didn't need to. Honestly, these kids seemed to think they'd invented drinking and kissing and driving fast, as if everyone who came before had spent their Saturday nights playing Scrabble.

How could it be that every generation of human beings believed it was original? Maybe it was part of the life cycle, like learning to walk, or to scramble an egg. Everyone had to learn things anew. She remembered the day Rosemary proudly showed how she'd discovered a way to keep summer tops and sundresses from falling off hangers: "Look, I bent the ends of the hangers up, so now the clothes don't slide off!" Millions of women had been doing that for years upon years, and Martina's own closet was full of hangers with their ends bent upward, but to Rosemary, it was all new. In that moment, Martina realized it would continue this way for the rest of her life—she would watch her children discover marriage, careers, parenting—even aging—anew. But was someone watching her? Her mother had been dead for twenty years, and her grandmother had also died young. Soon she would outlive them both. She sighed a familiar sigh—she was supposed to be a link in a chain of women, but the upward links of that chain were gone, and the lower link fancied herself to be the first link ever.

❧ ❧ ❧

Rosemary hoped to make it to her room without answering any questions, but her mother was on the couch watching a rerun of "The Carol Burnett Show."

"Quick, come quick!" Martina chirped, waving Rosemary in as she closed the front door. Her mother was wearing a thin powder-blue robe and white socks. The blue seemed to glow so intensely in the living room's low light that her mother's face was gray in comparison. "This is our favorite skit. With Eunice, remember? They're playing Sorry!" She barely looked up at Rosemary, a departure from her usual tendency to train her attention on her daughter like a searchlight. Rosemary sat down on the couch and looked toward the TV.

Carol Burnett and Vicki Lawrence were glaring at each other in a garish fake kitchen. One of them said something in a shrieky voice and the canned laughter erupted, a grating sound after the whooshing of the wind outdoors. Rosemary felt immediately repulsed but continued to stare, like an onlooker at an accident scene. Those actresses were pretending to be people—people in pain, family members who never listened to each other and were never honest with each other and harbored years of pent-up frustration. Here they were taking jabs at each other, and people were laughing.

Her mother, covering her mouth with her hand, also laughed, but it sounded like a burp. Now that was funny. Rosemary snickered and Martina said, "Oh my goodness, those ladies are funny." As the applause crescendoed, the screen flickered to a scene of a blonde woman in a black leotard lifting her leg up and down on a mat. Then she was on a beach, and there was a close-up of her butt in a pink bikini. Then she was back in the black leotard and there were large numbers on the screen.

"How was your evening?" Martina asked.

Oh yes, this was a commercial, for an exercise product, and she was expected to turn away from it. But it was even more compelling than the show. Faster, more lurid.

"Rosemary," Martina said, nudging her daughter's knee. "How was your evening?"

Rosemary forced herself to turn from the TV. "Nice," she said. "We met up with a few of Pete's friends and had dinner at Armando's. Then we went bowling."

"Out to dinner again? I don't understand where Pete gets the money to take you out so much. He doesn't seem to have a job."

"He's a musician, remember? His band gets paid to perform."

The show was on again, so they turned their attention back to the TV. A woman was on stage now, in a gold sequined gown that reflected so much light that she looked like a glowworm against the royal blue curtain. Then she sang sweetly into the microphone, and her face was huge on the screen. Her voice was clear and lovely, but then her eyebrows arched and her face looked like a cadaver molded into the expression *sad*. Then her face changed to *wistful,* and soon she was a full-body glowworm again, and the voice got louder and her face filled the screen again, only now the dial seemed to be set on *triumphant.* Rosemary was incredulous. Was this really what Martina and millions of other people thought was real and good and worth watching? She glanced over at Martina, who was engrossed in the performance, and then back to the screen. It was ridiculous, total bullshit. The audience clapped in approval, and then there was a scene with Harvey Korman and a short guy. Oh, now this was supposed to be funny again.

She stood up and kissed her mother's cheek. "I'm going to bed, Mom. Good night," she said.

"So soon? You used to love this show."

Did she? Really?

"Well, I'm tired, good night."

"Good night, hon," Martina said, her eyes returning to the screen.

❧   ❧   ❧

Dinner at Armando's—a restaurant that was closed for renovations all month long. Honestly, the girl could at least do some basic research before lying to her mother. But Martina instantly forgave her. Clearly, Rosemary wanted privacy, and as long as she was safe, Martina could live with that. Of course, she routinely checked through Rosemary's room—reading notes from girlfriends, birthday cards from Pete, the scribbles in the margins of her daughter's school notebooks. She had a clear line in her mind of which lies were "white" and which were dark and sinister. She could handle this. She was sure her daughter was OK.

❧   ❧   ❧

In the bathroom, Rosemary drank water from her cupped palm and then looked into the mirror with intense curiosity.

Her dark hair was untidy, and her mascara had run. Her pupils were a bit dilated, but her irises—now they were mesmerizing. She had always disliked her brown eyes—they'd seemed dull and colorless compared to Pete's green eyes, and her brother's blue. But suddenly they were deep and mysterious, like the desert night. She removed her makeup and washed her face, and was now even more taken with her eyes. Were everyone's eyes so amazing? Why had she been hiding them with makeup? They were perfect just as they were. With the sound of the TV persisting from the living room, she opened a window to hear the sounds of the night and was struck with the difference. Why would anyone choose that noisy bullshit when they could hear wind and leaves rustling instead? But even the quiet of the bathroom was not really quiet: There was still a hum—the light. She turned it off and gripped the cool vanity. Yes, that was better.

Rosemary felt her way out the door, down the hall, and into her bedroom, where she clicked on the bedside lamp. In its soft light she gazed about her room, at the stuffed animals, the checked curtains, a bird figurine, posters of rock bands, certificates from school, a miniature porcelain tea set, a pile of flip-flops. She moved thoughtfully from one item to the next, scrutinizing everything as she applied a new metric: Was it real, or was it bullshit? Jim Morrison and the Doors were posing for the camera, so that poster was bullshit, but the picture of Jerry Garcia was candid, so that was real. The stuffed blue dog, grabbed with a claw in a plastic booth at Armando's, was bullshit, but her well-loved Raggedy Ann doll was real. The fuzzy yellow area rug, with its synthetic fibers and plasticky backing, was bullshit; the tiny Navajo rug, a souvenir from a long-ago trip to New Mexico—that was real.

She ran her hand along the surface of the dresser, which she and her dad had painted together a few years earlier. The body of it was white with the drawers each painted fluorescent orange, lime green, and sky blue. Rosemary was suddenly drawn to a corner of the dresser where the paint had been damaged and a bit of pine showed through. She scraped away a little more paint with her thumbnail and was captivated by the wood's beauty. It was so quiet, so simple, an island of reality adrift on a fake sea. But just beyond the exposed circle, the pine was still trapped beneath the high-gloss paint. The wood was suffocating! How could she have been a party to this? This paint, it had to go, and it was urgent—the wood needed to be free. So she scraped it away with her thumbnail, thrilling as the patch of wood expanded, marveling that it seemed to shine brighter as it grew, like a nature preserve in the middle of a city.

As the pile of paint peelings also grew, her thumb was raw and aching. Soon she realized she could not free the wood that night. It was a bigger project, needing tools, drop cloths, and cans of whatever chemicals her dad had in the garage. She smoothed the spot lovingly with her hand, promising to return, and slid a ballerina music box over the spot. Then she turned to look at the rest of her room. This she could do.

When Martina knocked on her door an hour later, Rosemary was hard pressed to explain why there was a laundry basket in the middle of the room heaped with stuffed animals, knickknacks, clothing, and memorabilia.

"I was in the mood to clean," she said. "But now I really am going to bed." She switched off the light, leaving her perplexed mother in the doorway.

Rosemary climbed into bed imagining what a life without bullshit would be like. Scenes clicked through her mind like the frames of a Viewmaster: a cabin in the woods, a Japanese bath, a bowl of steaming soup, an acoustic guitar, a mountain stream, a sleeping cat, a garden bed, a barefoot child running through a grassy field. She lay awake for hours, imagining herself as an artist, a healer, a nun, a baker, a mother, a teacher, a farmer's wife—in the mountains, in the desert, in a small town in Spain, the alleys of Bombay, a fishing village in Mexico. She walked through scenarios and envisioned personas as if she were trying on cloaks from a rack.

But what were the criteria for Real and Bullshit? This she never truly determined, and had no way of knowing that this imprecise metric would stay with her for decades, informing her decisions in ways she could not fathom.

Chapter 3 | April, 1985

Eisenhower Medical Center, Rancho Mirage, California

It was hard to focus. Rosemary's eyes were blurry and the shapes in the room kept moving from left to right. Trying to discern those shapes was a struggle, almost painful. Then suddenly there were loud sounds and more movement, worse than before, so she closed her eyes. She needed the shapes to stop moving. It was dark again now. Better. Then hands, so heavy and insisting, grasping her own, and a wet spongy thing swabbing the inside of her mouth. She licked her lips in disgust and the sounds started again. Then something squeezed her arm and it hurt. But the pain and the noises made her curious. What was going on? She forced her eyes open again and the shapes had form. They were her dad, her mother, and her brother, right above her face. They shouted and smiled and the hands grabbed hers harder. They seemed so happy to see her. What was going on?

She turned her head to the left, searching for the source of the pain, and saw a black blood pressure cuff squeezing her arm. An IV bag dangled above her head. After a moment she realized that the sounds were directed at her.

"Rosemary, Rosemary honey, hello honey, hello. . ."

Another head crowded in. It was wearing a mask. The mask

yanked the blood pressure cuff away and peeled something off Rosemary's face. That hurt too.

"Rosemary," the mask said. "Do you know where you are?"

Well, this seemed to be a hospital. Perhaps she had been in an accident? She tried to reply but couldn't make a coherent sound. The swab returned, and this time she welcomed it. After clearing her throat—a painful task—she managed to say, "Hospital."

More shouts and cheers.

"What is your full name?" the mask asked.

"Rosemary Grace Sabin."

"What year is this?"

"1985."

"Who are these people?" the mask asked, pointing at her family.

"My mom, my dad, and my brother," Rosemary replied, suddenly aware of more pain, this time in her feet and ankles. "What happened?"

"Can you feel this?" the mask asked, squeezing her left toe.

"Yes."

"And this?" Now the right toe.

"Yes."

"Well, this is very good," the mask said. "The doctor will want to do several tests, but her cognition seems excellent. I'll check back in a little while." The mask left and her mother's face was back.

"Honey, what's the last thing you remember?" Martina asked.

She thought for a moment and replied, "After school." Her voice was raspy. "Thursday. What's going on? Why am I here?"

"What else do you remember?" her father asked.

There were pictures in her mind: she and Pete at the pizza place. She tried to say it aloud, but her throat felt like it was stuffed with sand. She remembered that she hadn't been able to eat the pizza because she couldn't breathe. All day she'd been tired and weak, walking slowly from class to class, finding it difficult to finish a sentence. The night before had been weird, too. As she rearranged her room, refilling the drawers of the furniture that she and her dad had just finished stripping, sanding, and staining, it had gotten harder and harder to get a deep breath. She'd been uncomfortable all night, tight in her chest.

"Rosie," her dad said. "You've had an extreme allergic reaction. You went into respiratory failure on Thursday. The doctors put you into a medically induced coma."

She looked around the room as if seeing it for the first time. This was not a normal hospital room. She searched her brother Deet's face for clues but he just looked at her with tears in his eyes, like an adult would.

"A coma?"

"Yes, a coma," her father confirmed.

"Where am I?"

"In the ICU, sweetheart, at Eisenhower. And we are so glad to see you." He squeezed her hand. "It's Sunday morning, Rosie."

"Sunday?" she gasped, raising her voice and feeling more pain in her throat. "My throat hurts."

Her mother quickly swabbed her mouth again. "That's from the breathing tube, honey," she explained.

"The breathing tube?" Rosemary asked and tried to sit up, but found her wrists restrained.

"Oh, I'm sure those can come off now," her dad said, releasing the Velcro bands. He rubbed her wrists soothingly as she looked at her arms. They were covered in bruises and bandages. An IV protruded from the back of her right hand. The cannula in her nose hissed with oxygen and the taste in her mouth was vile. She bent her knees up to stretch her legs, but winced.

"Why do my feet hurt?"

"You had several seizures," her father replied. "You injured yourself a bit, but it's nothing serious."

"Seizures?" Rosemary started to cry.

"You've been through a lot, Ro," Deet said. "Take it easy."

She laid back on the pillow and closed her eyes. At least everyone would stop moving left to right.

She tried to remember that day. In the pizza place, in the bathroom, she'd tried to calm down and breathe deeply. She was embarrassed to be such a downer around Pete. She looked into the mirror defiantly and told herself that she *could* breathe. She'd never not been able to breathe before, so of course she could breathe now. She brushed her hair, smeared on some lip gloss, and tried to smile as she walked back to the table. But Pete just looked at her and said, "Rosie, you don't look good. What is wrong with you?"

She focused her eyes on the crushed-red-pepper shaker and tried not to cry. But then she was unable to focus on it because of the noise, a steady, rhythmic pounding like someone was hitting railroad spikes with a giant hammer, over and over.

"What's that noise?" she asked Pete.

"What noise?"

"That noise, that pounding."

Pete pushed his chair back and pulled Rosemary out of her chair. "We need to get you to the hospital," he said.

"The hospital, why? It's only a noise."

"Call 911!" Pete shouted to the guy at the counter.

"The firehouse is a mile down the street," the guy said, pointing. "That'll be faster. I'll call and tell them you're coming."

Pete led Rosemary to the car and drove like a madman down Twentynine Palms Highway. Hang on, babe, he said, as she fought the rising panic. She could not get a breath. She put the seat flat and tried to lie on her stomach, but that didn't help. She put her head between her knees, but that didn't help either. She tried to pray; nothing helped. By the time they got to the fire station, she was writhing like a tortured animal, taking small breaths like staccato hiccups. Pete drove up on the sidewalk, honking the horn and shouting. A bay opened and an ambulance pulled forward. Pete led her to the vehicle and helped her climb in. The last thing she remembered was the bumpy pattern of the steel on that step.

And now it was Sunday.

Tears slid down Rosemary's cheeks as a hand rubbed her shoulder. A doctor came in, filling the room with his voice. She kept her eyes closed as he talked with her dad. But she could feel her mother's eyes on her face, could feel that beacon of attention trained on her. So she let her face go slack and pretended to sleep. She wanted just one more minute of quiet, just one more minute of solitude.

But what was that? Someone was sitting on her legs, mashing her calves and making a noise like a braking train. "What's on me?" she muttered. "My legs!"

"It's OK," Deet reassured her. "They put these electric tube things on your legs to help your circulation."

"It's so you don't get blood clots when you're in bed for so long," Martina added.

"Oh my God," Rosemary said, trying again to sit up. "I need to move."

"We can remove these now, Miss Sabin," the doctor's voice boomed. Reddish hair protruded from his nostrils. He was ghastly.

He unfastened the devices and she stretched, wincing again as she bent her ankles. "You sprained your ankle and you have some major bruising," he explained. "You'll need to rest it for a while."

As she tried to sit up she felt a tugging at her crotch. "Uck, what is this?" she whined, feeling for the tube that kept her tethered.

"Oh yes, the catheter!" the doctor said cheerfully. "We'll send the nurse in to remove that. Do you folks have any questions before I go?" Her father led the doctor into the hallway, and her mother followed. When the door closed, she turned to her brother, who stood erect with his hands in the front pockets of his jeans, his plaid shirt loose over a faded black T-shirt.

"Holy shit, Deet! What the hell?"

"It's great to hear your voice," he said, smiling through fresh tears and moving toward her. "This has been a brutal three days."

She looked at him tenderly. When was the last time she'd seen his face so close? They were always just passing in the hallway, shouting through doors, bickering across the dinner table.

"Did I almost die or something?" she asked.

"It was touch and go," he replied. "Pete pretty much saved your life. They say that if you had been oxygen deprived much longer, you would have had brain damage."

"Holy shit!"

"I know. Mom and Dad have been a wreck. Mom hasn't been home since Thursday, but Dad went home to sleep. Sorry, but I went home, too," he chuckled. "You're pretty boring when you're in a coma, you know? And they only let visitors spend like ten minutes in here at a time, and everybody always wants an update on your condition. Whenever I was home, all I did was answer the phone. You get so sick of saying the same thing over and over again."

Visitors? Oh, no.

"Who was here?" she asked, already embarrassed.

"Well, Pete came a bunch of times, and Alejandra, and those girls from. . . ."

"Pete!" Oh God, how awful, and shouting made her voice hurt again.

"Of course!"

"Crap."

"What would you expect? Don't worry, you look beautiful with a breathing tube in your face and an oxygen mask and wires sticking out everywhere. Just gorgeous."

"Oh shut up," she said, newly miserable.

"Look, Ro, you really almost died. Just be glad you're alive."

"I am, I am."

"Grandma and Grandpa were here too, but not for long. They had some trip planned."

"Huh."

"But look, the doctors ordered a pregnancy test for you because they were giving you a CT scan. Mom about lost it and wouldn't authorize it, so if you are pregnant, you'll be having a mutant kid."

"I'm not pregnant."

"And the doctor said you have 'glass' in your lungs, which isn't glass, but it's what certain stuff looks like on the CT scan.

I think it made Dad suspicious that you smoke. You should be really careful about all of this."

"Thanks."

"And they refused to rule out a drug reaction. Were you on anything?"

"Nothing."

"Okay, but that freaked out Dad also."

"Well I was not on anything."

"Dad has been weird all around. I've never seen him like this. He feels responsible, but the doctors keep telling him he didn't do anything wrong. He used that product according to the directions—you were just allergic to it."

"What product?"

"The paint remover, from your dresser."

"All this is from paint remover?"

"And dust and stuff. But look, they're on their way back in," Deet said, looking through the glass wall. "Anything else you want to know?"

At that moment she realized why she was steadily becoming nauseous. Deet's breath was awful. Sour, really gross.

"You need to brush your teeth," she said. "Your breath is really bad."

"Thanks," he said, rolling his eyes. "And you're fresh as a daisy."

When her parents pushed the door open they brought the nurse, who shooed them all out of the room.

"Let's remove that catheter," she said, yanking back the sheets and jerking the tube out of Rosemary's urethra.

"Ow!" Rosemary shouted.

"Oh, sorry!" the nurse said with a laugh. "I'm so used to my ICU patients being unconscious! And these EKG sensors can come off, too." She peeled the electrodes from Rosemary's body, leaning closer to her face to do it. God, the woman reeked, of body odor and mint gum. The adhesive smelled too, and now she noticed that she could even smell herself. The catheter removal had unleashed a wave of repulsive crotch odor.

"Is there a reason why everything smells so strong to me?" she asked.

"It's a side effect of the steroids," the nurse explained, coming closer as Rosemary pushed herself into the pillow to gain more distance. But a wall of sweat and deodorant stink soon washed over her like a putrid Santa Ana wind.

"I'm on steroids?"

"Oh yes, and several other medications. You'll be weaned off all of it by next week."

"OK, thanks," Rosemary answered, her voice still raspy.

"Would you like some tea? That should soothe your throat."

Rosemary nodded.

"You'll be hungry soon, too. That's another effect of the steroids."

"And can you tell me why everything seems to be rotating from left to right?"

The nurse laughed again, her throat fat shaking ever so slightly. Her skin was soft and pale, like vanilla pudding. "Those are the sedatives. They use some pretty strong drugs to keep a coma patient sedated, and they took a while to get the cocktail right for you. You were a tough case."

"I was a tough case?"

"Well the ambulance drivers didn't expect you to seize," she said, emitting a mint cloud that enveloped her words. "They gave you a heavy dose of valium to stop the seizure. Then the docs had a hard time bringing you back up in the trauma room. And your gases were off. Evidently you were not exhaling properly, so you had a CO_2 build-up in your blood. They had to put you in that coma to regularize your breathing and get the exchange of gases back on track again. But don't you worry. You'll be on your feet again in no time. Young people bounce back very quickly."

She handed Rosemary a food service menu. "Let me know what else you might like with that tea," she said, turning off the EKG monitor and gathering up a bag of urine along with the catheter tubing. "I'll let your family know they can come back in now."

But it wasn't just family who came back in. Their neighbor, Mrs. Lopez, came in with a cross for her bedside. "I did nothing but pray for you yesterday," she said.

Her science teacher came in with a Get Well card signed by her classmates from fifth period.

Her old friend Bernadette came in with a chocolate croissant in a white bag. "I remember how you love these," she said gently.

Alejandra came in with an empty vase. "They wouldn't let me bring in the flowers," she said with a shrug.

There were others, too. The guys from Pete's band, and their girlfriends. Several sheriff's deputies and their wives. The man from the pizza place. All the while her dad hovered, emitting a force field that admonished guests not to linger. Finally he announced that Rosemary needed to rest, and she was so grateful that she wept. He also convinced Martina that she needed to go home and get some sleep. It was decided that Deet would stay with Rosemary.

Once their parents were gone, Deet ordered the maximum number of items from food service and ate wolfishly while Rosemary forced down some chicken broth and tepid tea. They watched a Padres game, which was blurry and incomprehensible to her. In the second inning, with one out and the Padres at bat, she fell asleep. She dreamed she was chewing on an envelope thick with glue. The chewing went on and on. She worried that the glue would discolor her teeth. She awoke, conscious of a terrible taste in her mouth, as acrid as melted plastic. Tony Gwynn struck out. Now it was two outs.

She drifted in and out of sleep for the next few innings, in the room thick with smells, surprised every time she woke to find Deet still there. In the fourth inning, she dreamed she was in an empty apartment that began to rapidly fill up with cat hair. She ran outside in a panic and then got in line for a roller coaster, which she rode in a pizza box. As she lurched along the rails, she could feel cold steel push through the cardboard, pressing into her thighs. When she woke up next, it was the seventh inning and a butch-looking nurse was speaking loudly.

"Seventh inning stretch!" she barked. "I need to take you to Radiology." Alex, the nurse, smelled like cigarettes and coffee as she helped Rosemary into a wheelchair. "Hey!" she yelled to everyone they passed on their way to the basement. In Radiology, as Rosemary had another CT scan, a disembodied voice told her in a lilting tone when and when not to breathe. Back in her room, a respiratory tech gave her a steamy treatment of some sickening medicine as he watched the game over Deet's shoulder. When it was done, her mouth tasted like the inside of a gas tank.

"I need to brush my teeth and take a shower," she told the tech.

"OK," he said. "I'll get the nurse."

This one was young, blonde, and smelled of latex. Her name was Patricia, and she brought Rosemary a toothbrush and toothpaste. As Rosemary gratefully brushed and brushed, Patricia and Deet tried to figure out how the under-the-sink toilet worked.

"So no one pees around here?" Deet asked as he puzzled at the contraption.

"Sure they do," Patricia replied. "They just do it in their catheters."

"Everyone has a catheter?" Rosemary mumbled through the foam.

"Most people in ICU are unconscious," Patricia explained, abandoning the toilet efforts to Deet. "We're not even used to talking to patients around here. That's why it's so wonderful to have you here because we can see you're going to get well. So many of our patients never get well. Oh, look! The toilet is ready!"

"What an invention," Deet marveled. "An under-the-sink toilet that's totally plumbed. Unbelievable."

"It really is," Patricia said, turning to Rosemary as she rinsed her mouth. "But there are no showers on this floor. I can wash your hair and you can wash your face at the sink, but that's about it."

The "wash" she used for Rosemary's hair was actually a bottle of goo that was somehow supposed to clean hair without water. Several times when Patricia got called away, Rosemary was left waiting as the foamy slime dripped down her forehead and into her ears. Although it smelled like turpentine spiked with cherry cough syrup, Rosemary found herself enjoying the process. Patricia massaged her head and combed the goo through while chatting with her like a girlfriend. She was probably in her mid-twenties, and Rosemary wanted her to never leave. Was this what it was like to have a sister? When she was done, Rosemary's hair was a thousand times worse than before, but she thanked Patricia profusely and fought back tears as she left the room.

Deet was staring at her.

"What?" she said accusingly.

"Hey," he said. "I gotta tell you something."

"Oh God, what?" she said, suddenly exhausted.

"I'm moving out."

"What?"

"I'm moving to the coast."

"You're leaving home?"

"Yeah, like next week."

"How? What do you mean?"

"I know a guy who's gonna get me a job selling pools."

"What? What do you know about pools?"

"Nothing, but I'll learn. It's just selling. It's all just selling."

Deet, who should have been in Pete's graduating class, had doubled up on credits during his junior year, attended summer school, and received his diploma in August. He'd been working since then at a furniture store.

"But you're only eighteen!"

"Old enough. I want out of here so bad."

"Where are you going to live?"

"I have a room in an apartment. I'm taking over the lease from some actor who didn't make it."

"Who is this friend of yours?"

"Craig's brother."

"Who's Craig?"

"A guy I work with."

"Have you told Mom and Dad?"

"Nope."

"Are you going to ask them for money?"

"I've saved up some money, but hey, if dad wants to give me money, I'll take it. I figure I'm saving them a bundle by not going to college."

"Well, this sucks."

"Why?"

"'Cause now I have to be home alone with Mom and Dad. Great. Thanks a lot."

"You can visit me."

"Right, I'll just do that, every weekend. I'll run on out to L.A. and we'll hang out."

"Santa Monica, actually."

"Whatever."

"There are buses, there are trains. But listen—you have to help me tell Mom and Dad."

"What do you mean help you?"

"Be there when I tell them, and be positive about it. Say it's a great opportunity for me."

"Selling pools."

"In beautiful Santa Monica, four blocks from the ocean."

"Oh, for Christ's sake."

"I'm gonna do great."

"They're still expecting you to go to college."

"Puke. I am not going to college. I'll be fine without it."

"What's your big hurry? Why do you have to leave now?"

"I don't know, Ro, I just suddenly can't stand this place. I'm a legal adult, and Mom still expects me home by midnight. I can't have a girl in my room unless the door is open, and Dad sniffs all around me every night when I come home. He thinks he's so subtle about it. I mean, it's ridiculous."

"But what about me? How can you leave me alone with them?"

"Ro, I gotta get out of here. Maybe I'll move back to the area someday, but for now I have to leave. I don't want to end up in some crappy town like this, in some ugly little dump forever. I want to make a lot of money so I can do whatever I want."

"And you're gonna make that money selling pools."

"It's a start!"

"Oh, whatever."

"Now don't be negative. Help me out."

"This is the worst day of my life."

"Yeah, I'm sorry to spring this on you, but it seems like we never have any time to talk without Mom around."

"You suck, you know.

"I know."

"And I'll miss you."

"I'll miss you, too."

❧   ❧   ❧

The night seemed to last for weeks. Rosemary shifted around constantly, trying to find a position that didn't hurt. The bed, which was designed to prevent bedsores, shifted and adjusted of its own accord, periodically emitting strange groaning noises like distant helicopters. She was awakened by nurses taking her vitals, nurses giving her meds, and nurses changing her IV bags. She attempted to use the under-the-sink toilet but muffed the process, creating a puddle on the floor that she instantly stepped in. She was so overwhelmed by her wet foot that she considered waking Deet for help, but just then a respiratory tech named Molly came in to give her another dose of steamy, rank-tasting medicine. Rosemary wiped the pee on the sheets and listened to Molly, who chattered brightly about an upcoming wedding as if it were midday. At around 4 a.m. Rosemary was ravenous. She limped to the door, still bound by her IV tubing, and asked a nurse for food, feeling like a waif at an orphanage. After a turkey sandwich she fell back to sleep until 7:30, when her pulmonologist, a dark pointy woman who smelled of dry cleaning solution, woke her with a stethoscope.

"We're chalking all of this up to an allergic reaction," Dr. Chu said, listening to her chest.

"But I don't have any allergies," Rosemary said, instantly feeling stupid.

"That paint stripper you and your dad used had some strong chemicals. And he discovered that there was some work done on the ventilation system at your school last week. There's no telling what particulates were in the air there. All together, those insults to your lungs were simply more than you could handle."

By late morning, Rosemary was out of ICU and in a regular room. But the glory of a hot shower soon gave way to horror as she looked at herself in the mirror. The steroids had bloated her; she had a moon face and a round, puffy belly. Dotting her body were bruises, punctures, blood blisters, swellings from the seizures and the arterial blood draws and the IVs and the God knows what else, and she just cried and cried in the shower.

She also worried about how this incident would change her day-to-day life. What would her reentry at school be like? A thing like this could make a person more popular—"What happened? Did you really almost die? Do you need me to carry your books?"—or it could push her out of the herd—"I don't get what happened to her. It's just too freaky. I think she ODed or something." And what would this mean for her and Pete? Would it make them closer or drive him away? This felt like a big deal, an un-fun adult sort of big deal, like that freshman girl last year whose mom died, and who had to go live in Brazil with the father she'd never met. And then there was her weight. She didn't even know how to lose weight—her body always took care of everything. But now she had twelve steroid-driven pounds on her, and she was always hungry. Once she got out of these hospital gowns, her clothes wouldn't even fit. What would she wear to school? And when was she going back to school, anyway? Would she have to make up tons of work? Would she have to go to summer school?

Deet went home and her mother came back, this time with an armload of Good Housekeeping magazines and Lorna

Doone cookies. The day lasted another week as Rosemary was forced to interact with Martina and the multitude of nurses, orderlies, nurse assistants, respiratory techs, and janitors who marched through her room, all bound to their officious and mysterious duties.

Beneath the chatter, Rosemary speculated endlessly about why this had happened to her. All this from removing paint? And breathing in unknown crap? This was no accident, she came to believe. It was a sign.

She thought about that glorious night—the drumming in the desert, with the black bowl of heaven above and the hardscrabble earth beneath. It had all started that night.

Rosemary used to believe the desert was a wasteland, but now she knew differently. The desert was a world alive and infinitely more honest than some cozy green place like Oregon. The desert was reality; the rest was fluff. She was part of that tough, real world, she realized with pride, and she needed to get to know it better, needed to protect it. How had she disregarded it all these years?

She wished she were there now, away from the putrid medicines and the miles of plastic tubing and the people in uniform. She had seen what life could be like, the unity and beauty of people who chose to connect with each other in nature, and she wanted that for herself. Somehow she needed to create a life that was real, a life in which she would not feel sad or hopeless or disconnected.

She was halfway through a huge plate of pasta when Pete came to visit at dinnertime.

"Hey!" he shouted cheerfully, "Look at you! You're back!"

Her heart raced as he kissed her forehead. She was all too aware of her bloated face, her garlic breath, and Martina's gaze. But her mother surprised her by treating Pete with a sort of deference. "I'm sure Rosemary and you need to catch up," she said, gathering up her purse. "I could use a cup of coffee anyway."

After Martina left, Pete stroked her hair and sang softly to her. He smelled like man sweat and smoke—he'd been burning brush all weekend with his dad—and she drank in the first natural scents of the past thirty-six hours since she awoke. Suddenly she was crying, and she forgot to be embarrassed about it.

"I hate this place," she said. "It smells bad and it's noisy and I want to go home."

"Soon, babe. I'm sure you'll be home soon."

"They say I'll be here till the end of the week!"

"That's just a few days. You'll be OK."

"What if I have asthma forever?"

"You won't."

"What if I stay fat forever?"

"Don't worry, babe, you'll be fine."

"You don't know that."

"Yes, I do."

"How?"

"Well, what did the doctor say?"

"That I'll be fine," she said with a laugh.

"See?" he smiled. God, he was gorgeous, which made her cry more.

"You saved my life!"

"I drove you to the fire station."

"How did you know what to do?"

"When you said you heard pounding, I knew you were hearing your own blood and that you were going to faint. I think I learned that in health class, like in ninth grade, and it just hit me. And you looked so—so gray."

"I looked gray?"

"You just didn't look right, and your skin was clammy."

"Oh!" She suddenly felt protective of the person she had been four days earlier, that girl who didn't know she'd been poisoned, that she could soon become brain damaged or die.

The tears flowed harder now, and Pete gently cooed, "It's OK, babe, let it out."

"And Deet's leaving. He's moving to Santa Monica."

"What?"

"He told me last night. He got a job selling pools. He's leaving next week."

The weeping grew to sobs as Pete rubbed her back and tried to soothe her. But after a long while she quieted and felt herself able to breathe deeper, the way she felt after the steamy lung treatments.

"I want to go back to the desert," she said suddenly.

"Huh?"

"That night when we went to the drumming circle—that was what started the whole thing."

"I don't understand."

"It was that night I decided to strip the paint from my dresser because I didn't want to live around fake stuff anymore. It took my dad a few weeks to get to it, but I decided it that night after the drumming. I loved being out there that night. The whole thing felt so pure and beautiful."

"It was definitely a cool scene."

"I never appreciated the desert before. I always wished I lived some place more normal, with green lawns and big trees like on TV, but something happened to me out there. The open space, the rock, the sky. . . ."

"You've spent many nights out on Amboy Road."

"Yeah, but that place is not natural."

"True."

"This was different. And ever since that night, when I look around, all I see is stupid crap—fast food restaurants, bad TV, girls who think it matters whether they wear pink lipstick or red—"

"That's all you see?"

"No, I guess that's not all, but I don't want to get sucked into a bunch of stupid bullshit. I want a simple, natural life."

"Okay, we'll go back to the desert. Now relax and rest." He rubbed her shoulders and sang softly until her father entered the room, still in his officer's uniform, and broke the spell. She reluctantly roused herself as Pete stood up.

"Sir," he said, shaking her father's hand.

Sir? He'd never addressed her dad like that before, and her father had never looked at Pete that way. A new level of respect was in place now. It seemed things really did change when people almost died.

When Martina returned, they chatted about the weather, the Padres, the price of gas, and the nurse with the lisp. A few more visitors came bearing snacks and flowers and balloons and books, and by 9 p.m. she was finally alone.

As the ward quieted for the evening, Rosemary clicked off the lights and stared into the semi-darkness. She was off oxygen now, and off the IV. Untethered, she stood up and made her way to the west-facing window overlooking the roof of a lower floor of the hospital. She knew that beyond the hospital lay the San Bernardino Mountains, L.A., the ocean, and then Asia, Africa, the Atlantic, New York, the Rocky Mountains, and then back to this room. And she knew things had changed. She didn't know in what ways she was different now, or who she would become, but the fact that she had changed was something she could neither avoid nor control.

CHAPTER 4 | JULY, 1987

Twentynine Palms, California

MARK SABIN WATCHED HIS DAUGHTER AS SHE WEEDED THE garden bed on the side of the house. From his place at the kitchen table, with the prop of a newspaper in front of him, he could see her crouching at the zucchini plants, her beautiful face obscured one moment by a wide-brimmed hat and then revealed as she leaned back on her heels. She yanked at the moist soil, removing baby tumbleweeds and spiky goatheads, a task she attacked doggedly though it was nearly a hundred degrees outside. He admired her tenacity and puzzled again at the effort. The bed had once been a rock garden, a tasteful display of river cobbles over a layer of weed block that he'd created some ten years earlier. It had been simple and tidy, and required little maintenance, but she wanted a "growing space" that had afternoon shade, so he relented. As usual, as his wife would say.

But Rosemary, at eighteen, puzzled him in many ways he could not quite define. She kept out of trouble, did well in school, and had been accepted to Cal State San Bernardino. She was just eighteen, but sometimes seemed thirty. Her brother David had been a handful, and he expected the same from her. He was used to unruly teenagers, had arrested plenty of them over the years—seized their alcohol when they gathered at Chocolate Drop, broke up parties at the Sunset Motel, ran them down speeding, and of course scooped them up off the Amboy Road berms like armies in a game of Risk. But Rosemary—she had seemed to grow up overnight. She'd quit wearing makeup, quit watching TV, quit wasting her babysitting money on nonsense, and now she was growing this garden. She'd even rigged up an elaborate water-catchment system so that her garden would not "impact the desert's scant resources."

It was that science teacher of hers who seemed to put these ideas into her head. Ms. Othmar, Rosemary's sixth-grade teacher, had moved up to the high school and Rosemary had her for both biology and earth science. The woman, a big proponent of conservation, had led at least a dozen schoolwide and municipal water saving initiatives, but they always fell flat. But she certainly had influenced his daughter. Or was it Rosemary's freak coma that prompted these changes? It seemed that one day she was a typical teenager, and the next she was an environmental zealot who scrutinized everything—every drop of water expended, every food-purchasing decision, every cotton or polyester fiber in a piece of clothing. It could be exhausting to be around her.

And now she would be off to college in just six weeks, an event that had always represented a mythical deadline for him. "When the kids are grown," he'd say to himself, about so many things. He could retire from the sheriff's department any time now, and start a new career. It was too late for the Marines, of course, but he'd rebuked himself enough for letting that flame die, a dream first deterred by his parents' snobbery and second by his wife's inability to be independent. If only she had been more tough—able to be alone at night, to fill out insurance forms, to discipline the kids—if she could have handled his being deployed, he would have joined in a heartbeat. But he'd made his choices. Moved to this ridiculous town a hundred fifty miles from the coast because the Marine Corps Air Ground Combat Center was here. As if by being near the base, some general Marine-ness, some grandeur, would rub off on him. With a B.S. in Criminal Law he became a small-town cop.

But these were all his decisions and he had to live with that. He had no right to blame anyone for them.

He looked around at the kitchen of the house he almost owned—just thirteen more mortgage payments. The cramped kitchen, uncomfortably hot when the oven was on, should have been remodeled years ago. His mind clicked through the scenario he had imagined so many times: The side wall should be pushed out to encompass that garden bed, and they should install an island with an ice maker beneath and a place for four stools. He'd always imagined throwing parties with guests standing around that island, chatting as he mixed up the next batch of margaritas. Martina would be pressing avocadoes for guacamole and he would say, "Not too spicy, now," and she would say, "Why does everyone always congregate in the kitchen?" Then he'd usher the guests outside to the covered patio, where he'd grill the steaks. The conversation would be light, the laughter lilting. He and Martina would be relaxed, fun-loving hosts.

But he could never convince her that remodeling the house was a good thing, that it would add value to their home and expand possibilities. She'd always steadfastly refused to take on debt. The other deputies often envied him, decrying their spendthrift wives and their seemingly insatiable desires for new furniture, new shoes, and vacations they could ill afford. At first he loved Martina's simple ways. "I want what I have," she'd say, and that was a comfort for many years, but the kids were grown now, and here they were, living like old people. He looked with disgust at the electric stove that was original to the house—a Hotpoint. They didn't even make them anymore. And the gold refrigerator that was so loud you could hear it in the driveway. The ugly cabinets—dark wood with some sort of curlicue design. All of it needed to go. They should have stainless steel appliances, granite countertops, a tile floor.

The kitchen had looked the same, except maybe for the curtains, on the day Mark discovered whom he'd really married. It was their second wedding anniversary, and he'd come home excitedly announcing that he'd arranged for a sitter for their son, David, and that they would be going out to dinner to celebrate. But Martina refused, insisting that she already had a fine dinner in the oven and they could not afford such an extravagance. He protested, insisting they needed to splurge sometimes, but watched with growing dismay as she poked the chicken casserole, bending toward the oven in her slate-blue dress, her hair pulled back neatly, an apron tied around her slender waist. All the other women he knew wore shorts in the summer heat—it was 1968, after all—but Martina wore dresses. And shoes in the house.

Suddenly he saw his young wife anew, saw that she was not quite grown. How had he not seen this before? He took in her placid smile, her impassive face, and his forehead ran with sweat. She was a child, really, playing house, a sapling that still needed to be staked. He had driven home that evening dreaming about sex. There would be dinner out, a bottle of wine, the gift he had bought for her—a lace camisole—and then there would be sex. Maybe even hot, deeply satisfying sex. He had barely touched Martina since David was born, and he saw now that in his mind, this night was going to reverse that trend. And why not? They were adults, and this was their wedding anniversary. She had seemed to like sex at first, and he assumed it would only get better with time. But there she was with that God forsaken casserole, and his desire for her seemed wrong, almost deviant. A surge of anger swept through him as he realized his desire for her would soon turn to dust and that it would be a burden to him for the rest of his days. At this realization it was as if his legs left the linoleum and he was floating in the small kitchen, undulating in the stifling summer heat. He gripped the counter harder and forced his will against the rising panic. In the space of a few moments, the anger was replaced with protectiveness and a naïve hope. Maybe things would change.

She had not changed, but he had. He came to accept his lackluster marriage and grew to enjoy his children, his work, and his community. Family life had given him the opportunity to feel like a minor hero, but now that was ending. Now there really would be a change. He could run for sheriff, or maybe the City Council. Or go to law school—he'd always wanted to be a prosecutor. He was only forty-two. There was still time.

On the table lay a plate and fork with smears of chocolate frosting, the remains of a cake that now seemed like a pathetic symbol in a sad story. A few days earlier, Rosemary and her boyfriend Pete marked their two-year "anniversary," and Rosemary had baked this cake to celebrate. She had clearly expected her parents to relish being included, but he had found the commemoration silly, and it had rankled his wife to no end.

Martina disliked Pete for reasons she would not, or could not, articulate. Of course, they were both still grateful for his heroic actions a couple of years ago in getting Rosemary to the ambulance, but Martina had begun to downplay it lately.

"That boy saved our daughter's life," Mark frequently reminded his wife.

"He drove her to the fire station," she would counter.

And though she insisted that she did not have an aversion to his hair or his van or even his guitar, Mark had noticed a pattern: Her ire seemed to rise when Pete did something particularly whimsical or romantic. These were the times when her face would darken, and she would say she felt a migraine coming on, or that Mark needed to get serious and tell Rosemary that her nipples were showing through that ridiculous blouse.

For their "anniversary," Pete had written a song for Rosemary and was reckless enough to sing it for his pretend in-laws. Afterward, Martina set down her coffee cup and said, "How nice" and "if you'll excuse me." She then slid the phone book from its shelf, called the Pennysaver, put in an ad for a garage sale and spent the next seventy-two hours violently sorting through every box, drawer and closet in the house, unearthing all manner of detritus to sell on Saturday morning.

The whole garage sale incident convinced Rosemary that her mother did not want her to be happy. As soon as Martina left the house to take the unsold items to Goodwill, Rosemary found her father in the kitchen and confronted him.

"Don't you see, Dad?" she insisted. "Don't you see how she is?"

Mark sighed, as had become his habit when his daughter challenged him. He ran his fingers through his close-cropped hair, the black now showing gray at the temples, and looked at her. His dark brown eyes were weary.

"I don't always understand her either, honey," he said soothingly. "But I do know she wants you to be happy."

"Happy how?" Rosemary fumed. "Happy on the couch with her? Doing word searches?"

"Go easy, Rosie," Mark coaxed. "She means well."

"Why don't you tell her to go easy on me?" Rosemary whined.

"She's just a nervous person, Rosie."

"She's weird and getting weirder, Dad."

"You're not being fair, Rosie."

"Dad, Mom has no friends. Have you ever noticed that?"

Of course he'd noticed that. "Mrs. Lopez is her friend," he offered weakly.

"Mrs. Lopez is our neighbor," Rosemary said, hands on hips. "We have a key to her house and sometimes she borrows our folding chairs."

"Come on, honey. They're friends."

"Dad, Mom has no life."

"She's shy is all, Rosie."

"Dad!"

He began smoothing his eyebrows. How had they gotten so bushy? He'd have to trim them soon or he'd start looking like an unkempt Yorkie.

"Dad!" Rosemary insisted again as she sat down imperiously in a chair across from him. He suddenly felt drained.

"She's been praying again."

Mark's head snapped up. He stared at his daughter wordlessly.

"She's doing it again."

He dropped his gaze to the Formica wood-grain table. After a heavy silence he asked, "What have you seen?"

"Last night, Pete was coming down with a cold, so he took me home early. It was around 9:30 and she was saying 'Hail' on you guys' bed."

Mark rubbed his temples and leaned his elbows heavily on the table. He knew that when Martina said "Hail," she was reciting the Hail Mary over and over, a behavior that he and the kids had dubbed "power-praying."

The first time this happened was about seven years earlier when David got caught stealing a bike from Reese's Bike and Sport. The shop owner recognized David and called Mark at the sheriff's office: "Your boy just helped himself to a new Schwinn from my shop." Mark was silent, stunned. "Now I'd like to let you handle it," Reese said. "I don't need to file a report. If you get the bike back to me right away we'll just let it lie." Reese continued to talk over the silence. "I want you to know that I would do the same for any of these kids from decent families. I'm not doing it just because you're a deputy."

Mark thanked Reese, rushed to his car, and drove around town until he found his son under a highway bridge. He and his friends were standing around the bike, admiring it and high-fiving David. As Mark pulled up in the squad car, the other boys scattered and David froze.

Mark stepped out of the car without a word. He eyed his son with a level gaze, picked up the bike, placed it in the trunk, opened the back of the squad car, and looked again at his son. David, then thirteen, began to weep, smearing his tears with the back of his hand. He considered handcuffing the boy but decided against it. Soon the weeping escalated into a wail as Deputy Sabin continued to watch.

Eventually David got into the squad car and Mark drove to Reese's shop, where David returned the bike and apologized. Mark and Reese left him in the back of the shop where the bike mechanics gestured toward him and snickered. David struggled to hold back his tears as Mark and Reese worked out a schedule for the summer: He was to work from 8 to 11 a.m. Monday through Friday for six weeks, cleaning the shop and running errands. There would be far heavier consequences if he screwed it up.

That evening when Mark told Martina, his shame over his son's actions was eclipsed by the pride he felt in how he'd handled the situation. But Martina could not appreciate his cool-headed response. Instead, she started praying for forgiveness from God. As the days went on she prayed more and more, sometimes saying the rosary twice at a sitting.

After a week she began to shorten the prayers, saying only the initial sounds of the words. Soon after, she abandoned that for the current method of drawing out one representative word and reciting the prayer in her head. Mark, Rosemary, and David were stunned by Martina's newfound piety, but she would not answer questions about her behavior or let herself be dissuaded from it.

Since then, she'd been through two more spates of power-praying, once when Rosemary got caught hanging out on the Amboy berms, and again when she found a lighter in David's coat pocket. The praying episodes seemed to last about a month, and they were grueling for the family. Mark expected her to launch into another when that crazy drunk shot at him last Christmas, but that passed without incident.

"Why do you think?" he asked Rosemary.

"I don't know," she replied. "Is someone sick?"

"She's never done it for sickness or death."

"Well, when does she do it?"

Mark hesitated, wondering if it was appropriate to tell Rosemary what he had discovered. But the girl had asked, with her clear, brown eyes and smooth-skinned face like a picture-frame insert. He breathed deeply, exhaled slowly, and answered, "She does it when her kids screw up."

Rosemary's forehead wrinkled in confusion.

"I figured it out," he said. "She's asking for forgiveness."

"But who screwed up?"

"You tell me," Mark said, looking her full in the face.

"What did *I* do?"

Mark realized at that moment that the praying was indeed about Rosemary. It was about her and Pete having sex. The girl was way too smart to get caught, but that stupid song Pete had sung for him and Martina was just too much. Just too much, about the softness of her lips and the sheen of her hair and the curve of her this and that. Honestly, the kid was just plain stupid. Or, Mark realized with a start, stoned. Of course, the kid was stoned. He was always chewing gum and squeezing Visine into his eyes, claiming to have allergies, and he guzzled all of their iced tea whenever he walked in the door. He was ashamed for not figuring it out sooner.

He felt his eyes narrow.

"Dad, what?" Rosemary demanded.

Mark's heart raced as he struggled to breathe deeply, staring at the napkin holder to maintain a focal point. Years of keeping his cool under pressure, of resisting impulsive behavior and reactions, served him now.

"Rosie, your mother thinks you and Pete are getting too serious." He realized that the power praying had begun the night of the garage sale, a few days after Pete sang that damned song. Mark had noted the same pattern the time before: First she gets busy, then she prays.

"Now I'm not allowed to have a boyfriend," Rosemary said, folding her arms in front of her and settling into a pout.

Suddenly Mark hated the boy. Hated his handsome GQ face and his ingratiating ways. Hated his confidence, his way of taking up space. What *was* he doing with his daughter? He was twenty years old. What exactly did they do when they were together? There were always explanations: We're going to check out a club that Pete's playing next week, Alejandra's mom invited us for dinner, there's a basketball game at school. But did he really know what she was doing? What went on between them? What did they talk about? Did she smoke pot? Did she perform oral sex? He nearly wretched in sudden revulsion. He shoved his chair back and crossed the room to the sink, filling his hands with water and splashing his face.

"Dad, what's wrong?" Rosemary followed him to the sink.

He began running his wet hands through his hair, filling his hands again and again with the cool water.

"Dad, she'll be OK," Rosemary soothed. "She always comes out of it eventually, right?" Rosemary rubbed his shoulder as he stared blankly into the sink. "Right?"

"Yes," he said, turning off the tap. "Yes, honey, she'll be OK."

At that moment Martina was not at Goodwill, as she had told her husband and daughter. She was kneeling at her mother's grave, power praying the Lord's Prayer over and over again. She knew that Rosemary was fornicating with Pete, and she was praying for forgiveness. She was not exactly clear who needed to be forgiven—her, for not instilling the values of the church in her daughter, as she had also failed to do with her son, or Rosemary, who was weak and seemed to have no shame.

It was exhausting to pray like this, but Martina welcomed that drained feeling. It was better than the frenetic activity that came first. And she was comfortable in this state, familiar with it, like a childhood home she returned to every few years. The only hard part was finding the privacy to pray. It was easier now that David no longer lived at home, but she hated summer, without Rosemary's regular school schedule. At least her mother's grave was secluded at the back of the cemetery, and here she could relax. She had already prayed the rosary once and was pausing before the second round to chat with her mother.

"Mama," she said to the low headstone. "Mama, I need your help. My daughter has lost her way."

Martina used prayer both as a shield and a supplication. While uttering the prayers, she felt protected from harm, and also that she was doing all she could to beseech God to forgive her. Ever since her wedding night, the thick hide of fear had been forming.

Martina was named after a martini, her worthless father's favorite drink. She was also a Catholic, and feared retribution for having married a Jew. Of course there was always a chance Mark was not really a Jew, since he had been adopted, but his parents insisted he was. When she first started dating him, she felt she had really grown up, like she was living dangerously. Mark, with his dark eyes and olive skin, was handsome, exotic —an intriguing contrast to her pallid, Scotch-Irish looks. He was from the coast and he'd graduated from college, which meant that he was comfortable in worlds that were completely unknown to her. He was also a law enforcement officer—she felt safe with him—and her mother did not hate him. Marrying him seemed inevitable.

She told herself that it was how a person lived, not what he or she believed, that mattered to God. And Mark said she could baptize their children, as long as she never told his parents.

But once they were married she began to feel a yoke of doom. The ceremony had been at the Sabins' home in Santa Barbara, not in the church, and shortly after their honeymoon, Martina began to fear that the civil ceremony had been a terrible mistake. Every week when she asked Mark to attend church with her, he simply smiled and said, "No, thank you." And when their son was born, just ten months after the wedding, they named him David, a name Mark said was a brilliant compromise—the Old Testament was always a crowd pleaser. But after months of attending Mass alone, Martina soon began to believe the parishioners were gossiping about her, so she stopped going. Then the weekly guilt of skipping Mass began to mount. By the time their daughter was born two years later, she insisted on naming the child some form of Mary. A New Testament name, she thought, might position her soul a few steps farther from hell.

Martina's mother, Deedee, had worked all through Martina's childhood as a hotel maid. Abandoned by her husband at twenty-six, she spent the best years of her life resenting the mothers who got to stay home, women with soft hands who leisurely drank coffee in the mornings as she hauled ass to work.

She imagined they were cooking fine meals for their loving husbands while she boiled hot dogs for her bickering children; that they dusted their fine furniture as she plucked milky condoms from brown, low-pile carpet; that they spent the month of December shopping for lavish gifts they bought with their husbands' fat paychecks while she worked extra to pay for the Easy Bake Oven and the Rock'Em - Sock'Em Robots.

Deedee was lonely, though she would never admit it, and automatically deflected any suggestion of it with the retort, "I got my kids and I got God. What else do I need?" She was looking forward to grandchildren but instead dropped dead of an aneurism a month after Mark and Martina's wedding. She never knew what hit her.

Martina always said that when she was a mother, she would not work, would not farm out her kids to the care of strangers or leave them home to rot. And she was able to keep this promise. The problem was that she had absorbed large chunks of her mother's unfortunate mind—the same resentments and jealousies toward the other stay-at-home moms, considering them lazy and privileged. On the other hand, she avoided the working mothers too, believing in her own mind that they were poor parents who neglected their children. When Mark asked why she didn't go shopping with friends as he recalled his own mom doing, or why she didn't spend time chatting or gossiping with the neighbors, she would repeat an updated version of her mother's response: "I've got my husband and I've got my children. That's all I need." The God part she would keep to herself. After all, Mark was Jewish—or sort of.

So she kept her love for her husband and children quiet. At first this was a conscious modesty, a practiced reserve that made her feel mature and worldly. She'd seen a movie once about a family struggling through the London Blitz and liked to imagine that she was that mom. There she was, clad in a wool A-line skirt and a much-worn cotton blouse, walking with dignity through the bomb-pocked streets of London, wisely spending her ration tickets, keeping a brave face for her children as she collected them from school. Some days she'd imagine that her husband, her tall-dark-and-handsome husband who touched her at night with restrained desire, was in the RAF. She didn't know where he was deployed because it was all top secret. For all she knew he was behind enemy lines, fighting for his life in some city her limited knowledge of history couldn't quite pin down. Would it be Paris? Rome?

But it was too hot for wool skirts in Twentynine Palms, California, and her husband came home every night. He was also less than impressed with her elegant martyrdom and could never understand why she took the time to sew her own cloth napkins and make homemade mayonnaise.

Over time, Martina's love for her family became a badge she wore like a scout's square-knot insignia. But her faith, kept close and dark, began to molder and turn rank. While Deedee had believed in what she could see—shrines, paintings of the Stations of the Cross, the Bingo Bash the parish brought in twice a year—Martina believed in what she could not see: tapeworms, child molesters, Muslims, hell. When searching for guidance in her religious vacuum, she relied on a simple formula: Take the seven deadly sins and do the opposite. Gluttony? Eat little. Sloth? Get busy. Wrath? Suppress anger. Envy? Want nothing. Greed? Own only what was necessary. Pride? Get smaller. Lust? Pretend your husband was in the RAF.

Living small carried her for a long while, until David hit puberty and started to stray. Then supplication was the only path. She would pray a path straight to the afterlife for herself and her children.

∽ ∽ ∽

Rosemary peeled off her gardening gloves and gathered up her tools. She clattered through the kitchen door, looking surprised to find her father still at the table.

"Dad," she said. "What's so bad about getting serious with Pete? I'm happy."

He traveled in his mind from the earlier kitchen scene to this one and stared at the newspaper in his hands. "I see that, honey," he said, absentmindedly straightening the pages. "But you're very young."

"I'm eighteen, Dad. I'm an adult."

"You're very young. When you go away to college, you'll see. There are other fish in the sea."

"What's wrong with Pete?" Rosemary demanded, her voice rising. She threw her gardening gloves on the table like a gauntlet. "You know, sometimes I think I should just go away to college and never come back—just leave, like Deet. Maybe he had the right idea."

Mark winced at her words and looked back down at the newspaper. Grills were on sale at Benton Brothers.

Suddenly they heard Martina's Impala pull into the driveway, heard the door clunk closed and the keys jingle as she came in the kitchen door.

Mark turned toward his wife with a ready smile. "How did it go, hon?" he asked.

Martina looked from her husband to her daughter and back again, her forehead creased beneath her auburn hair. "How did what go?" she asked.

"Goodwill?"

"Oh," she replied. "I guess I don't know."

CHAPTER 5 | MAY, 1989

Joshua Tree National Monument, California

THE UNCOMPLICATED MUSIC OF CRICKETS SANG IN THE desert night as Pete and Raul flicked their cigarette lighters, struggling to ignite the Duroflame logs. Rosemary sipped a Negro Modelo, her feet stretched against the fire pit. It was illegal to gather wood at Joshua Tree, so Rosemary always brought fake logs, maintaining that the campfire added to their authenticity. They would spend the night here in the tent as they did every two or three months when Raul came, bringing with him two pounds of fine Mexican marijuana for Pete to sell. Spending the night at a campsite, she believed, provided good cover for the drop. Didn't they look like they were just here for a weekend getaway? The pile of climbing ropes and harnesses in the back of the Chevy Blazer, bought secondhand and completely unused by any of them, was, she believed, nothing short of genius.

She was humming a song that Pete had written, running through tomorrow's play list in her mind. Pete's band had a gig the next night in Twentynine Palms, the first there in several months since he had moved to Riverside. They'd been touring small clubs in the desert towns of southern California's Inland Empire for about a year now.

"Babe, you gonna cook?" Pete asked, straightening up. The logs at his feet were beginning to blaze. Raul was rummaging in his car, sifting through stacks of handmade clothing stored in ramen soup boxes. He sold embroidered cotton blouses and beaded necklaces to tourist shops north of the border, but it was the pot hidden in the door panels that really supported his family. Since his father died, the needs of his mother and siblings seemed to be endless.

"Yeah, in a minute," she answered, watching with excitement as the fire consumed the shiny Duroflame packaging. She went to take another sip of her beer but found it empty. Instead she drained a nearby water bottle and splashed a bit of it on her face.

She watched as Raul opened and refolded the flaps of each box, clearly looking for something. "Ah!" he shouted and approached her with an open palm, smiling proudly. He handed her a small pipe, a snake carved from onyx.

"For me?" she asked.

"Yes," he replied, pronouncing the *y* as a *j*. "I hope you like it."

"It's beautiful, Raul!" she exclaimed, standing up to give him a hug. "Thank you so much!"

"We'll be back soon," Pete said, signaling Raul to follow him. The men walked to the edge of Campsite 38, up to the road where the cars were parked near the trash cans, and around to the footpath that people used to enter the panoply of rock that made this park so famous. She watched them walk away, in their dusty jeans and hiking boots.

But the crackling fire reclaimed her attention. She crouched down again and fed it a few dry sticks, enjoying the feel of the smooth stone pipe in her hand. Then she sat back and surveyed the campsite with an approving gaze: picnic table, fire ring, tent, and the smooth inset rock ledge that was cool and shady in the mornings. They could have stayed at more-secluded sites, but Rosemary insisted that would make them look suspicious. Better to be conspicuously public, smiling and making friends with the neighbors in one of the park's best sites, than skulking in the shadows with the gnarly creosote bushes.

Thirsty again. She opened another beer and sighed, knowing this would be another hundred fifty calories and that the diet plan she and her roommate had created included only one beer or one piece of chocolate per day. But the joint they'd smoked earlier had made her hungry, and her mouth dry. She was frankly ravenous, and not terribly excited about the bean burrito dinner she had planned, but it was cheap. Nearing the end of the spring semester, her money was about gone, and Raul's arrival was two weeks later than expected, so Pete was also low on money.

The ramen boxes were on the ground by Raul's 1978 Datsun, and she looked at them with sudden interest. The packing tape on the sides of a box was tattered. It was a much-used box, and Rosemary thought of the Chinese worker who had last handled it before the box was loaded on the ship in—where? Shanghai? Like she knew. What did the worker look like, she wondered. What was the factory like? Could she somehow, by the force of her mind and the strength of her compassion, connect with that person and his or her experience of life? She stared and stared at the box, trying to picture the hands that had pressed the tape into place amid the noise of relentless machines.

But the whine of a bug broke her concentration and she began to scratch her head violently. She looked down at the bulge of flesh that spilled over the waistband of her jeans and squeezed it in contempt. How could she have gotten so fat? How could this be her? Why couldn't she be lean and trim? Some women made it look so easy. She was stuffed into size-ten jeans—stuffed! She was bigger than her own mom, for God's sake. But then, Martina had always been a wraith, devoid of all pleasure-detecting sensors. Rosemary had been sensuous and shapely, believing it was attitude that kept you slim and pretty, not something as mundane as dieting and exercise. But she realized she'd been dead wrong.

OK, change the scene. Thinking of Martina was a sure buzzkill.

Rosemary sucked in her stomach and smoothed her hair. She was sure, really, that she looked pretty in the firelight, and perhaps even earthy. There were women, she was well aware, who were confident in their beauty even if they were not thin. They presided over strong, sturdy bodies that could double-dig garden beds, make bread, carry babies. She stopped her movements and was truly struck by this idea. Maybe that was who she was becoming. Maybe this was what that "Desiderata" thingie talked about—"gracefully surrendering the things of youth." Maybe she was maturing.

She prepared dinner with a newfound sense of purpose, laying out the paper plates, grating cheese, and folding tortillas around logs of refries with a lordly air. She opened a third beer—it was petty, really, to count—and sliced the avocadoes with Pete's pocketknife. She looked around for Pete and Raul and saw them high up on a rock above the campsite, their heads bent close in conversation. They weren't really drug dealers, she assured herself. Pete was a musician and Raul was an importer who worked hard to support his family. They were just working men who needed a little extra to get by.

She was really hungry, but was reluctant to shout in this quiet place, so she left the food on the table and returned to the fire. A half hour later, with the beer and a bag of cashews long gone, she grew irritable. Pete and Raul were nowhere in sight. She ate her burrito, opened a fourth beer, and squeezed her stomach again. God, was she ever fat.

Rosemary was working hard at making her last piece of chocolate last when Pete and Raul returned to the campsite, well past dark.

"Babe!" Pete called out in the overly jovial manner he used when he knew Rosemary had good reason to be angry with him. He crouched down to kiss her. "Hey," he said tenderly, taking her face in his hands and kissing her briefly, softly, on the lips. She turned toward the fire. He knew how much she liked it when he held her face in his hands, and she was determined not to fall for it.

"Where have you been?" she asked with a whine that she despised. "I've been sitting here alone forever."

"I'm sorry, but Raul and I have been talking about a business proposition that you're gonna love."

"The food's cold," she said, struggling to hold back tears.

Raul joined them at the fire pit, adding some twigs he'd found around the site. The flames momentarily surged.

"Let me explain," Pete said, straightening his knees. He opened the cooler, muttered "Whoa," and took out the last two beers.

"Make it last," he said to Raul, who nodded in thanks. "Rosemary's been thirsty."

She looked at him balefully but suddenly felt a stab of pain in her gut. She saw how easily he handled her anger, his utter lack of defensiveness, the confidence he exuded as he pushed his hair back from his forehead. He was certainly beautiful in the firelight, with his worn jeans hanging loosely from his slender hips, and she instantly became convinced he was cheating on her. That was why, she was suddenly certain, it didn't matter to him whether he was with her by the fire or out talking with Raul, or whether she was too busy with schoolwork to make the trip to Riverside. He was getting it somewhere else!

She turned her gaze back to the fire and felt her face grow hot and red. How could she have been so stupid? In a moment her mind marched from Shock to Stinging Betrayal, stopped for a few minutes in Sadness, and then landed squarely in Fury. Who was the bitch anyway, or were there several? Probably one of those little shits who hung around as the band was breaking down. The seventeen-year-olds with their flat stomachs and their boobs hanging out of their halter tops, laughing loudly in the parking lot as the equipment van was loaded. Pete probably picked up a different one in every little club he played. He probably caught their eyes while he was singing, or thrust his hips toward them ever so slightly during a guitar solo, and that was enough. She knew how easy it was to fall for his penetrating eyes and just-scruffy-enough looks—she did it every time she saw him play.

All those guys she had passed up, being faithful to Pete. Guys her own age, college guys with similar interests. She thought of Brent, her buddy in plant biology class who'd also been in her freshman comp. with her the year before. He was easy to talk to, and he made her laugh. He was a little dorky, but he had a kind face and she was at ease with him. He'd confessed to having a crush on her more than once, but she had remained loyal to Pete. Why?

"Rosie!" Pete said loudly. "Earth to Rosie!" He shook her knee. "Have you heard one word I've said?" Pete and Raul were halfway through their burritos, sitting cross-legged on the pad that Rosemary had spread before the fire.

"Huh?" she asked. As she turned toward him, she sniffed loudly and wiped her moist eyes with the back of her hand. "What?"

"I'm telling you that Raul is getting out of the weed business."

She ran her sleeve over her face. "You are?" she asked Raul. He nodded.

"It's getting harder and harder," Pete continued. "And more dangerous. All that mandatory sentencing stuff coming down from the feds is crazy. Even I'm spooked by it."

Her brow furrowed and she looked squarely at Pete. He was spooked? She'd never heard him once admit to being scared of anything. He was always cool on stage, smooth in social situations, and bold with her dad, scoffing at the many precautions she took to hide his pot dealing. He seemed to have turned confidence into an art, and that confidence had made her feel safe, made her believe in the magic of him. She was torn now by two desires: She wanted to challenge the idea that he was spooked—return him to his magic state, because if he wasn't magic, then she was certainly an idiot for staying with him so long—and she also wanted to challenge his confidence altogether, to tear it away and reduce him to shit, to prove it was an act put on to impress, obfuscate, inflate. Her mind suddenly turned this into a defining moment. Turning to face him, she thought: Either you're brave or you're not, you're for real or you're full of shit. Either I've been in a meaningful relationship with a gorgeous guy who doesn't mind that I'm fifteen pounds overweight, or I'm just another brainless band groupie and I've wasted four years of my life.

"Yeah," Pete continued, speaking for Raul. "He knows this area on both sides of the border so well that he's ready to expand. He wants to help people instead of just distributing weed."

Her curiosity momentarily eclipsed the defining moment. "Help people?"

Pete shifted so he was facing her fully, a gesture that ten minutes earlier would have appeared thoughtful, but which she now saw as a ploy to manipulate her. "He's going to help poor people who want to get into this country, underprivileged people who can't find work in Mexico and can't wait for papers."

"What?" Still incredulous, Rosemary turned to face Raul. "What are you talking about, illegals?"

"You don't have to label them like that, Rosemary," Pete said reproachfully. "They're human beings."

"You're going to smuggle in illegal immigrants, Raul. Is that correct?"

"Jes," Raul nodded.

"This is your new business?"

"Jes."

"So you'll be a coyote."

"A guide."

"You'll take money from these poor people and lead them into the desert to die."

"People do it every day, Rosie," Pete interjected. "They cross the desert without dying, and then they work their asses off in lousy jobs. Probably half the people that cut the grass and wash dishes at Cal State are here without papers. Or they were, until the amnesty. Get real, Rosie. They even pay taxes, most of them—you know that. The writing's on the wall. Immigration is changing, getting easier."

"They can't do it alone, Rosa," Raul said. "My cousin came over that way. He survived and he has a good life in Tucson. His coyote did not leave him to die."

"And people aren't contraband," Pete added. "It's safer than weed."

"It's human cargo, Pete. It's ugly."

"And pot's so pretty, I forgot. Drug dealing is a beautiful thing."

"It's not drugs, it's a plant!" Rosemary said, reciting the familiar litany. "There's no reason for it to be illegal. Pot's never killed anyone. It's safer than alcohol."

For a moment Rosemary saw a scene in her freshman dorm room after Pete had been fired from H & H, a beer distributor, for showing up late to work about a billion times. Rosemary had put on classical guitar music, lit a stick of incense, and filled his imagination with explanations fit for a New Age king: "Security is an illusion," she cooed. "This is the catalyst you've needed all along. Now you can work on your music without distractions." Rosemary assured him that having "the wolf at the door" would stoke his creativity, and that "When God closes a door, he opens a window." Wow, was she ever a jerk. She pumped him up to believe all that shit and made sure she believed it too. But he wasn't magic, he was just a guy. A lying, cheating, piece of shit guy.

"But it *is* illegal," Pete continued. "It *is* risky, and the laws are getting tougher. And I'm sick of it. It never stops. Someone's always knocking on my door at four in the morning all drunk and stupid, wanting a little baggie to help him sleep or to go watch the sunrise with. And now I have to move again because the landlord is on to me. It's nickel and dime money, Rosie, not worth the headache. With this I could bring over a group of people a few times a year and have the rest of the time for the band, and for you. Why are you being such a downer?"

Rosemary rose to her feet and started cleaning up the plates and food. She put the crusty bean pot to soak in the dishpan.

"What are you doing?" Pete demanded. "I thought we were having a conversation."

Raul stared into the embers.

"What is there to talk about?" Rosemary said, rummaging in a box for lantern fuel. "It sounds like you've already made up your mind. Just don't expect me to visit you in prison."

"You suck, you know that?" Pete said, jumping to his feet. "I support you in your decisions, but you don't support me in mine."

"Oh, you call this a decision?" Rosemary retorted, unscrewing the lid of the metal can. "It sounds to me like suicide. You're just too lazy to work, is all. You only started dealing because you were too lazy to show up to work every day!"

Raul got to his feet and headed up onto the rocks.

"What the fuck is with you?" Pete demanded, his voice rising. He grabbed her by the shoulders.

Rosemary wrenched away from him, slammed the can on the table, and faced him. "You've been screwing around on me, and now you're becoming a criminal. I can't deal with this."

"What are you talking about?" Pete shouted.

"Are you really going to stand there and tell me you've never slept around? That you've been loyal to me all these years?"

Pete stared into her face, trying to control his breathing. "I have never screwed around on you."

A high animal sound slipped from Rosemary's throat. "You're a goddamned liar!" she shouted, shoving him backward into the picnic table. "I hate your fucking guts!"

He fell heavily into the table, sending the propane stove and fuel can and a jug of water clattering to the ground.

"What the fuck?" Pete shouted, straightening up. "You're totally fucked up!" He leaned over to pick up the fuel can, scanning the ground for its lid as Rosemary patted down her jacket pockets.

"I saved your life, you know!" he shouted helplessly, still searching for the lid.

"You drove me to the goddamned fire station!" Rosemary shot back. She found her keys and made for Pete's Blazer.

"What the hell are you doing? Where are you going?" he barked, slamming down the fuel can.

"Fuck you!" Rosemary shouted as she climbed into the driver's seat, shut the door, and started the engine. She put the truck in reverse, backed up a few feet, and stalled with a violent lurch.

"Fucking stick shift!" she shouted. As Pete ran toward the truck, she locked the door, restarted the engine, and skidded out of the campsite, spraying dirt and gravel onto his legs, and knocking over a trash can. In the rearview mirror she could see him chasing his truck in the glowing red of the tail lights. She tore along the narrow campground road, choking on tears.

Chapter 6 | June, 1993

Joshua Tree National Monument, California

E VERYTHING WAS POSSIBLE. MORNING SUN BATHED THE Camry like a cherished child. Dried salt lakebeds gleamed as if they'd been whitewashed for royalty. Ravens, lords of the desert sky, greeted them from telephone poles, cawing their welcome.

Life was bright, rollicking, something to laugh along with. Since Rosemary met Liam, the puzzle of the world had become ever easier to solve: Everything came down to either love or fear, and she chose love. Tonight she would introduce him to her parents, but first they would set up camp and spend the day at Joshua Tree. Liam, who'd been playing around on these rocks for years, had been amused to find that one of the West's premier climbing spots was Rosemary's old teen-age hangout, and a largely unappreciated one at that. It was that "So where are you from?" conversation that started everything, carried them from dirt-covered co-workers at High Desert Landscaping to friends to lovers to fiancés. It had all been so easy, so graceful. At twenty-four, Rosemary was blessed.

As she stepped into the park visitor center, she suddenly felt a rushing flow of energy course through her body. She gasped, closed her eyes for a moment, and listened to the white noise of blood rushing through her ears. Her fingertips tingled as she reached for Liam, but he was not within reach. When she opened her eyes, he was already stepping forward to shake the hand of a park ranger. He didn't even notice the uncanny occurrence, which Rosemary quickly decided was part of the plan. After all, when you're stepping into your divine destiny, it is your own individual journey.

She found the restroom, splashed water on her face, and paused to look at herself in the mirror. With her clear skin, tan, and curly dark hair framing her face, she was striking. About a year earlier, she had let her heavy eyebrows grow in and stopped trying to straighten her hair, which gave her a dramatic, almost-exotic look. She noted with pleasure how the skin under her eyes was tight and supple. She looked better than she had in years—a world apart from the bloated, dissipated college student she had been just two years earlier. She had spent four years in air-conditioned buildings living on coffee and beer, working on her pretty much worthless degree in environmental science with an equally worthless minor in hydrology. But her landscaping job in Santa Fe had sculpted her body; she was strong, slender, healthy—and amazed at how fast her life had changed once she left Southern California.

The heavy restroom door suddenly swung inward, startling Rosemary. She turned to see a large woman, probably about sixty, enter and glance toward her. "Hello," Rosemary said automatically. The woman smiled, chimed back a hello, and approached a stall. Rosemary's gaze followed the woman's wide bottom, squeezed into elastic-waist capris, and she pitied her. She glanced again at her own flat tummy and tried to lock the image in her mind.

In the visitor area, she found Liam looking at displays of flora and fauna. He had bought a map and gathered a fistful of brochures on the park's climbing and camping areas.

"I'll go fill up the water jugs," she said. Absorbed in a poster about the Oasis of Mara, he grunted assent and kissed her on the cheek.

As the water at the shady spigot outside splashed into Rosemary's five-gallon jug, she felt amazed as always at the tap's clear gushing amid the harsh, sere desert. People walked around with bottles of water, took showers, washed their clothes, and clinked their ice seemingly without regard to how none of those things should have been possible. Fifty liters a day. That was what a human being was said to need to survive: five liters for drinking, ten for cooking, fifteen for bathing, and twenty for sanitation. But most Americans used more than that in one shower, and that was before they watered the lawn, washed the car, and ran the dishwasher. It was something that kept her awake nights long after she'd written her papers and charted her graphs on how fast the planet's freshwater supply was being depleted.

"Hot enough for you?"

She looked up, surprised to hear a voice that was not Liam's. The elderly man standing behind her with an empty water jug smiled broadly, his ruddy face shaded under a khaki hat.

"Oh, this is nothing," she replied, noting the small Band-Aids on the man's neck and forehead. "Wait till three in the afternoon—then we'll really fry."

"Aw, that's for lizards," the man said. "Me, I can't be in the sun like that anymore." He indicated the Band-Aids on his neck and forehead. "Just had some cancerous growths removed. We'll be in the cool enjoying the view before long." He pointed toward an RV. "That's got A/C and a fine awning."

Rosemary looked over at the Winnebago and chuckled as she said automatically, "So what does that get, like twelve blocks to the gallon?" The man's brow wrinkled as he looked at her wordlessly. She quieted herself abruptly and felt a stab of shame. They looked up when the woman from the bathroom approached with a brown bag in her hand.

"Got some more sunscreen!" she called as she passed. "And a couple of cold Cokes. I'll be in the RV."

"All right then, love!" he replied with a smile. Rosemary busied herself screwing on the jug's lid and wiping down its sides with her T-shirt. "So long," the man said, touching her arm. "Have a good day." She nodded and smiled, awash in a nameless disappointment.

Liam was already at the car when she returned. "The ranger suggested the Jumbo Rocks campground," he said, stowing the water container in the trunk. "Do you know it?"

"Yes," she said, recognizing it as the area where she, Pete, and Raul had spent so many evenings. "It's beautiful."

As they snaked through the narrow roads at 10 MPH, Liam's voice, deep and rich as a bassoon, lulled her back to the perfect feeling she had enjoyed since they left home. How she hated high voices in men! She looked over to appreciate him, her prize: solid, stocky, tall enough, and unaware of his good looks. Hair crammed under a Yankees cap, powerful legs in loose, worn shorts, a T-shirt advertising Yum Yum Mix fertilizer. So sweet and so damned capable. Liam could handle anything that came his way. A rock face, a car engine, a baby, an artichoke, whatever the challenge, he approached the world with an attitude that said "of course." He was by far the best thing that had ever happened to her.

They'd driven eight hours the day before, stayed in a motel in Kingman, gotten an early start, and arrived at Twentynine Palms when the morning was still sweet and cool. Not much had changed since she'd been there last. She had scanned instinctively for her father's police vehicle as they made their way through town, and worried they'd bump into her mother in the grocery store, but they had emerged undetected.

Rosemary was nervous about the evening. Deet, who had been living in L.A. for years, doing something with hedge funds that no one could quite understand, was in Phoenix now, working for a golf course developer. Desperate for a buffer, Rosemary had begged him to make the trip, but he said he was close to closing a deal and couldn't get away.

She assumed her parents would like Liam—who wouldn't?—but she was also enjoying a subtle defiance. She was an adult—a college graduate with a job and a fiancée. No, she was not exactly using her degree and she was not long on money either, but she was on track for success. Liam would be leaving High Desert soon to start his own landscaping business. They would be able to buy a house and raise a family. Liam was her destiny. If they didn't like him, tough.

Rosemary sat in the car with the engine idling while Liam checked out one campsite after another. She knew most of them but wanted him to choose. Returning to the driver's seat at Site 22, he told her, "The people at the next one over have a ladle dogged."

"A little dog?" she asked.

"That's what I said, isn't it?" he asked straight-faced as she threw her head back and laughed. "Don't want to hear that thing yipping all night long, and the one next to it has absolutely no shade." He inched further along, rejecting four more until they arrived at Site 38. Her heart raced as they approached it.

"This looks nice," he said, pulling up the emergency brake and getting out. "Be right back." Could this be happening? A park that covers 560,000 acres and they end up camping in the same place she had spent so many nights with Pete?

Liam returned to the car excited. "This one is awesome!" he said beaming. "Do you want to check it out?"

"No, I know it," she said. "It's a great site."

"Then we're home!" Liam said, backing the car in. "Come on, sweet thing. Let's move in."

Liam set up the tent facing east so they would have morning light, and Rosemary set up the camp stove and unpacked the food. She made them each an almond butter sandwich, sliced some peaches, and brought their lunch to the shady rock ledge where they could stretch out.

"Well this is cool," Liam said, running his hand over the smooth rock. "You've stayed at this site befuddle?"

"Yes, before," she smiled. "With Pete, several times."

"With Pete? No kidding! Well that's as weird as it gets," he said without a trace of rancor. "So what am I up against? Do you think his ghost is around here?"

"He's not dead, Liam."

"Ah, but his spirit might be malingering." He chuckled as he devoured his sandwich. "God, I'm starving. So tonight's the big night, huh? Mark and Martina Sabin meet Liam Ellis. What are we going to talk about?"

"Well, the weather for starters."

"Hot and sunny. Then what?"

"Your work."

"My work, right—about how I yank weeds out of gravel and pick up dog shit in rich people's yards."

"Stop, you do more than that."

"Not lately. Juanito has been giving me total crap work ever since I gave notice."

"Well that's temporary. You can talk about your business plans."

"Maybe your dad has some good cop stories."

"Sure, get a few beers in him and he'll loosen up. As long as we can keep Mom from getting too bizarre."

"But you said she's been pretty normal these days."

"According to Dad she is." When Rosemary called to say they would be visiting, her dad had sounded upbeat. "All is well here," he'd said, which meant that Martina was not power-praying or scrubbing the paint off walls.

"So why are you so normal, anyway?" Liam asked, licking his fingers. "Why aren't you dangerously religious or relentlessly law-abiding?"

"I don't know, and Deet's fairly normal too."

"The mysterious David, with the nickname reminiscent of a Raid can."

"Hey, that name is his own fault. He spent his childhood torturing bugs."

"Here's a question—do they think we're out here sleeping in two separate tents?"

Rosemary laughed. "Probably, but it won't come up. Nothing uncomfortable ever gets discussed. Don't worry, they'll love you."

Liam shifted his body so that his head rested against her leg. She leaned back on the rock and began massaging his head, surveying her surroundings. The site, the park, the town were all the same as they had been four years ago, but the world was such a different place now. She could scarcely believe she had been at this very place fighting with Pete about cheating and Mexican immigrants and what all. The picnic table the old Coleman stove was on before it came crashing to the ground was still in the same spot, but Liam's Coleman stove was on it now. The firepit was still there though they had not brought any fake logs for it. This flat, shady rock ledge was still a magical perch. It was all such a still, expectant place.

Liam's regular breathing told Rosemary that he was asleep, and she smiled. Only Liam could fall asleep on a rock. Her mind drifted back to Martina, which always made her unaccountably sad. Her mother lived such a small life. Rosemary could not remember a time when she didn't feel sorry for her, when she didn't feel guilty for having a boyfriend, for leaving the house on a Friday night, for going away to college. She'd had to tell Martina some time during fifth grade that she wanted to walk to school with Sheila instead of her, and that she didn't want Martina to volunteer in her classroom anymore. While her classmates complained that their mothers were grumpy or self-absorbed, Rosemary complained that hers was a leech that cramped her style. The guilt to which she was so accustomed stirred in her heart like a hibernating skunk disturbed in its sleep.

But this was negative and unproductive. She pushed the thoughts aside and replaced them with an affirmation: Everything unfolds as it should.

Rosemary rubbed her index finger where a cut was healing from an accident with pruning shears the week before. The slice had been so clean she'd barely felt it at first, but it had bled like crazy. Just looking at it made her shudder. This and every laceration she had seen since her first semester of college had made her shudder, as they reminded her of her old roommate, Janine. She waited for the stomach-tightening spasm that always came with thoughts of Janine—there it was, deep in her gut. She breathed through it and repeated soundlessly to herself, "Everything unfolds as it should. Everything unfolds as it should." But that mantra never worked with Janine. Again Rosemary lost control of her thoughts and the dark scene played itself out in her mind, as it had so many times before.

She'd returned to her dorm room earlier than expected one Friday night after some boring talk and heard voices through the closed door. It cheered her to hear that Janine—nearly always alone—had a friend over now, and she thought the evening might turn out to be fun after all. When she opened the door, she saw a bottle of vodka on Janine's nightstand. And then she saw the blood. A heap of sodden, red paper towels lay on the rug, and a small collection of knives was spread out on Janine's Hello Kitty bedspread.

"Shit!" Janine shouted.

"Shit!" the other girl shouted.

"My God!" Rosemary cried. "What happened? Are you hurt?"

Janine scrambled to cover the knives with her pillow, but the sudden movement made a paper towel fall from her forearm. A bright red drip of blood sprang loose and raced toward her wrist.

"Janine!" Rosemary shouted. "What happened?"

The other girl jumped to her feet, clutching a paper towel to her own forearm. "Sorry," she said, her hair covering her face as she struggled to step into her sneakers. "I gotta go."

Janine put her head in her hands as the door slammed. Rosemary stared at her in stunned silence.

"Janine, what the hell?"

"Look," Janine said after a moment. "I didn't want you to see this."

"See what? What is this?"

"Me and Annika," she said, fresh tears streaming down her cheeks. "We sometimes cut ourselves."

"What?"

"Cutting. We cut ourselves."

"You cut yourself? On purpose?" Rosemary's grew louder and more shrill. "What the fuck are you talking about?"

"It's not that uncommon, Rosemary. Calm down."

"People do this?"

"Yes, people do this. Please stop shouting."

"But why?" Rosemary asked, managing to speak more quietly though her heart was racing.

"You wouldn't understand. Just forget you ever saw this. It's a private thing. You shouldn't have seen this."

"Buy why do you do it?"

"Sometimes," Janine said, wiping her face with a corner of her blanket. "Sometimes it's something I need to do. It's part of my depression."

"You're depressed?" Rosemary looked at Janine's face and suddenly saw a world of pain in her tear-filled eyes. Did she always look like this?

"Yes, Einstein, I'm depressed, OK?" Her voice grew sharper. "I've been depressed as long as I can remember. And sometimes when the pressure builds up, it's the only thing that relieves it." She methodically wiped the knives clean and slid them into a plastic makeup bag. Rosemary saw a serrated steak knife and an X-Acto with blue paint on its handle. As Janine put the bloody paper towels into the trash can, Rosemary saw successive stripes of scars on her arms. They were mostly the same length, but were at different stages of healing. Rosemary realized she had never seen her roommate's arms before. Janine always wore long sleeves, even on the hottest days, and went to and from the shower every morning in a bathrobe.

"It's not polite to stare," Janine said, pulling on a hooded sweatshirt.

"Sorry," Rosemary whispered.

"I'm sure it's hard for you to get this," Janine continued. "But cutting brings peace. For a while."

"You cut your body and feel peace from it?"

"Shit, will you ease up? Not everyone is like you, OK? We're not all happy and pretty with nice families and gorgeous boyfriends, OK? Some of us have problems."

"Well how can cutting yourself solve a problem?"

"It doesn't solve it," Janine said wearily. "It doesn't solve anything. It just makes it easier for a while."

"Pain makes it easier?"

"The pain is. . .it's a distraction, a distraction from my emotions. For a few minutes, when the shock of the physical pain hits, there's relief from the emotional pain. Can you understand that?"

"I guess so."

"Sometimes it's just a pressure that needs to be relieved. I don't do it every day. It's just something. . .look, I wish you'd just forget about it."

"How can I ever forget this?"

"And don't tell anyone you saw Annika here. Like I said, it's a private thing. I should have locked the door."

Rosemary sat on her bed stiffly.

"I guess I should have knocked."

"No, it's your room too. Listen, you want some vodka?"

That was in early November. They were cordial for the next few weeks, but Janine didn't return from Thanksgiving break. Sometime over Christmas vacation, her things disappeared from their dorm room and Rosemary never learned what happened to her. In January she had a new roommate, Melinda, who was none too bright, but at the time Rosemary was just so relieved that she was normal.

And she had felt guilty about it all ever since. She should have been a better friend. She should have asked Janine what made her so sad. She should have been the one Janine could open up to. She probably should have alerted some authority at Cal, or found a way to contact Janine's parents to tell them their daughter was a cutter. She should have stretched out her hand to a drowning soul. But she did nothing. She treated Janine like some exotic creature with a rare disease that might be catching. She gave her a wide berth and kept things light, telling herself she was respecting her roommate's privacy, but really she was just being a selfish, shallow jerk. No, everything had not unfolded as it should have, but she believed she had learned something from the experience. She knew she would be a better friend the next time someone needed help, that she would be a responsible adult in the next difficult situation, not a selfish, shallow jerk.

"Hey!" Liam had been coming awake slowly, rousing himself like a cat in the sun. Suddenly he lurched and sat up abruptly. "You said Pete was a dealer, right? And that he used to meet his connection at Joshua Tree, right?"

"Huh?" Rosemary blinked away the old scene. "What?"

"Pete. He was a dealer, right? Did he ever hide his stash here?"

"Not really. He usually wasn't too worried about being caught."

"But did he ever?"

Rosemary thought back to a time when Pete had gotten more cautious, a short while after his bass player was busted, and he did have a hiding place. "A few times he hid some baggies when he thought the park rangers might be onto him," she said.

Liam jumped down from the rock ledge and was instantly grinning. "Can you find the spot? Let's see if there's any hidden."

"Liam, after all these years? I doubt there would be any, and I probably couldn't find it anyway."

"Well let's try. Come on, it'll be fun."

"I thought you wanted to climb."

"It's too hot to climb now anyway. I'll hook up with some people in the morning. Come on, let's go on a pleasure blunt."

"Oh, a treasure hunt! And what if we find the treasure?"

"We'll smoke it! Come on, sweet thing."

"Wait, let me get oriented," she said. She stood still, imagining the site the way she and Pete used to set it up, and stepped slowly toward the rock face. After studying the ways up, she chose a path with vegetation—such tenacious vegetation!—growing from its shaded, miniature crevices. She scooted up and pulled herself through a small space between two huge boulders high above the site. Yes, this was the route, she was sure. "I think I can get us there. Why don't you grab a water bottle."

Rosemary scanned the expanse ahead of her, taking in the vast field of towering rock slabs and jumbled boulders that somehow created one united landscape, like a collection of stepsiblings in a blended family. When Liam returned with a water bottle and their hats, he followed her toward a rock formation about a hundred yards away that stretched high above the others. If she was right, there would be a small cave at the base of that rectangular rock jutting up like a miniature office building.

"Is this it?" Liam asked as she crouched in front of the shaded opening while her eyes adjusted.

"Yeah," Rosemary answered, peering in cautiously. "But it's spooky. There are probably spiders and stuff."

"You want me to go in first?"

"Please," she breathed with relief, stepping aside.

Liam crouched down and ran his hands along the small opening, little more than a triangle of space between two slabs of stone. As he reached into the darkness, muttering a confident "No webs here," a lizard skittered out of the cave and ran over his foot. In an instant he was up, shrieking and dancing a graceless jig. "Aah!" he shouted, hopping up and down. Rosemary burst into laughter and he soon joined her, tears streaming down their faces.

"My God!" Liam said, wiping his face with his hat.

"Oh," Rosemary echoed, still giggling. "That was fun! Do it again!"

They laughed uproariously until Liam said through a sigh, "Okay. Let's check this out." He got down on his hands and knees and moved slowly through the opening.

"Looks OK," he called. "No monsters!"

Rosemary crawled in after him. "It's so good to get out of the sun," she said.

"Yeah, it must be like twenty degrees cooler in here."

They moved their hands along the walls, trying to get their bearings in the relative darkness.

"Can't be more than eight or ten square feet in here," Liam said. "Are you sure this is the place?"

"Yes," Rosemary answered, feeling for the boulder that she knew was part of the cave's interior. "There's a sort of ledge here somewhere." She raised herself up, ran her hands along the upper walls and found the rounded place on top of the boulder. She spread her hands along its surface, following the slope to where the boulder met the slab wall. "OK," she said when her hands found some loose stones, "this is the place."

"Yeah?" Liam replied, joining her on his knees.

Rosemary began handing the stones to Liam, who piled them on the ground. Her fingertips touched something soft. "This might be something," she said, pressing her hands into the soft mass. "Holy shit, this might really be something!"

"No way!" Liam breathed excitedly.

"Way!" she replied with a laugh. "And it's big!"

She lifted the plastic mass from its crevice, made sure there were no others, and crawled out through the triangle of light. Liam scuttled after her into the sun.

"Well?" he asked.

She leaned into the rock face waiting for her eyes to adjust. Liam watched patiently as she opened the Ziploc bag and pulled from it four small, heat-sealed plastic packages.

"Oh my God!" Liam shouted.

"Shh!"

"We found the treasure!"

"Shh!"

"OK, OK, let's open one." With his pocketknife, he slit open one of the packages and drank in the pungent scent of marijuana.

"It's wonderful! Look at these beautiful buds!"

"Totally," she agreed, fingering the moist clumps in a reverential tone.

"What's with the packing?" he asked. "Either Pete was here just yesterday or there's some magic about this plastique."

"Pete had a seal-a-meal thing," she explained, laughing a little. "He had other guys selling for him and was getting paranoid that they were stealing from him, so he'd weigh out quarter-ounces, half-ounces, or whatever, and seal them. He could guarantee weights then and no one could say he sold them short."

"An honest dealer, I like that," Liam said. "I've been ripped off by dealers—hasn't everyone?—but what are you gonna do, call the Better Business Bureau?"

"So these are four quarter-ounce bags."

"Could they really have been sitting here for years?"

"Who knows, could be years, could be yesterday."

"Well I'm sure I have some papers in the car. Let's fire it up."

"You want to get stoned now?" Rosemary asked. "We're going to see my parents soon."

"We have like four hours," Liam countered. "That's enough. Come on, we're on vacation and we were just gifted with an ounce of what promises to be great weed. Shouldn't we accept the gift?"

Rosemary paused and said, "Well, we can't keep it all. Let's just take a quarter-ounce and leave the rest where we found it. We can't be sure this is a forgotten stash."

"Fair enough," Liam agreed.

She resealed the Ziploc, crawled back into the cave, replaced the baggie and covered it with the same rocks. When she emerged, Liam was smiling. "Come on, sweet thing," he said. "Let's spark it!"

Rosemary felt the mixed emotions she had become so familiar with in high school, the blend of daring and dread, thrill and fear. Liam certainly expected her to smoke with him, but she knew she'd just overeat, feel stupid, and fall asleep. She hadn't smoked since college. And then there was all the crime caused by the drug trade. Didn't he know how the power of the Mexican drug cartels, not to mention gang violence in the U.S., was fueled by American demand? Should she tell him?

Rosemary said nothing as they descended to the campsite and settled back onto the shady rock ledge, where Liam began examining the buds.

"It's art," he gushed, "pure art."

"It's a plant."

"We are fortunate people."

As Liam broke up the tight, compact buds and separated out the seeds, she found herself thinking about Pete. Where was he? Should she have answered his phone calls four years ago? Did she screw that whole thing up or was she right about her suspicions? She remembered his professions of innocence. She'd assumed it was an act, but could she have been wrong?

Liam got rolling papers from the car, deftly rolled a joint, looked around, and lit up, drawing carefully and shielding it with his hands.

"Oh yeah, this is delicious," he said, holding in the smoke and handing her the joint. "Fine weed, probably Indica."

She waved the joint away.

"No?" Liam asked, exhaling.

"Nah."

"Okay."

Well, that was easy.

"So tell me about tonight," Liam began. He took another toke. "What are they hoping for right now?"

"Well right now my mom is cleaning, and feeling hurt that we're not staying at their house." She paused to picture Martina vacuuming, shoving the upright before her in short, angry bursts. "And she is surveying the refrigerator to make sure all the food is ready."

"It's ready now?"

"Definitely. She would have done it all yesterday, and last night. 'It's a poor hostess who entertains her guests in the kitchen,'" she said in her best Emily Post voice.

"So what will she be serving, o psychic one?"

Rosemary pictured her mom looking into the fridge and tried to imagine what she would be seeing, cloaked beneath waxed paper. "Shrimp cocktail and raw vegetables for starters."

"And?"

"Horseradish sauce."

"And?"

Again, Rosemary pictured the refrigerator and peered beneath the waxed paper.

"Chicken parts, marinated in a sticky teriyaki sauce, which she will broil." She paused. "A rice pilaf with scallions and pineapple bits. And green beans amandine." She chuckled a bit and sighed. "My mom has three set company meals that she rotates through. They're like suits hanging in her closet—a bit outdated, but sensible just the same."

She thought of her father's parents, and how clearly unimpressed they were with those company meals on the rare visits they made to Twentynine Palms, and then of those strange, disorienting visits the family made to Santa Barbara every summer. They would drive hundreds of miles to stay with strangers, it seemed: the fancy house, the lush green yard, the well-dressed grandparents who looked at the her and Deet like they were unusual breeds of koi that mysteriously showed up in their backyard pond. Who were those elegant people?

Her most persistent memory of those visits was of Ruth throwing away food. "These don't keep," she'd say, pushing a plate of kosher franks, grilled just an hour or two earlier, into the trash. While she was scraping the plate, she would intone, "As Ira would say, when in doubt, throw it out!" Hours later Ira might do the same thing, standing in front of the fridge with his large rectangular butt protruding: "As Ruth would say, when in doubt, throw it out!" And there would go yesterday's chicken lo mein.

Suddenly she wondered how her mother felt about the annual Santa Barbara trip. She never complained, but she certainly didn't seem to enjoy being there. Funny, Rosemary had no idea how her mother felt about those visits, or even about her grandparents themselves. Did she enjoy the break from routine, the visits to Disneyland, the time at the beach, or was she also counting the days? Rosemary had always resented her mother's reticence, her stoicism, but suddenly she saw their merit. There was value, sometimes, in keeping your feelings to yourself. Martina would probably have made things worse by groaning about those visits, might have turned Rosemary and Deet against their grandparents if she carried on about their wasteful lifestyle, their liberal politics, their golfing.

"Seriously, though," Liam said, pulling her back to the present. "Do you think they'll like me?"

"Of course."

"When I walk through the door, what will they want to see?"

Rosemary turned her eyes toward the rock face she was leaning on and ran her fingers along the cool stone. "They'll want you to be stable," she answered, studying the tiny fissures in the basalt. "Steady and sensible. Someone who reads newspapers. Someone who plans for the future."

Liam took another puff. "Well I guess they'll like me then," he said, coughing as he exhaled.

"As long as you don't smell like pot smoke," Rosemary said, nudging him playfully.

"It's plenty windy here," Liam replied, stubbing out the joint. "I won't smell like smoke." He leaned back, close to her. "Long live Pete what's-his-face."

"Dean."

"Dean."

They were quiet for several minutes, and Rosemary grew languid in the heat, feeling her heartbeats slow. Soon she felt a flood of warmth, of forgiveness, toward Pete. Even if he had cheated on her, they'd still had some good times.

"Pete saved my life once, you know," she said drowsily.

"I thought you said he just drove you to the fire station."

"Yeah, well, if he hadn't, I would have died."

"Well long live Pete Dean again, then," Liam said with a lazy thumbs-up.

She breathed deeply and turned her attention again to the landscape, fascinated anew by the way the rocks stacked up against each other. How permanent they seemed, but of course they were in transition. Some day they would slip, shinny, tumble to the ground, succumb to the siren call of gravity, lament their fate as they fell. But it was all as it should be. And the desert itself was as it should be. Thank God nobody was irrigating it here, trying to coax flowers and grass from its alkaline soil, pretending it was Atlanta or Charlottesville or Eugene. She had grown to despise places like L.A. and San Diego, desert cities that pretended they weren't. Those places should have been tiny coastal towns with a few thousand people making their living as fishermen—that's all the climate could truly support. But instead they were metropolises because the cities had stolen water from other parts of the state—and the Colorado River as well. And while she usually got riled up by what to her was a human rights violation perpetrated against the residents of Owens Valley and the like, today she saw it as a metaphor for the way people in America's media-soaked, anxiety-ridden society perceived themselves. It wasn't OK to have a wide nose or thin hair or full thighs or a gap in your teeth—these things were wrong and must be fixed. Just like it wasn't OK for a landscape to have sparse vegetation or bare soil or trees that bloomed only once every ten or fifteen years—these things were wrong and must be fixed. And the only way to fix them was to destroy rivers and deltas and lakes and aquifers so that desert towns could recklessly become cities. That narrow idea of what was beautiful ran much deeper than she'd realized, deeper than women getting nose jobs or starving themselves; it had destroyed a whole chain of ecosystems.

But this was not the time for these thoughts, she scolded herself, taking a deep breath. She was here to enjoy her fiancé and her favorite place. And with the sound of a raven's wing beats above, the weight of Liam's body gently pressing against hers, and the rock face in front of her, it seemed nothing could satisfy her more than sitting there, running her hands along the smooth stone. She grew drowsy and began to drift until Liam's voice startled her.

"You know," he said. "Why is it that I like raspberry flavored things, but I hate raspberries?"

"Huh?"

"Come on, let's do something."

She reluctantly broke out of her reverie.

"Let's go for a walk," he continued, straightening up and reaching for a water bottle.

"Sure," she said, stretching. She stuffed a fanny pack with peaches, put it on, and followed Liam out of the campsite into the miles of rock and sky.

They walked in silence. As Rosemary looked around, she searched for nooks she could take a nap in while Liam looked for places to climb. He stopped a few times to boulder up a particularly tempting face while she waited in the shade, musing on a creosote bush and its microcosm: how the shade moved through the day, how tiny weeds had taken hold in one spot and not another, where lizards and rodents could find refuge from predators.

She climbed up to a flat ledge and settled in while Liam bouldered around nearby. Looking out over the great open expanse, she followed the movement of distant cars and of birds on the cliff formations. Her nervous system alternated between the calm and quiet of the familiar place, and doubt—another familiar place: Was she boring Liam? Should she be bouldering around with him? Should she be more interesting right now, more daring, zippy, and fun?

❧ ❧ ❧

At the top of the spires, Liam was whooping with satisfaction, a nimble mountain goat free under the desert sky. His life stretched out as far as he could see: a new business, a beautiful woman, a place like this. How wonderful to have escaped the East, the old moldering East. "Back east" or "out west," people said. And he was out. Never would he get sucked back into that old, decaying world. A few more hours and they'd be back on the road, back to the life he couldn't wait to build. Suddenly he felt like it was Christmas Day and he wasn't allowed to play with his toys until after breakfast.

The in-laws. Knock out this meal tonight, maybe brunch on Sunday, and they were back on the road. Mark and Martina were like clients, he decided, clients he needed to win over. They were clients who, say, had ten acres of land out Old Santa Fe Trail. People who wanted a stone driveway entrance, a butterfly garden, and a fountain. Big clients he needed in the worst way. "Sweet thing!" he called down to Rosemary, who was staring at something. "We should get going!"

He scrambled down, leaping to a graceful, bent-knee landing. Then he straightened up quickly, arched his back, and thrust his arms out like a gymnast, pivoting around to accept applause from all corners of the stadium.

"A perfect ten!" Rosemary announced. Liam laughed and reached for her, running his hands down her torso, feeling her pleasing shape and firmness. Here was the woman he'd chosen. She was pretty, good-hearted, strong, and she made him laugh. She was also good in bed.

"Okay, darlin'" he said. "Let's clean up and go meet the folks!"

❧   ❧   ❧

The street was as it had always been, tidy and bland, with the houses varying only slightly from each other. But as they pulled into the driveway, Rosemary saw that Mrs. Lopez's front yard next door had become a dazzling garden. Cactus and succulents filled the area that used to be covered with white, angular stones.

Rosemary got out of the car and stepped toward it, completely engrossed. Some plants were six feet tall, with narrow paths snaking around them. Others were flowering, and some created a ground cover. Low stools and ceramic ornaments were tucked in among the plants. Mrs. Lopez had created a desert world comfortable enough for a person to dwell, a tiny world that worked. It was arresting, beautiful.

"Ro!" she heard Liam's voice. "Babe! Over here!"

She turned to find Liam with Mark and Martina. They were smiling at her indulgently. She was embarrassed but felt suddenly warm. Only Liam could do this: In one second, he had made her happy to see her mother.

She walked over and hugged her parents. They commented on her lean frame, shaded their eyes and smiled at Liam.

"That garden," Rosemary pointed. "Who knew Mrs. Lopez could create such a thing?"

"She didn't," Mark replied. "Don't you remember the Lopezes moved? Betsy did that, our new neighbor."

"I told you about her," Martina said. "She's a single woman, from out of state."

Mark wrapped his arm around Martina's shoulders. "And she's Mom's new best friend." Mark smiled at Rosemary, holding her gaze in a pointed way, and Rosemary realized that Betsy's presence was why he had been so upbeat about her mom.

"Oh, you make me sound so silly," Martina scolded him. "Let's go inside. I've got some snacks waiting for you."

"Would you like a margarita?" Mark asked.

"A margarita?" Rosemary stopped, ripping off her sunglasses. "Since when do you drink margaritas?"

"Since I bought a snazzy blender," Mark responded. "Is that OK with you, dear daughter? Or is there a law against your parents drinking delicious drinks?"

"Sounds great!" Liam exclaimed, holding the door open for the three of them.

Over gazpacho and scallops marinated in lime juice, they discussed political changes in Twentynine Palms and the price of gas. Over well-brined chicken parts blackened with Cajun spices, seared on Mark's gleaming new gas grill, the conversation turned toward desert landscaping, along with possible names for Liam's new business. The salad, Rosemary noted with disbelief, was leaf lettuce with baby greens, rather than the usual iceberg. Who were these people?

Rosemary drank steadily, thirsty from the spicy food, but mostly to revel in feeling free and loose—with her parents, of all people. Imagine, being treated like a guest in her childhood home, like an adult, and her parents were actually interesting. They looked older, but they were relaxed. More alive, really, than ever. They'd taken a trip to Vegas, just three hours north, a place they'd never been before, and among other adventures had had an encounter with a pickup truck full of people with blue-tinged skin. "No joke, they were blue," her dad laughed. "The truck had Kentucky plates. What they were doing in Vegas I can't imagine."

And the Sabins had bought new carpeting. "Now that Little One is gone, it seemed like time for new," her mother explained. Little One, their ancient Scotty dog, had finally croaked. They'd also painted the living room and dining room, not white again, but different shades of cream and beige, and the walls were bare. "You'll have to excuse us," her mother said. "We haven't hung the pictures up again." This meant that the photos of her and Deet no longer filled the wall area above the piano, the piano that she'd never played enough. All those lessons with Mrs. Shoen, all the études and sonatinas. She imagined playing it now: She'd sit down casually on the Naugahyde bench and improvise something, a rich conglomeration of chords with a mysterious melody that sprang from a secret place within her. She'd play just long enough to suggest that there was more where that came from, and then seem a little embarrassed at the attention she'd drawn. Liam would be awed, moved. She'd take a sip of her drink and drift coolly away from the piano.

"Rosie? Rosie!" Liam nudged her. "Your dad asked you a question." The reverie dissolved.

"How's your job?"

"Work?" Rosemary recovered quickly. "It's OK. I'll miss working with this guy." She elbowed Liam. "But I like it. I like being outside. I like being around plants."

"Good for you, honey," Mark said.

She braced herself for the question: When will you begin using your degree?

"You know," Mark said. "I never paid much attention to gardens and landscaping until Betsy moved in next door. She transformed that pile of rocks into such a beautiful place. I have a new appreciation for it all."

"Oh, that garden is really something," Martina agreed. "You should see it in the morning light. And Betsy is such a delightful person."

Delightful. Again, who were these people?

It turned out that Betsy, whose last name was Ross, really, was from Minnesota and had moved to Twentynine Palms to escape those endless northern winters. Betsy was back in St. Paul at the moment, visiting her aging mother. Rosemary assumed that the fresh, flavorful food was somehow due to her influence.

By the third margarita, Mark started in on his "world's stupidest criminal" stories. Since Rosemary and Martina had heard them all before, they both leaned back and smiled as Mark put on his show and Liam enjoyed it. A feeling of contentment settled over Rosemary like morning dew.

But Mark had saved his big news for dessert. Over coffee and fruit he announced that he was retiring the following month from the sheriff's department and would be entering law school.

"It's time for a change," Mark said to Rosemary, whose jaw had dropped and stayed dropped. "I know I'll be nearly fifty when I'm done, but what the heck? I'll still be nearly fifty if I don't do it, right? I'd like to be a prosecutor. I'd like to help put those bastards away."

Rosemary was astounded. Her dad, her sweet dad, was taking a risk. He was growing, and her mom beamed with pride.

"Your dad is very excited," she said. "The fact is, we saved this money for David's college, and he never went, so now your dad can use it for his own."

"There'll be a lot of driving, but your mom says she can handle me being away."

Martina popped up from her chair and started clearing the dessert dishes.

"Law school?" Rosemary asked, incredulous. "You're going to law school?"

Now Mark beamed with pride. "Yes, I am. And this will give your mom more time to visit with Betsy."

"More decaf anyone?" Martina interrupted. There were no takers.

"So I figure I'll study criminal law and hopefully work for the D.A.'s office," Mark explained. "I look forward to being more than a witness in those court rooms."

Rosemary helped her mother scrape and stack the dishes while Mark and Liam chatted. But when talk turned to spending the night, she rebuffed the offer, and Liam took her cue.

"It's late," she said. "Thank you so much for dinner. It was just delicious, Mom."

"We never see you. Why can't you just stay here?" Martina encouraged. "Your room is just as you left it, and so is David's. You two will be plenty comfortable here."

"Well now," Mark said, beginning to construct the shield that he so often erected for his daughter. "As long as they're not above the legal limit."

"I had only one drink, sir, and that was two hours ago," Liam assured Mark. "I'm fine."

"I don't know why you prefer to sleep on the ground and use a public bathroom when you can stay here," Martina huffed.

"That's just fine, honey. Camping is always fun," Mark said with exaggerated enthusiasm.

"I like waking up outside," Rosemary said, running defense. "It's special, and it's what we've planned."

"You've done this together before?" Martina asked.

"We've been together for two years, Mom."

"It's been well over a year since we've seen you. Oh, I don't know." She began waving her hand across her face, as if to wave away her feelings.

"Call us tomorrow, honey," Mark said. He kissed Rosemary on the cheek and shook Liam's hand. "You kids enjoy the park!"

CHAPTER 7 | APRIL, 1995

Palm Springs, California

T HE GUESTS STOOD WITH CHAMPAGNE FLUTES POISED, READY to toast the new couple. Someone made a joke at David's expense, and although she couldn't hear it, Martina laughed along with the other guests. Isabelle, her daughter-in-law-to-be, threw her head back and laughed loudly, her white teeth glinting sharply as a camera flashed. She had not quite closed her mouth when David turned to kiss her, causing them to fumble and poke their lips at each other like confused chickens. Martina snickered.

"To Isabelle and David!" shouted Heather or Haley or some other blonde H- woman, raising her glass in an expansive gesture. "Congratulations on your engagement. May your love be as deep as the ocean, and your sorrows as light as its foam!" The guests clinked their glasses and the band struck up a two-step version of "Come Rain or Come Shine."

"C'mon, babe," Liam said, taking Rosemary's hand. Rosemary looked around for a place to set her glass, and Martina reached out her hand. Rosemary handed the empty to her mother with an apologetic smile and followed Liam to the dance floor. Guests smiled and clapped as Liam led Rosemary around the floor in a flamboyant Western two-step.

"Woo-hoo!" shouted the H, who was Isabelle's sister— they'd been introduced; Martina really should know her name.

The woman dragged her father onto the dance floor shouting, "Come on, Daddy! Time to enjoy your party!"

Guests filled the dance floor of the sumptuous country club ballroom. Everywhere waiters were offering pork medallions, duck confit, blackened shrimp, and more champagne. David was marrying a hotel-chain heiress and the family had spared no expense for their engagement party.

Martina watched her daughter whirl around the dance floor, aglow in her husband's arms. Her cobalt blue dress sparkled beneath the light of the chandeliers like brush strokes on a glittering black canvas. She was gorgeous, so young and full. Martina could remember how it felt to be twenty-six, that feeling of bursting with possibility. Of course she was never as beautiful as Rosemary, but she was firm and trim, and when dressed to the nines could turn a few heads. Mark had seemed to think she was beautiful.

And he was still handsome. At that moment he was standing near his mother and aunt on the other side of the dance floor, clearly not paying attention to the conversation. Ruth was probably going on about her golf game, or Ira's back pain. Martina turned her attention back to the dance floor, where Rosemary and Liam were embracing. Soon David and Isabelle joined them, and there they were in one frame: her children, all grown up. They were complete, done, like cakes ready to be taken out of the oven. Done and done.

A few years ago she had been angry at how they'd seemed to cast her aside, especially Rosemary. "They look at me like I'm a part of their past," she'd said to Mark, "like I'm out of style."

"They're growing up. They'll come to appreciate you again, honey. Give them time."

"But don't you see? They're these healthy, strong young adults, and I'm a faded middle-aged woman. It's like they're these beautiful tomatoes, or bell peppers, fresh from the garden, and I'm the tired soil. They don't realize that they're healthy and beautiful only because they took everything I had to give!"

"Well they didn't ask to be born," Mark said. "We chose to have them. It was our job to raise them."

"And it's their job to care about us."

"They do care about us."

"If I could have one minute with my mother again I'd be the most grateful person in the world. Yet here I am and they barely call or visit."

"How much time do I spend with my own parents?"

"Probably not enough, but that's different—they're not terribly interested in us, have you noticed?"

"Martina, you're wrong about this. People grow and change, and relationships change too. Be patient."

"Patient is all I've ever been. You know, my mom had so little to give to me and my brother. All she did was work and all we were was poor. Here I've had everything to give to our kids and they don't want it. They never really have."

"Of course they have."

"It's been years."

"Well. . . ."

"And my poor mother died before she even got her first Social Security check."

"I know."

"I wonder if she was angry when she realized what a rip-off it all was."

"A rip-off?"

"Yes, being a parent is a rip-off."

"Now Martina. . . ." Mark had argued that she was mistaken about it all but she'd tuned him out.

In truth, though, she was no longer angry. Things did change, and not always for the worse. Her life had become much richer in the past year since Mark had begun law school. At first she dreaded it, and had started praying for hours at a time again, but Betsy had convinced her to volunteer at the neighborhood elementary school. Four mornings a week, she and her neighbor walked to the school and helped struggling first- and second-graders learn to read. They were so sweet, the kids, and always seemed excited to see them. They called Martina and Betsy "Auntie M" and "Auntie B" and clamored for their turn to read with them. The teachers said she and Betsy were a godsend, that the kids were progressing well, and "what would we do without you"?

It was so simple, what they did each day, and it filled so many needs for so many people. Martina felt like she'd stumbled upon some new miracle cure for every negative emotion she'd ever felt.

The band segued into a slow song and soon Mark was at her side.

"May I have this dance?" he asked.

She smiled as he led her onto the floor and settled into a gentle swaying motion that required no proficiency in actual dance steps.

"Look at them, honey," he said, turning so Martina could see David and Rosemary dancing with their partners. "Look what we did."

"We did do that, didn't we?"

"We did, and I'm so proud."

They sat down as a Western swing started up.

"I can't get over how fancy this is," she said to Mark, taking in the sit-down dinner for sixty, the live band, the open bar, the lavish flowers. "The whole thing is a bit much, don't you think?"

"For an engagement party? My God. And I can't find a thing to talk about with Isabelle's family. I'm looking forward to going home tomorrow, getting back to my normal routine."

◈ ◈ ◈

As her silk dress swirled, Rosemary's thoughts swirled too, back to that morning, back to her and Liam's first instance of Baby Sex. Although they'd decided to wait to start a family until Liam's business was more established, suddenly—here in Palm Springs on a long weekend, in a charming inn with the springtime sun warming the linen sheets and the heavy scent of calla lilies filling the room—the time seemed right. And what if it worked? What if she were pregnant right now?

After a few songs they left the dance floor, eager to replenish their drinks. Liam pointed toward a table festooned with roses, a four-tiered cake sitting on it surrounded by fine chocolates.

"Check this out!" he exclaimed, "That cake is about ten times bigger and fancier than our wedding cake."

"Unbelievable."

"And the vodka is all Gay Gosling."

"Grey Goose, you dork," she said, playfully shoving him. "I can't imagine what the actual wedding will be like."

"Totally," Liam agreed. "But Deet sure looks good."

"Yeah, money becomes him."

"Your mom looks a bit out of place."

"A bit? I tried to talk with her for a while and she just kept saying, 'How very fancy this is' and 'I hope they're happy.' And my dad looks like a security guard they hired for the event. I've never seen him so stiff."

"Well I could get used to this—this opulence."

"Yeah. Sorry I'm not a hotel-chain heiress."

"No problem," Liam said, sliding a hand down her butt. "You're a great lay."

"Liam!" she shouted, slapping his arm. "You're terrible."

"Just doing my job. You want a baby, right?"

"God, did we really do that this morning?"

"We did, Mrs. Ellis, we did," He reached over to kiss her lightly on the lips. "I just hope it takes a while for us to get pageant."

"Liam," she scolded, shoving him slightly.

"Fine, I hope it takes us a while to get *pregnant*, because doing it without a condom—wow."

"Yeah, it's nice when you don't smell like a balloon."

He laughed and kissed her again. "Be right back."

Rosemary scanned the crowd and found Deet and Isabelle talking with two men in impossibly expensive suits. This would be her brother's world now, a world she could hardly imagine. Just like that, he would be wealthy, secure, connected to powerful people. Of course *she* didn't want this life—it would entail boatloads of bullshit—but she sure wouldn't mind the money.

The inn they were staying at cost $350 a night, and the whole tab was being picked up by Isabelle's family. What other goodies would come Deet's way? And Isabelle already owned a gorgeous house that she inherited from her grandmother. She and Deet would just move into it without even a mortgage, while she and Liam struggled to save a down payment for some small, boxy, fake-abode house in Santa Fe.

But Deet and Isabelle would be living in the L.A. area, which she had come to regard as a nearly immoral act. Unless you caught every bit of water that fell from the sky, cultivated nothing but native plants, eschewed backyard pools, and took only a few showers a week, she believed living in those coastal cities was downright wrong. And even if water were plentiful, how could anyone cope with all the driving?

Now, Santa Fe was a perfect place. With a population of about sixty thousand, it was a manageable size, yet there was so much to do. You could ski, kayak, hike, or spend days daydreaming in museums or visiting Indian ruins. It had theater and dance, great restaurants, a charming downtown, natural groceries, and a thriving farmers' market. People there were much more open-hearted, and not so caught up in their appearance. They let their hair go gray, they wore last year's fashions, and they certainly did not flaunt their wealth. A Santa Fean would be embarrassed to drive around in a Jaguar convertible with a jaguar-fur interior, like Deet's father-in-law-to-be did. God, the man was odious. Santa Fe, ringed by mountains on a high desert plateau—it was beautiful. In all four seasons it was blessed with clean air and a brilliant blue sky. And it cared about how it used its water.

It had been nine months since her own wedding, a modest, lovely affair at the estate of one of Liam's clients. The reception was small and tasteful—Liam's sister had called it exquisite—and Rosemary had loved its simple elegance. But this engagement party made her wedding look like some hick backwater affair. How did Deet *do* this? What magic did it take to walk into this kind of money?

No, no more thinking like this. She had a beautiful wedding and she'd married a wonderful man. They were happy together and soon would start a family. It might be a struggle for a while, but that would only bring them closer together. There would be none of the darkness, the sorrow or regret, that so many people lugged around. She and Liam were living in the light.

Deet caught her eye and headed her way.

"Having a good time, baby sister?"

"Of course," she smiled.

"Good." He drained his glass.

"So you're off to Mexico tomorrow?"

"Yup."

"When are you going to start working for Mr. Hotel Honcho?"

"I already have a career."

"Yes, but you're going to have to support your wife in the manner to which she is accustomed."

"Thanks for that."

"Or be a kept man."

"Please."

"I cannot believe she inherited a house in Malibu."

"I know, I know. Don't remind me."

"What do you mean?"

Deet scanned the room, located Isabelle, looked back at Rosemary and said, "Well, her grandma, Oma, was a piece of work. Did I ever tell you about the Thanksgiving I spent with Isabelle's family?"

"No."

"Well Oma also had a house up near Mount Shasta. Do you know, she would never turn the heat on. . . . Here it's late November, there's a foot of snow on the ground, we're all inside wearing ten sweaters, but she won't turn the heat on. It was the most miserable holiday I've ever spent."

"Seriously?"

"Yeah, it was some Old World macho thing. Everybody acted like it wasn't a problem. I just kept stoking the fire, but it's a big house—the bathrooms and bedrooms, they were like forty degrees. Finally I asked her to turn the heat on, and she looked at me like I was the wimp of the century. It was one of those room-clearing moments, and suddenly I start apologizing. Finally I make some excuse to go to bed early and turn on the baseboard heat in our bedroom, but it makes a god-awful smell and she caught me."

"Get out!"

"Yes."

"No way!"

"Yes! They all still rag me about it. Then at Christmas the family is together again, this time in Malibu, thank God, and I bring her a huge Tower of Treats from Harry & David, the biggest one they make, and you know what Oma gives me? A handkerchief, a black handkerchief."

"What?"

"A fucking handkerchief, with a note that says, 'I have no idea what to give you. Come by some time and rummage through my garage and take whatever you want.'"

Rosemary nearly spit out her goat-cheese canapé. "No!" she shouted, laughing and sputtering.

"Yes. Totally bizarre. And then she went and croaked on Valentine's Day. Had a stroke. And I'll tell you what, I won't miss her."

"What a story."

"Isabelle is the eldest of her grandchildren, so she got the house. That's just how the will worked. I think Hillary and the others got a wad of cash instead."

"Who's Hillary?"

"Isabelle's sister. You've asked me that like twelve times."

"Right, sorry."

"So that's the family I'm marrying into."

"Jeez."

"I know. Look, I'll see you in a minute. I gotta take a leak."

"Do you have your black hankie with you?" Rosemary asked. "You know, just in case they're out of TP?"

"Very funny."

⋘   ⋘   ⋘

In the men's room, Deet saw Liam at one of the urinals and sidled up next to him.

"Hey, bro," Deet said.

"Hey yourself," Liam replied, zipping up. "Great party."

"Thanks."

"So you guys are heading to Mexico?" Liam asked, washing his hands.

"Yeah, but just for a long weekend."

"Be nice to relax after all this."

"Relax? Not likely. Isabelle never sits still. You and Rosemary look great, you know? Marriage seems to agree with you."

"We're doing pretty well, thanks."

"So listen, let me ask you something." Deet zipped up, checked under the stalls, opened the men's room door and looked into the hallway.

"What's up?" Liam asked.

Deet pressed the door closed behind him and leaned against it. Then he folded his arms in front of his chest and stared at Liam.

"What?"

Deet paused for a moment, shifting his gaze to the floor. After a minute he said, "How do I say this."

"What's going on? Are you OK?"

Deet exhaled loudly. "Fuck. OK, I'll just say it. Look, Isabelle is great and everything. We get along great."

"Seems like it."

"But you know how she inherited that house from her grandmother?"

"Yeah, you lucky shit, of course I know about that."

"OK. So Oma dies suddenly, on Valentine's Day, and a few weeks later we're cleaning out her stuff, sorting and packing things for the cousins and for Goodwill and whatnot, and I start to find some stuff that just creeps me out."

"What, like old-lady bras? Fake teeth?"

"No. . .Look, I need you to not tell anyone this."

"No problem."

"I'm serious, no one, not even my sister."

"No problem, man." Liam mimed locking his lips with a key.

"Thank you." Deet exhaled loudly. "Here's the deal: Oma was eighty-two when she died, which means she was born in 1913. She left Europe when she was nineteen. The story is that she moved to California 'cause some cousin had already moved here, and the cousin got her a job as a hotel maid. Then her uncles move here a year later and they lend her money to buy the damn hotel. By age forty she's a millionaire."

"OK. . . ."

"That's the family story, from maid to CEO, the immigrant drama. She paid her uncles back every cent and built an empire. But you know what I found in her garage?"

"What?"

"Money. Boxes of cash."

"No way!"

"And antique guns."

"Seriously?"

"Yes. I think Oma and whatever business her and her uncles were in was a whole lot more than hotels. Who keeps boxes of cash in a garage? And there's a lot of other funky stuff I've seen. Basically, I'm convinced the fortune I'm marrying into is dirty money. It's organized crime or something."

"Holy shit!"

"Yes, but I think to myself, well, Isabelle is innocent of whatever this is. I'll make my own money. I don't need to be a part of it. And when it's just the two of us, it feels possible. But when the whole family is gathered in one place like this, and when I think of actually living in Oma's house, I'm totally creeped out. I don't know if I can do it."

"Could you sell the house? Move somewhere else?"

"Isabelle says that's out of the question."

"What did she say about the money and guns?"

"She refused to acknowledge what it could mean. She said her uncles were able to buy that first hotel because they worked hard, and Oma was a child of the Depression—she hoarded things, she didn't trust banks. She was pretty offended that I even brought it up."

"What are you going to do?"

"I don't know. What would you do?"

Liam rubbed his jaw, staring at the tile floor. "It's sort of a chilling prospect, isn't it."

"Yes."

"I think I'd tell her we would have to at least rent out Oma's house and live somewhere else."

"She certainly doesn't want to."

"She doesn't care that you don't want to live there?"

"Oh, she'll find some way to win the argument. She thinks new drapes and new kitchen cabinets will change my mind about the house."

"Isn't that a problem right there?"

"Probably."

"You know, you should feel on top of the world right now, but instead you seem totally down. Down and—trapped or something."

"Is that how I sound?"

"Yeah."

"Fuck. I don't know what I'm doing here."

When they got on the plane two days later, Rosemary was dreamy with expectation, nursing her secret hope, while Liam, nursing a secret burden, thought about the many outcomes conception could lead to. A family like Isabelle's—even gangsters, ax murderers, Nazis—were all begun with the same act: plain, simple, wonderful Baby Sex. What the fuck did that mean?

Chapter 8 | September, 1997

Twentynine Palms, California

S HEILA, EXHAUSTED FROM THE EFFORT OF LABORING WITH her first baby, dozed between contractions against Rosemary's bent knees. Trapped against the headboard for hours, Rosemary stoically supported a hundred seventy pounds of the crankiest, sweatiest pregnant woman the world had ever known.

When a contraction ruptured her endorphin-clogged sleep, Sheila would slump forward onto her hands and knees and pant like a drugged dog while Rosemary stretched her own legs and took a sip of water. Then she would reassemble the heating pad and memory-foam pillow like a feverish catcher's mitt and receive Sheila's body back onto her own. Sheila would moan "I'm so tired" while slipping back into her prickly sleep, and Rosemary would fantasize about snow and ice.

At 3 a.m. Rosemary's tank top was drenched with sweat and the room smelled of hamsters and sage. Sometime before midnight, Max, Sheila's husband, had burned a bundle of sage to "cleanse the energy" in the tiny room, and the two hamsters who scritch-scritched through the night emitted their own aroma of urine-soaked straw.

It was amazing that she was here for this birth. Sheila and Rosemary, who had been best friends in elementary school, had rekindled their relationship a couple of years earlier. They'd run into each other at a water conservation expo in Sedona, Arizona, and learned that they still shared a fondness for each other.

Sheila and Max were eco-activists (*not* environmentalists, thank you very much), and were building a house—actually a geodesic dome—outside of Taos, New Mexico. But it was costing more than they expected, though, so they'd moved back to Twentynine Palms to work and save enough money to continue construction. They refused to go into debt for the dome or anything else.

When Sheila told her of her pregnancy, Rosemary was shocked to hear the due date was September 6, the same as her own baby's birthday. Her son, Dylan, and Sheila's baby would be just a year apart. And, if Sheila's baby really came on time, then Rosemary and Liam would be in town for the birth, since they were planning to spend Labor Day weekend with her parents. And it had actually happened that way.

At twenty-eight, Rosemary was determined to be a good friend. She was honored to have been invited to the birth, and had done a lot of reading to prepare for it. She'd planned to serve not just as a friend, but as a doula, a woman who provides support to the mother during childbirth. Sheila's labor had begun Thursday, just before midnight—the timing was perfect. Rosemary imagined she'd spend some part of Friday with Sheila and Max helping out, have a mind-blowing experience witnessing a birth, and then go back to her own family for a nice mini-vacation.

But somehow, in her mind, the whole thing was supposed to take much less time. Her own labor had taken twelve hours, which seemed like forever, but Sheila had already been in early-stage labor for twenty-six hours. Rosemary had been there since 7 p.m. or so, just a few hours after she, Liam, and Dylan had gotten into town. Silva, the midwife, had gone home for the night, saying Sheila was only two centimeters dilated.

During a particularly weak, short-lived contraction, Rosemary let the warm pillow arrangement slide to the floor and flicked on the breast pump on the bedside table.

"Let's try this now," she said over the machine's whirring sound. "Silva said this might help bring on stronger contractions."

"Stronger?" Sheila murmured. "They already feel pretty strong."

"But Silva said they're not dilating your cervix very much, remember?"

Rosemary moved stiffly away from the headboard, adjusted the controls and attached the tubes to the suction cups. "This is supposed to stimulate your hormones," she said, and arranged Sheila against some pillows. She placed the clear, plastic cups over Sheila's immense breasts, drew the hoses over her belly and sat alongside, holding the cups in place while Sheila drifted off again.

Like an ocean in slowest motion, Sheila rose and receded again and again, hardly speaking, while the pump pulled ceaselessly at her breasts. Occasionally Rosemary removed the cone-shaped cups she was holding to lick them for a better seal. She watched in sympathy as Sheila's nipples became distended and blue-ish, looking more and more like bruised udders every moment.

Rosemary had never been away from Dylan this long, and just the thought of him made her own breasts swell with milk. She surveyed the bedroom in the low light. A poster blared "Stop Welfare Ranching," and another shouted "Fuck Bechtel!" On a small piece of parchment on a table, Edward Abbey's words exhorted the reader to get outside, to remember what the fight was all about. There were the baby things on the dresser— stacks of clothes, receiving blankets, and cloth diapers—and of course the hamster habitat on the dresser. Sheila had always loved hamsters. Rosemary smiled at the memory of waking up at Sheila's house after a fourth-grade sleepover and their discovering together that one of the females had had a baby overnight.

But she was getting so tired, and soon her mind snared her in a small, wearisome circle of thoughts: The breast pump should be set to LOW during contractions and HIGH in between, the bedspread was hand-quilted but machine-stitched, the wood floor needed oiling, and Sheila's pumpkin face called for longer hair, rather than the short, rounded cut she'd had for years. Then back to the pump.

"Oh!" Sheila shouted.

Rosemary roused herself. "You OK?"

"Yeah, I guess I was dreaming." She rubbed her eyes and then her belly. "When will this be over?"

"You're doing great," Rosemary struggled to appear cheerful. "This baby is just in no hurry."

"I want this to end."

"I know you do, and it will. Let's try something else." She clicked off the pump, turned on the bedside lamp, and began massaging Sheila's lower back as she remembered her midwives doing during her labor.

Dylan's had been a good birth, a textbook perfect birth, also at home, but it was no fun at all. She thought she'd be one of those goddesses who would love her contractions, who would be radiant and powerful and graceful as she became a mother, but instead she loudly announced over and over that this would be an only child, that she was trapped in a body of pain, that there was nowhere worse she could imagine being. And she puked about ten times.

"Oh, here's another contraction!" Sheila dropped her head abruptly, breathed through it, and when it was over, panted, "That one was really hard. Do you think I'm getting close?"

There was no way Sheila was close. Rosemary accepted the fact with dismay. What was she going to do? In just a few hours, it would be Saturday. She was supposed to spend the day with her parents while Liam climbed, and now she would be exhausted.

She called up a line from her doula book and cooed, "Every contraction brings you closer to your baby."

Sheila slumped to her side and dozed.

Rosemary, pressing her thumbs along Sheila's spine and coaxing her through another weak contraction, heard movement in the living room, a muffled fart, and Max clearing his throat. She heard him shuffle to the bathroom, pee, drop the lid without flushing, and shuffle toward the bedroom.

"Hey," he said, entering the stuffy room, greeting Rosemary with eye contact and climbing onto the bed. He began to rub Sheila's upper back in broad, circular strokes.

"No." Sheila shoved his hand away. "Don't touch me, and don't talk to me."

Max sighed, turning toward Rosemary. "How's she doing?"

"She's tired. Are you ready to be with her now?"

"Yeah," Max said, pulling his long hair into a ponytail.

As Rosemary stretched out on the couch, she focused on her breath and the blackness of her eyelids, told herself she would feel rested and refreshed in two hours, and sank into sleep.

She woke to the sound of Sheila shouting from the bathroom, "This hurts so bad!" Rosemary sat up heavily, her damp shirt clinging to her soaked nursing bra.

Sheila was shouting, "Shit! This sucks!" as Silva pushed through the front door.

"Morning!" Silva chirped, a loud paper grocery bag under her arm. "You're still here! What a trooper. Any action in there?"

"I doubt it," Rosemary yawned, rubbing her eyes with an allergic intensity. Damn hamsters. Her watch read 5:45. "I need to get home. My husband has plans. I never dreamed this would take so long."

"Yes, this is one of those long, slow births that we all dread."

After Silva checked Sheila's dilation—three centimeters— she assured Rosemary she could leave for several hours without missing the big event.

"No one ever knows for sure," she said, slurping coffee from a travel mug. "But this is still early labor."

Rosemary gathered up her shoes and purse and knocked on the bathroom door. Sheila was leaning over the bathroom sink while Max massaged her lower back. She stroked Sheila's hair, saying, "I'm going home for a while. I'll see you later, OK?"

Sheila shifted her arms to Rosemary's shoulders for a few moments, whispered "Thank you so much," and went back to the sink for another contraction.

Speeding through town, Rosemary drank in twenty minutes

of solitude. Cool air pumping through the windows of the car woke her up some, but she longed for a shower and for luck— that Liam would be pleasant, that her mother would be relaxed, that Dylan would be easy-going today.

She parked the Camry in her parents' driveway and quietly opened the front door. As she walked down the hallway, she heard the shower, and then Liam's voice.

"Yeah, almost, little guy," he said. Dylan whimpered as the water was turned off. Rosemary slipped into the bedroom, smelled poop, grimaced at the mess in the port-a-crib, and opened the bathroom door with a singsong hello.

"Mom-Lady!" Liam called, toweling off Dylan in his arms. "Look, little guy, Mama's home!" Dylan reached for her, beginning to cry. Rosemary clasped him close and kissed his neck.

"OK, OK," she cooed as he grabbed at her shirt.

"Morning," Liam said, kissing her on the cheek. "Oh boy, Dylan, the twenty-four-hour, all-you-can-eat milk bar! Step right up!"

She sat down on the toilet seat and began to nurse Dylan, breathing with relief at the pressure release in her breasts. He caressed her back with one hand and squeezed her breast with the other. "Easy, baby," she whispered, grasping his hand.

"So his diaper blew out, huh?"

"Yeah," Liam said, dragging a towel across his back. "That was some moop. Sorry, but the crib's a pit. I don't have time to clean it."

"Did the rest of the night go well?"

"Oh yeah, he slept right through. Your parents and I watched a Dodgers game and that was about it." He picked up Dylan's dirty pajamas. "Can I leave these too?"

"Yeah, don't worry about it," Rosemary said, looking into Dylan's clear eyes, running her hand over his perfect skin. "Hello, my beautiful naked boy. I missed you." Dylan looked up at her, exposed his two teeth in a smile and hooked a hand into her mouth.

"So? Is it a girl or a boy?" Liam asked.

Rosemary expelled Dylan's hand with her tongue and tried to sound casual.

"Sheila's still in labor. I'll be going back later, sometime this afternoon."

"You're going back?" Liam shoved the towel into the rack. "After being there all night?"

"Yeah." She shifted Dylan to her other breast and grabbed his hand before he could start squeezing.

"You know I have plans, right?" Liam picked up the floor towel, draping it over the tub.

"I know. I'll see if my mom can take him. It'll work out."

"But he misses you," Liam argued.

"He was sleeping nearly the whole time I was gone, Liam. He seems fine to me."

"Well I don't see how you can go back there," he said, working a comb through his hair. "How much did you sleep?"

"Four hours," she lied. "I'll leave if it's too much, don't worry."

"Yeah," Liam said, squeezing shaving cream into his hand. "And monkeys are gonna fly out my butt."

"It'll be OK," Rosemary insisted, switching Dylan back to her left breast. Liam stood at the vanity in his boxers, leaning into the mirror. He had put on about fifteen pounds since they were married three years before, but carried it well. He simply got bigger, like a carp.

"I'll be home around skinnertime," he said, rinsing the razor.

"OK." Rosemary stood up to make it uncomfortable for Dylan to nurse and he pulled off. "I assume my dad will grill something." She shifted the baby to her hip and followed Liam out of the bathroom, stopping at the crib.

"Well you've really outdone yourself, boyfriend," she said, sighing at the poop explosion. "Let's get started on this."

Bending over to peel back the sheets made Rosemary dizzy, but she kept at it, keeping a conversation going with Liam as he dressed.

"So where are you climbing?"

"Not sure. Jaco's picking me up in a few minutes. We'll sort it out on the drive."

Rosemary began to feel nauseous with exhaustion and set Dylan down. "Just a minute, pal," she said, walking to an open window. Dylan cried out in protest as she breathed slowly, using a plant pot outside as a focal point. He continued to cry as Rosemary returned to the crib, able now to wrestle with the foam mattress. She felt like she was in tenth grade again, arriving home after a night of drinking on Amboy Road, attempting to appear sober in front of her mother.

A car horn sounded as Rosemary stuffed the bedding and pajamas into the washer. Still naked, Dylan held himself up on the dryer door, pulling on her shorts.

"Well, have a good day," Liam said, kissing her quickly.

"You too."

✍ ✍ ✍

Mark listened to the voices rise and fall, blend and become distinct as his daughter and her family began their day. How wonderful to hear a child's voice in the house again, that high-pitched cheeping that supplied a song of new life to remind you that that was what it was all about—life, whether you enjoyed it or not, understood it or not.

Martina lay against his chest as he stroked her bare back. A few years ago he never would have tried to seduce his wife on a Saturday morning—his chances were bad enough after wine and dinner out. But this had become almost a norm, like the pancakes she used to make on weekends when the kids were little.

He used to regard his sex life as one of life's greater ironies. Men often said that while marriage could be both burdensome and boring, at least you could count on regular sex. But that was never true for him. In his own home with his own wife, he'd felt like a man hanging out in a bar, hoping to get lucky. How to say the right thing, strike the right tone, create the right mood? And you had to change it up—she wasn't stupid.

If she suspected his intentions, thought he was buttering her up for sex, she'd shut down instantly. He had to make her feel attractive, but not like an object; sexy, but not cheap; safe, but not so safe that she just curled up and went to sleep. Sometimes it angered him, all of this, and sometimes he took it as a challenge. Regardless, it seemed to be over, and he felt like he'd hit the jackpot.

He was relieved beyond measure that Rosemary seemed happy, and that Liam felt like a son to him. He loved the boy—admired him, actually. It took guts to start your own business, to raise a family without the security of a regular paycheck. He himself certainly didn't have that kind of courage.

And David, well, he wished he were closer to his son. How could the boy not tell his own father the real reason he and Isabelle had broken their engagement? His vague line, "It didn't work out," was nonsense. Something happened. Something had soured David on his fiancée. What could drive a man so resolutely from a woman he seemed to love?

❧　❧　❧

Martina was growing restless. Lollygagging in bed on a weekend morning was all well and good when just she and Mark were home, but not with others in the house. She'd enjoyed Mark's amorous advances—even in the daylight hours—ever since the kids had moved out. Somehow she could never reconcile it before, influenced by that confusing dichotomy that both revered mothers and regarded sex as sinful. But enough of that. If she thought about it too much, she would be sucked back into her old ways.

"This is a busy day," Martina said, slipping out from under Mark's arm. "We should get up."

"Huh?" Mark asked.

"Time to get up. Come on now, Grandpa. Chop chop."

❧　❧　❧

Liam grunted as he climbed into Jaco's Humvee. "Why do you drive this goddamn monster?"

"Nice to see you too."

"Sorry." Liam reached over with a fist bump. "How you been?"

"Good, you?"

"OK. Glad to get out for the day."

"Had enough married bliss?"

"Rosemary's impossible. She was out all night at her friend Sheila's house."

"Sheila Simpson?"

"I don't know—Sheila."

"The one we graduated with?"

"Yeah, from high school. You know her?"

"We all know each other—Twentynine Palms is a pretty small place. What was she doing there all night?"

"Sheila's having a baby, and Rosemary has decided to be some martyr friend of the century. She was there all night while Sheila was in labor."

"Wow! No kidding! A boy or a girl?"

"It's not even close to being born, and she's going back there later today."

"Ro was always a nice person."

"Gimme a break! All night, and more time there today. We're here to spend time as a family. I'm going climbing, but just for a few hours. I'll be back by dinner, and I won't be all exhausted and strung out. She looked like shit this morning, but she just kept pretending she was fine."

"Well, I'm sure it's pretty cool watching a baby be born. It's not like it happens every day."

"Oh, forget it. Let's get some food."

Jaco slipped a Bob Marley disk into the CD player. As the sound of reggae relaxed him, Liam was embarrassed to have complained about his wife. He sometimes forgot that although Jaco was his climbing buddy, he was Rosemary's high school friend first, and the guy clearly felt some loyalty to her. Bitching about her was bad form.

And the truth was he didn't know why he was so annoyed. He didn't like worrying the night before that Dylan might wake up and he'd have to get him back to sleep without Rosemary's magic boobs, and he'd been bored hanging out with his in-laws, but that wasn't enough to piss him off so much. Rosemary pretending to be fine this morning irritated him— how stupid did she think he was, anyway?—but he could blow that off.

As Jaco turned into the parking lot of the Carousel Café, Liam suddenly realized what had angered him so much—it was that squinty smile Rosemary had given him in the bathroom. When he told her they'd watched the Dodgers game and Dylan had slept through the night, she did that thing—smiled a placid little smile and quickly scrunched her eyes at him. It was her "I approve" face, her "This is exactly what should have happened" face, and he hated it.

Liam was also upset about a conversation he'd had with his father-in-law. Deet had never told the family why he and Isabelle had broken up, though he'd told Liam and sworn him to secrecy.

"I guess it just wasn't meant to be," Liam said lamely to Mark, ashamed by the lie. "Who knows about these things?"

"Well, I'm sure there's more to it," Mark said, "but David certainly won't tell us."

Five months earlier, Liam had been speeding down Interstate 25 from Santa Fe to Albuquerque when he got a frantic call from Deet.

"There is no question her family's business is dirty!" Deet shouted as he sped west on Interstate 40 through Arizona. "Fuck, fuck, fuck! I can't have people like that in my life! It's just too fucking slimy for me!"

"Like what exactly?" Liam probed.

"Like they pay off inspectors, they hire illegals, they dump cash in offshore accounts. The list goes on and on. The whole hotel chain is dirty!"

"It's not like it's the only dirty business on the planet," Liam reasoned. "You can ignore it, or maybe even work to change it from within."

"No way, man. I can't get that close to it!"

"Why are you being such a drama queen about this?"

"Look, bro, you know I love money."

"Who doesn't?"

"I just know I can't be around this," Deet continued, growing hoarse. "It'll do me in. It's like having an alcoholic work in a brewery or something." He began to sob.

"Maybe you two can move somewhere else, just remove yourselves from the business."

"She won't do it."

"And you think she knows nothing about this stuff?"

"Who the fuck knows what she knows. I gotta break it off. I don't want to spend my life looking over my shoulder. I gotta break it off! It's over. I'm telling her tonight." The cell connection abruptly cut out, and a few days later Rosemary told him that Deet had called to tell her he was no longer engaged.

"Wow, just like that, huh?" Liam said.

"Yeah, so sudden," Rosemary agreed.

As Jaco cut the engine, Liam shuddered. He exhaled long and slow, then set the thoughts aside and slammed the heavy steel door. He was determined to have a good day.

❧   ❧   ❧

Rosemary heard her parents' voices in their bedroom as she got ready to shower. She ran the hot water as Dylan held onto the tub, peeing on his feet. "Hey, thanks," she said, wiping it up with the floor towel. "Let's not tell Grandma about that, OK?"

As soon as she stepped into the shower, Dylan began tossing his bath toys into the tub, singing, "Yuh, yuh, yuh." She quickly rinsed the shampoo through her short hair—no time for those long curls anymore—and stepped onto the floor. Looking around for the floor towel, she saw that Dylan had gathered it up and was chewing on it.

"Dylan, yucky!" she said as she tugged at the towel.

"Dis!" Dylan shouted, holding on tighter, which made him fall on his butt. He crawled over to her and smashed his face into her shins, arms up.

"I'll pick you up in a minute, sweet stuff. Just let me get dry." Now whimpering, he grabbed the backs of her calves, pinching her flesh.

"Ow, stop!" she yelped, swatting his hands away. How could a one-year-old's grip hurt so much? She could tell full-scale wailing would begin soon, so she scooped him up and distracted him instead with a playful toss. Immediately he began to heave his body up and down, imploring her to bounce him. So she did, with one hand behind his head and another around his hip.

"Bounce-a bounce-a baby boy. . . ," she sang, bouncing him as high she dared, his blond hair flapping like prayer flags in the wind. He squealed until she set him on the vanity and then settled into a "maw" mantra as she quickly dressed.

"Maw," meant "more." Along with hi, bye, Mama, Dada, and "dis" for all points of interest, Dylan managed to get his needs met.

Rosemary set an open box of tampons in front of him as she brushed her teeth. One by one he dropped them to the floor, laughing and looking at her each time.

"Yeah, pal," she said through minty foam. "Gravity is so cool."

She slipped the toothbrush into her toiletry bag, took her vitamins, and stopped to examine her face. Dark circles rimmed her oversized brown eyes and her arched brows were overgrown. Still ten pounds over her pre-pregnancy weight, Rosemary viewed her appearance in its present state as a fall from grace.

"You know, Dylan? I used to be pretty." He looked up, chewing on a tampon. Like Rosemary, his eyes were his most striking feature, a deep brown with lashes like a camel's. He looked very much like she had as a baby. "I hope you enjoy my face," she said to him. "It was great while it lasted."

Rosemary sighed, parking Dylan on her hip. "Let's get you dressed. And help me out, OK? No kicking. Let's have an easy time of it."

In the bedroom she pinned on Dylan's cloth diaper and velcroed the cover against a steady stream of kicks and writhing. "No!" she shouted repeatedly, feeling a hot plume of rage course through her. "It is not OK to kick!" He wailed as she gripped his legs, but he managed to sit up as she yanked his shirt over his head. "Damn it, Dylan!" she hissed, setting him on the floor. "Why do you have to make it so hard?"

"Dis!" he shouted tearfully, crawling to the bed and grasping frantically at the covers. "Dis!"

Rosemary stood, holding her head in her hands, dizzy again. She really needed to sleep.

"You want to be on the bed?" she whispered. She laid him on the bed. "Dis," Dylan said, patting the bed beside him. "Mama." She collapsed beside him and he reared up in triumph, tugging at her dress, threatening to wail again when it wouldn't yield.

"OK, OK," she sighed, rearranging her sun dress and bra. She lay on her side, arranged pillows between her legs, under her head, and against her back, and then positioned Dylan so he could latch on. Once he started nursing, she felt instantly drowsy. Suddenly she tripped and fell off the roof into a snowdrift, her book bag landing on the back of her head. She lurched awake and reoriented herself. Dylan tried to switch to the other breast by climbing across her with a knee in her sternum. She instantly drifted off again.

The nap ended with Dylan prodding her navel. "Mama, Mama."

"Oh, Dylan honey," Rosemary groaned. "What is it?"

"Mama," Dylan repeated, still prodding.

Rosemary looked at the ceiling and figured out what he wanted. "Ah-ooo-ga!" she called out. He laughed, prodding harder. Rosemary repeated her version of a hokey car horn over and over as Dylan poked her belly and pleaded "maw."

"OK, buddy," Rosemary yawned. "We should make breakfast and say hi to Grandma and Grandpa." She sat up and felt her hair—it had dried smashed into the pillows. Dylan held onto her neck from the back, dancing to his yuh-yuh song. At just 7:40, it was probably eighty degrees in the room.

"Here they are!" her dad exclaimed as she entered the kitchen with Dylan on her hip. He gave them both a kiss. Her mother spread her hands and crooned, "There's our boy!" Rosemary handed him over and started coffee for herself.

"There's some in the pot," her mother said. "Oh, I know," she replied to Rosemary's look. "You like your fancy stuff."

Rosemary poured boiling water over the finely ground French Roast and felt instantly cheered by the aroma. While the quick oats boiled, she rinsed fresh blueberries in a strainer and watched her parents delight in their grandson. Mark and Martina had always been reserved with their own children, but were downright effusive with Dylan. Who could understand people?

As she plopped the steaming cereal into the bowl, the same Jemima Puddle-Duck bowl that both she and Deet had grown up with, Dylan erupted in shrieks.

"Oh my goodness, someone's hungry!" Martina said, settling him into the highchair—the same chrome and plastic highchair she and Deet had used as babies.

"Sweetie, you know the oatmeal is too hot—we do this every day," Rosemary said, sliding the bowl into the freezer. She shook a few Cheerios onto the highchair's tray. "You can start with these."

Almost instantly Dylan scattered the cereal with angry sweeps of his hands, crying and sending most of it to the floor.

"Hey!" Rosemary shouted, her index finger an inch from his nose. "We do not throw food!" Dylan waved his hands in front of his face screaming, batting her hand in the process. She grabbed his hands and held them as he shook his head from side to side, his cries escalating. "And you do not hit me!"

"Oh, he's just a little guy," Mark said softly.

"Yes, but he can still learn."

Dylan's cries subsided as she retrieved the bowl from the freezer and set it in front of him. "Here you go," she said, though she knew that if her parents weren't in the room, she might have said something evil, like "Choke on it."

Dylan scooped up handfuls of oatmeal and smeared them over his mouth, with about a third reaching the target. Martina picked up the spoon and tried to scrape some off his cheeks, but he shook his head away in defense.

"Fine," Rosemary said, scalding her tongue on the coffee. "Wear your breakfast. See if we care." Dylan strip mined for blueberries and then pushed aside the last of the oatmeal, working to expose the picture of Jemima Puddle Duck and the Fox underneath it.

"Dis!" he laughed, pointing to Beatrix Potter's handiwork. "Dis!"

Rosemary smiled reluctantly and then ended the meal with the washcloth torture. Over Dylan's screams, she and her parents planned their day: Martina and Rosemary would take him to the pool while Mark caught up on some yard work and made dinner.

"I'll grill chicken," he said decisively.

"Sounds great, Dad."

❧   ❧   ❧

As she packed the diaper bag, the pool bag, and the lunch bag, Rosemary felt a familiar reluctance—time alone with her mother was always so awkward. But Martina smeared sunscreen on Dylan and entertained him while Rosemary packed the car, which raised her spirits—it really was nice to have the help. As they drove to the Luckie Park pool, Rosemary hoped she wouldn't see anyone she knew—not with her strung-out, tired face and this extra ten pounds. She had not gone to her ten-year high school reunion, but she knew many of her classmates still lived in town.

"You were just like this when you were a baby," Martina said, turning toward the back seat to toy with Dylan's feet as he sang "yuh, yuh, yuh" in his car seat.

"I was?" Rosemary asked, feeling a pang of tenderness. She had often wondered what she was really like as a baby. The pictures didn't tell her much, and her parents just shared the same old stories—the spaghetti bowl on the head, the time the swan bit her at the zoo, the song she made up about the June-bug birthday party.

"You were so curious, so alert. Your father and I enjoyed you so very much."

"What was Deet like?"

"David? David was quieter, more independent. He liked time to himself."

"Really?"

"Yes, he would want to be set down after a while, but you were always so social."

Rosemary smiled as they drove, imagining herself as a baby in a car seat as her mother drove them to the pool. She tried to picture the scene—she would be wearing a tiny cotton dress, and the car seat would be made of chrome and fake leather. Deet would be looking out the window, shooting things with his finger, making "Pshew!" sounds. But what would her mother be thinking about? Would she be planning dinner? Would she be thinking about the weather, Watergate, the price of gas? Would she be worrying about her fading looks? Would she be thinking about her own mom or her brother, who had both died so young? Would she be longing for the freedom she'd given up to become a mom?

"Mom," Rosemary asked cautiously. "Was it ever hard for you?"

"Was what hard?"

"Being a mom, especially with two kids so close in age?"

Martina paused. "Oh, I suppose there were some tough days, especially when you two were sick, or when Dad was working long hours. Sure, it was hard sometimes."

She wanted to ask, "Were you ever mean to us?" but she knew the answer. It was Rosemary who was the mean mom, snarling at Dylan over his endless demands, yelling when he wouldn't leave her alone for even a minute. She longed to be more patient, like her mother, but she knew it would just be fake. She was not interested in applying a thin veneer of bullshit on her very real emotions. What good would it do to pretend to be nice when she was really seething?

She pulled into the nearest parking space at the pool, braked the car with a jerk, and realized with a sickening start: The good it would do is that Dylan would be happier.

"Honey," Martina said, "let's park in the shade. The car will be hotter than blazes if you park here."

He would be less fussy if she were more tolerant, and she would like herself better.

"Dis!" Dylan trumpeted.

She had to try harder. He deserved better.

"Rosemary, what's wrong?" Martina asked.

Rosemary turned to look into her mother's face—the fair skin, so poorly suited to the harsh desert sun, now growing more and more lined; the silver-streaked hair, which had never once been dyed or permed; the thinning lips, now pursed in concern—and felt ashamed. Martina always tried so hard. Couldn't *she* try that hard?

"Honey?"

Rosemary stared ahead, hardly seeing the scrubby vegetation that lined the parking lot, and felt a new sense of resolve. She would be a better person. She would learn to be both truthful *and* kind—it had to be possible. She would give more to Dylan and to others.

"Hey, my little daydreamer," Martina repeated. "Let's park in the shade."

"Sorry," Rosemary said, starting the car.

The pool was crowded. Martina took Dylan while Rosemary headed for the bathroom. She had a new spring in her step as she tacked through the sea of lounge chairs—she was beginning a new time.

The smell of the bathroom—chlorine and a certain mustiness she had never smelled anywhere else—made her smile. She peeked into the shower room and remembered how she and Sheila used to take showers together after swimming. They would run the water forever with no regard for the desert's scant resources, taking handfuls of shampoo from the wall dispensers to make crazy hairdos. Or they'd drive the women there crazy by seeing how high their voices could go in the shower room's echo.

It was amazing to think how much time had passed. Now here they were moms, or about to be. And they were still friends. Yes, last night had been a grind, but she'd happily do it again for Sheila.

Martina settled into a lounge chair in the shade with Dylan in her lap. The boy was so beautiful, so perfect and new. She could feel his whole body grow heavy and still as he became mesmerized by the water. He looked into her eyes for a few moments, examined the buttons on her blouse, and then went back to watching the water. She felt him settle more and more as she let herself sink heavily into the chair.

Her daughter was a devoted mother, to be sure, but she worked Dylan up with her constant attention. Many times she watched Rosemary talk or sing to him when she might have let him be. Then he would demand her attention and she would fume about being overwhelmed by his needs. Dylan was clearly not an easy baby, but Rosemary made it harder on them both by constantly feeding his need for interaction. What she and Liam really needed was a second child. Otherwise this baby would have to absorb the full attention of his mother forever, like a sun that never set.

Rosemary, putting on sunscreen at the sink, could hear a woman on her cell phone in a toilet stall. A cell phone—how ridiculous!

"Raymond, I don't understand," the woman said. "You said you were just going to stop by your brother's house, and you've been gone all morning."

And how absurd to be talking about personal stuff in a public bathroom.

"I'm confused as to why that was more important than spending time with Jonathan."

She didn't sound confused, Rosemary thought. She sounded annoyed.

"I'm saying this because I really support you in having a strong, fulfilling relationship with your son."

Oh, for God's sake. You're pissed off. Just say it already.

"He seems disappointed. He needs clearer communication. When you tell him an hour, he expects that. If it were open-ended, he needed to hear that."

Come on, tell him you're mad as hell.

"Well, I guess I'm irked," the woman said.

Irked? Please.

"But I'd rather process this more fully later."

Ugh.

As Rosemary washed her hands, the woman stepped out of the stall with tears in her eyes. She was nearly six feet tall and stunning.

"You OK?" Rosemary asked.

"Yes, thank you," the woman answered, sniffling. "Marriage is just hard sometimes, isn't it?"

"Yes, it is."

The woman slipped off her lovely, flowing dress to get into a two-piece bathing suit, and Rosemary was instantly jealous: flat stomach, firm legs, breasts that faced forward like a pair of glowing headlights.

But the woman was so sad. And so wimpy.

Rosemary looked at her own image in the mirror. Sure she looked tired, but she'd been up all night helping a woman through labor, a far more worthy task than working out at the gym. And yes, she was a little chunky, but she was still nursing. She'd lose the weight soon, and at least *she* could stand up to her husband.

"I hope it gets easier for you," Rosemary said.

"Thank you," the woman replied, wiping her nose with a wad of toilet paper.

Rosemary found her mom at the kiddie pool, trying to get a hat to stay on Dylan's head.

"Hey, buddy," Rosemary said, feeling newly encouraged. "Ready to swim?"

"That pool looks none too clean," Martina said, looking critically at the greenish water. "Do you think it's safe?"

"Let's just tell ourselves it's all the sunscreen," Rosemary said with a smile. She lowered Dylan into the shallow end next to the overflow return pipe. Martina rolled up her khaki capris and sat down on the pool's edge with a few Tupperware containers and an empty shampoo bottle.

"These were your favorite sorts of things to play with when you were small," she explained, dipping her feet in. She lowered the open shampoo bottle into the water and Dylan quickly became fascinated by the air bubbles glupping out as the bottle filled and the water rushed in. He spent the next hour filling and emptying cups of water at the pipe or pushing the shampoo bottle under to watch it fill. Rosemary drifted next to him, her hands on the pool bottom, as he chased down cups and returned again and again to the pipe, brushing against her like a wisp of kelp. As moms chatted and children played all around them, Rosemary had an image of a bunch of hippos passing the heat of the day in a river filled with water lilies. She smiled and absorbed the ease like a massage. At least for today, she was a part of this tribe.

They headed back home for naptime with the idea that Rosemary would go back to Sheila while Dylan slept. She felt guilty that she hadn't checked in with her all morning, and guilty too for leaving Dylan again. He'd fallen asleep in the car, and she'd managed to lay him down in the crib without waking him.

Martina was clearly nervous about being left with her grandson. "How will he react when he realizes you're gone? What do I feed him? When will you be back?"

"How about you feed him some yogurt and fruit and call me at the number on the fridge if he seems unhappy," she replied. "I really need to be there for Sheila."

"But you're already so tired," Martina protested.

"I'll be OK, Mom. Thanks."

But she wasn't OK; she could barely stay awake for the drive. When she pulled up in front of Sheila and Max's house, she lowered the windows and allowed herself to fall asleep. Forty minutes later she woke in a panic, drooling and sweating. What if they needed her in there? What if she'd missed the birth? Rosemary scrambled out of the car, ran up the front walk, and pushed the door open with great expectation.

And there was Sheila, naked on her hands and knees, panting through a contraction as Silva rubbed her lower back. Shoot me, Rosemary thought—it's a freeze frame. It was like returning to the page you'd left off at in a novel and finding the rest of the book glued shut.

"She's six centimeters dilated," Silva told Rosemary in the kitchen. "I just told them we're going to have to start talking hospital. She's been laboring for nearly forty hours. I can't let it go till she's too tired to push."

Rosemary's stomach tightened. The hospital? She knew Sheila and Max had no insurance. She also knew she was supposed to bake a birthday cake that night for Dylan. And she was already running on about three hours sleep. She felt like a high school athlete suddenly dropped into the Olympics.

"If the baby isn't born within five hours she'll have to go anyway, since at that point her water will have been broken for twenty-four hours, and that's part of home birth law," Silva said. "The baby's position is just not facilitating dilation. At the hospital they'll give her some Pitocin, which will bring on stronger contractions."

When Silva explained the same thing to Max and Sheila, they nodded and stared at her slack-jawed. "If you choose that route sooner than later, you'll be certain to still have the energy to push the baby out," she added. They went back to the bedroom to talk.

"The hospital will cost them at least four thousand bucks, after already paying me fifteen hundred," Silva said quietly. "Four thousand bucks for some Pitocin in an IV drip."

"Well that's bleak," Rosemary said, knowing too well the crushing feeling of debt. She and Liam had been mired in thousands of dollars of debt, along with a towering mortgage, ever since they'd bought their house two years ago.

Down the hall they heard muffled voices and soft crying. "Good," Silva said. "A few tears might clear some blocked energy."

A few minutes later Max called the women into the bedroom. Silva marched in easily, but Rosemary stopped at the doorway, overcome by a wall of stink—a sickening, yeasty combination of sweat, feet, and fear. It was as if someone had emptied an aerosol can called "Human" into the room.

"Please check me one last time," Sheila said, panting on the tail end of a contraction.

"OK," Silva sighed and helped Sheila into position. Max slumped in a folding chair, staring straight ahead.

With two gloved fingers in Sheila's vagina, Silva stared down at the striped bed sheets, feeling for Sheila's cervical opening as the laboring woman groaned in discomfort. They all waited silently.

"Well, my dear," she said, withdrawing her fingers and removing the glove. "I would say you are a tight seven."

"Oh!" Sheila began to cry.

"Jesus," Max grunted.

"Okay," Sheila said, "Let's go."

Silva called ahead to the hospital while Rosemary helped Sheila into a maternity dress and Max packed an overnight bag. When Silva returned, she was full of urgency.

"Remember," she said. "Although I'm licensed, home birth is still foreign for the hospital staff. As far as the OB-GYNs are concerned, I'm a quack, and you guys are nuts for wanting to have your baby at home. A doc named Compton is the OB on duty today, and Elsa is the charge nurse. Look, Compton is a jerk—he hates midwives—and Elsa is old-school. Don't expect much empathy or gentleness. And Sheila, I must tell you that he does routine episiotomies."

Sheila winced at the mention of having her vaginal opening expanded with scissors.

"Let's try to let the small stuff slide and maybe you can convince him that all your prenatal yoga and whatnot will allow you to stretch without being cut. He'll be expecting a non-compliant patient, so it'll be up to you to charm him."

"OK," Sheila and Max said in unison.

As Rosemary helped ease Sheila into the car, she recalled her own time delivering Dylan, when after eight hours of back labor, she looked at her midwife and said, "I can't do this anymore." But when she imagined the agony of sitting in the car for the twelve-mile ride to the hospital, she just said, "Oh, forget it."

"I'll lock up the house and see you there!" Rosemary called out as Silva's car backed out of the driveway.

Back inside, Rosemary surveyed the messy house in dismay. How depressing it would be to come home to this place with a new baby. She remembered when Dylan was tiny, how Liam would always tell her to let it go when she complained about their untidy house, but she never could. Was that really just a year ago?

She spent the next half hour straightening up the bedroom, changing the sheets, airing out the rooms, sweeping, and washing the dishes. Then she followed the others to the Naval Hospital a mile away.

On the drive, she felt overcome with heaviness. Dylan's empty car seat made her unaccountably sad, as if she were mourning a stillbirth and couldn't bear to return the shower gifts. It was nearly 3 p.m.—on Saturday, right? She realized now she should have left the car seat with her mom, and also should have called from Sheila's house. But this birth was like a black hole of time. She'd call from the hospital.

Rosemary caught a glimpse of herself as she walked through the glass doors of the hospital: flowered sun dress, Birkenstocks, pool hair. She had never been to a hospital birth, but assumed that looking like a disheveled hippie was the worst way to approach a hostile obstetrician.

Rosemary was directed to Sheila's room, where she found her panting on her hands and knees on the bed while Elsa stood with her back to her, having Max spell their names for the newspaper announcement. Sheila was wearing wool socks and a short hospital gown with the back mostly open, and was already hooked up to an IV and an external monitor.

The doctor walked in and exclaimed, "Whoa, what a group of spectators!" His shiny head gleamed in the fluorescent light. "I'm Doctor Compton. Sheila, isn't it?" He ruffled through some papers on a clipboard.

"Yes," Sheila answered, picking her head up to make eye contact, though Rosemary could tell she was still feeling the contraction.

"Please lie down for a vaginal exam so I can check your dilation," he said, sliding a sterile glove onto his right hand. Silva helped Sheila lean back as Compton probed with his latex fingers.

"According to your chart you were told that you were a tight seven at your last exam, but you are really at five centimeters dilation." He withdrew his fingers, peeled off his glove and scribbled onto her chart. Rosemary shot an indignant glance toward Silva, but she was staring as if in a trance. "Elsa will administer Pitocin and you will progress faster." Elsa nodded and left the room.

"So," Compton continued. "Sheila Simpson, eh? Any relation to Marge and Homer?" As Sheila entered her forty-second hour of labor, the man was attempting to make jokes. Sheila and Max looked at him blankly as Silva laughed obligingly. "Don't worry," Compton continued. "Your next baby will be easier."

"I'm not having another baby," Sheila spat. "But I need to discuss something with you."

Compton looked annoyed. "And what is that?"

"My biggest fear of childbirth is getting an episiotomy. I just want you to know that I've done months of various exercises to allow me to stretch naturally, and I'd like to be given the chance."

"Well," he smiled. "Most women at the last minute just want

to get it over with. Chances are you'll do the same. We'll see what we can do."

Rosemary felt like crying when the door closed, but she seemed to be alone in this. Sheila looked stoic, Max was a stick, and to Silva, this sucking up was all in a day's work.

"My dear," Silva addressed Sheila. "You are most likely to get what you want from Compton if you call him 'doctor' or 'sir' whenever possible."

Sheila nodded.

"And if you have a problem with anything Elsa is doing, let me know quietly and I'll try to talk to her. She doesn't take well to being told what to do by patients."

"Even though it's my body."

"Correct."

"OK," Sheila replied, dropping her head to breathe through a contraction.

"And the Pitocin might be rough. It's going to make your contractions stronger and harder. Just remember that each one brings you closer, and you're on the home stretch now."

"At five centimeters?"

"His fingers are a different size than mine and he wants to cut me no slack, but that's between him and me."

Elsa entered the room with a vial in her hand. She was squarely built. Wearing gray scrubs and with her gray hair pulled back tightly, she looked like a large walking cement block. She emptied the vial into Sheila's IV bag and recorded some information on her chart.

"It's a busy day, but at least you've got this nice birthing room."

"Yes, this is great," Silva said.

"This thing feels horrible," Sheila groaned, tugging at the monitor that was attached to a large belt wrapped around her lower abdomen. "I can hardly move."

Elsa left the room without a word and let the door slam behind her.

"Oh," Sheila whispered, sliding into another contraction. "Oh, shit." The Pitocin was kicking in quickly. "Oh, shit!"

Sheila yelled. Soon, a pattern began. Rosemary and Silva took turns rubbing Sheila's back through the increasingly stronger contractions while Max watched dully from a chair.

The contractions were coming hard and fast. Conversation stopped and an endless tedium set in, to the mesmerizing soundtrack of the blips from the fetal monitor. Like the night before, Rosemary settled into a torpor, trapped in another airless room with people who were like mismatched guests on a lost ark.

After a while Silva glanced at her with a smile and said quietly, "You're quite a friend. Not many people could stick this out for so many hours."

"That is so true," Sheila said, her first words in over an hour. "You are a true blue friend, Rosemary. My first friend, and my best friend. I don't know what I would have done without you."

Rosemary gave her a squeeze in acknowledgment and felt a swelling of pride. But soon she sank back into her taciturn misery. She glanced at the clock—Liam would be getting home soon, and her dad would be preparing the grill. What was Dylan doing? How was her mom holding up? She realized with horror that she not yet called home, and her mother couldn't reach her. She needed to find a phone, but Sheila's contractions were getting harder and more frequent, and the two women had a system—Rosemary massaged the right side of her lower back, and Silva the left. The contractions were endless waves—if she left it would be even harder for Sheila. Max had fallen asleep, and Rosemary had a hard time not hating him for it. Soon. She'd make the call soon.

Another surreal hour passed as Sheila descended deeper into hard labor. It was like the legends of fairyland where a year passed as a day.

When the contractions began to escalate in intensity, Sheila soundlessly propped herself up on pillows, and everyone else soundlessly changed places. Max woke up and relieved Silva, Silva took Rosemary's place, and Rosemary sank into Max's chair.

When Elsa came in to check Sheila's vital signs, she broke the spell.

Crap, the phone call!

Rosemary left the room and called her mom from the nurses' station.

"Hi!" she tried to sound cheerful.

"Honey, where are you?" Martina asked. "I've been calling that number for hours. Your little guy has been unhappy for some time."

Rosemary felt her breasts fill up with milk as she fought back tears. "We're at the hospital."

"I thought Sheila was having her baby at home."

"It was taking too long, so we had to transport."

"Well Liam just got back and the baby's a little better now, but he's been fussy since he woke up at 2 o'clock."

"That was a long nap," she said, shifting the nursing pads in her bra to absorb the leaking milk.

"Yes, but when are you coming home? Your father is ready to put the food on the grill."

"It's getting closer."

"But when? I'm afraid Liam is annoyed with you. He's not saying so, but he seems it."

"Oh Mom, how can I leave? She's getting so close."

"Do you want to talk to Liam?"

"No! Go ahead and eat without me and I'll be home as soon as I can."

Martina sighed. "We thought we'd see more of you this weekend."

"I know. This isn't what I planned either."

"Well, why can't you leave? You're at the hospital. She's in good hands."

"She seems to need me."

Another sigh.

"I'll be home as soon as I can, Mom. I have to go."

"Bye-bye, honey."

When Rosemary returned to the room, things had changed.

Sheila plunged into a contraction that lasted nearly four minutes, and came out of it shouting, "I want to push!"

Silva left the room to find Elsa.

"I'm scared!" Sheila squeaked.

"There's nothing to be afraid of," Max said firmly.

"Shut up!" Sheila shoved him away and began to hyperventilate.

"Good," Rosemary cooed. "That's right, this is the way we breathe when we can't push." She pivoted to the foot of the bed where she could meet Sheila's eyes and began to hyperventilate with her. "Yes," Rosemary continued in a calm voice, blowing along with Sheila. "We blow, we breathe high and shallow and we open, we open for the baby."

Silva returned with Compton, who began speaking while Sheila was spiraling into another long, hard contraction.

"So you're wanting to push, Miss Simpson?"

Sheila managed a jagged "hmm" in response.

"When you're through with this contraction we'll check your dilation," he said, pulling on a glove.

Max wondered over to Rosemary and squeezed her hand. "Thank you for being here," he said.

"Hey," she said quietly, leading him away from the bed as Sheila let out a deep, guttural growl. "Can I give you a word of advice?"

"Sure."

"When Sheila says she's scared, don't tell her there's nothing to be afraid of. Try telling her you understand, but that everything is going to be OK. Tell her she's safe, that she's strong, that she knows just how to push her baby out."

He looked into her face for a long time and finally said, "Tell me again."

"Don't tell her there's nothing to be afraid of. It feels lousy to have your feelings denied. Tell her she's safe and strong, that she can trust herself."

Staring at Rosemary's chin, he replied, "OK."

Compton withdrew his fingers and wrote on Sheila's chart.

They all looked at him as if he were about to call out the winning door prize number.

"Nine plus," he announced. "There's a little cervical lip left. No pushing till it's cleared."

"Thank you, Doctor," Sheila said breathlessly, then quickly began contracting again. She had a look of desperation in her eyes that Rosemary could well remember. Trying not to push was like trying to stop a sneeze and an orgasm at the same time. During a tornado.

Sheila ended the contraction with a howl and shouted again, "I want to push!"

"Do you suppose Doctor Compton is available?" Silva asked Elsa.

"I'll get him," Elsa replied. "I think she's ready."

"I'm so scared!" Sheila shouted at the end of another contraction, and Max repeated what Rosemary taught him. Sheila allowed him to remain at her side while she rode the waves of her final contractions.

Compton returned promptly. "I understand you're ready to push," he said. "Let's take a look." Sheila leaned back into Max's arms as Compton performed a vaginal exam. Again the Master of Ceremonies reached into the fishbowl for the winning ticket. Rosemary smiled, wishing she could shout, "We have a winner!"

When Compton withdrew his fingers and finally said, "You are indeed fully dilated," they all exhaled together. "The baby is already through the mid-pelvis," he continued. "You can push now. But if you're serious about not getting an episiotomy, I suggest you push only during contractions and allow the shoulders to deliver slowly."

Rosemary and Silva exchanged wide-eyed looks of disbelief. Sheila began repeatedly saying, "OK, OK, OK," digesting the fact that forty-five hours of labor were actually about to end. "OK, OK, OK," and the long, seamless grunts began. She locked in eye contact with Silva between contractions when she needed help to control her urge to push.

"Don't clench up your whole body," Silva coached. "Let your jaw drop and use the same muscles you use to shit."

Rosemary wrinkled her eyes shut for an instant at those words, remembering how she'd hated to accept that she had to "poop" Dylan out, but this was indeed how it was done. She stepped over to Max now and grasped his hand. He clutched hers in return.

"I can't do this!" Sheila shouted. "I can't do this!"

"Yes, you can!" they all shouted back.

"This is the time when you feel you're going to split in two," Silva soothed. "But you will not. You will birth this baby beautifully. You are a strong woman and you know just what to do."

Sheila took those words back to an eternal secret place and grew quiet. With the next contraction she returned growling and pushing.

"The head is crowning," Compton reported. Rosemary felt a wild leap of excitement when she saw the small tuft of black hair protrude and then recede back.

"It has hair!" Max shouted. "It has hair!"

Another powerful push, and the baby's head protruded a little more before receding. "Is it out yet?" Sheila shouted.

"It's crowning," Silva answered.

"The head isn't even out?" Sheila bellowed.

"So close."

Sheila moaned and grunted through the next six contractions, and the head was almost through.

"I'm gonna tear!" Sheila shouted. "It hurts! I'm gonna tear! It burns! Up high! Don't cut me!"

"You're not going to tear," Compton said calmly.

Elsa firmly pressed a warm washcloth under Sheila's clitoris. Rosemary watched as Compton deftly eased the head out and Elsa suctioned the baby's nose and mouth. A face! With masses of black curls! The baby rotated its head toward Sheila's right thigh.

"The head is out!" Max shouted, pumping Rosemary's hand up and down. "The head is here!"

"Head delivered at 8:32," Elsa said aloud.

"Ms. Simpson," Compton began. "Now is the time for control. I want you not to push during your next contraction. Just let the first shoulder slide itself out and the next will follow." Rosemary and Silva shared incredulous looks. The routine cutter was handling this birth as gently as a midwife would have.

"Look at me, Sheila," Silva said, and Sheila stared into her eyes as if they contained all the secrets of the universe. When the next contraction came, she resisted the urge to push, matching Silva's high, fast breathing blow by blow as Compton slowly eased the shoulders out. The baby let out a cry and its body slid out like a buttered water balloon.

"Sheila!" Max shouted.

"It's a girl," Compton said with a smile. He placed the baby on Sheila's belly as Elsa wrapped a warmed blanket around her.

"Oh!" Sheila shrieked, staring agape at the wet, softly crying infant in her arms. "Oh, Max, look, a girl, a baby girl." Max buried his wet, weeping face into Sheila's hair. "Max, a baby girl!"

Sheila's voice grew softer as she touched the baby's face. "She's here, our baby girl. Hello, sweetie," she whispered. "Oh little girl, oh look, oh welcome, baby girl." Max stole another look and then pushed his face back into Sheila's hair, sobbing. The baby looked into Sheila's face and began sucking on her little fist. "Are you hungry, little one?" Sheila tried to aim her huge nipple into the newborn's mouth.

Compton placed a stainless steel bowl at the bed's edge to catch blood and other fluids and then checked Sheila's swollen labia for tears.

"I can't believe she's finally here. I can't believe there was really a baby inside me," Sheila said, beginning to weep.

"You are quite a steadfast individual, aren't you," Rosemary said to Sheila with a kiss. "I can't believe how long you kept it up."

"Tell me what choice I had!" Sheila laughed.

"Well, you're still amazing," Rosemary said, awed by the baby and by the everyday miracle of birth.

"So are you," Sheila kissed her cheek. "Thank you so much. I would have been so much more scared if you hadn't been here."

"Ms. Simpson," Dr. Compton announced loudly. "Your peritoneum is intact. You have not torn. No stitching will be necessary."

"Thank you so much, Doctor," she said with a long outward breath. "I'm so grateful."

"I'm glad you came through so well," he replied. "And now I am applying traction to the cord to force the placenta to detach."

Sheila shrieked as he slid the placenta out, which looked like a hunk of liver the size of a dessert plate. When it was over Sheila was wracked with an after-contraction so strong that six hands reached out to steady the baby on her abdomen.

"Well, congratulations," Elsa said to Sheila. "She's beautiful. Do you have a name chosen yet?"

"No, we don't," Sheila answered.

Max said, "How about Elsa?" spurring a cathartic laugh from everyone but Elsa.

"I'll be back in a few minutes after I dispose of the placenta," Elsa said.

"Dispose of it?" Sheila looked aghast.

"Actually," Silva interjected, leading Elsa by the elbow toward a corner. "They were hoping to take it home to plant it beneath a tree."

Rosemary glanced out the window, saw that it was dark outside, and the magic of the birth cracked like an egg. That meant Dylan was either asleep or miserable. She could feel her breasts harden.

"Sheila," she said with a quick embrace and a last look at the baby. "I need to go."

"I understand," Sheila said. "I'm sorry I ruined your weekend."

"Not at all," Rosemary said. "This was an honor and a privilege."

She slipped into the elevator and nodded in greeting to an ashen-faced man with slumped shoulders. His meaty hands held three vases of flowers past their peak, with the string of a wilted "Get Well Soon" balloon around one thumb. She realized with sudden horror that someone he loved had just died.

Rosemary watched the lighted numbers change as tears streamed silently down her face. At the lobby she left the elevator, but the man remained. Where was he going? To the basement? To the morgue?

A warm wind blasted her face as the automatic door released her into the young night. She inhaled deeply, wiping tears with the back of her hand, grateful to be breathing air that had not been exhaled moments before and recirculated through a building full of sick and injured people. New air that couldn't possibly have been the last breath of a dying person.

But there was no saving the evening at home. They all sat stiffly in the living room watching an Angels game as Rosemary ate leftovers and Dylan nursed fretfully. Liam, stony and aloof, stared at the TV while her parents sat in quiet embarrassment. When Rosemary took Dylan into the bedroom at bedtime, she dozed off as he nursed. By the time she emerged an hour later, her parents had gone to bed and Liam was watching "Saturday Night Live."

"I'm sorry," she said, sitting down heavily next to him. He muted the TV and turned to face her.

"We drive seven hundred miles to spend three days with your parents and you spend half of that time with a person you'd forgotten existed until two years ago."

"Sheila's not just anyone, she's an old friend. She was very important to me when I was a kid."

"And now? What's important to you now? I really can't tell."

"I had no idea it would take that long."

"There are clocks, you know. I'm pretty sure the hospital and even Sheila's house had a clock that you knew how to read."

"How was your day?"

"It was fine. Tell me, why did you even go to the hospital? It's not as if you were needed, what with Max, the midwife, the doctors, and the nurses. Why didn't you just leave?"

Rosemary looked at him as if across a vast plain on a moonless night.

"It never occurred to me."

"It never occurred to you? It never occurred to you that since you'd been with these people the whole night before and you were tired and you were supposed to be spending time with your own family that maybe it was time to say 'so long'? That your one-year-old son was missing you and we were supposed to be having a vacation? None of that occurred to you?"

"Birth casts a spell on people," she said, looking at a muted Will Ferrell. "I did feel torn and guilty, but I never seriously thought about leaving before the baby was born."

"Birth casts a spell? I don't remember it that way."

"You slept through most of Dylan's labor."

"Because you told me to! You only wanted the midwives!"

"That's true."

"So I just don't understand, right?"

She looked at the TV screen. Will Ferrell glanced at her with his left eyebrow raised, and then the camera cut to Tracy Morgan, who looked shocked. She wanted to know what he'd said.

But instead she turned back to Liam and replied, "Yes, it seems you just don't understand."

"Well, I think that's total bullshit," Liam snapped.

And then she wanted to mute Liam. She imagined seeing his mouth suddenly stop working, like a cartoon character. He would be confused at first, then angry. Steam would shoot from his ears. She would laugh at him.

"I'll tell you what I do understand," Liam continued. "That Dylan should have a nice first birthday celebration, and your parents should not be utterly disappointed with this weekend. I would like to have a good day tomorrow with my family. And I understand that I need to go to sleep."

No, he didn't get it. She had done something wonderful that day. She knew what an important role she'd played, and so did Sheila. It wasn't her fault that Liam couldn't see that.

He stood up and straightened the ottoman. "Good night," he said and left the room.

She continued to stare at the muted "Saturday Night Live" until a commercial came on. Then she went to the kitchen for a glass of water and stood there feeling lost. It was just past 11 o'clock.

She stepped outside. It was cool and lovely, as still and soothing as a mountain lake. Was it really only that morning that she and her mother took Dylan to the pool? So much had happened since then. She'd helped her friend through a birth, a tough birth; she'd gotten to witness a new life entering the world, and now Sheila and Max were parents. They would be negotiating all that newness right now: Is she nursing right? Should we change her diaper? Can you hold her while I go to the bathroom? She remembered those surreal first days, just a year ago. They were wondrous, and exhausting, and scary, and—everything all at once.

A sudden wind startled her, rustling through the palo verde tree on the border between her parents' house and Mrs. Ross's. She watched the tree kick and sway in the wind, responding anew to each gust. She imagined that it wasn't merely getting jarred when the wind blew but that it sensed its arrival the way a dog senses its master's footsteps. Maybe the tree looked up and greeted the wind, waving its arms and rustling its branches to show its welcoming joy.

She smiled at the thought and wished she could curl up under that tree. Just sleep outside all night in the bed created by fallen leaves, with the curved dome of stars as a blanket. The earth would lie beneath her like a lover, quietly filling her empty places with the soft serum of life. And in the morning, the sun would caress her awake, whispering, "Come, love. Walk with me."

But now the sound of water, pattering on leaves. Rosemary looked toward the sound and saw Mrs. Ross in the moonlight, emptying a watering can onto a plant at the edge of her yard. Clearly she had been thinking about a particular plant, some plant that was more vulnerable to the arid climate, or was perhaps newly planted. Mrs. Ross, who had no children of her own, treated the plants as her babies. Rosemary's eyes teared up at the tenderness.

Suddenly her body felt heavy and she went back inside and got ready for bed. "Tomorrow will be a good day," she said aloud, quietly, in the bathroom. "I will wake rested and there will be harmony in my family."

CHAPTER 9 | MAY, 1998

Joshua Tree National Park, California

ROSEMARY SHIFTED IN HER SLEEPING BAG, REFORMING HER jacket into an even worse pillow. She'd been awake for hours, forever. How could the night be so long? She had to pee, but could ignore that. What she could not ignore was the fear. Twenty-nine years old and still afraid of the dark. Imagining knives thrust through the tent, a stalker on the ridge behind her, a deranged drifter who knew she was alone. What an idiot. Leaving Santa Fe at noon to drive ten hours to Joshua Tree. Stuffing her face with Doritos and Chips Ahoy and Diet Mountain Dew. Now all that crap food and caffeine had fed her stupid brain with endless anxiety and here it was what, three in the morning? She desperately needed at least four hours of oblivion to reshuffle the deck, to reset the mental trip meter.

She should have taken those cucumbers and sliced them up for the trip. Liam would never even look in the produce drawer. Left alone with Dylan for the weekend, he'd probably waste money taking him out to dinner and renting movies and be Awesome Dad—the big bastard. Then there was the leftover chicken and some even-older enchiladas. More wasted money. She should have put it all in the freezer before she left. She also should have paid bills. Probably some were overdue. She wondered if Dylan, now twenty months, missed her, if he'd cried for her at bedtime.

She belched and tasted Doritos. Oh, how could she have done this to herself again? She reached for her stomach, gripping a good four inches of flab. Here she was again, a fat shit. The kid was nearly two years old—she couldn't blame this on pregnancy anymore. It was four inches was microbrewed ale and Hershey's Special Dark and hunks of aged cheddar inhaled over the kitchen sink. Or homemade cookies, when she was happy enough to bake them. Was she ever happy? Yes, there were good days. Good days when she liked her kid and liked being a mom and even liked Liam. Was it really as bad as she thought?

God, she had to pee, and it was so damned windy. She'd considered skipping the tent, since sleeping under the stars was wonderful, and setting up a tent in the dark was miserable. But she had been—and still was—too spooked. But now the wind validated her decision. She imagined telling Liam, "I wanted to sleep out, but it was so windy." If she'd been brave enough to sleep outside without a tent that would please him, or at least stave off the disapproval he seemed to constantly exude around her but would never admit to. It might make him think she wasn't a total wimp, not completely tamed by middle-class life.

And she, he said, exuded resentment. But she knew it was true. To Liam, it was as if he handed her a gift every day, this gift of being an at-home mom, but she was always glancing at the receipt, wondering if there might still be time to exchange it for a life that fit her better. It was hard for him to work so much, but it was their decision that Dylan would not be dumped in day care.

But she expected to be happy in it, expected to be fulfilled. Making homemade play dough, painting the bathroom, pawing through hand-me-downs, reading picture books, splashing at the pool, watching the budget, going to the Children's Museum, making nice dinners, keeping a vegetable garden—she thought it was what she wanted. She thought she'd have lots of mom friends and a happy marriage and would feel complete.

But instead she was a wreck, one day telling Liam they had to make big changes, had to rethink everything, that she felt she would crack, and the next saying, "Don't worry, it's all OK."

She wished Liam would have a hard time this weekend with Dylan, that when she came home he'd utter some pat phrase like, "I don't know how you do it," or "Now I see why you've been having a hard time." But she knew she wouldn't hear that. Even if any of it were true, he'd never say it. My God, when had they become so competitive! When had a lack of empathy become the norm! She balled up the jacket into her face and screamed. Screaming was better than thinking. She sat up and punched her duffel bag, punched it again, punched it and kept punching until her wrists ached. Why did she even bother living? There was no greatness in her. She was a blob of mediocrity, a pointless almost. An impatient, angry, bored parent. A sullen, resentful, stingy wife. She did not deserve Liam, who was a good man, or Dylan, a pure being who was unfolding like an exotic flower. No, she probably did deserve Liam, the judgmental shithead, and Dylan, the spoiled brat who never gave her a moment's peace. She fell back into the sleeping bag and wept.

Morning at Joshua Tree was always glorious. It didn't matter the time of year or the company or the occasion, as long as there was coffee and the rock and the wingbeats of ravens under a still desert sky. This was Rosemary's favorite landscape. She looked around at the jagged outcroppings and sloping inclines, the spare but thriving vegetation, and considered how so many people thought the desert was a dead, barren place. But to her, the rock formations were like bones—the bones that remained after some lush, green landscape had been boiled down for stock. But the rock still had marrow, still had nourishment; it was not lifeless. Those greener places were beautiful—the humid coastlines, rolling prairies, and old mountains covered with trees—and certainly more comfortable, but they didn't let you think. Only the open deserts, and especially the Mojave, gave her enough space to remove her head, shake out its contents, and set it to rights again.

It was Saturday morning, 7:15. She would have forty-eight hours here, an enormous, gluttonous hunk of free time for someone used to having it doled out in one- and two-hour slices. It was Liam who had suggested she take this Memorial Day weekend for herself, to get a break and relax. At first she was leery, and slightly insulted. He didn't want to be with her? He didn't think Dylan needed her? He thought she was wacked? Liam suggested she visit friends in southern Colorado, just three hours from home, or head up to a campground in the national forest above Santa Fe. But she wanted to come to JT. And she would not be telling her parents she was here. She was here to breathe, to think her own thoughts, to sleep.

What was it about morning that made everything better? Morning, with a good cup of French roast, brought hope. If ever she were too poor to brew a good cup of coffee in the morning, she would most certainly lose all faith.

Seven hundred miles from home—or seven miles, depending on where home really was—in the Indian Cove campground. Not her favorite campsite but pretty good for a holiday weekend. She ate a yogurt and a banana and stared at the dirt, at the line of shade and sun. This was the time of day when she emptied the dishwasher, threw a load of laundry in the washer, and made Dylan breakfast. Even at home, morning was the best time. Everything fresh, everybody still behaving well.

Rosemary walked down to the bathroom—really a pit toilet—with a bottle of Purell in her hand. It was occupied, so she waited in the shade and considered how to spend her day. She'd brought a book, a sketchbook and pastels, a set of runes, a journal, and a little pan flute she was learning to play. But a hike would come first, before it got too hot.

She suddenly needed the bathroom urgently and stood up, trying to negotiate with her guts. Things had never been quite the same since Dylan's birth. Since then it was like she and her body were on speaking terms but no longer best friends.

Finally the door opened and a tall man came out. He nodded at Rosemary, and as he walked away she was completely disgusted—no Purell, no wipes of any kind. He'd probably go make breakfast now for his wife, and the poor woman wouldn't realize he'd just wiped his butt with those hands.

Afterward Rosemary tidied up the campsite and put on sunscreen. By now Dylan had probably climbed into bed with Liam. They'd read some books together and then Liam would make pancakes. He'd help Dylan flip them and everything would be sweet and perfect. But that was because Liam would never think to dust, or mop the floor, or fold laundry. He never understood why she was stressed out being an at-home mom because he treated time with Dylan like a vacation day. And a weekend without her would not change that. She wished she could be gone for two or three weeks, enough time for the toilets to stink and the mail to pile up and the take-out meals to get pathetic. Then maybe he'd get it.

She breathed in and out deeply. "I am love and light," she said aloud. "I am love and light." She'd gotten that affirmation from her friend Lara, and sometimes it helped. It was a complete lie, of course, but it tended to calm her a little.

Rosemary set off in the direction of Pete's stash cave, about a mile away, where she and Liam had found the weed five years earlier. She went inside, felt around in the same places, and found nothing, but the memory of that day made her smile. She wondered if Pete had retrieved the baggies or if they'd been stolen by someone else.

She had actually seen Pete last summer, an altogether bizarre experience. Mikaela, a friend from college, was passing through Santa Fe. She'd been Rosemary's dancing partner of sorts at Cal State. Back then, they would drive far and wide to hear any band they could dance to, sometimes sleeping in the car if the shows ran late, getting home just in time for morning classes. So when Mikaela called to say she'd be in town, Rosemary bought tickets to the Igbo Beats.

Rosemary was ridiculously excited for a night out with a girl-friend, her first since Dylan was born. She'd dressed in a loose, flowing skirt and a tight tank top, with her nursing boobs giving her what the Commodores would call a mighty-mighty-brick-house look that made her strut. She couldn't wait to dance, as she and Liam had a year earlier when the Beats played on the Santa Fe Plaza. She had been hugely pregnant then, and felt singularly blessed to be dancing under an evening sky to the powerful earth rhythms of nine African men drumming and singing.

That's what she expected, and had led Mikaela to expect, but instead they walked in and found Pete—on stage in Santa Fe, in her town. Pete, with his acoustic guitar, was the warm-up act. She was speechless. He actually sounded good, sort of like Leo Kottke, and he was still handsome, though he'd buzzed his hair and put on some weight. She was completely dumbfounded.

She and Mikaela ordered beers, and Rosemary tried to act nonchalant, but she was fascinated by Pete's ability to charm the women in the audience. She could see them staring at him thoughtfully, could practically hear them wondering what he was like in bed, especially when his face contorted during riffs and when he uttered a long "oohhhh." She watched those women more than she watched Pete, and felt a cackling cynicism rise inside. When she was supposed to be asking Mikaela about her life, about her tour in the Peace Corps, Rosemary was instead fantasizing about walking from table to table, telling the fawning women that Pete was really just a so-so lover, that he wasn't magic, that she'd seen bits of toilet paper stuck in his pubic hair more than once, that he was really just an everyday schmuck.

And while Mikaela pretended to be interested in Rosemary's life, she spent most of the time urging her to talk to Pete.

"Fine, I'll talk to him later," Rosemary said. "First tell me about Africa."

"Oh, Africa was amazing," Mikaela gushed, taking several

long sips of her beer. Rosemary remembered this behavior—Mikaela was forever getting someone's attention and then pausing, building suspense as she readied her delivery. It was annoying.

"The people are so loving and open. They have nothing, yet they are so open. But I have never been so sick. All of us had some form of intestinal virus the whole time. I shit more in the last two years than I have in my whole life. You can't imagine it. I've seen people sticking their asses out of moving cars to shit."

Mikaela paused, waiting for a shocked response, but Rosemary was distracted by Pete and was late with the oh-my-God that was clearly expected.

"Oh my God!" she sputtered, trying to recover.

"It was unbelievable," Mikaela continued. "You go to squat at a pit toilet and you can see intestinal worms moving in the shit."

That got Rosemary's attention.

"Oh my God," she said genuinely. "That is so gross."

"I'm telling you, it was unbelievable."

"So there's no sanitation? What about protecting drinking water?"

"Well what we mostly did was dig and case wells because the surface water is so contaminated. There's actually a huge movement of people raising money to construct wells in these remote villages. Someone in the States can raise as little as three thousand bucks and there are donors who will match it. It doesn't take much to radically improve life for these villagers."

"Wow, that's amazing."

"It truly is. That's why I'm here, just visiting friends before I go up to Laramie to talk to a few people at the university who might want to start a foundation for this."

"Seriously? You're going to start an NGO or something?"

"Well, I'm trying to."

A robust round of applause shifted their attention to the stage, where Pete had just finished a solo rendition of "Layla." Rosemary felt herself softening toward him. He had not given up on his music—he really was quite talented—and if he was touring with the Beats, then he was probably not smuggling drugs or illegal immigrants into the country. The beer brought on a sense of nostalgia and forgiveness, and she found herself feeling proud of him. She began to relax and plan what she would say to him after the set. First, she would have to get backstage somehow. No way would she stand near the stage while he was playing, waiting at his feet for him to look down and notice her.

"I'd like to play an original song now," he said to the audience. "It's on my new CD, which is available tonight."

Rosemary smiled generously—a new CD! Good for Pete.

But once he started singing, she soon recognized the words as having sprung from a conversation she'd had with him years ago, after her first year of college. Rosemary had bought a new address book, and Pete walked in as she was copying names from the old book to the new. She'd remarked at how surprisingly difficult it was, how what had begun as a clerical task had turned into a soul-searching afternoon. Which names should get copied? Who was really her friend? What did it mean to be a friend, and was she a good friend? Did she have enough friends? Who should be left out of her new address book, her new life? Pete had been deeply moved by it all, and now here he was singing about it.

"Carey, where have you be-en?" His voice rose up with the question. "Should I write you i-i-i-i-n?"

As the "in" went on and on, in an oh-so-sincere tone, Rosemary shouted out, "That bastard! This song was totally my idea!"

"What?" Mikaela asked, and Rosemary explained.

"So?" she said. "What were you going to do with the idea? You probably wouldn't even have remembered the conversation if you hadn't heard the song tonight."

"Yes, I would have," Rosemary insisted. "And it might have made a nice poem."

"Do you write poetry?"

"Not now, but I have."

"Oh, let it go," Mikaela said with a wave of her hand. "The guy saved your life, remember? You owe him one."

"He drove me to the goddamned fire station!"

"What is it with you? You never should have left him. You know that, don't you? He was crazy about you."

"He was cheating on me."

"How do you know that?"

"I just know it."

"No, you don't know, you just believed it. I knew plenty of musicians back then, and I asked around. He was true to you, and you wouldn't even pick up his phone calls."

"You're wrong."

"No, you're wrong, and I'll tell you another reason I know—because I tried to get him into bed more than once, but he turned me down."

"What?" Rosemary slammed her beer on the table.

"Yeah, I tried, but he wouldn't go for it, while you two were together and even after."

"I thought you were my friend!"

"I was, and I am. It was just gonna be sex. He's hot, is all. But it never happened, so forget about it."

"Forget about it?"

"Yeah, now you can hate me instead of him, 'cause he never cheated on you."

"I can't believe this," Rosemary seethed, staring into Mikaela's defiant face.

"Thank you and good night!" Pete called out as his set ended.

"Now's your chance to go talk to him," Mikaela said.

"No way."

Mikaela shoved her chair back and wandered over to the stage as roadies in black T-shirts began setting up for the Beats. Rosemary chugged her beer and watched her with disgust. She didn't know what to do—stalk out of the bar, find Pete and apologize, sob in frustration, or scratch Mikaela's eyes out. So she ordered another beer.

But when the Beats came on, the night completely collapsed. In the time since she'd last seen them, the band had transformed itself into a sad joke. The guy who had done most of the singing the last time, the one who'd appeared only slightly to be the lead man, was now wearing a white, rhinestone-studded suit. The other men were still wearing fezes and flowing colorful robes, but the dude in the center looked like some goofball Elvis impersonator. He was also playing a saxophone, badly, just wailing on a few disconnected notes. Rosemary's jaw dropped in shock and Mikaela stood with her arms crossed.

"So this is what passes for African music in the States?" she asked.

"You should have seen them last time," Rosemary whined. "They were amazing."

The eight men were still smiling, they still had beautiful blue-black skin, they still played rich complex rhythms and swayed joyfully, but Mr. Elvis—he seemed to want to transcend them, to move on, to what, being white? American? A rock star? It was a bleak sight.

After a few disappointing songs, Mikaela said, "I've had enough. I have a long drive tomorrow."

"You're leaving?"

"Yeah, I'm tired. I'm driving up to Wyoming in the morning and I need to sleep."

"But this is the first time I've gone out with a friend since Dylan was born!" Rosemary blurted out.

"Look," Mikaela said. "I'm really sorry, about everything."

"Uh-huh."

"It's been great seeing you, and you know—" she touched Rosemary's arm gently. "You should get out more."

"Yes," Rosemary replied. "And you should go fuck yourself."

Rosemary stayed for a while longer, thinking it meant she was grown up and confident if she could hang out alone at a nightclub, but she was miserable. When her breasts started to fill up with milk, she suddenly missed Dylan so much she ran out of the club and sped home. Dylan woke up as she walked into the house.

"Perfect timing!" Liam said as she entered the bedroom. She could tell he was smiling as she kissed him with relief. "You have some amazing Mama Radar."

Rosemary sank into the sweet joy of nursing Dylan. She was home, nestled in the goodness of her family. And the pathetic Elvis dude, Mikaela, Pete—they were all just part of her beer headache. A quart of water, a few hours of sleep, and they would all be gone. This was where she belonged.

❧   ❧   ❧

Rosemary smiled at the memory as she walked away from the cave, closing her eyes to appreciate it fully. "Hah!" She said aloud with a laugh. "I'm sure I won't be copying Mikaela's name into my new address book."

But whose name would she have in her address book? Rosemary was aware that Sheila was her only close friend, and she still lived so far away in Twentynine Palms. And Lara—well, it seemed that Lara was pretty much full of shit. Lara was the first friend she'd met in Santa Fe, and Rosemary had bought into all her New Age schtick, but lately Lara's life was falling apart, and she couldn't face any of it head on. She had breast cancer, but wouldn't say the words. And although she had spouted dogma forever about people bringing on their own "work"— what the rest of the world called misfortune or bad luck— suddenly Lara's "healing opportunity" had arisen from environmental factors. And when Lara went through an ugly divorce, her story was not that her marriage had failed but that her ex was "not committed to growth." She seemed no different from the people who, when they get what they want, say, "God answers prayers," and when they don't, say instead, "The Lord works in mysterious ways." Rosemary once had a landscaping client who would claim with confidence that while God brings rain, Satan brings floods. Suddenly, both women seemed nuts.

Rosemary had tried to help her through the cancer, only to be informed that her energy was "cloying" and "dampening." Lara said she would call her in a few months. Rosemary had effectively been dismissed.

But it was hard to meet people in Santa Fe, which was a much smaller town than it seemed. Since the local Hispanics and Anglos rarely mixed, and the Native Americans kept completely to themselves, her town of about sixty thousand was really more like twenty thousand. And it was an angry place. The locals watched as their culture faded and their relatives could no longer afford to live in town. They felt robbed of their way of life by newcomers fleeing the coasts and the Midwest to buy up houses in spacious suburbs like Cielo Vista.

Their resentment was almost palpable. But that barely touched the ancient bad blood of the place. "There are a lot of discarnate souls here," a spooky shaman lady told her once. "For centuries, this was a crossroads and battleground for many tribes, and the Spanish conquistadors wielded control over the Pueblo Indians for so long, and then you have the weapons labs up in Los Alamos—there are many ghosts here who don't know how to move on."

Ghosts or no, Rosemary needed a friend.

❦   ❦   ❦

A red-tailed hawk swooped overhead, riding the updrafts of the cool morning air, and a sudden surge of joyful energy filled her body. She turned to the rock face that had been shading her as she walked, and climbed up to a higher vantage point. The sky was clear enough that she could see Mount San Jacinto, and wasn't that Mount San Gorgonio? God, it was beautiful.

Rosemary breathed out a long sigh and felt. . .big. She thought about what had driven her here—the stress, the drudgery, the isolation. Didn't everyone say being a parent was hard?

Didn't half of all marriages end in divorce? So why was she surprised that it was tough?

Well, she'd been surprised because she had thought "hard" meant simply being tired, or short on money, or sick of housework. She'd never dreamed that "hard" would mean imagining—every day—the satisfaction of throwing chairs through windows, or fantasizing about walking away from your kid and never returning. People didn't talk about that. When you're pregnant, they smile and congratulate you and say you look beautiful. They did that on your wedding day, too. Why didn't anyone tell her what was really down the pike? So the newly minted idiot could enjoy her last moments on an Earth she still recognized? The conspiracy of silence was cruel.

But she was part of that conspiracy. Rosemary had decided that she would be truthful and tell women what it was really like only if they asked. She hadn't even told Sheila, before, during, or after her endless labor last year. The same was true regarding her sister-in-law, Gwen, who was expecting her first child in just a few months. The women never asked.

So why did she smile at their news? Because she hoped that maybe it would be different for them. Maybe this birth, this baby, this family, would be different. Maybe this would be what, the Christ child? The Buddha? Maybe they would figure it all out and light the way for her and the others. Maybe they would change everything. It was the same way she felt on the first day of school, or the first day of a diet. Liam called it her Fresh Start Syndrome.

OK, so it was hard. Her mother liked to quote her own mother, Deedee, the grandmother Rosemary had never met, with the question, "Who ever said life was easy or fair?" That was always cheery. Why did benighted people quote other equally benighted people and derive solace from it?

She stood up, scrambled to the ground, and landed with a graceful thud, automatically striking a gymnast's pose. She looked from side to side with a triumphant smile and dropped her arms and giggled. She suddenly found herself missing Liam.

It would be nice to have someone to talk to. That's a good sign, she recognized—missing him. Maybe it meant that all was not lost, that she didn't really want to push him off a cliff. Or, maybe it just meant she was a bigger jerk than she'd feared. All she ever wanted was time alone, and here after one day she was looking for conversation.

The time alone thing—what was that about? If she loved Dylan, and she knew she did, why did she always want him to go to sleep? All the moms she knew spoke greedily of naptime, gushing over the long ones, whining and sometimes even weeping over the short ones. Some of them woke up at 4 a.m. just to ensure a little time alone, moving soundlessly through their houses like shadows. But Dylan slept too lightly for that. Just getting up to pee in the night was a challenge. Although his bed was on the far wall of their bedroom, if she stood upright, no matter how dark it was, the kid would wake up. So she would crawl on her hands and knees to the bathroom every night. Once in the bathroom, she would straighten up slowly, carefully grasp the doorknob, and silently close the door. Then, because the sound of her urine hitting the water would often wake him, she put her hand in the toilet to break up the stream, which made far less noise. She also had a method for washing her hands silently. It just took longer.

Rosemary thought objectively about the peeing routine and realized for the first time how ridiculous it was. Looking pointedly at a creosote bush, she said aloud, "I crawl to the toilet and pee on my hand every night." Well, that was hilarious. Really, really silly. "Can you believe I do that?" she said laughing. "It feels good to tell someone, Bushy. May I call you Bushy?" She giggled. "Thank you for not judging me. I'm here for you too, any time you need to talk." She threw her head back and roared.

"Excuse me?"

Oh shit! Someone's here! "Oh," she said and looked toward the voice. Above her, near the place from which she had just descended, was the tall guy with the poop hands. Another human had seen her talking to a bush. "Oh," she said again.

"I wonder if you've seen anyone around here," he said loudly. "I was supposed to meet some friends here, but I think we might have missed each other."

"No, no one," she replied.

The man scrambled to the ground next to her, drew a map from his pocket, and spread it out. It was a topo full of concentric circles and hand-written notes.

"Are you familiar with the park?"

"Yes, very" she answered. "What do you need?"

He didn't know Joshua Tree all that well. Rosemary explained how to find the climbing pitches he was looking for and directed him to some others. It was fun to talk, and gratifying to be consulted. Imagine—a guy who asked directions. He was probably forty, his face lined and sunburned, with sprays of gray at his sideburns.

Once he walked away, she noticed how hot it had become and began hiking back to her campsite. By now Liam and Dylan would be dressed and ready for their day. What would they do? She wanted so badly to be a fly on the wall and see what they were really like when she wasn't around. Was Liam really so engaged, or did his attention drift like hers did? Would Dylan be whiny and clingy? This was all *schadenfreude,* she knew, and she was ashamed.

"I am love and light."

She was also a space case, missing trails and landmarks and taking an hour more to get back to camp than she should have. By the time she returned, she was hot and thirsty and strung out. In a shady corner of the site, she devoured a bag of grapes and then found a place under a Joshua tree to lay out her sleeping pad. It gave her little shade, but lying down outdoors was always a huge pleasure. She saw that the tree had a few clusters of white-green blossoms, a stunning fact, considering that for a Joshua tree to bloom, it needs both a winter freeze and a well-timed spring rain.

Rosemary stretched and loosened in the heat, feeling blessed to have discovered those flowers. Her breathing slowed as she looked up at the tree arching over her, its branches gently nudged by the light breeze. Watching the long stalks move in their spare, ineluctable way was suddenly all that mattered.

Then, like a gift from a secret admirer, a yucca moth alit and began to move delicately from flower to flower. It nosed into the blossoms, its fine legs traveling nimbly over the compact petals. She could not see its determined proboscis probing and gathering nectar, but she knew it was there, and she wondered if the flowers enjoyed this. Was it tickly or painful? Gratifying or invasive? Lovemaking or a simple transaction? She recalled her early knowledge of plant sex, long before the college biology courses—the old science units on pollination in fifth grade, all that pistil and stamen stuff. She'd found it fascinating because she had the feeling there was more to it. She didn't yet know how babies were made, but those lessons seemed to be edging around the question. Now she felt herself turned on by the simple word "nectar." An instant throb began low and deep, a rich primal energy rushing like rainwater against a sluice. Why couldn't a man right now be drawn to her the way that moth was drawn to the flower? Why couldn't he just follow some instinct, some scent, without knowing why, like a dowsing wand—find her next to the cool of the rock and join her? She tried to put a face on the man. Liam? Brad Pitt? Mick Jagger? No, it needed to be someone new, a stranger. A stranger with strong rough hands, piercing eyes, and hair that would flutter in the wind. Oh yes, that worked. That worked really, really well.

She napped for a while and awoke sweaty and disoriented, the shade long gone. With the sun high she returned to the tent to savor her drowsy, drugged feeling, spreading out her sleeping pad to enjoy the luxury of wasting time. One of the many go-to-sleep songs she'd made up for Dylan came to mind: "Your so-ft eyelashes, a ne-ew spring leaf, come little baby, let's drift to sleep. . . ." She loved the heaviness of a sleeping baby—the even breathing, the sweet smell, the surrender. But there was more—it was trust. Dylan trusted her. She had earned that trust, and she was suddenly proud of it. She sat up, abruptly alert. Why wasn't that a big deal? Why didn't people put this stuff on their résumés? "Despite loneliness, sleep deprivation, springtime allergies, cheap shoes, credit card debt, and regular run-ins with poop, boogers, and vomit, I have not bailed or hit anybody or become a crackhead. I have earned my son's trust."

OK, enough sleep. Time to do something. She finished unpacking the car, made herself lunch, and got out her sketchpad. For Christmas last year Liam had given her this sketchpad and a beautiful box of pastels. Sweet William, she often called him.

Swirls of yellow-green took shape as the résumé issue took hold. She didn't have much on her résumé, and this made her resentful for so many reasons. First, few people appreciated what it took to do a job like landscaping, especially in the harsh climate of northern New Mexico. Understanding plants, bugs, and micro-climates, and also dealing with employees and clients, was not easy, and she was good at it. But what she did best was read the movement of water. She studied the terrain of each job carefully, seeing it as a stage on which the main character, water, would play. Where would the star enter the stage, and where would it exit? How would it behave while on that stage? How could it be coached to stick around longer, to play the largest role possible? She had worked for High Desert Landscaping for five years, until she was too pregnant to lift sacks of mulch and manure, but only recently did she realize she should have been paid twice as much as she had been. Her old boss paid her like a job foreman when really she functioned as a landscape designer.

Then there was parenting a kid, something nearly everybody did but so many people did poorly. Shit, if you included that on a résumé it would actually work against you. She often wished she could tell people everything she did well in a day. "And then, even though Dylan was upset from the bug bite, I was still able to give him a bath without crying." But no one wanted to hear that. And no one but another mom knew what it was like.

She had met some other moms in the neighborhood—the Park Posse, as she called them—though none were close friends. It was easy to feel lonely in Cielo Vista, a spread-out subdivision ten miles outside of Santa Fe where she and Liam had bought a small, boxy, fake-abode house. She could map Cielo Vista in a minute, with its grocery, park, coffee shop, pizza joint, real estate offices, pool, and bank. It was quiet, safe, dark at night, and not the suburban trap it might have been—at least there were no lawns—but it could be isolating.

It seemed the Park Posse women spent most of their time sizing each other up. Nursing your baby ranked high in social status, as did being relatively thin. Fat women in elastic pants who carted around bags of bottles were pariahs. Women whose kids were always sick were also to be avoided. Who wants that oozing kid in a play group? And why is he sick so often, anyway? They probably eat too much sugar. And then there were diapers: cloth, with expensive, breathable covers, were best, especially if you used the diaper service. Buckets of stinky diapers soaking in vinegar were not a status symbol but were more acceptable than disposable—think of what that woman is doing to the earth! Babies should sleep with or alongside their parents, or at least in their room on an all-cotton sleeping pallet. And working mothers? Forget them. They had no idea what they were missing; their priorities were totally screwed up. By the time you paid the day care center to ignore or abuse your kid, how much money did you really earn anyway? And how could you cook a decent dinner? The part-timers could be OK, especially if they worked from home and had a loving family friend to care for the kids. Then you could be friends with them.

It turned out she qualified on all counts. Not too fat to be gross, or too thin to be dangerous. Cloth diapers? Breastfeeding? Working in the family business? Check, check, check. She and Liam did not have a grand house, or go to the hottest restaurants, or take the vacations some of these women talked about, but that somehow worked in her favor—it meant she was making sacrifices for the good of their son. She was in if she wanted to be, but the Park Posse looked to Rosemary like a sorry excuse for friends.

There was one mom, though, who was different. Colleen seemed restless in her life, which appealed to Rosemary, and she lived just down the street. Maybe she had some spunk, an edge. At the park, she always had a cup of coffee in her hand, a takeout cup from some gas station, and would talk about how she'd been up since 5 a.m. baking cookies from a recipe on the corn flakes box, or drawing up plans for a backyard fort for her boys. She also knew where all the sales were. "There's a door-buster at Mervyn's tomorrow," she'd tell the Park Posse. "I'm planning on getting there at six—I need a new bread machine. Anyone game?"

When Rosemary arrived at her house with Dylan for their first official play date, she found a rain-soaked L.L. Bean delivery on the porch and handed it to Colleen when she opened the door. "You got a package," she said, incredulous that Colleen had not brought it in earlier.

"Thanks!" Colleen chirped, dropping the sodden box in the foyer next to a jumble of bags from the mall. In the living room, a dusty blue sectional couch framed a round coffee table with four remotes on it. The table faced a home entertainment center six feet high, shrouded in smoked glass. Along the wall stood a bookshelf of VHS tapes and family photos. Rosemary looked through a window to the back patio, where a new set of table and chairs, still choked in their wrapping, stood next to another set of table and chairs that looked a whole lot better than the crappy plastic ones she and Liam owned.

"Well hi, Dylan," Colleen said, taking his hand. "Let's go find your buddies."

Rosemary followed as Colleen led Dylan down the hall to the kids' room, where four-year-old Matthew and three-year-old Christopher stared at him from within a maze of train tracks.

"Look who's here," she announced. "Your friend, Dylan. Can you show Dylan the trains Daddy built for you?"

"My trains!" Matthew barked.

"My trains!" Christopher repeated.

"Yes, but we're sharing," she said, letting go of Dylan's hand.

"My bunny!" Matthew said, snatching up a stuffed rabbit from the carpet.

"Mine!" Christopher shrieked.

"No, son, *this* is your bunny," Colleen said, reaching for an identical rabbit nearby. "You boys can hold onto your bunnies, but everything else we share with our friend, right?"

Rosemary walked toward the boys, crouched down with a smile, and began moving the trains. "Choo-choo!" she sang. The boys watched her impassively and Dylan wandered away to the plastic bins stacked four feet high and crammed full of toys. Rosemary began to follow him, but Colleen waved her away.

"They're fine," she whispered. "Let's go have a cup of coffee."

Despite her reluctance, Rosemary followed Colleen, experiencing something akin to peer pressure: Clearly, staying with the kids was uncool, and having coffee was cool.

"You'll have to forgive the bunny thing," Colleen said as Rosemary followed her down the hall. "Our pet rabbit, Charizard, died a few days ago, and I got them those stuffed ones to make them feel better. They're not quite ready to share them."

"Oh, that's fine."

"You should see how cute—at night, they've been putting the stuffed ones into Charizard's hutch."

"Oh," she said again, managing not to say what a bad idea she thought that was.

"It's a whole lot easier cleaning up after the stuffed kind, I'll tell you," Colleen said with a chuckle.

In the living room, Rosemary stopped to look at a large photo of Colleen and her husband, Matthew. They stood on the shore of a sunny lake, facing each other, holding both of each other's hands. Rosemary stared for what was probably an inconsiderate amount of time, intrigued by their facial expressions. Colleen, dressed in mid-thigh denim shorts and a tank top, her hair several shades darker than it was now, looked resolute, almost defiant in her lopsided smile. Matthew, slim and boyish, his hair cut in a Bee Gees shag, smiled broadly, confident.

"How did you and Matthew meet?" Rosemary asked.

"We grew up together," Colleen answered, sponging a counter in thoughtful circles. "In Topeka." She picked up the sponge and tossed it into the sink. "And I can't wait to go back. I hate this place."

"You hate Santa Fe?"

"I hate New Mexico—all this dryness. I'm sick of this scratchy place. I want my boys to have grass to play on, and trees to climb."

"There are trees here," Rosemary countered.

"Real trees," Colleen said resolutely. "Not these scrubby things."

"Well, I grew up in the Southern California desert," Rosemary said with a smile. "This is a lush forest for me. All these piñon and juniper, the aspen and ponderosa in the mountains, the cottonwoods along the river."

"Well you've lived a deprived life," Colleen replied. Her bangs, carefully engineered to look tousled, spilled onto her forehead. Her khaki pants bulged at the waist, and a magenta top, designed to flounce, pulled against her tummy. A Size 10 woman smashed into Size 8 clothes, Rosemary surmised, and quickly hated herself for it.

Colleen's watch sounded a tone. "Boys!" she shouted. "Arthur's on!" The brothers' bedroom door flew open, slamming into the wall as little Matthew slid into the living room in his socks. He snatched up the remote and clicked on PBS in time to hear the "Arthur" song beginning: "Hey! What a wonderful kind of day!" Christopher screeched and grabbed unsuccessfully for the remote.

"No!" Matthew shouted, thrusting his hand above his head. "You're too yittle!"

Dylan walked into the living room with a rubber T-Rex in his hands, confused. Rosemary crossed the room to stand next to him, rubbing his back. "Christopher and Matthew are excited to watch a story on TV," she said. "That was surprising, wasn't it?"

Christopher gave up the struggle for the remote, delivered a perfunctory punch to his brother's abdomen, and settled into a bean bag chair inscribed with his name.

"TV story," Dylan said.

"Yes," Rosemary crouched down to look in his face. "Would you like to watch also?" Dylan nodded and turned his attention to the TV, where Arthur the aardvark was taking a photo of his family at the beach.

"You can sit down, sweetie," Rosemary said, but he remained standing, riveted. She returned to the kitchen.

"He doesn't watch much TV," she explained.

"Of course not," Colleen said, which pulled Rosemary off center. How was she supposed to respond to that? She decided to pick up the earlier conversation.

"So then why did you move here?" she asked.

"Matthew's job," Colleen replied. "He got recruited by Greenwell. He's a mortgage guy. He works mostly with jumbo loans."

"I guess this is a good place for jumbo loans."

"Shit, I cannot believe what passes for a million-dollar home here. Tell me why you would want some mud hut on a dirt road, where you can't hardly park, and can't remodel because your dumb mud house is in some dumb-ass historical district."

"You mean a 'must-see adobe treasure on Acequia Madre, walk to school and shops, just minutes from the plaza?' "

"Yeah, like that. What do you do, read the real estate ads?"

"I've worked on the grounds of plenty of those houses, and I'd take one any day. I love those old adobes—cool and quiet, lots of rounded corners, deep-set windows, stone floors."

"You can keep 'em. OK, OK, you win," Colleen said, waving her hand at Rosemary. "But I still wouldn't want one of them."

"Well I can see why you're happy with your house," Rosemary cooed. "It's quite lovely."

"Oh," Colleen waved her hand at the kitchen with its granite countertops, brushed steel appliances, and gleaming white tile.

"This is all Matthew. He's a nut about this house. He does most of the cleaning, you know."

"No way!" Rosemary shouted.

"I kid you not," Colleen said. "Nearly every night, after the kids are in bed, he pours himself a scotch and cleans. Pulls apart the toaster oven, flushes out the sink disposal—whatever catches his eye."

"What do you do?"

"While he's cleaning? I don't know, what do I do?" She cocked her head to the right. "I guess I watch movies, or work on some project. Or I just go to bed."

Rosemary was intrigued. "Does he cook, too?"

"I do most of the cooking, but he'll even wash up a lot of those dishes, too. Apart from the laundry and the vacuuming, he does all the cleaning. It's great most of the time, but sometimes it can get on your nerves."

"And the yard?"

"I'll water, but he does the rest."

Rosemary had winced when she first saw the border beds of annuals baking in the sun—none of them drought-tolerant, none of them native. "Wow," she said. "I don't even know what I'd do with my time if Liam did all that."

"Good question, huh?"

The question disturbed Rosemary, reminding her of the message she'd seen on the Unitarian Church marquee in town: "How you spend your days is how you spend your life." Did that mean she was really spending her life picking up toys, pulling weeds, and mashing potatoes? Her life? Was that all there was?

"Well, we moved here when I was pregnant with little Matthew," Colleen said. "And I'll be honest, it has pretty much sucked ever since. I hate living so far from my mom and the rest of my family, don't you?"

Rosemary thought of Martina— her praying, her meekness, her smallness. No, she didn't miss her all that much in the day to day. Of course she missed her dad, but did she miss Deet?

He was living in Tucson, doing something else she didn't understand, this time with real estate. And of course his fiancé, Isabelle, was long gone, whatever that was about. She wondered what it would be like for Dylan to have Uncle Deet nearby. Would he teach Dylan to fish? Take him bowling? What exactly did uncles do with their nephews?

"No, I don't mind being far from family," she answered, suddenly jealous of Colleen. She had a husband who cleaned, and she missed her mother.

"Well, Matthew knows that we will be out of here by the time little Matthew is ready for kindergarten," Colleen asserted. "We're going back to Kansas. And to be honest, I'm having a hard time meeting people here.

"The people Matthew meets through work are just gross. The men either have sticks up their asses and are so damned boring, or they're arrogant jerks trying to one-up each other about their hunting cabins or their mutual funds. And their wives—most of them are older than me, and they drink like crazy. I have gone to parties where the women are doing Jell-O shots in the kitchen. I mean, hello? And out here, the moms are so full of themselves. You're like the first woman I've ever had a normal conversation with."

"Well," Rosemary responded. "I'm honored."

Pulled from the memory by a persistent fly, Rosemary said aloud what she'd known for some time: "Colleen is my friend." She turned the page to start another drawing. "It might not be a perfect match, but I'll be a good friend."

Other issues stepped up next. They were not making it on the income from Liam's business, Ellis Landscaping. Even though they lived simply, and she economized so much, the income was erratic, and it seemed they could never get ahead. It was a constant disappointment for her—when you did the right things, wasn't your life supposed to work out well?

The temptation to work grew every day, so much so that she believed the universe was testing her. In the past six months she had turned down three jobs, all in landscaping, and all well-paid. The thought of having more money was so seductive. She resented that she could never buy something unnecessary, like placemats or a new dress, without being plunged into uncertainty and guilt. She knew too well the feeling of entering a few weeks of deposits and checks and then seeing the shocking result—the negative sum, or the tiny sum that was supposed to carry them through the end of the month. It was the same sickening feeling she had as a kid when she did something wrong—yes, Mom, I'm sorry I dug that hole in the yard, right through the weed block, so I could bury the time capsule I'd created inside a plastic Easter egg. Please forgive me. Yes, Mr. Bank Guy, I'm sorry my car payment will be late. Please forgive me.

But the biggest draw was having firm ground beneath her feet again. She would know how to spend her days. She would understand her role. She would not look at a day spreading out before her with trepidation: What if Dylan didn't nap? What if that little cough didn't abate, and they had to stay home all day? ("Only ten hours till Daddy comes home!") What if she yelled at Dylan, and started another downward spiral?

But the individual days were nothing compared to the question that caused her the real grief: Who should she be? Should she be the thrifty mom, selling outgrown baby stuff to the consignment store and researching energy-saving lightbulbs? Should she be the hot mom, working out to exercise videos, cutting carbs, and wearing form-fitting spandex to the farmers' market? Or how about the moody and mysterious artist mom, the highly-involved-with-the-extended-family mom, the fixing-and-painting-the-Sheetrock-myself mom, the scrapbooking mom, the volunteering mom, the perfect-house mom, the activist mom, the look-how-many-pets-we-have mom, the going-back-to-school mom, the starting-a-business mom, the shopping mom, the home-schooling mom, the book-club mom? So far she just seemed to be the cleaning-cooking-doting mom who needed to justify her existence every day with busy-ness and devotion to Dylan. At least she wasn't the drunk mom, or the abuser mom, or the affair-having mom. She was better than some, but who was she really?

Rosemary stopped drawing, searching for the term she'd read in a parenting magazine: She was a "child-centered" mom, attempting to follow and support Dylan's interests with unwavering attention. She couldn't quite pull off the "immersion" or "continuum" parenting thing, with the kid nursing till junior high and in his parents' bed forever, but she tried to be child-centered, at least between bouts of resentment, boredom, and rage. But the whole thing exasperated her. How were women ever happy in this role? How did they sublimate everything in themselves that did not serve the child, or the family? She hated how one magazine article would profile a goddess mom like these and the next story would be about "making time for you," the endless admonishment to sleep when the baby sleeps, or reserve naptime for your "special time." Then when do you prune the fruit trees or call the insurance company? It all seemed impossible.

But if she went back to work, Rosemary knew, she could escape all these questions with an explanation that most of the world would accept: "We needed the money." Her mother wouldn't accept it, and neither would the Park Posse, but oh well. Liam would also object, but she knew he'd relent. But when she imagined dropping Dylan at day care, it looked like failure. She and Liam could survive without a second income; the real reason for her working would be to escape the emotional challenge of being with her kid all day.

Once, when Dylan was having a meltdown in the grocery, an older woman had turned to her and said, "Kids are terribly strict Zen masters, aren't they?" And it was true. Staying patient and loving as you cared for someone twenty-four hours a day, especially in the beginning when you're exhausted and healing from childbirth—it was crazy difficult. But she knew, despite all her bitching and conflicted feelings, that she needed to do what she was doing now. If she could parent Dylan, she could do anything. And if she didn't parent Dylan well and completely, then she would be missing her big chance at becoming . . .someone. She closed her eyes and heard herself say, "I am Dylan's mom."

Rosemary set down her pastel and found her velvet bag of Viking runes and its companion book explaining how to interpret the oracle. It had been years since she'd pulled a rune, since before Dylan. They always made her a little afraid. What if one portended some sort of doom?

"Show me what I need to know for my life right now," Rosemary said aloud, thrusting her hand into the bag. She shuffled through the stones until one seemed to stick to her index finger. Yes, this was the one. She withdrew it carefully, set it on the ground before her, and looked it up. It was Mannaz, "The Self."

The book's explanation read: *A correct relationship to our self is primary, for from it flow all possible correct relationships with others and with the Divine.*

Well, duh.

Remain modest. . . . Regardless of how great may be your merit, be yielding, devoted and moderate, for then you have a true direction for your life.

Oh crud, the devotion thing.

Be in the world but not of it. . . . Strive to live the ordinary life in a non-ordinary way.

Great. It all smelled like another unattainable version of motherhood: Spend your days washing diapers, but do it with some godly presence, some divine light.

If she wanted to take this to heart, then she was clearly being told to put off working, to lay low and be humble. It all sounded reasonable from the outside, and to be expected. "Once you have kids, your life is not your own anymore." Her mother had told her that, as had her mother-in-law. Her midwife told her to "surrender." Liam told her to enjoy her time with her son. But what if she died young? It could happen to anybody, and she knew that if it did happen to her, people would pity Dylan and Liam as the Christians moaned and the Jews ate. But would anyone say, "I wonder what her dreams were? I wonder what she hoped for, what she put off until Dylan grew up?"

Well, this was morbid. But more important, it was telling: What were her dreams, anyway?

Maybe it wasn't a dream, but the ranching family that owned the water rights to Cielo Vista were looking to sell them to a European corporation, and a group of residents had gotten together to investigate the possibility of setting up a water co-operative instead. Corporate control of water was growing more and more common, and Rosemary was shocked to see it rear its head in her own backyard. In developing countries, privatization improved infrastructure and water quality but could make water so expensive that people spent up to half their incomes to buy what their families needed. International corporations were quietly buying up water rights all over the globe. So far the Cielo Vista Water Coalition was just a ragtag group of volunteers, but she found that her passionate commitment and degree in environmental science were more than a lot of people in the group had to offer. They were meeting with the ranch family the following week. Maybe something would come of all that.

As she put the runes away, the smell of coals and lighter fluid blew toward the tent. Someone was starting a cooking fire. Ah, a holiday cookout. What fun.

But she wasn't invited. She'd chosen to be alone, chosen to eat instant noodles like some wannabe monk while families nearby gathered for their outdoor feasts. Whatever. She pulled out a bottle of Schnapps. At least she'd brought that.

But it was such a small bottle of Schnapps, and it was gone so fast. It was barely dusk when she began to feel restless. She pulled out the dull-as-dirt book she'd brought: *Relationship Dynamics in the Modern Marriage*. Right. Like she was going to read that.

Soon she heard guitars tuning up someplace nearby. No fair! She wanted to hear the music, too! After a while, bits and pieces of a song filtered in, but the gusty evening breeze interrupted it. Why not take a little walk right now? She set off singing along with what she heard, in the happy freedom of being a little drunk.

> *Good morning, America, how are you?*
> *Don't you know me, I'm your native son. . .*

The narrow road snaked through the campground. She walked with a bounce in her step, feeling lightheaded and suddenly exuberant.

> *I'm the train they call the City of New Orleans.*
> *I'll be gone five hundred miles when the day is*
> *done.*

She'd never been to New Orleans, but she imagined stepping off a train there right now. She would meander through the sultry streets, music spilling from the bars, sidewalks filled with people out for a good time. Men would turn their heads to watch her pass, but she would glide by, her body light and free under a loose summer dress. She'd stop for some crayfish and jambalaya, chat with people at the bar, finish up with a cold beer, and keep walking. A sound, at once primal and sophisticated, would draw her toward a club with its doors and windows open to the night, strings of colored lights illuminating the faces of musicians as they played with their eyes closed, playing with one mind. She would stay a while and then walk on, stopping in at the next club, and the next, surrounded by music and good will, living her private life in a public place.

> *Halfway home, we'll be there by morning*
> *Through the Mississippi darkness,*
> *Rolling down to the sea.*

An RV generator revved up, drowning out the snippets of guitar. Rosemary could see a family eating dinner at a folding table beneath the awning of their camper. The kids were around nine and twelve, and as Rosemary stopped to watch, the girl yelled, "Ew!" and the others laughed. She couldn't hear what was so gross and funny but continued to watch anyway, captivated by their movements, the passing of ketchup and the opening of sodas. Would she and Liam ever have a second kid? Could this be them in a few years? After a few minutes she walked on, excitement growing in her as she realized she'd watched the family undetected. What else might she see tonight?

Up ahead, at a site near the recycling bins, a solitary man primed a gas lantern. To her left, on a footpath, someone filled a dish tub with water from a spigot. A Chevy Suburban came up slowly behind her and passed, the kids inside staring out dully. At the next site, a man and a woman, probably in their fifties, sat silently in identical camp chairs, their books illuminated by small lights. At another site, men sat on coolers around a fire, drinking beer. Kids dashed past her, looking for marshmallow-roasting sticks under the scrubby creosotes. A woman called for her dog in a singsong voice: "Moosey! Moosey!" At the next site, two people were unpacking their car in the dark, their tempers short. "I do not know where the tarp is," the woman said. "I never saw it at all." The man barked, "Goddamn!" and Rosemary hurried on.

People were just living their lives here, the same lives they lived in their houses and apartments, only without the buildings. This could be her street in Cielo Vista, or her parents' street in Twentynine Palms, except that it was out in the open. It was like some goofy old movie, and she was the character with the x-ray vision. The place was really like a suburb—cars parked in the driveways, trash cans out front, the sites numbered, the ranger patrolling periodically, the rent due. Yet it was so beautiful. Why not live here all the time? Did anybody really need all the crap they filled their houses with? Did she really need a closet full of clothes? Shelves of books? A garage full of tools? What would it be like to really simplify? Would she and

Liam be happier, more relaxed? Or, without the distractions, would they quickly realize they had nothing in common?

She stood still in the road, listening to the small sounds of humanity, and felt so tender toward it. Everybody was just trying to get by, doing their best to hit the highlights before they ran out of time, and it all suddenly looked so fragile. Even the campground looked fragile. She could imagine the park and others like it as a permanent settlement. The scenario wasn't really so hard to see. The cities becoming too toxic, the country plunging into a depression, the unemployed as modern no-mads, people displaced by war; the nation so crowded that land couldn't just sit around unoccupied. They were chilling thoughts, but they seemed possible, even inevitable. The park, her own home, the plenty, the comfort, the predictability, the safety, even the Earth itself—could it be so fragile?

Rosemary walked on, beginning to feel tired as she passed by dark sites, their occupants either asleep or elsewhere. She could tell by the numbers that she'd almost circled back to her own site, and when the wind gusted toward her, she heard the guitars again. Up ahead was an open fire illuminating adults and chil-dren. She slowed her steps and crept closer, watching through thin stands of yucca. She recognized the kids as the ones who'd passed her earlier, looking for sticks, and now they were roasting marshmallows, shouting about the best way to blacken them without dropping them into the fire. There were five of them, and a few adults. Two men with their backs to her were playing guitars softly, and the others were moving back and forth be-tween two sites—the women, cleaning up and getting things settled for the night while the men sat on their lazy asses.

Just families camping together. She felt her chest fill with longing. It would be nice to have Dylan and Liam here, to see Dylan's little face aglow by the fire, to watch him play with the other kids, all dirty and happy, and to feel she belonged in this scene. These people didn't need to know how grumpy she usu-ally was, or how short Liam's temper could be, or how high their credit card balances were. The Ellis family could just be part of the gathering. But if the Ellises were there, who would the other families be? Colleen and Matthew? No way. Deet and his girlfriend du jour? Yeah, right. Sheila and Max? Nah. Liam talked about old friends, but they'd all scattered after college. She and Liam only had acquaintances, not friends close enough to travel with, not like this.

She buried herself deeper in the yucca, though it was scratchy and uncomfortable. Soon the women came to the fire, and chairs and people were rearranged to make room for them. She counted two men, three women, and five kids. Quite a crew to cook for.

The men launched into "Like a Rolling Stone." The guy on the right sang the verses and then nearly everyone joined in for the chorus. Rosemary sang along in her head.

What would it take? What would it take to be a part of this? People did these things. They walked over to groups of other people and were welcomed. She'd heard that in many parts of the world, a campground was a social place where you were expected to meet people, not a suburban analogue where people kept to themselves.

If only it were daytime, she could feign a need for something—a can opener, some cooking oil. Or Dylan would run toward the other kids and would lead her in. But here she was lurking in the bushes like a goddamned stalker. She extracted herself and hurried down the road, her head feeling dull. Back at her site, she dragged the sleeping bag and pad out of the tent, stared up at the stars, and said aloud, "Please lead me where I need to be."

Birdsong awoke Rosemary before the sun. The air was cool, like a whispered secret, and as she gazed up at the lightening sky she realized she'd slept the whole night without waking. She felt thoroughly rested. When was the last time? She faced the east, wondering what she would do if she were someone else. Her mother would say a Hail Mary. A Navajo would toss some cornmeal. A Muslim would wash her hands and feet, cover her head, and pray. After a long pause she began the ritual of making coffee.

She sipped her coffee as the morning sounds began—car doors opening and closing, pans clattering, people's voices. She used the pit toilet right after a ranger cleaned it, feeling triumphant about that luck, and set out on a walk. She headed west, walking quickly.

The sky was a flawless turquoise, as it should have been in Santa Fe, but it had been a bad fire season already. A blaze in the Jemez Mountains had exploded earlier in the spring and was still smoldering, keeping people off the hiking trails and turning the sky an oppressive milky gray when the wind was out of the west, with the sun glowing like an inflamed egg yolk. With the forest fire raging, the smoke hid the mountains, and the sky hung low like an ashen blanket.

Rosemary got back to the campsite about an hour later and was startled to see a woman walk toward her.

"Good morning!" she chirped as Rosemary searched her face. She was one of the women from around the fire the night before!

"Hi!" Rosemary replied with an air of familiarity that was instantly embarrassing.

"I'm sorry to bother you, but we were wondering if you might have some tools," the woman said. She was about Rosemary's age, smiling with a wide jaw and big teeth. Rosemary took in her brown eyes, sunburned face, and green sundress, and instantly liked her.

"You're not bothering me," Rosemary assured her, trying to conceal her rising excitement.

"Our pop-up camper is stuck halfway up," she explained, "and somehow none of us have any tools. We have three first aid kits but not one screwdriver. We were in such a rush to leave that my husband left his tools at a job site."

"Let me see," Rosemary said, making her way to the car.

"Well, you're far from home," the woman said, looking at the New Mexico plate. "How far a drive is this for you?"

"About ten hours," Rosemary replied, rooting around the back of the Subaru.

"Wow, we just drove four hours from San Diego, and that was murder for the kids." She looked around the campsite. "Are you here alone? I'm Andy, by the way."

"I'm Rosemary," she said, struggling with the latch of a forgotten compartment. "My son and husband are home in Santa Fe."

"You have the whole weekend to yourself?" Andy asked, her jaw gaping.

"Yes, can you believe it? With the driving, three days."

"Three days." Andy closed her eyes and shook her head.

"I know. It's unbelievable. I guess all you have to do is appear to be losing your mind, and you get time to yourself. Hey! Look at this!"

Rosemary extracted a roadside emergency kit and opened it on the ground. Wrenches, pliers, and screwdrivers spilled out, along with a lighter and flashlight.

"Awesome!" Andy exclaimed. "It's like Christmas!"

"Who knew I had this?" Rosemary asked, surveying the contents.

"Why don't you come on over and have some breakfast with us?"

Rosemary felt like whooping and dancing on the table. "Breakfast?" She tried to act nonchalant.

"Well, brunch. We're getting a late start. Oh, come on, it's the least we can do."

"Sure!" Rosemary agreed. At the road, she let Andy lead the way, as if she didn't know where their site was. "What a beautiful morning, huh?"

"It's perfect," Andy agreed. "So how old is your son?"

"He's almost two," Rosemary replied, and suddenly felt like something was missing. It was wrong that Dylan was not there to stretch her hand out to, that she couldn't hear the little songs he always sang, the songs that narrated his life just above the level of a whisper. "I'm starting to miss him," she said, and was amazed by the pang of longing that passed through her. She had never missed Dylan before. He had always been right there.

"I bet," Andy replied. "I took care of my mom once when she was sick, and I left the kids with my husband. By the time I was on the plane heading home, I felt physically sick, I missed them so much."

Wow, physically sick.

"Hey!" Andy shouted as they approached the campsites where Rosemary had crouched in the yucca the night before. She put her arm around Rosemary's shoulders. "We're saved!"

A man who was lighting a stove looked up and said, "Great!"

"Wade, this is Rosemary," Andy said. Rosemary was horrified to see he was the guy who had seen her talking to a bush.

"You're kidding!" Wade exclaimed with a smile. He wiped his hands on his khaki shorts before shaking hers. "This is the lovely lady who helped me out yesterday!" He had a day's growth of beard on his tanned face and a pair of sunglasses propped in his thinning hair.

Andy gazed at Rosemary in appreciation. "My goodness! You must be our guardian angel!"

"Will you have some coffee?" Wade asked, reaching for the French press on the table.

"Sure!" Rosemary replied, looking around in wonder, as if she'd been given backstage passes at a concert. Near a flattened box of graham crackers and a copse of empty beer bottles stood a diaper pail and a cardboard box of pots and pans. Two guitars and two smaller cases were stacked a few yards from the fire ring. A heap of climbing ropes and harnesses spilled from the open hatchback of an old Toyota Tercel. Children's voices lilted from a large tent nearby.

"The kids are playing Candyland," Andy said. "God, I hate that game."

"It's the worst," Rosemary agreed.

As they talked, she dug into the eggs and thick slabs of whole grain bread, melting into the comfort of these people. There were two couples: Andy and Eric, who had Asher, four, and Layla, two; and Carl and Liana, who had Maya and Mikey, five-year-old twins, and fifteen-month-old Lily, whom everyone called Peanut. Wade was a friend who had a twelve-year-old son in Santa Barbara. "He's too cool for climbing with his dad anymore," Wade said. "My ex-wife made sure of that."

The camper, a used pop-up that Liana and Carl towed from San Diego on its maiden voyage, was the focus of all attention after breakfast.

"I knew that guy was a crook," Liana said. "I didn't trust him."

"It'll be fine!" Carl said with a smile that Rosemary recognized. It was that same Please-Be-Happy smile that Liam shot her way whenever things were sucky—especially when the sucky situation was his fault. "We can fix it."

As Carl worked on the extension mechanism, several people were needed to hold up parts of the camper and the kids were bored with sit-down games, so Rosemary took them to the toilet, helped wash the breakfast dishes, and finally took the older ones on a walk. She smeared sunscreen, filled water bottles, packed snacks, insisted on hats. She was Instant Auntie, and it all seemed so natural and unremarkable.

After the camper had been fixed, it was expected that she would stay for dinner. While the men went to town for more beer, taking Layla and Peanut so they could nap on the drive, Rosemary, Liana, and Andy made dinner.

Rosemary cringed as the twins scrambled on the rocks around the campsite. "Don't look at them," Liana advised as they leaped to the ground from a precarious height. "They know their own limits. When we interfere, we mess with their mojo." She and Andy shifted so they couldn't see the kids and Rosemary did too, although she was nervous.

"I know," Liana said. "It's hard to do, but it's better all around."

Rosemary thought of Dylan and how she always felt a tug in her gut when he was climbing a ladder at the playground or jumping on a trampoline. She imagined being one of the moms who sat on the benches chatting, looking relaxed as her kids played, but she couldn't bring herself to do it. The "what-ifs" made her hover over him though she wished she were not so fearful of his getting hurt.

"I always want to trust Dylan," she said, "but then I imagine what people would say if he got hurt: Can you believe she let that tiny boy go down that huge slide? Can you believe she let him jump off those monkey bars? That woman should have her kid taken away!"

"Those voices will kill you," Andy said, shaking her head.

"Those voices make you live your life in fear," Liana added.

"But it *would* be my fault if Dylan got hurt," Rosemary argued. "It's my job to keep him safe."

"It's also your job to help him reach his potential," Liana countered. "And he won't be able to do that if he's full of your fear."

"Well, there's fear, and there's caution," Rosemary ventured.

"Yes, there's nothing wrong with caution, when it's needed," Liana replied. "If there were unseen dangers here, like bears, or even poison ivy, I would be more cautious. But this is just their bodies and their environment. It's simple physics. They're testing themselves. I shouldn't be holding their hands."

Rosemary watched as the kids approached each potential jumping-off place, sometimes leaping with confidence, sometimes looking over the edge, reconsidering, and moving down to a lower point first. They were so happy, all on their own! If Dylan were here she'd be entertaining him constantly and turning the whole afternoon into another episode of the Mommy 'n' Dylan Show. To some extent, she would enjoy it, but she'd also need a break afterward, and he would want her to keep entertaining him, and then she would try to reason with him ("We just played for an hour!"), and then he would whine and cling, and then she would feel trapped and resentful. That was the sequel to the Mommy 'n' Dylan Show, and it played out day after day after day.

"Don't you think so?"

Andy had said something, but Rosemary missed it. "Sorry?"

"I said I believe it's my job to let go and let them lead."

"To let go? At two?"

"Once they're able to walk away, I start following," Liana asserted.

"Yup," Andy agreed. "What she said."

Rosemary looked at them with both longing and incredulity, recalling the Park Posse and its competitiveness and backbiting.

"And how did you all find each other?" Rosemary asked.

"Right here!" they sang together.

"We've been coming here since before we had kids," Andy said with a smile directed at Liana.

"The guys climb, and we hike," Liana explained.

"And talk," Andy said.

"And party!" Liana added.

"I hate climbing," Rosemary confessed.

"Me, too!" Liana said. "All that damned equipment."

"It's sooooo slow," Andy added.

"Hey, it's past five o'clock," Liana said, flicking Andy's ponytail as she got up from the table. "Who wants a beer?"

That night Rosemary sat around the fire, included in the circle of light with these lovely people, marveling that the night before, she'd been huddled in a scratchy tree stalking them. They sang for hours, and she felt like she was along for the journey as her idols searched and quested and discovered: Joni Mitchell came upon a child of God, Bob Dylan was tangled up in blue, Neil Young burned his credit card for fuel, Jerry Garcia played songs on the harp unstrung, and Greg Brown played the poet game. There were even some early Rolling Stones and Carly Simon thrown in, and plenty of songs she'd never heard before, but she would pick up the chorus anyway. She recalled the many nights she'd spent under these stars in this place and could not recall ever feeling so connected. She felt like she'd found her tribe, like a wolf welcomed back to the pack.

As the night wore down though, and the kids were put to bed and the campground's quiet hours approached, Rosemary knew she would soon be going back to her solitary tent. So what did that mean? Was this really a tribe, or just another posse? She thought about the day and realized it was indeed a posse, and to belong to it you had to meet certain requirements: You couldn't hover over your kids, you couldn't request to sing the Bee Gees around the fire, and you probably couldn't vote Republican. It was her kind of posse, but it was a posse just the same.

"OK, one more," Wade said, reaching for Carl's guitar. "This is by my hero, Mr. Greg Brown." No one knew the song, so it ended up a solo:

> *You're a tempting little morsel on the*
> *corporation's fork.*
> *If we show up with the right bits and bytes,*
> *they'll fatten you like pork.*
> *And America will stretch her maw and show you*
> *her white teeth.*
> *It's only when it's much too late you'll see the*
> *cancer underneath.*
>
> *Oh, America will eat you,*
> *Oh, America will eat you,*
> *Oh, America will eat you. . .up.*
>
> *Everything has a number, and we all must drink*
> *our cup.*
> *All I ask is to know, when my number's up,*
> *Looking at these corpses talk and laugh it up on*
> *TV—*
> *All I want is to never have to ask, "Lord, which*
> *corpse is me?"*

There was a long silence as Wade strummed the last few chords. "Well on that cheery note—" Andy began.

"Jeez, Wade," Liana said, rising to her feet. "Could you depress us any more?"

"Huh?" Wade responded. "You want another? Greg has like twenty albums."

He played a more upbeat tune next, but Rosemary was too preoccupied to notice it much. Those lyrics—they had articulated what she'd been thinking for some time. If they weren't careful, she and Liam would end up "eaten" by America. She felt it more and more these days, ever since Dylan had been born. They had consciously bought an overpriced house in Cielo Vista because the school was good. But couldn't they just live anywhere and home-school their son? They paid hundreds of dollars for health insurance every month, but couldn't they just put that money into being truly healthy? They went into more and more debt every day, for a car, for repairs for that car, for dinners out. And last Christmas, they'd bought a dishwasher. How pointless was that? It seemed that every day, she made one more weird little compromise, some largely unconscious decision that made her fear she would become just another suburban mom, just another consumer.

When she was younger, she had prided herself on her decisions: what to study, where to live, what to eat, what to plant, who to marry. But was she still living consciously? She had always assumed she and Liam would rise above the social and economic garbage strewn about the American landscape. Was she kidding herself?

She could remember a few years earlier, when they had first come to Joshua Tree together. She'd walked into the Visitor's Center and was overcome by an intense, overpowering feeling—a rush of energy, a blinding, whooshing force—and she took it as a sign. She'd asked Liam once, during some harrowing fight, why he'd married her. He thought about it for a while and answered, "Because I thought my life would be better with you than without you." That was all. And when she told him about that moment at the Visitor's Center, he looked at her blankly and said, "Maybe your eyes just took a while to adjust, or the air conditioning was a shock after the summer heat."

"I believed you were my destiny," she sobbed. "I believed you were my soul mate."

"And who says I'm not?" he asked.

Was he? If so, why was everything so hard? And why did she feel like she had accomplished absolutely nothing in her life? How could a young, healthy person feel so lost?

Andy and Liana yawned and grew quiet; it was clearly time to go. Rosemary stood up, stumbled on the fire ring, participated in several hugs, and found herself back on the road, next to her yucca. The air was chilling, away from the fire. She tried to maintain a feeling of ease and contentment as she hurried toward her campsite, but soon the images took hold—marauders with knives, poised to lunge at her from the bushes. Men with empty eyes ready to clamp one vise-like fist around her wrist and the other over her mouth.

She imagined herself in a slasher movie on a screen in someone's den, and a girl with a Diet Sprite and a bag of Cheetos in her lap was whispering, "No, don't go that way. It's a trap!" But she didn't know the script, so she went that way.

And ended up safe at her campsite, warm in a sweatshirt, with a lantern glowing and a box of really good licorice to chomp on as she stared up at the brilliant stars.

So this was it. She still had the drive home tomorrow, but these were her last great moments of contemplation. She was sleepy, but fought it, because now she was in a different movie. This was when everything was supposed to come together, when she was supposed to feel comfortable in her own skin, accepted by the universe, infinitely patient with its processes. She should be inhaling the Earth's breath, singing to the lost chord, laughing as her path opened before her. It was all so simple, she'd say to those who were still lost, so very simple. Don't you feel God's love? She'd look kindly at those who had not yet discovered these same truths, and smile compassionately as their busy minds struggled with what she already understood.

She leaned over and scratched her head hard, working up a story so her time there would seem worth the trouble. "How was your weekend?" Liam would ask. "It was awesome," she would reply. But how was it really? Twenty minutes earlier, sitting around the fire, she had felt elated, connected, at home.

That was rare in anyone's life, she would guess. But it was over. If it didn't last, did it mean anything? If she were ejected from the tribe simply because it was time for bed, had she ever belonged? Flowers didn't bloom for long, but they were beautiful and brought joy to people, and food for bees. They were needed to create seeds for the plant. So, even though they were ephemeral, they still mattered, right?

So the time around the fire was a flower. But what was the seed that flower would drop?

Ah, now that was a question worthy of the movie that had just gotten really boring because all she was doing was scratching her head at a picnic table in the desert.

She stood up and stretched, working the muscles that had grown sore from hiking and bouldering. As she bent over her outstretched leg, a thought occurred to her: Maybe she was OK. Maybe nothing was wrong.

Footsteps crunched in the dark. She whirled around with a fist.

"Hey, it's OK," a man's voice said, and Wade stepped into the lantern light.

"Oh," Rosemary exhaled, relieved.

"I'm sorry for frightening you." He clicked off his flashlight.

"Oh, that's OK," she said, smoothing her hair.

"I know I'm intruding, but I was so glad to find you awake. I went for a walk—it's such a beautiful night."

A walk? Well that was a flattering lie. No chance this guy wasn't looking for her. He knew her site was nearby and probably just looked for a New Mexico plate.

"No, you're not intruding," she insisted. They sat down across from each other at the table.

"I loved hearing you sing tonight," Wade said.

"Well, back atcha."

"No, I really mean it. It was great. I didn't know how much I needed that."

Ah yes, he's been divorced, Rosemary recalled. Perhaps recently, and he's hurting. She hadn't tuned into him much during the day—had consciously avoided all the men, actually, not wanting to be perceived as an interloper—but he really was handsome, and he had a rich, deep voice. She noted his muscular arms and weathered face. Nice. Probably worked construction, maybe landscaping.

She thought of Liam and imagined how he would feel about this encounter. She'd cut this scene from the movie. Might as well let it roll, though.

"You headed back tomorrow?" she asked.

"Yeah, back to it."

"What do you do?"

"I own a concrete cutting business."

OK, so construction. Owner, even. But she knew that could mean a lot of things. She and Liam owned Ellis Landscaping, and they were always broke.

"What's that exactly?" she asked.

"Mostly what we do is earthquake preparedness. We retrofit public buildings, reinforce bridges, that sort of thing."

Oh, big stuff. Bids, contracts, suits.

"So do you work for the state?"

"Yeah, and townships, and the federal government when it comes to interstate highways and the like."

But his ex-wife is probably sucking him dry. Ugh, when did she start thinking like this? She was like some hideous crone, counting coins with her pointy fingers.

"I'm always under a lot of pressure, which is why I like to come here. It's just a few hours' drive and I get to feel human again."

"I know how you feel," she agreed. "I grew up nearby, and this place only gets more important the older I get."

He was forty-one, divorced for four years after being married for nine. He lived in San Diego in a house he inherited from his father, who died a few years back. He read a lot, mostly nonfiction, with a particular interest in the Southwest and a passion for reading old travel books and then trying to duplicate the journeys. He was learning to parasail. He didn't see his son enough, but don't get him started on that. He liked simple food. He was tired of the dating scene.

"It's enough to turn a guy into a monk," he said. "I can't describe how miserable it is."

"Try," Rosemary said. "I'm curious."

"God," he answered, rubbing his eyes with the heels of his hands. "Women my age are like rhinos. They might be intelligent and attractive, but they have so much armor built up that you can't even connect with them."

Rosemary furrowed her brow in confusion.

"You sit there having to prove that you're not their emotionally abusive ex-husband, or their cold, distant father, or even their shiftless teen-age son. And all the while, you're trying to eat your grilled halibut and comment on the wine and ask about her work. It's torture, and then you get to pay for the meal. I can't even remember their names half the time. And the younger ones. . . ."

Rosemary looked pointedly at Wade and realized that either he was an extraordinarily skilled con man, or he was being candid in some true, rare way. Maybe it was the beer, the music, or the stars, but there was something naked and honest happening here. Her instinct told her to trust it.

"All the women I've dated who are younger, around thirty or so—they don't have the armor so much as they have intense expectations. They're either looking for a husband and kids—the whole scene, now, before they get any older—or they're aimless and boring, clinging to some freedom they don't even seem to enjoy. Either way, it's like you fit into their ready-made picture, or you don't. There's no, like, 'Here we are, let's see what happens.' But those are better than the ones that are totally whacked. I went out with a graduate student once who was eight years into writing her dissertation on something she couldn't even explain to me. Another one was a vegan who wouldn't sit on my leather sofa. And one girl, I think her name was Tamela, wanted us to go into therapy after our first date."

"No!"

"I kid you not, our first date, so we could 'be in beauty'" he said with air quotes. "'Be in beauty,' with no 'imprints' from our earlier relationships. It's a freak show out there. Like I tell you, I'm considering becoming a monk."

"You should write a book about this."

"Right, and cry all the way through it."

"You could examine modern society through the window of the first date," Rosemary said.

"Huh, that's an interesting idea."

"Seriously, you could contrast all this stuff with what it was like when you were a teen-ager, or when you met your wife."

"Ex-wife."

"It would certainly be cathartic."

"And it would give me something to do on lonely Saturday nights."

"And with the money you make on it you could start a home for stupid single women."

"A re-education camp!"

"Yeah. You could figure out how Pol Pot did it. Teach the women to want something other than marriage, or revenge, or whatever."

He clapped his hands together and laughed. "Oh yeah, that's the stuff! And you could run the home for me!"

"Hah!" Rosemary laughed. She got up to find a water bottle and shared it with Wade. "I'd be one of your students."

"Yeah, right. You."

"Yeah, right, me. I don't know the first thing about what I want. In the big picture, I mean. If it weren't for my son, I'd be utterly lost. I'd be as aimless as one of your little dates."

"Well, I can tell you're an awesome mom. I saw you with the kids today."

That was nice to hear, really nice to hear. She considered her response. "Well, you could say that I am devoted. I have a lot of rough edges with my son in the day to day, but I am certainly sincere."

"That's all that really matters, isn't it?"

"No, I don't think so," Rosemary answered emphatically. "A lot of sincere parents screw up their kids. The whole thing actually scares me to death. I mean, if you had a surgeon who was sincere but he removed your kidney by accident instead of your liver, would that be good enough?"

"True, but it's not all parenting. There are genetic factors, environmental factors—"

"Yeah, but," she paused, "to be honest, I think most parents don't try hard enough and that's why so many people fail."

"Fail?"

"Struggle unnecessarily. Fail to meet their potential."

"Shit, who meets their potential?"

"Some people do! People do amazing things, but most of us just bumble along."

"And you think you're just bumbling?" he asked.

"Totally."

"Is it your parents' fault?"

"No, it's my fault. I'm nearly thirty, and it's my fault that I'm just taking up space on this planet. Other people have goals and they strive to make them happen. I just exist."

"So what are you meant to do?"

"Something great, I'd like to think," she said with a shrug.

"Like what, discover a cure for cancer?"

"Come on, why are we all just bumping around from one day to the next? We have our relationships, we make some money, we have some fun. For what?"

"Sounds like *you're* ready to become a monk."

"I had a friend in college who declared herself a Buddhist. She would always talk about right actions and right livelihood and right intentions and whatever the other rights are. She liked to say, 'Don't just do something, sit there!' It was funny, but after listening to her for so long, I grew to believe that if I just made the right decisions, my life would take care of itself—it would unfold in all the right ways."

"And it hasn't?"

"God, no."

"But there are many right ways. You can't think there really is only one right way."

"Maybe not, but if I do what is right, shouldn't my life be better?"

"Oh, now that's a big-time trap."

"What?"

"My mother used to pray for one thing, and one thing only: 'Please God, keep my boys safe.' She went to church and raised us in the faith and lived a righteous, humble life. And what happened? My little brother dies at nineteen."

"Oh God, I'm so sorry."

"Me too. It was just an oops on the freeway, you know? Just driving in someone's blind spot and boom, gone. We were all devastated to lose Patrick, but my mom—she lost her faith that day, too. She did everything 'right' and God couldn't do the one thing she asked in return? Nah, there's no rhyme or reason to anything."

That statement terrified her. If it were true, then she was truly lost.

"Rosemary," Wade said, "you know, I watched you all day today, and I have to say, you are wonderful."

"Huh?"

"Look, you're beautiful, you're smart, you're articulate, you're passionate—"

"And it all means squat if I don't do something extraordinary with it."

"But what is extraordinary? Look around you," he said opening his arms. "Look at all the rocks and plants and animals that make up this place. Is one thing here more important than another? Is that monzogranite formation wishing it were quartz? Are these juniper trees failures because they're not giant sequoia?"

"Maybe. I can anthropomorphize anything."

"Well they're not. Look, if that California juniper were a giant sequoia, it would take up all the available water and still be half dead. And if the gneiss didn't have its exact properties, then that monzogranite wouldn't be able to thrust up, however many millions of years ago. They're all perfect just the way they are. Everyone is perfect in their own way."

"Even the pedophiles."

"Look," he said sharply. "I don't pretend to have all the answers, but this is how I see it. I spend a lot of time dealing with rock. Now you know that some rock can support a climber and some can't. We always focus on the rock that can hold us, but the one that can't might have vegetation on it, and those bushes and trees are providing habitat for wildlife and holding water in the soil. Or someone wants to build a ten-story building somewhere, but the underlying rock can support only a two-story, and that's fine. If all rock were some intense quartzite that takes forever to break down, we wouldn't have some of the simple things we take for granted, like a sandy beach, or even concrete. When you're skipping a stone into a lake, you know that some work and some don't. But the ones that are not small, smooth and flat—the ones that are failures as skipping stones—are what you want to build a garden wall with. Sometimes a rock's greatness is not readily apparent, but it's always performing a function that someone or something needs. There is no *one* perfect. There is no *one* right way to be."

When he was done speaking, Rosemary looked away from him and into the lantern's glow. Could anything really be that simple? Of course, if you were a skipping stone trying to be a hunk of bedrock, that could be a problem.

"So," she said, "then a rock's only job is to understand its nature and accept it."

"I'm not here to make some proclamation," he replied. "I just think it's possible to be happy with who you are. So maybe we have ordinary lives—we're not movie stars or Olympic athletes or millionaires—but we can live our lives well. You know, like maybe you live in an ordinary house on an ordinary street," he continued, "but you have a really strong, happy family, or you help people out in some big way, or you do some creative thing you really enjoy, or—I don't know. I just think any of us can be great in our own way. Someone said, 'Art is doing well what needs to be done.'"

"Huh."

"And I think it's true."

They paused as a moth circled the lantern, butting its head at the glowing glass.

"And don't tell me," he said with a laugh, "that the moth seeks enlightenment and gets killed in the process."

"Hey!" she returned the laugh. "That's my favorite cliché!"

He yawned. He was clearly past his talking limit. He was a guy, after all, and it must be nearly midnight.

"Thanks for listening to me," she said, shifting her body. "I'll figure it out."

"Yeah, it's late."

He stood up, stretching his arms and shoulders, and she stood as well. They made their way to the edge of the site and lingered at the car.

"I sure am glad I took that walk tonight," Wade said.

"I'm glad you did, too."

"The stars are awesome."

"I bet you don't see them so much in San Diego."

"Not like this. Look, that's Orion."

She smiled. Of course that was Orion.

Wade pointed out Orion's belt, his head, his bow, all of which Rosemary was well aware of. But when the stargazing was over there was an awkward silence. She knew she should make her way back to safe territory, but the temptation to stay was too great.

"Look, I'll be honest," Wade said abruptly, grasping her hands. "I hate to leave you. I can't remember a time when I've enjoyed being with someone as much as tonight."

Whoa, now this was big, a potential life-changer screaming down the pike, careening toward her at the speed of light. And, just as quickly, she heard the stories she might be telling in five years: "We met at Joshua Tree. I went there to get my head together when my marriage was falling apart, and there he was." Wade would kiss her and say, "I took one look at her and knew I could never let her go."

Or:

"I blew it. I had an affair on this little weekend at Joshua Tree, with a guy I had just met. I actually thought it meant something, but it didn't, and I destroyed my marriage."

Decide, Rosemary, decide.

Wade put his hand under her chin and turned her face toward him. "I know I shouldn't do this," he said, and kissed her.

A tongue! A tongue, ever so light and graceful, gently swooping, just dipping its toes in the pool. He pulled away and looked at her astonished face, the face that did not withdraw, and sent the tongue in again, this time probing the deep end of the pool, while the hand left her chin to take her in a full embrace.

Hands! And a long, muscular back beneath a neck that smelled of rock and sweat.

And moonlight. And serendipity. And newness.

But that was enough. She pulled away, her hands on his face now. She smiled and said, "I have to go."

He exhaled loudly and said, "I know." He was quiet for a moment. "I hate to let you go. You're—you're pretty much everything I want."

She took her eyes off his face and looked to the right, down the road, and in her mind's eye saw an image of destruction: jagged hunks of broken concrete, twisted rebar, shattered glass. She stepped back resolutely.

"Thank you," she said. "You're wonderful."

"Will you be around tomorrow?"

"No, I need to leave early."

"Rosemary. Rosemary what?"

"Ellis."

"If I'm ever in Santa Fe, can I look you up?"

"Sure, that would be great."

"Good night," he said, giving her a peck on the cheek.

"Good night, Wade."

She watched as he walked away.

CHAPTER 10 | MAY, 2000

Twentynine Palms, California

M ARTINA FILLED THE POT WITH TAP WATER, LEVELED EACH scoop of coffee grounds with a butter knife, filled the metal basket, and snapped on the lid. She centered the electric percolator in front of the toaster and plugged it in. She loved the sense of purpose that mornings brought.

As the pot burbled and cooed, she opened the kitchen window. It would be hot today, at least eighty, but Rosemary hated air conditioning, and Martina knew that if her fussy daughter woke up in a house with the air on, she would whine, "Mom, can't we let the world in?"

Mark had already left. He'd have his coffee at the diner as he had for decades—a wasteful habit that irked her every day. His law studies had proved more demanding than expected, and she found herself alone nearly all the time. She thought it wasn't too much to ask that he have his coffee at home, but he refused. With a smile.

She peered through the window at the house next door and felt the familiar swelling of sadness. Betsy Ross was gone. She had moved back to St. Paul to care for her mother and had rented out her house to an unfriendly couple, people who rarely said hello and who had let the garden run down. It was a shame, such a shame. She missed her friend.

Martina had also stopped volunteering at the elementary school. A new principal, Ms. Teag, had mandated that teachers use only research-based reading strategies, and Martina—well, she was not a research-based strategy. But would she like to help out with the PTA fundraisers? No, she would not. Oh that woman, that awful Principal Teag.

But no more mooning over what could not be changed. She had work to do today. Rosemary and Dylan were here, and that was a treat. Rosemary had called the day before yesterday, asking if they could come and stay for a few days, and had arrived late last night—without Liam. Martina was confused. She and Mark had visited them in Santa Fe just a few months earlier, and thought everything was going fine. Liam had been digging a giant hole in their backyard for a cistern that would hold umpteen gallons of rainwater, and Rosemary was busy with a group that was trying to gain control of the community water system.

Martina bowed her head, said a Hail Mary for her daughter and son-in-law, and then waited for the urge to say another. It would come, she knew, like the pulsing of peristalsis or the successive waves of a tsunami. When the impulse came, she breathed deeply and it passed.

Breakfast next. She sliced up lowfat cheese, steamed some onion and bell pepper slices, and opened a carton of fat-free egg substitute. She would make omelets in a non-stick pan that required only a spritz of oil. For lunch she'd planned a whole-grain pasta salad, and for dinner, grilled chicken breast and tabouli. The PBS show on cholesterol a few months back had made a big impression on her. There would be no more fatty foods in her house, just fruits and vegetables, lean meats, and whole grains. But she *had* bought some lemon sorbet for dessert that evening, in honor of the visit. She could hardly wait for her daughter, and especially her grandson, now nearly four, to wake up.

❧   ❧   ❧

Mark, settled into his favorite booth at the Carousel Cafe, was relishing his bacon, eggs, and home fries with biscuits and gravy on the side. He'd been coming to this diner nearly every morning for a good ten years, first just for coffee, but now for a meal that actually left him feeling full. He'd known the waitress, Lena, since she was pregnant with her second child, and now she had five kids at home, and the youngest retarded. He tipped her well.

This business with Rosemary was a worry. "It's a long story" was all she'd say last night. He hated to leave today, but he believed she was OK. Shaken up by something to be sure, but she always landed on her feet. He said he couldn't miss class, and that was true, but there was something else pushing him out the door this morning. He just could no longer stomach running interference between his wife and daughter. He was tired of shielding Rosemary from Martina's kneejerk reactions, from her simplistic view of the world, and just as tired of shielding his wife from Rosemary's abrupt, imperious judgments, which cut Martina to the quick. When Liam was there, they tag-teamed it, something they had never discussed but both seemed to understand. But without his son-in-law, Mark felt like a piece of taffy smushed and pulled by the two women. His anger at his son rose anew like familiar bile—would it kill David to be a true member of this family? To be a man who showed that he cared about his parents and sister?

But this thinking would get him nowhere. He turned his thoughts to his class later in the day: statistical analysis in criminal justice. Law school was turning out to be his new lease on life. He even enjoyed the commute, listening to books on tape from the library and planning essays in his head. It wasn't easy, being at least twenty years older than the other students and often older than his professors, but he had never enjoyed anything more. At fifty-five, his life was starting anew. Suddenly he was an actor on a huge stage, rather than a member of the audience.

❧   ❧   ❧

Rosemary had been awake since 5:15, listening to the birds bicker and claim their territory. She'd hoped to sleep longer, maybe even till noon, but this was better than the last six days, when each nightmare-studded night seemed to last a week.

Dylan continued to sleep, stretched out next to her on the sofa bed in what used to be her bedroom. Her parents had finally turned her old room into a guest room, and Deet's into a craft room. The thought of her mother pursuing a creative hobby in that boxy little room made her smile. Yes, smile. It had been a while.

She'd heard her dad in the bathroom earlier, performing the three S's—shit, shower, and shave—and knew he was already out of the house. Her mother was in the kitchen now, producing comforting, familiar sounds that soothed Rosemary like a lullaby. She heard Martina crank open the casement windows and place last night's clean silverware in the drawer with delicate clinks. The water ran, and then a metallic snap told her that Martina had placed the lid on that infernal electric percolator of hers. She made the worst coffee ever—weak and thin, like a picked-clean skeleton.

Dylan lay on his back, his arm across his forehead like an opera singer who had just learned of his lover's betrayal. His hair, streaked blond from the summer sun, fell across his clear round face, his sweet-sour breath moving the hairs slightly with every inhale and exhale. The flowered sheet was wrapped around his waist, revealing dirt-stained knees and feet tanned brown in the pattern of his sandals. She marveled that he was still sleeping, considering he'd napped for most of the drive yesterday. It seemed the events of the past week had exhausted him as well.

The clock reported 7:35. She couldn't stay here all day, staring at the ceiling. Soon she would have to face Martina and tell her why she was here. It would shock her mother deeply, and confirm for her that the world really was as dangerous as "Law and Order" made it appear. At first she had decided never to tell Martina, but she needed to get away. From her street, from her house, and from his ghost. If only for a little while.

❧   ❧   ❧

It had started in mid-May, with a phone call from Colleen's mother.

"Is this Rosemary Ellis?"

"Yes," Rosemary answered warily.

"I hate to bother you, but are you a friend of Colleen and Matthew Wooster?"

"I am."

"Well, thank heaven," the woman said with a sigh. "I am Colleen's mother, Yvonne, calling from Topeka, Kansas. We've never met, but my daughter speaks very highly of you, and I need your help."

"Is something wrong?"

"I hope not, but Colleen's line has been busy for days, and I'm worried that something might be wrong. May I ask you to walk down to Colleen and Matthew's house and see if everything is OK?"

"Of course," Rosemary replied.

"And then ask her to call me?"

"Sure."

"I will be in your debt," Yvonne said.

Rosemary found Colleen at home, covering a tremendous cardboard box with red-checked contact paper. She'd already cut a rectangle for a door.

"Hey," Colleen said when she opened the door. When Rosemary told her of the phone call, Colleen shrugged off her mother's concern. "Yes, I unplugged my phone because I'm sick of hearing her say I told you so." She continued her task, carefully peeling the backing off the sticky paper and smoothing it with her manicured hand. "I told her that Matthew and I were having some problems and she had a field day reminding me that she'd predicted that my marriage would end in disaster. Hold this, will you?"

Rosemary steadied the paper roll as Colleen tugged on it to cover another side of the box.

"But she beat me to it, by calling you. I was going to ask you if I could give your number to my lawyer. I don't want Matthew to know I've contacted a lawyer."

"You already have a lawyer?" Rosemary was stunned.

"Just to learn my options," Colleen said. "I'm taking the kids back to Kansas, and that's it. I'll be staying with my sister."

"But what happened?"

"Oh, what hasn't happened," Colleen said, her casual facade slipping. "Matthew does nothing but work and drink. If he's not at the office, he's home drinking, and doing some unnecessary thing to this stupid house. I've been on him for this for years. I might as well be a single mom. The boys need him. It hurts them every day to be blown off by their dad."

Tears streaked her face as she dropped the paper roll, sank down heavily and covered her face with her hands. "I can't take it anymore. He's an ugly drunk. All he does is criticize me and yell at the boys. We can't do anything right."

Rosemary sat on the floor next to her and rubbed Colleen's back. "I don't understand," she said. "When did all this start?"

"You know it's been building for a while."

"No, I didn't know that."

"Well, it has. It's embarrassing, you know? I don't talk about it much. But at Easter time it really came to a head." Colleen wiped her face with the bottom of her tank top and listened for the boys. "The boys are on my bed watching *Aladdin*," she said. "I think Christopher might actually be asleep.

"Anyway," she turned to face Rosemary, "my parents came to visit for Easter. They got in to the motel late the night before and were coming for brunch on Easter morning. I made this really nice brunch—I even made bunny cupcakes—and I wanted to wait for them to start the Easter egg hunt, but Matthew wanted to do it as soon as the boys woke up. He was furious. I didn't know it, but he'd bought one of those things that you go around the yard making Easter bunny prints with, you know? He hid the eggs early in the morning and then spread sand all over the patio and made these prints. But it got

windy that morning and the wind was ruining the footprints.
I had no idea. He wanted it to be a surprise.

"So it's like 10 a.m. by the time my parents finally get here,
and they have no idea we're even waiting for them, and
Matthew is fuming. We finally go outside, and of course it's
windy and cold like every spring day in this lousy place, and
the prints are all but gone, and the boys don't care about them
anyway. All they want is the chocolate, and Matthew, my God,
the whole time the boys were searching for the eggs he was like
a caged animal. He went around the front and tried to recreate
the prints, but they wouldn't show up anywhere, so he chucks
the thing in the garage and hunkers down in a chair and just
stares at his feet for like an hour, ignoring everybody. The boys
were so confused. Here's all these pretty eggs they colored, and
the plastic eggs with treats, and Grandma and Grandpa, and
here's their dad acting like a total freak. So we go in for brunch
and Matthew can barely sit still, but he does manage to drink
gallons of mimosas. He was such an ass all day. After my parents
left for the motel he switched to scotch, and that night he
busted up an old chaise lounge. Just took a bat to it and wailed
on it. He actually screwed up his shoulder from it. Since then
it's just gotten worse and worse."

"Holy shit," Rosemary said.

"Holy shit is right," Colleen agreed. "I mean, it hasn't been
like that the whole time. He apologized for that, and he bought
a new lounge chair, and he managed to be nice and not drink
for a few weeks. He knows how to behave when he wants to,
but I have had enough."

"I take it counseling is not an option?"

"He will not go. I'm hoping if I leave for a long while it will
scare him into getting himself together. I can't live like this
anymore."

For the next few weeks Rosemary carried messages to
Colleen from her lawyer, all the while keeping Colleen's secret.
But when the Woosters came to a party at Rosemary and Liam's
house, Matthew was a perfect gentleman—he drank only one

beer, made favorable comments about their garden, and took several shifts at the trampoline, keeping the kids from landing in the surrounding cactus. "I read him the riot act last week," Colleen whispered to Rosemary in the kitchen. "He's trying." Colleen knocked on her head with two knuckles. "We'll see."

But everything was different just a week later when Rosemary, Liam, and Dylan marched down the street for Christopher's fourth birthday party. The living room was knee deep in balloons. Matthew forced fresh drinks on guests who had barely finished the one in their hands. He did his Archie Bunker imitation repeatedly, saying to Colleen, "Isn't that right, deah?" with his forehead scrunched up. He insisted that Rosemary try the frozen grapes. "Aren't they refreshing?" he demanded, bearing down on her with his six-foot frame, his balding head like an uncooked sausage. "Aren't they refreshing?"

The next day, late in the afternoon, Colleen stopped by to return a toy that Dylan had left at her house. "I'm taking the boys for ice cream," she said. "Would Dylan like to come?" Dylan was thrilled as Rosemary buckled his car seat into Colleen's mini-van.

"Whoa," she said to Colleen, pointing toward Los Alamos where a plume of smoke showed that the Cerro Grande fire was growing. "That was half that size just a few hours ago. It looks like it's exploded."

"My God, I hope it doesn't get too close to Los Alamos—those poor people."

"And the wind up there is changing," Rosemary added. "They say it's already threatening some structures." The fire, which started as a controlled burn, had been spread by high winds and was now edging closer and closer to the town that had gifted the world with the atomic bomb. For the past several nights, she and Liam could look toward the Jemez Mountains and watch the flames. In the day, though, when the wind was low, the fire was a tidy plume, something that people who lived thirty miles away could somehow disregard. But the wind was picking up now out of the west, which meant that soon the plume would widen, the whole Santa Fe area would smell like a campfire, and a pall of smoke would obscure the mountains in all directions.

"God, I can't wait to get out of this place," Colleen said.

"Do you ever wonder what's actually burning up there? The lab has stuff buried all over those canyons. What the hell are we breathing?"

"I repeat: I can't wait to get out of this place."

Colleen backed down the driveway as Rosemary poured buckets of cooled cooking water on her lavender plants.

She didn't know what the worst part of all these fires was— that after decades of aggressive fire suppression, they burned so hot they exploded trees and filled the streams with ash, or that firefighting efforts required millions of gallons of water people needed to live.

Thinking about how all that water was being used reminded her that she needed to send another email to the homeowners association urging it to support creation of a local water coop. Since its inception two years earlier, her group had successfully urged the ranching family that owned the subdivision's water rights to give it time to find a way to buy those rights rather than sell them quickly. It had been a tremendous undertaking, a grass roots effort in which Rosemary had played a huge role.

When Dylan came home forty-five minutes later, sticky and happy, Rosemary was slicing cucumbers for a noodle salad, sipping a glass of Chardonnay, and listening to NPR. As she washed Dylan's hands and face, he regaled her with a detailed description of his new favorite ice cream flavor and then began jumping on the mini-trampoline in the living room, singing, "Cherry berry bunch! Cherry berry bunch!"

An hour later, he was still singing his ice cream song, with many variations on the theme, when the phone rang.

"Cherry berry bunch!" Dylan sang as he jumped. "Berry ferry chunch! Crunchy bunchy wunch!"

"Rosemary! Rosemary!" Colleen screamed.

"Smunchy lunchy scrunch! Lunchy munchy spunch!"

"He's dead!"

"Dunchy grunchy zunch!"

"He's dead! Matthew's dead!"

At that moment, as Colleen screamed into the phone, Liam walked through the door and Dylan leaped off the trampoline to body check him. "I got ice cream!" he shouted as Liam struggled to steady himself.

"Whoa!" Liam crooned as he set his keys down.

Colleen screamed, "He shot himself! He's dead! He shot himself! Matthew's dead!" Rosemary stared at Liam wordlessly.

"What the hell?" he asked.

Colleen continued to shriek. Rosemary heard a wail go up behind her. One of the boys began screeching and Colleen hung up. It was quiet.

"I have to go down to Colleen's."

"What happened?" Liam asked, shifting Dylan into a potato sack hold over his shoulder. Over Dylan's whooping laughter she whispered into Liam's ear: "Matthew just shot himself. He's dead. That's all I know."

"Holy shit!"

"I need to go down there."

"Holy shit!"

"I know."

"Call me when you know more."

Rosemary ran down the street in shorts and flip flops beneath a smoky haze. How could Matthew be dead? They were there just last night. Dylan, her own son, was in that house just last night, and in Colleen's car an hour earlier. Holy shit. Who knew they had a gun? Should she have known that?

She heard the howling from the street. When she opened the front door, Colleen was sitting on the sofa with both boys leaning on her. Little Matthew was silent, but Christopher was crying loudly.

"Daddy got very sick and died and we couldn't help him," Colleen shouted over his cries. She stared at Rosemary, who stared back, breathless. At the sight of her, Christopher buried his face in his mother's breasts and quieted down.

"Can't we give him medicine?" little Matthew asked.

"No," Colleen replied, still staring at Rosemary's stricken face. "I wish we could, but we can't. Sometimes when people get so sick, medicine can't help them anymore."

Sirens wailed in the distance, a sound that jarred the women into the same thought: Get the kids out of here.

"Can Dylan play right now?" Colleen asked Rosemary.

"Of course, Dylan would love to play with his pals. How about we walk down to my house?" Rosemary asked the boys, reaching out her hand.

"I want Mommy!" Christopher shouted, burying his head deeper.

"I'll be down as soon as I can," Colleen said, prying him away from her. She placed the boys' hands in Rosemary's and stood up. Christopher continued to resist, but as the siren got louder the women shoved him forward and Rosemary headed toward the back door with them.

"Let's go this way," she said. She looked back at Colleen, who stared after them. Rosemary hated to leave her alone. "This is the cool way, behind all the houses," she shouted, as if she could overpower the sound of the sirens. "It's like a secret passage!"

"Why did Daddy get sick?" Matthew asked, struggling to look over his shoulder as Rosemary pulled him forward.

"I don't know," she answered, suddenly aware that everything she did in the next few minutes was going to matter a lot. What would Colleen want her to say? That the Lord worked in mysterious ways? That God needed mortgage brokers in heaven, so Daddy had to leave? Her whole body flushed hot, as if a flame were suddenly ignited at her feet. If this were her own kid, she'd hug him, or look him in the eye and say some perfect, life-affirming thing. But it wasn't her kid, and she had no instructions from Colleen.

"You'll be OK," she said to Matthew.

"I want Mommy," Christopher whimpered.

"You're both going to be OK," Rosemary insisted. "And none of this is your fault."

They walked on in silence. When they got to her backyard, Dylan was swinging and Liam was sitting on the other swing, staring at his feet. Dylan ran toward the boys and Liam rose, clearly uncertain as to what to do.

"The police are just arriving," Rosemary told him. "I still don't know anything." Matthew held her hand for a moment and then broke away to follow the younger boys.

"How old is he—was he?" Liam asked.

"I guess thirty-ish."

"We were there last night."

"Yeah, and how many times has Dylan been there, and I had no idea they had a gun."

"Me either! What are you supposed to do, ask people? Like when you have a cat allergy?"

Liam held Rosemary briefly, but they broke off to watch the boys. All three were in the sandbox, though Matthew was staring at his feet.

"What an asshole," Rosemary said. "How could he do this to his kids?"

"She shouldn't be alone," Liam said.

"What did you tell Dylan?"

"That Colleen was having a problem and she needed you."

"How do we explain this to him?" Rosemary asked.

"We can talk about this later. One of us should go down there."

"I'll stay with the kids."

"OK."

After Liam left, Rosemary stood in the yard in a glassy daze, squinting in the sunlight as the smoke steadily diffused it. She stared at Matthew until he seemed to sense it and looked back at her. She looked at Christopher, sitting listlessly in the sand. Finally she went inside. In the kitchen, all was as she'd left it, just twenty minutes earlier. Twenty minutes. One bullet was fired, and now the world was a different place—yet everything looked the same.

She switched off NPR, poured another glass of wine, and finished making the noodles. Then she baked a bag of French fries and a box of fish sticks, assuming the Wooster boys would prefer that, and cut up peaches and nectarines. Not knowing what else to do, she set the table and called the boys in to eat. She imagined little Matthew saying to his therapist years later: "My dad had just blown his brains out, and here we were eating fish sticks." But what was she supposed to do?

At the table Dylan chattered about Legos, the three boys ate French fries, and she sipped her wine. Nobody touched the noodle salad.

After dinner, she put on a Winnie the Pooh video and watched it with the kids. About an hour later, Liam and Colleen came through the door. The boys ran to greet their mother, and Liam shot Rosemary a wild-eyed look.

"Is Daddy better yet?" Matthew asked as Christopher buried his face in her thigh. "Can he come back now?"

Colleen shook her head as tears streamed down her face. "No, love, he can't."

"Then when can he?"

"He can't," Colleen said through her tears. "He can't."

Colleen pulled away from the boys and said, "I need to call Grandma." Liam hurried to hand her the cordless phone. "Stay here with your friends, son," she said, pulling away from the boys and heading down the hall. The boys wailed and chased her, but she locked the bedroom door and Rosemary led them away.

"Why are they crying so much?" Dylan asked Liam. Before he could answer, Dylan turned to the boys: "Why are you crying?"

"Let's bounce!" Liam shouted. He scooped up Dylan and dropped him on the mini-trampoline. "Who's next? Christopher? Matthew?"

❧   ❧   ❧

Sprays of blood darkened the walls of the master bedroom. Blood, now dried and dull, had flown over the things Colleen had been packing, splattered across open suitcases, coated a grocery bag full of shoes, pooled in an infant car seat. Chunks of flesh dangled from the ceiling, crusted and dull. Stitched sunflowers on the bedspread gleamed yellow here, dirty black there where blood had soaked through twelve hours before. The open closet door, more red than white, dumped an arc of light into the room, exposing the cement slab inside the closet where the carpet had been cut away.

Rosemary stood in the doorway of Colleen and Matthew's bedroom with a kitchen sponge in her hand. The carpet cleaners had already been to the house. There was no saving the carpet, they told Colleen, but as a courtesy they removed the worst of it. They explained the same to Rosemary outside, their faces ashen, their plastic sacks heavy. Gerhard and Bjorn. They were from Germany. But Bjorn was a Swedish name, Rosemary thought dumbly. They tossed the bags over the wire fence into the unused dog run at the side of the house—the bags with the oatmeal-flecked, tan Berber carpet—now stained crimson.

She had come over thinking she would clean up the room for Colleen, bring some order to the place, make it so she could pack for her return to Kansas. Rosemary had expected to wipe down a few surfaces, fold some clothes, box up some books. But this. This!

The night before, when the kids were asleep, Colleen told Rosemary and Liam what had happened.

After she and the boys returned from the ice cream shop, she began to cook dinner. Pork chops with a cajun rub, corn on the cob, coleslaw from the supermarket. She expected Matthew to grill the chops when he came home.

Colleen was mixing up some iced tea when Matthew slammed into the kitchen, an envelope in his hand.

"What's this?" he demanded, waving the envelope in her face. "Griego and Associates Law Firm. What's this?"

There was no way to hide it anymore, so she told him. Told Matthew she was leaving him. Told him it was over, that he had pushed her too far for too long. Told him she was done believing his empty promises.

So he punched a hole in the living room wall and stormed out. She assumed he was going out to get good and drunk, and would probably be gone a few hours. She'd have time to pack, to grab clothes and necessities for herself and the boys. The other stuff she'd worry about later.

Colleen set the boys up with a movie and fell to the task, dragging things out of the walk-in closet and out from under the bed, piling shoes, clothing, and toiletries into bags, suitcases, boxes. She'd drive all night and be in Topeka the next day.

But Matthew came back sooner than expected, not even an hour later. He found her rummaging in the hall closet and pleaded with her to be reasonable, to sit down and talk it out. She could smell the scotch on his breath and refused to talk. He began to weep and beg. When he followed her into the bedroom and saw how much she'd already packed, he pushed into his side of the closet, fumbled with some keys, and came out with a hunting rifle.

"Matthew, no!" she shouted. She hadn't seen that gun for years; he hadn't gone hunting once since they'd moved to New Mexico. But she knew it was loaded. He always kept it loaded.

He leaned against the closet doorway, bent his knees, and slid down, his back to the jamb. Then he slouched down farther, propped the gun to his right, and pointed the barrel at his right temple. The butt of the gun rested on the carpet outside the closet. "Don't leave me," he said calmly. "Colleen, do not break up this family."

Why didn't you run? Just take the kids and run?

Because I was afraid he'd do it. I couldn't let him do it.

But what about you? What about the kids?

You don't understand.

But Colleen!

You don't understand. Matthew is my family.

Yes, but. . . .

No, Matthew is my family.

And then she told them. Told them how Matthew was her foster brother. How he had joined the family when he was sixteen and she fourteen, like so many kids before him. Colleen's parents had fostered eight children in all throughout her childhood. Her parents were Christians who walked their talk. They gave kids a leg up. Matthew was supposed to be just another kid, just another casualty of drugs and poverty, this time from East St. Louis. She was expected to crochet him a Christmas scarf, help him with his homework, introduce him to her friends. And she did all that, but she also fell in love with him.

They hid their relationship for nearly a year, where it ripened in a cocktail of comfort and the forbidden that always confused her but never lost its appeal. But they had to confess when her parents were taking steps to adopt Matthew.

Peter and Yvonne, were horrified, hostile even, at the news. But they eventually accepted it.

They would arrive at the house in a few hours. This house with the horrible bloodied room.

The women had walked down the street about an hour earlier to meet the carpet cleaners.

"I haven't slept at all," Colleen said dully. "Every time I closed my eyes I would see it all again, hear that shot."

Silently they cleaned up the kitchen and the dining area. Threw away the chops that had sat out all night, the corn in its cold, filmy water. Put away the unused silverware, the glasses, the salt and pepper shakers.

When the deputy came by to ask Colleen a few more questions and get the gun, Rosemary slipped away to the bedroom. With the sponge. To stand in the doorway frozen in horrified wonder. How could one body have contained this much blood? How could one head have contained this much—meat?

She inched toward the closet. A clump of hair, attached to a curl of flesh, clung to a lavender blouse. Her eyes slowly clicked from one piece of clothing to the next, seeing the blood and bits of—head—studding the sleeves of nearly all of Colleen's tops and jackets. On Matthew's side of the closet, the blood was mostly on one tweed sport coat near the door. Two hangers down, though, a slice of bone dangled from a navy blue cuff.

Rosemary stared at the bit of bone. It was white—seemingly the only thing in the room not bloody. It seemed ready to fall. All night long that shard had been collecting its potential energy, anticipating a transfer into kinetic energy, so it could fall. It didn't know or care what it was. Its work was to fall. And when it hit the concrete floor, then its job would be to rot. But that could take years in the desert.

On the floor of the bedroom was everything Colleen had begun to sort through the night before. Two open suitcases full of clothes, balled up and shoved into all compartments. Photo albums, zipped duffel bags. The pile between the bed and the closet was clearly what she had planned to leave behind—a port-a-crib, an unopened down comforter, pink ski boots. All splattered with blood and. . .head.

Colleen skied?

Rosemary looked down at the sponge in her hand. She needed a plan, guidance. How the hell was she going to do this?

Rosemary heard the deputy say, "All right then," and heard the front door close. She stepped out of the room in time to see Colleen rush into the bathroom, and, through the door, heard her vomit. Rosemary followed the sheriff out the front door and into the sunshine of the morning.

"Sir!" she called after him.

The deputy turned and squinted at her, peering from under the brim of his hat. "You the neighbor where she's staying?"

"Yes."

"Well, God bless you. That young lady needs a friend right now."

"Yes, I—"

"She's lucky to have you. I tell you she's lucky, period. I'm just glad I'm not here on a murder-suicide. Most guys woulda shot her first."

Lucky. Rosemary could find no response to that.

"Look, when her folks come, have them call me, will ya?" he asked, retrieving a card from his jacket. "I'll need to return the gun at some point, and I don't want to hand it to the young lady."

"Sure," Rosemary replied, taking the card. "But I need some information before you go. We need to clean up that bedroom, and I'm wondering if you could recommend a service that does this sort of thing."

"A service? For cleaning up all that blood?"

"Yes, it's awful in there. I don't even know where to start."

"The families do this," he said matter-of-factly. "No one's gonna touch blood. You think a housecleaning service is gonna touch a mess like that?"

"Well I just assumed that somebody would, some service."

"No, there's no service. The families do this, but here, let me give you some equipment."

Suddenly a creeping headache from last night's wine surged to her forehead, and her stomach churned. The families do this. But there was only one family here, no distant in-laws who might approach it coolly.

She followed the deputy to his car. He popped the trunk, placed Matthew's gun inside, and pulled a bagged kit from a side compartment.

"Here, wear this," he said, thrusting the bag at her. "It'll keep you safe." He closed the trunk, walked to the driver's door and nodded to her. "Like I say, she's lucky to have ya."

Rosemary watched the car back down the driveway, feeling like a little kid who didn't want to be left alone. In the bag were a white paper suit, paper booties, three pairs of latex gloves, and a pair of throwaway goggles.

Suddenly Colleen was at her side, startling her. "Hey," she said, and Rosemary screamed. They both laughed, and Rosemary grabbed her stomach again.

"I know," Colleen said, serious again. "Mine hurts, too."

"I need to know what you want me to do in there," Rosemary said. "Do we want to take all those clothes to the cleaners? Just haul in a giant bag to the dry cleaner? Or do you want to try to launder them yourself?"

"I wish we could burn it all. But we'll just have to throw it all out."

"We could at least donate them."

"Donate them? Would you want to wear something that had some bastard's brains splattered on them? Forget it. Matt doesn't need his suits anymore, does he? And I will never wear a stitch of clothing that has had his blood on it. Anything that has blood on it, I want it gone."

"OK," Rosemary agreed.

"Maybe my dad can help haul all this shit to the dump. I don't ever want to see it again. Can we borrow Liam's truck?" The phone rang. "I gotta get that," Colleen said, turning toward the house. "It's probably my sister."

Rosemary watched her go, hating again to be alone. She glanced toward the dog run, at the bags the carpet cleaners had left. She walked slowly toward it, wending her way through the scratchy native grass that Matthew had insisted on mowing.

The bags were a clear, thick plastic. Through the film she saw blood and the same sort of gore that was in the closet, only larger pieces. But then she saw something else. Something different. Whitish stuff, coils of whitish stuff. Oh God, she thought—brain! That's Matthew's brain. This was where he thought his thoughts. This was where he made his decisions, the tiny ones and the huge ones. Decisions to approve loans, to order a burger or a Caesar salad, to have another drink or to stop for the night. Decisions to punch holes in walls, to press a rifle to his head. We make so much of our decisions, Rosemary thought, so much of our intelligence, our beliefs. Such a big thing of our ideas, our opinions, and there they lay. Coils of putrefying muck stuck to hunks of torn carpet.

She went back into the house and heard Colleen sobbing into the phone: "Holy fucking shit. What am I gonna do? What am I gonna do?"

Colleen would have to face all of this alone, and Rosemary had to help. She was her friend. She could do this.

She rummaged around the garage and found a bucket, a gallon of bleach, a spray bottle of Windex, a box of Hefty bags, and several rolls of paper towels. She put on the paper clothing and strode into the bedroom with a renewed sense of purpose. This was what friends did for each other.

But after a few hours she was getting lightheaded. It was so hot in the suit in the south-facing bedroom. She knew she could drop the temperature by ten degrees if she lowered the shades, but she couldn't bear to darken the room.

Rosemary had three trash bags full of shoes, books, blankets, and clothing and another filled with scary trash, but there was no sense of accomplishment. There was so much left to do. She'd heard Colleen's parents arrive, felt the house fill with both grief and reproach. She didn't know what to do. She probably needed to eat, but the idea was repulsive. She couldn't imagine touching food after handling all this—this.

She felt trapped, utterly trapped by this endless blood, this circumstance and obligation, and she began to worry about Liam and the boys. It was Sunday, after all. She had the makings of a strawberry shortcake in the fridge, organic turkey sausage, pasta, and local salad greens for a nice dinner. It was spring, warm and lovely. She was not supposed to be trapped in a hot, bloody house.

There was a knock at the door.

"Rosemary?" a woman's voice called. Rosemary assumed it was Yvonne. She removed her gloves and dropped her sponge in the bucket. It was strange to open the door as if this were her own room. How in the space of a few hours had this somehow become her realm?

She opened the door slowly, peering out carefully as if the room were under quarantine.

"Yes?" she asked.

Yvonne gasped at the white suit and the goggles, putting a hand to her lips. "Oh, my," she said. Then, looking past Rosemary at the room she exclaimed louder, "Oh, my!"

"It's pretty bad," Rosemary said, closing the door behind her. "You might not want to look in there."

"Well, what matters most is that Colleen and the boys are safe."

Huh. What had been mattering most to Rosemary was that she remove the blood from that room and get out before she either melted from the heat or went insane from the fear of Matthew's ghost.

"You are a trooper," Yvonne said, leading her away from the room by the elbow. "And I think you need a break."

It was a relief to leave the room, but disturbing to be in the grip of Colleen's mother. "My grandsons, how are they?"

"Well, I don't really know. They're with my husband, ma'am."

Ma'am? Where did that come from?

"Well I am thinking that they might need to come back home and see their mama and their grandparents," Yvonne commanded.

"Yes," Rosemary said, sensing an escape from her morbid task. "I think that would be good. I can go bring them down."

"That would be fabulous," Yvonne said with a brief, shiny smile.

Rosemary took off the hot crunchy suit and left it crumpled in the hallway. Colleen ventured toward her with a concerned look. "Are you OK?" she asked.

"I don't know."

"God help me, I don't know what I'm gonna do," Colleen said, choking back tears.

"You'll make it," Rosemary assured her. "You're strong."

"Yeah, I'm strong, but I'm also angry. How am I gonna parent these boys?"

"You'll be OK," Rosemary said, aware that she was talking out her butt. "When God closes a door he opens a window, right?"

"Well, I'd like to think so," she said. "My God, if Matthew weren't dead right now I'd kill him."

The women laughed and instantly hushed themselves.

"I'll go get the boys," Rosemary said. "And the truck. I'll start getting this stuff out of here."

"You are the most amazing person, Rosemary," Colleen said, looking into her face.

"Oh, you'd do it for me, wouldn't you?" Rosemary asked.

Colleen opened her mouth to respond, but closed it again, wordless.

Rosemary walked out the front door. Birds sang, bugs hummed, dirt crunched. It was the most glorious day ever. She began to skip, and soon the skipping turned into a sprint. She reached home breathless, and found Liam exasperated.

"Stop throwing away that fruit!" he was shouting at Matthew. "You can't take one bite and throw the rest away. The second bite is just as good as the first! Oh, thank God you're home," he said to Rosemary as she burst through the door. "You running from a ghost or something?"

"No," she said. "I'm just so happy to get out of there."

"I want Mommy!" Christopher shouted when he saw Rosemary. Matthew just stared at her.

"How about if we walk down to your house to see your mom?" she asked.

"I want Mommy!" Christopher shouted again, pulling his face away as Liam washed him with a cloth.

"I was supposed to do billing today," Liam said to her. "You can take these guys home?" Liam closed his eyes and scratched his head vigorously, a gesture she recognized as his head-clearing mechanism.

"Where's Dylan?" she asked.

"Asleep on our bed. He crashed right after breakfast."

"Weird."

"Yes."

As she rounded up the boys' shoes, Liam whispered to her, "How's Colleen? What's going on down there?"

"It's gross and bad. I'll tell you later. For now I need to do a dump run."

"A dump run?"

"Hello, anybody home?" It was Ed Grisham, their neighbor, calling through the screen door.

"No, Ed!" she called back. "We're all away on a trip!"

"Do you know what happened last night?" he asked as he pushed the screen door open. "I heard a shot and I saw the ambulance, but I don't know what happened." She opened her eyes wide, nodding toward the Wooster boys. "Oh," he said.

"I'll walk the boys home," Liam announced loudly. Rosemary was not surprised. He couldn't stand Ed.

As Rosemary told Ed what had happened, he exhaled loudly, shoving his right foot into and out of his rubber gardening shoe. "My Lord," he said. "That poor woman. No one should have to witness that."

Instantly her mind drifted to the odd fact that the boys had only one set of grandparents. Then she remembered the splatter of blood in the closet and the room.

"Hey, you're a paramedic," she began.

"Used to be."

"OK, and you know about bodies and things like that."

"Of course," Ed said, looking to the porch to make sure his ugly shar-pei was still there.

"Well, I've been at the scene of this suicide all morning, and I can't figure out what exactly happened when Matt pulled that trigger."

She explained what she knew, and Ed filled in the rest: There would have been a small hole, charred around the edges, in Matthew's right temple, where the bullet entered. From that hole, the blood, under great pressure, would have sprayed out, hence the splattering across the room. The left side of his head would have been gone.

"How gone?" she demanded.

"Gone. Not a hole, just gone."

"Would his face have been recognizable?"

"Maybe."

"Would his eyes have stayed in their sockets?"

"Certainly not the left one."

"Would there have been coils of brain streaming from the hole, or would they have been blown clear away from his skull?"

"Oh, for Christ's sake, Rosemary! I don't know."

"I wonder where the bullet is now," Rosemary went on. "I wonder if it lodged in a roof beam or passed through."

"Was Colleen in the room?" he asked.

"No." Christopher was calling for her and began pushing

the bedroom door open, so Colleen rushed to the door and got him into the hallway. She'd just gotten him to the living room when she heard the shot."

"Good God, the kids were in the house?"

"Yeah."

"For Christ's sake."

"I guess one thing just led to another."

"Well she's lucky she wasn't in the room," Ed said, again shoving his right foot in and out of his clog. "At least she didn't get sprayed with blood."

Or gore, Rosemary thought. No chunks of flesh to wash off and get clogged in the shower drain. All morning long, every time she'd dumped a bucket of bloody water down the sink, bits of flesh had clogged the shower drain. She'd repeatedly had to lift out the stopper, pick off the pieces, and then wipe her gloves on a damp paper towel. She had a system.

"Yeah," Rosemary agreed. She imagined what might have happened in that moment had Colleen been in the room. The shocking sound of the shot, the spraying of the blood— still warm from Matthew's arteries—splattering onto Colleen's arms and legs. On her face. Blood under pressure, as if from a hose. "Yeah," she said again, as if in a daze. "At least Colleen didn't have the taste of Matthew's blood in her mouth, since it would have been open, since she would have been screaming."

"Jesus Christ, Rosemary!" Ed interjected. "Can you get any more graphic?"

"Huh?"

"This is a little more than I can take on a Sunday morning."

"Sorry, but it's what I've been doing all day."

"Well, I should shove off."

"Wait, I have to go to the dump," Rosemary said, feeling the same panic at being left alone. "Colleen wants me to throw away anything that has blood on it."

"You know that's illegal, don't you?"

"No, tell me."

"Blood-soaked materials are hazardous waste."

"For real?"

"You're supposed to call the county and arrange for a special pick-up."

"Oh, come on."

"I'm just telling you. But really, this being Sunday, it would be days before you got that pickup, or the permission, or whatever, and I have no idea what it would cost."

"Well that's not happening," Rosemary said resolutely. "Colleen has got to get this stuff gone. It can't sit around for days or whatever. And where would she keep it? Outside for the coyotes to tear into? Or wait for the maggots to infest it?"

"OK, take it easy," Ed said, thrusting his open palms toward her. "Don't worry, I'm not telling on you or anything. Just don't get caught. Let's just say it wouldn't play well in the papers." The shar-pei barked. "I sure don't envy you," he added.

"Yeah, I'm not looking forward to it."

"Call me if you need anything."

She suddenly wanted him to leave. She was getting light-headed again and her stomach hurt. She heard the bedroom door open and was thrilled at the thought of seeing Dylan.

"OK, you take care," Ed said, turning to let himself out.

"Thanks."

"Mama!" Dylan shouted, running toward her. She crouched down to bury her head in his hair.

"Hey, buddy!" she exclaimed. "I missed you." She hugged him tight, drinking in his wonderful aliveness.

"I'm hungry," Dylan said.

"Me too. Let's make some lunch."

She washed her hands for five minutes straight, scrubbing with a nailbrush, feeling like something between a surgeon and Lady Macbeth. She fixed a sandwich for Dylan as he chattered and sang, and managed to eat something herself. By noon— noon! was that all?—when Liam returned, she was feeling a little better. But Liam was shaken.

"This is horrific," he said. "Criminal. Look, I think she needs you back again, and she asked about the truck. Can you do this? 'Cause I'm telling you, I cannot."

"Yeah, I can do it," Rosemary answered, marveling to herself that it was true, she could.

"I'm telling you, I glanced into that room and nearly puked. I'm still nauseous. I can't believe you were in there all morning. Can you find someone else to help you? Someone with a strong stomach? Doesn't she have any other friends?"

Rosemary thought of the park posse, ran through the list of women in her mind, and knocked out all of them. Then she thought of Martha, one of Liam's part-time workers. Martha was pretty down to earth, and Rosemary had really grown to like her. She was actually a forest ranger and picked up a few hours with Liam when her parents could take her daughter, Maya.

"I have an idea," she told Liam.

❦   ❦   ❦

Later that afternoon, Rosemary and Martha were bouncing toward the county dump in Liam's truck, with the shock absorbers shot and the radio blaring.

"Yo, Ro, you plan on shifting any time soon?" Martha shouted above the whine of the truck engine.

Rosemary turned to Martha, confused.

"Shift!" she yelled.

Rosemary shifted up to fourth and lowered the radio. "Sorry."

They drove in silence, with heaps of bags, baby equipment, and a roll of bloodied carpet in the back.

"You have a dump pass, right?" Martha asked.

Rosemary nodded.

"What the hell is your friend gonna do now?"

"Move to Kansas."

"And be a single mom? It's harder than you think." Martha had been raising Maya alone since her husband was sent to prison two years earlier. He'd lent his car to a friend who'd used it for a drug deal and got caught. Her husband, who said he'd known nothing of the deal, was convicted as an accessory.

"What a selfish fuck this guy must have been," Martha said. Rosemary nodded.

They pulled into the dump and queued up behind a line of pickup trucks hauling yard waste, trash, and recycling.

"I wish I was hauling weeds right now," Martha said.

"Thank you so much for coming with me," Rosemary said, her eyes welling up. "I really needed someone."

"It's just lucky my parents could take Maya. And I gotta say, you were pretty hard to turn down." She raised her voice to imitate Rosemary: "Hey, Martha, can you help me out? My friend's no-account husband blew his brains out last night and I need to dump his body."

"I did not say that!" Rosemary laughed.

"Close enough," Martha said, rolling down the window. "Turn off the A/C."

They opened the windows, letting the heat of the day rush in as they crept toward the booth. Finally it was their turn. Rosemary handed the dump pass to the attendant. The man, the same old, sunburned guy who had been there forever, with his shirt buttons open well below his nipples, handed her a clipboard. Wordlessly Rosemary showed Martha the categories. Martha grabbed the pen and checked "Household Trash." The women cackled in sardonic glee.

They followed the line of vehicles to a tremendous open pit and slowly backed up close to the edge. Below, a Dumpster the size of a train car nestled in a pit ringed with parking slots. People to the left and right were throwing green trash bags and tall white kitchen bags into the Dumpster. Rosemary unhitched the tailgate and looked up to see Martha staring into the truck bed, transfixed.

"Holy shit," she said.

Rosemary realized then that she had loaded the truck before picking up Martha, and that Martha had not yet been acquainted with Matthew's head.

"Are you kidding me?" Martha said to Rosemary, the clear bag from the carpet cleaners not twelve inches from her face. "What the fuck?"

"Yeah," Rosemary confirmed. "That's the guy's brains."

"Holy shit!"

"Yeah."

"Is it legal to dump this here?"

"No."

Another truck backed in next to them.

"Sshh!" Rosemary hissed, grabbing the bags. "Hurry!" Together they began hurling the bags over the edge, and Martha got into the truck bed to shove the carpet to the edge of the tailgate.

"Ladies!"

The women stopped their work, staring wildly at each other.

"Ladies, let me help you!" boomed a bearded, barrel-chested man approaching the truck. He took off his baseball cap and wiped his brow with it. He smiled, revealing yellow teeth. Martha shoved the rug harder and Rosemary hoisted it onto her shoulder.

"We got it!" Rosemary said with a grunt.

"Yeah, we're good," Martha declared with a broad smile. She scooted out of the truck bed and helped Rosemary hurl the carpet to the Dumpster. They watched it drop and exhaled together as it landed in a way that hid the blood.

They looked back to see the man peering at the port-a-crib, the baby swing, the laundry basket full of suit coats.

"Can't I help you with this?" he asked again.

"No, no," they said, clamoring into the truck bed.

"A lot of people could use these things," he said. "You know, you can put it over by the guard shack—that's the unofficial scavenging place."

Over the years Rosemary had found plenty of goodies by the shack, and it was killing her to throw all this stuff away, but Colleen wanted it gone.

"OK, thanks," Rosemary said. "We'll consider it, but. . . we're moving, and we don't have a lot of time."

Martha glanced at Rosemary and then back to the man. "Yeah, we need to just get it done," she said, hurling a sun-yellow snowsuit into the pit.

"All right then," the man said, walking away.

"Jeez, I feel like a criminal," Martha said. "But he's right. Look at this crib. There's nothing wrong with it."

Rosemary looked at a hunk of gore clinging to the blue nylon frame.

"Would you want your kid putting her mouth on that?"

"No, but what would it take to clean that off?"

"It could be sanitized."

"Here," Martha said, flicking the piece of mystery flesh from the crib with a stick. "Now it just looks like a lugie."

"A lugie."

"Yes, a lugie!" Martha laughed. "Your garden variety phlegm wad."

"Oh, whatever," Rosemary said with a sigh. "Save the crib." A woman pulled up next to them in a Subaru Forester as Rosemary threw a baby swing over the edge.

"Hi," she said to the woman, wearing a floral dress and sneakers. The woman smiled as she looked at the two of them. Wow, Rosemary realized, she thinks we're gay.

"Okay, that's it!" Martha shouted as she hurled the suit coats into the pit. Rosemary loaded the crib back into the truck bed and they drove off, leaving the damned thing at the guard shack.

"We need gas," Rosemary said.

"I would really like a beer," Martha added.

"I would really like ten beers," Rosemary said as she pulled up to a fueling island at the Conoco. She slid her Visa card into the slot as Martha headed toward the store. A truck pulled in on the other side of the tiny island.

"Well, hello again!" shouted the man with the yellow teeth. Unbelievable.

"So, where are you two ladies moving to, anyway?" he asked pleasantly as he inserted his card.

"Tucson!" Rosemary replied with a sunny smile.

"Arizona, huh? Not hot enough for you here?"

"Well, I've got a good job offer," she said, pausing for just a moment. "I'm going to be running a café, a start-up downtown. I'm looking forward to the change." How easy it was to say this. Why?

"Sounds great," the man replied, "if you can stand to leave a great place like this. My wife and I retired here last year, from Texas, and I hope to never leave it."

Rosemary was aware of Martha approaching the truck, a paper bag crunching under her arm. "Santa Fe is lovely," Rosemary agreed, "but I can't pass up this opportunity."

"And you?" he asked Martha. "Do you have a job waiting for you in Tucson, too?"

Martha looked at Rosemary quizzically.

"Well, she's a publishing agent, so she can work anywhere," Rosemary replied loudly. "She'll be taking all her clients with her, working online and all."

"Well, God bless you," the man said, turning back to his vehicle. Lesbians, a publishing agent, the internet. He'd had enough.

"Hello?" Martha said as she climbed into the truck.

"He wanted to know where we were moving to and all."

"Oh, good grief."

❧   ❧   ❧

That night, after she and Martha laughed at the thought of eating the turkey sausage that Liam had grilled—sausage, of all things, after the day's gore fest—after lying in the hammock with Dylan and looking up at the stars, and after drinking nearly a six-pack, Rosemary sat on the couch, staring into a candle. She had not spoken to Colleen again and was glad to be away from that scene there, but she was spooked. She and Martha had trashed Matthew mercilessly as they downed beers on the porch, and now that it was quiet and she was alone, she expected to be punished for it, fearing she'd find

Matthew's menacing spirit around every corner, behind every closed door.

Some time around midnight, she opened the bedroom door to watch Liam and Dylan sleep, to listen to them breathe. Such an ordinary act, sleeping, but so much was still going on. Their cells were regenerating, their intestines were breaking down food, their blood was delivering nutrients, and Dylan was undoubtedly growing. Were they dreaming?

She looked closer at Dylan and suddenly imagined Colleen's husband as a four-year-old. If Matthew had been eligible for adoption as a teenager, there was no telling what his life was like as a toddler. Were his parents abusive? Neglectful? Well-meaning but unfit—drug addicts, perhaps—or were they depraved criminals who had lost their humanity? And if they'd lost their humanity, then why? How did their own parents fail them? She shuddered at that thought, at the responsibility of parenting and how its effects, good or bad, reverberated for years, decades, maybe even centuries.

Or maybe Matthew's biological parents were simply dead. But if they were dead, then where was the extended family? Were they estranged? Were they mentally ill? Were they illegal immigrants who couldn't come forward to claim the child? Children were so vulnerable; it was almost more than she could stand to realize how vulnerable every child was. Every teen-ager, even.

Rosemary imagined again the moments before Matthew pulled the trigger, just thirty hours or so earlier. She realized suddenly that for him, losing Colleen and his sons meant losing the only people he could call his family. The specter of his wife packing held a horror that only he could fathom. He had done his best; he had been a good provider. Yes, he had his demons, but he had tried to build a family the only way he knew. And there was Colleen, taking away more than he could bear to lose. Only a bullet stood between him and that pain.

Rosemary was overcome with choking sobs as she left the room. All day she'd thought only of Colleen and the boys, but now she wept for Matthew. It was 3 a.m. before she fell asleep.

The next day, hungover and disoriented, she walked down to Colleen's house to find a huge truck in the driveway, throbbing with a deafening roar.

"They're sandblasting the bedroom!" Colleen shouted over the noise. "My dad found these guys in the Albuquerque phone book. Can you take the boys tonight?"

"But the sheriff said no one would touch all that blood," Rosemary protested pointlessly.

"Well, he was wrong."

Rosemary was speechless.

Her headache started to lift at around 4 p.m. when Colleen dropped the boys off, and by 5 she'd opened another beer. So cold, so fizzy, so promising. Colleen returned to pick up the boys at about eight. Colleen and her relatives had all gone to dinner at Geronimo, a $50-a-plate restaurant on Canyon Road. The next day would be the memorial service, with lunch afterward at the rooftop cantina of the Coyote Cafe.

"What is this, a vacation for these people or something?" Liam asked.

"Seems like it," Rosemary replied.

"I mean the guy is what, thirty? He kills himself and there's blood and brains everywhere and the kids are fatherless and all they can think about is fine dining?"

"They'll be gone soon, and at least we get to eat at the Coyote Cafe."

The memorial, a bland, generic service at a dark, velvet-draped funeral home, went quickly, with the family gathering around the coffin for a few group photos. Rosemary was asked to take the pictures, and everybody smiled. She noted that some managed a not-too-happy smile, sort of a dignified smile-ette, but others, especially Yvonne and Colleen's strangely hairy brother-in-law, smiled broadly.

Afterward, Rosemary picked up Liam and Dylan downtown, and they made their way toward the restaurant amid the tourists.

"These people are so strange," Rosemary said, telling Liam about the service. "Who stands around a coffin for a group shot?"

"And a closed coffin at that."

Just then the Grateful Dead song "He's Gone" came on the radio and Liam threw up his hands. "Honestly, what is going on?"

"I think Matthew is playing head games with us."

"Tell you what, how about I take Dylan to a park and you go to this lunch thing without me?"

"Park!" Dylan shouted.

❧   ❧   ❧

At the restaurant, Rosemary ordered a margarita and duck tacos and tried to make conversation with one of Colleen's cousins, Peg, who worked as a chemist in a Purina factory.

"What does it smell like?" Rosemary asked, but before Peg could respond, Yvonne descended upon them with her arms outstretched.

"There she is!" Yvonne crooned. "It's Rosemary! Colleen's friend extraordinaire!" Yvonne was dressed like a cruise director in a shiny blue dress with oversized pearls. "Can you believe this? I was just talking to a colleague of Matthew's, and she had the same situation!"

"What?" Rosemary blurted. "Suicide by hunting rifle?"

"Oh, no!" Yvonne said waving away Rosemary's response. "I mean adopted siblings marrying each other! That woman over there, the one with the spiky hair, she worked with Matthew, and she said a friend of hers married a boy who was about to become her brother, just like Colleen did!"

Peg looked blank-faced at her aunt, and Rosemary took a long pull from her margarita.

"It's always like that, isn't it?" Yvonne continued. "I remember when I first learned I had diverticulosis. I had never even heard of it before, but suddenly it seemed everyone I met had it. Well, ladies, enjoy your lunch."

The women watched wordlessly as Yvonne sashayed to the next table. Peg looked back to Rosemary, raised her glass with a wry grin and exclaimed, "To family!"

๖ะ   ๖ะ   ๖ะ

Now, in her old bedroom, watching Dylan sleep and listening to Martina in the kitchen, it seemed even more surreal, like a Halloween tale. Colleen and the boys were gone, and she'd probably never see them again. Before they left town, Colleen had stopped by to give her a set of crystal candlesticks.

"May these bring light to your home," she said, "and may you never forget me."

Oh yeah, she'd forget all about this real soon. It happened all the time that a person who once viewed humans as sacred beings now thought of them in terms of their blood and guts. And it was every day that a mom watched toddlers sing songs that went, "Clean the walls, clean the ceiling. . . ."

The last day the boys had played together, Christopher sang that song and then looked Dylan squarely in the eye. "Daddy got very sick and died," he said.

"Can't you give him some medicine?" Dylan asked.

"We did but he still died."

"But you can buy a new daddy."

"No, Dylan," Liam said. "People only get one daddy. You can't buy daddies."

"But they *can* buy one!"

"OK, buddy," Liam said, roughing up his hair like Andy Griffith. "You can wish it if you want to."

A medical investigator informed Colleen that sorry, the incident would not be recorded as accidental. The gun pressed up against the victim's temple was conclusive evidence of suicide. The life insurance company, citing the investigator's report, denied Colleen death benefits.

The deputy came by the house also, to return the gun.

Who would want that gun back?

"Matthew was proud of that gun," Colleen's dad told her. "I gave it to him as a wedding gift."

"Maybe the boys will want to hunt someday," said Colleen,

agreeing with her dad that the gun should return to Kansas with them.

It was clear that for Colleen, who had no job, no child support, and no life insurance payout, rebellion was a luxury she could no longer afford.

≼ ≼ ≼

OK, Rosemary resolved, time to face the music. She extracted herself from the bed, slipped on last night's shorts and T-shirt, and made her way to the bathroom. There she looked with distaste at her bloated face, her eyes ringed in puffy gray. "Liver stagnation!" the vitamin guy at the co-op had proclaimed when she was shopping for B-12. "You don't need vitamins, you need a cleanse," he said, his arrogant eyes gleaming.

"Rosemary!" Martina exclaimed as she entered the kitchen. Martina gave her daughter the Concerned Hug, which came with a pat on the back at no extra charge. "Are you OK, honey?"

"Yes, Mom, I'm fine."

"Well, what is going on?"

So she told her, told her everything, from the secret lawyer communications to the birthday party to the ice cream to the hidden rifle to the bloodied room to the gruesome cargo and onward through the fine dining and keepsake photographs.

"But why did you do all that? Why was it all up to you?" Martina asked.

"I didn't *have* to," Rosemary answered in the patronizing tone she reserved for her mother. "I *chose* to. It's what friends do for each other." But as she said those words, she wondered if they were true.

And while her mother cooked the blandest breakfast in history (only Martina could suck the fire out of an onion), and as they tut-tutted together about Colleen's lousy luck and daunting fate, Rosemary did not tell Martina how the night after the funeral service, she had scared Dylan with her stony aloofness. "Mama!" he'd shouted into her flat, impassive face, but she would not respond beyond a mechanical word or two. She simply had no interest in him. She wanted to be left alone, but he would not comply, would not amuse himself, so the stone face gradually changed to a quiet seething. He cried to Liam that Mommy was mean and Liam finally became disgusted with her.

"Where are your priorities?" he'd demanded. "Look at your son. He's distraught, and you're totally drained. And for what? If you hadn't been Colleen's humble servant, she would have managed some other way."

෯   ෯   ෯

Just then Dylan entered the kitchen and he and Martina shared a warm, gushing hello. Rosemary was ashamed to see how much he needed his grandma right now. But why shouldn't he? Why was she such a jerk?

Although Dylan disappointed Martina by picking at his pallid omelet (Rosemary had at least feigned a lusty appreciation), the two kept up a cheerful prattle that allowed Rosemary to practice her old skill of carrying on a conversation with her mother while thinking of other things.

A week or so earlier, shortly after Matthew had pulled the trigger, she'd been in the grocery with Dylan, Christopher, and Little Matthew, and had run into Lara, the ex-friend who never did get back in touch after her first round of chemo. She was bald and down to about ninety pounds, and was living in a small apartment. But she still had her story: "These challenges are a gift," she said with a weak smile. Rosemary was aghast. There was nothing she could say—to express compassion would be perceived as negative, and to confirm Lara's story was patently ridiculous. She managed to utter, "I wish you well," and got away fast. Clearly, both Lara and Colleen had nuclear-bomb-sized holes in their lives, no matter what stories they did or did not conjure up. Watching Colleen's boys poke at the cantaloupe display, Rosemary said aloud, "What a load of bullshit this all is."

"Have some fruit," Martina offered, placing a bowl of sliced peaches on the table. Peaches were her dad's favorite, she recalled, which unleashed a pang in her gut. Rosemary had spent much of yesterday's drive anticipating her father's reaction to the tale of Matthew and his bullet.

"You should have called me," he would say.

And she should have. She could see that now. And she could also see another unwelcome truth: Her mother and Liam were right—she'd given too much. Again. She'd depleted herself because she had wanted to save Colleen. She thought she was just helping a friend through a tough time, but she saw now that she was trying to restore Colleen's faith in life, to swoop her up and protect her from becoming bitter. It had suddenly seemed her responsibility to do this. "Come on," Rosemary had silently exhorted. "Life is good—come with me and you'll see." Falling into despair had seemed like a danger she should prevent Colleen from facing. Because if Colleen, her everyday friend from down the street, could fall into despair, then it was possible Rosemary could end up there too one day. Had she truly saved Colleen? Or had she simply cleaned up a bloody room and done some baby sitting?

Are do-gooders good, or are they absurd?

As she wiped down the table, she wondered, What was Matthew doing right now? Had he gotten a good look at that horrible room? Had he been present at his wretched memorial service? Had he watched his boys try to make sense of how there was a loud bang and then Mommy screamed and the police came and they slept at Dylan's house and now they moved to Kansas and this was all because Daddy got very sick and died? Had he discovered yet that you can't drink when you don't have a body? Was he being reincarnated? Was he being punished? Or was he simply gone?

CHAPTER 11 | APRIL, 2003

Interstate 10, Blythe, California

"I'M SMACK DAB IN THE MIDDLE OF HUNGRYVILLE," DYLAN announced, thrusting his head into the front seat between his parents.

"What are you doing out of your seatbelt?" Rosemary demanded, turning toward him.

"Mom, the car's going like two miles an hour."

Liam pulled the Jeep Wagoneer into a parking space in front of Blythe Ranch Market.

"Can we get soda?" Dylan asked as they got out of the car.

"No, you already had a sweet today," Liam answered.

"But we're on vacation!" Dylan countered.

"Yeah, and?" Liam shot back.

As they browsed the grocery, a strange affair with lots of beef jerky and refrigerators stuffed with homemade tamales, Rosemary tried to pre-think what they would need while camping at Joshua Tree, as she had already done over and over at home.

"Do we have matches?" she asked Liam.

"Yes."

"A ground tarp?"

"You packed it yourself."

"Lantern mantles?"

"Yes. Relax, Ro. We're not going to the wilderness. We'll be a half hour from town."

"Marshmallows?" Dylan asked with a grin.

"Harshfellows?" Liam asked. "OK. Now c'mon, let's go."

Rosemary threw in an extra tube of sunscreen as they waited to pay for their cold drinks and chips.

"Why don't they call your big toe your thumb toe?" Dylan asked as Liam dug for cash at the register. The cashier laughed, and Liam and Rosemary joined in.

"A thumb toe. That's not a bad idea, buddy," Liam replied.

"But it wouldn't be the only thing that needs a new name. What about the Islets of Langerhans? Isn't that weird?" Dylan said.

"They were probably named after the person who discovered them," Rosemary offered.

"But that's not fair. It doesn't make sense to people. Cells in the pancreas should be called something that sounds like that. But skin, now skin is the right word. It sounds like what it is, doesn't it? Ssskiiiinnn. . .it sounds thin and smooth, like skin is, doesn't it? What if everything sounded like what it was?"

The cashier said, "I've never even heard of the islets of whatever he said."

"Welcome to my world," Liam said.

"We don't need a bag," Rosemary said, smiling as she scooped the items into her arms.

They crossed a side street to a gas station. Rosemary cleared the old wrappers and trash out of the car while Liam started gassing up.

"Can I clean the windows?" Dylan asked, a filthy squeegie in his hand.

"No!" Rosemary shouted. "Look at that thing!" The squeegie dripped a blackened stream of foamy fluid.

"You shouldn't even be out here anyway," Liam added. "Get back in the car."

"OK, OK," Dylan relented, placing the squeegie back in its grimy receptacle. He got into the car but began pointing and shouting, "Look, a stick bug!" He flung the door open, scooped the bug up from the pump island, and scrambled toward Liam with his hand outstretched.

"Dylan, wait!" Liam shouted.

"A stick bug!" Dylan yelled again, hooking the hose with his foot.

"Dylan!" Rosemary shouted as Liam tried to grab hold of the nozzle.

But before he could, it pulled out of the tank, spewing gasoline on the three of them like a furious snake. Dylan screamed as Liam grabbed the handle, still shooting gasoline out at their feet and legs.

"Goddamn it, Dylan!" Liam shouted.

"Is there any on your face or in your eyes?" Rosemary shouted, searching Dylan's face.

"No," he answered, starting to cry.

"Are you OK?" she asked Liam.

"Oh, yeah, I'm great," Liam said, shoving the nozzle back into the pump. "Just fucking great."

"Liam!"

"Oh, gimme a break, Rosemary. Look at us! Take a whiff!"

Dylan buried his head in Rosemary's waist and wailed.

"Great, now we can smell like shit and listen to him cry, too. A bonus."

"Oh come on, Liam, he made a mistake."

"And as usual, if he listened to me, this wouldn't have happened."

"He's only six and a half! He's a little kid!"

"Yeah, a kid who doesn't listen! I told him to stay in the car! We're going to smell like this for the whole trip."

"No, we won't. Come on, Dylan, settle down. We need to find some clean clothes." She tried to pry him away from her, pushing him away by the shoulders, but he wouldn't budge. Still wailing, he clung harder. "Dylan!" she shouted, reaching behind herself to separate his hands, which were clenched at the small of her back. "Dylan, let go of me!" she shouted.

Liam, wiping his hands on a paper towel, stepped behind her, grabbed Dylan's hands, and pulled them apart. Dylan wailed louder, but Liam stepped between the boy and his mother, held his face in his hands, and said in a commanding voice, "Enough." He wiped Dylan's face with a fresh paper towel as his cries began to subside. "We need to do certain things now to take care of ourselves, and if we're careful, we can make it so everything is OK."

Dylan looked into his father's face and said, "I'm sorry."

"I know you are. Now please do as I say. Do not touch your eyes or mouth."

A Food Mart worker passing by with a bag of trash. "Your best bet is the truck stop at the next exit," she said. "They've got showers and everything there."

"Oh yeah? Thanks," Rosemary answered.

They lowered the car windows, laid out paper towels for their feet, and drove out to clean up at the truck stop. After they'd all taken long showers and changed, Buck, a cashier who used to drive "all forty-eight states" until his back gave out, told Rosemary how to wash gasoline-splattered clothes.

"It happens," he said, drinking from a half-gallon tankard of coffee. "It's no big deal."

Following his advice, she created a concoction of dish soap, hydrogen peroxide, and baking soda, and ran the clothes through a washing machine twice. She also bought a spray designed to neutralize tough odors which they sprayed all over their shoes and around the car, and it mostly worked. Four hours later, they were back on the road, with the thunderous noise of driving seventy-five miles an hour with the windows wide open.

"Do you think we'll laugh about this someday?" she shouted to Liam, who was reclined in the passenger seat with his arms crossed over his chest.

"Please!" he shouted back. "Just drive!"

◈   ◈   ◈

Liam woke to the sound of female voices, Rosemary and Martina in the kitchen with Dylan's high-pitched lilt added to the mix. It was just 6:45, but they were already so damned active. He and Rosemary hadn't planned on staying at her parents' house, but they'd gotten into town so late after the gasoline fiasco, and setting up camp in the dark would have been too big a pain in the ass. Now the trick would be getting out of here at a reasonable hour. He knew Martina would find many reasons to detain them.

It was already warm, like a summer morning, which he welcomed after the spring snow they'd left behind in Santa Fe. It was their first spring-break vacation ever. Though it was a busy season for Ellis Landscaping, Liam's job foreman had proven he could manage important work, even installations, on his own. Liam was pulling back more and more these days, and he had to admit it was getting easier. Rosemary was a big help to the business now that Dylan was in school all day, and Liam even had time to coach Dylan's soccer team—plus enough flexibility to donate time and materials to the elementary school. Last year Ellis Landscaping planted shade trees at the playground and installed a drip irrigation system in the courtyard, which a group of second-grade teachers had transformed into a bird and butterfly garden.

He wondered if his father-in-law were home. It was Sunday morning and he didn't hear his voice, which probably meant he was out getting fresh bagels, or whatever passed for bagels around here. He'd wait to join the others in the kitchen until Mark came home. He needed Mark as a counterweight to Martina, with her tedious conversations and worn-out observations about "this thing called life."

In fact, he needed Mark, period. Liam regarded his father-in-law as a windfall in his life. The guy was so damned—what, sensible? reasonable? responsible? He just did the right things. Rosemary liked to say her dad had "a steady wisdom." That was fine, but for Liam, it was his basic integrity that he appreciated—so different from his own dad, who had been such a fuckup. Well, a fuckup to him, his sister, and their mom, at least. His dad, Nate, was twenty years older that Liam's mom, and had three families, one before Liam's and one after. Nate had died the previous August, which led Liam to understand two big truths: Divorce was weird forever, and people really could change.

Nate had left his first wife for Liam's mom, Jean, who was ashamed to this day to have been "the other woman," especially when it netted her a failed marriage. Her only defense was the enigmatic, "Your father was very persuasive." When they met, Nate already had two kids, who were twelve and fourteen when he walked out. The scuttlebutt was that the girl, the older one, swore the day he left never to talk to him again. But the boy hung on until Nate refused to pay for him to attend an expensive private college; they hadn't spoken since. Nate had never met his half-siblings, though their absence at Nate's memorial service was well noted.

But Liam and his younger sister, Gwen, were there, and Gwen even stood up and spoke. "Dad didn't believe in an afterlife, but I like to think he was wrong," she said, connecting the sentiment with some anecdote or other that made his life seem all wrapped-up and thematically tidy. Liam had to hand it to her—it took guts to speak in front of all those people—but the cozy witticisms were patently ridiculous.

After the service, they all gathered at Nate's house, where Liam had only been once or twice before. After Nate and Jean were divorced, when Liam was eight and Gwen five, his dad was single for about a year before meeting his third wife, Renee, who had three kids of her own. But they were never included in his new family; there were no attempts at a blended one-big-happy thing, and Liam realized now that he'd never even wondered why.

When he and his sister were in their twenties, Gwen managed to pull all the stepsiblings together for some meet-and-greet thing at a local restaurant, and he managed to get through it, but really, who cared? He didn't need these strangers in his life. But Gwen kept in touch with them, and would update Liam on their lives.

"Candace is expecting her second boy this summer," she'd tell him.

"Who the hell is Candace?"

"Your *sis*ter."

"You're my sister."

"Your *step*sister," she'd scold.

"Oh, boy!" he'd snap back, aware that he was behaving badly. "Shall I knit her a blanket?"

In what had been Nate's living room was a wall of framed photographs of him and this third family. They lounged in chaises on tropical beaches, stood in size order at weddings, crouched behind cakes at birthday parties, smiling, smiling, smiling. There was even a team picture from Nate's high school baseball team: 1945, Peekskill, New York. It was too much trouble to figure out which one was his dad.

For weekly visits, back in those confusing post-divorce days, Nate usually took Liam and Gwen out to a burger joint and then to some amateur sporting event. Nate was nuts about sports, any sports. They'd go to high school baseball games, city basketball games, co-ed softball games, racquetball tournaments, or sometimes drive for hours to Amherst to watch the UMass ice hockey team play. Nate didn't like professional sporting events as much. "This is where the passion is," he'd say, cheering on the thirty-somethings as they slid into home and stood up dazed and teetering. "These people are playing for free. That's how you know they're doing it for the pure love of the game."

Pure love. Yeah, he was a regular expert at that. Liam looked over at Renee, the last wife, with her shiny black hair pulled back in a severe ponytail, her mascara blotchy. She sat in an armchair, surrounded by people he didn't know, one minute extolling the virtues of vodka as a balm for grief, the next minute dabbing her eyes when talking about Nate. The circle of sycophants all took their cues from her, laughing or tearing up like an audience of shills. Some of those people were probably his stepsiblings, but Liam couldn't be sure.

Renee had found Nate dead just six days earlier, floating in their backyard pool. The coroner said he'd had a stroke and drowned.

"I have such anger," she said, forming an impotent fist. "Why should he go that way? He was a great man."

A great man. Oh yeah, Liam thought. Let's have some of that magic vodka and think about that.

At the bar—yes, a wet bar, in the corner of the den—he mixed himself a vodka and tonic and studied the icemaker. "Always Fresh"it said on the front. Liam read the print on the side of the machine and realized the thing didn't just make ice; it also steadily melted the old ice so that the ice was always fresh. For Christ's sake, was there anything more decadent than an icemaker that could also apply heat and melt its own ice? We wouldn't want the lord and lady to suffer the hardship of stale ice, now would we? That would be unthinkable. Holy fuck, whoever even heard of stale ice? Nate was such a dick.

A tall dude in a suit appeared, thrusting his hand toward Liam. "Liam, right?"

Who the fuck was this?

"Yes," Liam replied, mechanically shaking the smooth, slender hand.

"Holden."

Right. So who the fuck was this?

"I'm Renee's son, her oldest."

Oh, one of the steps. "Of course," Liam said. "How are you?"

"Well, I've been better. I'm sorry for your loss, or should I say, our loss."

"Oh yes," Liam said.

"You know, I just have to tell you how important your dad was to me." He stopped to weather a sudden outbreak of tears. "My own dad was pretty much absent," he continued after a few deep breaths. "Once my parents split, he moved to London. I guess he sent child support, but we only saw him once or twice a year. But your dad—" again, the tear wiping—"I was twelve when he married my mom, and he was a whole lot more of a father to me—to all of us—than our own dad ever was. He was always there. Once I got mixed up with the wrong crowd and got into a lot of trouble—a lot of trouble!—and he really turned me around." Holden paused again to collect himself. "He would *not* let me go down that path, he would *not* let me fail. I mean, he walked Candace down the aisle, he bailed out Michael when his business hit hard times, he came to our games and piano recitals when we were kids—I mean, he was there. I don't know where I'd be today if it hadn't been for him."

Liam stared at the man, at his reddish ears and his sincere, squirrel-like face, and wanted to clock him. How satisfying it would be to knock the fucker's teeth down his throat.

"Well," Liam said, at a total loss for an appropriate response.

"Look, I don't want to keep you. I just thought you should know how grateful we all are, and how much we'll miss him."

Liam nodded and drained his glass.

"I've really enjoyed being involved in Gwen's life all these years, too," he continued while Liam poured himself another drink. "I would love to get to know you and your family as well." He looked around the room. "Are they here?"

"No," Liam replied, relieved to be able to speak again. "This is the first week of school for my son, Dylan, and he hardly knew my dad, so it seemed unnecessary to disrupt his life for the funeral."

"He hardly knew Nate?"

"Well," Liam said, aware that he was talking louder now. "We do live twenty-two hundred miles away, and Nate was pushing eighty, so no, we didn't see him much." And don't you get it, asshole? Where was I when he was busy being there for you?

"Well, that's a shame. I do hope, though, that we can stay in touch. I'm in Phoenix a lot on business. You're out that way, aren't you?"

"Sure, Santa Fe is just five hundred miles from Phoenix." Dickhead.

"We could perhaps meet for dinner sometime."

"Yes, we could." We could also poke sharp sticks in our eyes.

"You take care," Holden said, briefly grasping Liam's upper arm before walking away.

Liam left soon afterward, driving his rental car to the airport eight hours before his flight. Gwen was disappointed in him, but that was nothing new.

But after telling Rosemary about the Holden conversation, after the sting had passed, she helped him see his dad in a different way.

"Don't you see?" Rosemary said, her eyes bright with epiphany. "He redeemed himself. He totally blew it with his first family, then he was lame but at least he tried with you and Gwen, and he was a hero in his last family."

"Third time's a charm?"

"It's actually a great story, if you can step back and look at it," she said lovingly, and he decided she was right.

To make it up to Gwen, he agreed to meet her in New York the following summer. She had a plan for scattering their dad's ashes in some meaningful, thematically tidy way.

When Liam heard the wheeze of the screen door and Mark's deep voice, he got up and got dressed. Rosemary was right—the gasoline thing would not ruin their trip, and yes, they would laugh at this someday. Probably today, when she told the story to her parents. She could be quite a hoot, his wife, especially when she wasn't being a crazed zealot. Her work with the water coalition had been a great accomplishment, and it turned out to be good for his business, but when she was fired up like that, she was nearly impossible to live with. And if he wasn't right there matching her enthusiasm, she was heartbroken. Once he said to her, "You know, you and the water coalition—it's kind of like your personal religious crusade. Is this how your mother was back when she used to power-pray?" That offhand comment enraged his wife and drove a wedge between them that lasted for weeks. And although they'd talked about it and she seemed to forgive him, it seemed to him like that wedge might still be there. Or maybe it always had been there, at least since Dylan was born. Hard to tell.

"There he is!" Mark said with a smile as Liam entered the kitchen.

"Morning!" Liam replied, engaging in brief hugs with his in-laws.

"You don't smell like gasoline," Mark said.

"So you've heard the story?"

"Not the details yet. We were about to. Dylan was telling us his dream."

"Well, that could take all day," Liam said, hugging Dylan briefly and giving his wife a quick kiss.

Rosemary turned her whole face toward Dylan, a gesture that Liam knew gave his son the green light to continue.

"It was about over," Dylan said, glancing at his dad.

"But you were telling us about the giant cave and the sound of the airplanes," Martina encouraged.

"Done?" Liam said jovially. "Well those bagels sure smell great."

Over breakfast, after Rosemary did a fine job of telling the gasoline story, she and Liam tried to convince Mark and Martina to drive out to Joshua Tree the following evening for dinner.

"You'll be our guests," Liam said.

"We'll have a nice meal for you, I promise," Rosemary coaxed. "We'll grill something."

"Grill? You brought a grill?" Martina asked.

"There's one at each campsite."

"A public grill? You don't know what's been on that surface!"

"That's what the fire's for," Liam explained.

"OK," Rosemary said. "Then we'll boil something in a pot."

"We'll make sure it's clean and nice for you," Liam assured. "We're the modern stone-age family."

"Yes, we'll be Fred and Wilma and you can be Barney and Betty," Rosemary said.

"And this here is Bam-Bam," Liam added, pointing to Dylan.

"What are you guys talking about?" Dylan asked as he arranged the fruit salad on his plate into the outline of a car.

"Just being silly," Rosemary answered, and turned her attention back toward her mother.

"Come on, Mom. You've never even been to the park, except for the Visitor Center, and it's practically in your own backyard."

"Just say yes," Liam said.

"We'll be there!" Mark announced decisively.

⤚ ⤚ ⤚

At the grocery they bought steaks, teriyaki sauce, baking potatoes, a prepared salad, two bottles of wine and a huge bag of ice, along with grill cleaner, a wire brush, and several sponges.

"I'm really looking forward to roughing it this week," Liam said.

Rosemary punched him and replied, "Come on, Fred, let's get out of here."

At the park they cheered when they were able to get their favorite campsite, Number 38, in the Jumbo Rocks campground. Liam and Dylan instantly scrambled up a rock face.

"I'm a lizard!" Dylan shouted, posing on all fours on a broad rock, his eyes squinting into the sun.

"I'm a vulture!" Liam shouted, perching above him in a scowling hunch.

"Mom, what are you?" Dylan shouted.

"I'm amused by my favorite dorks!" she shouted back.

They broke their poses and continued scrambling further while Rosemary unloaded the car. She gloried in the familiar scent of the place—the dusty blend of warmed stone and bleached soil, the modest perfume of desert shrubs.

"Rosemary, come with!" Liam shouted from a ledge above. "We'll do it when we come back!"

"Nah!" she replied, waving her hand. "You go on, I'm fine!"

She set up the kitchen first—spread the plastic tablecloth, set up the dish washing tubs, iced down the food, filled the stove's small fuel tank. Next the chairs, set in a circle around the fire ring, with a cloth bag full of books. Dylan had brought *Stephen Biesty's Incredible Cross-Sections* and *An Illustrated Guide to Desert Dwellers.* Liam brought *The One-Minute Manager* and a few back issues of *The Atlantic* and *Outside.* And Rosemary had brought Margaret Atwood's *The Blind Assassin*—plus another books she'd left hidden in the car: *Gifted Children: Myths and Realities.* She didn't want Dylan to see it quite yet. He'd just recently been identified in school as gifted. Highly gifted, actually. It was quite daunting—how were they supposed to parent him? How could they ensure he was being challenged?

Next the tarp for the tent and the sleeping bags. She considered setting up the tent but decided it could be an excellent project for Dylan, requiring him to follow written directions and use his spatial intelligence. Next came the lantern, head-lamps, and flashlights, and a trash bag, secured by a five-gallon jug of water.

She tidied up the car and lowered the windows—it needed to air out more. Then, after scanning the rock ledges to make sure she was alone, she reached under the passenger seat to retrieve a black, zippered bag. She withdrew three pill containers—they'd cost a fortune, and she had high hopes for them, but if Liam found them, he might be disgusted by her inability to accept herself. She'd already taken the colon cleanse that morning. Now, at midday, she took the appetite suppressant, and before bed, she would take the fat-burner. The herbal weight loss system was her last best hope for looking halfway decent in a bathing suit this summer. She looked around, saw no one, and replaced the bag under the seat.

The boys were still gone when she was finished setting up camp and began to feel restless. What should she do with this free time? It could be ten minutes or an hour. If she were home, she would clean something, check her email, or join Dylan in whatever he was doing. But here she was, instantly at loose ends, and scolding herself for it.

She spread the Therm-a-Rest in a shady spot beneath a Joshua tree and launched into her stretching routine. A few minutes later she was on her back with large rocks in her hands, pumping them like free weights. She visualized herself as lean and trim, like she was at twenty-three. Could she ever get that body back? Yes, of course she could—no more negative thoughts. She had to believe, she had to be grateful, and she had to affirm everything she wanted all the time.

Well, that took ten minutes. Now what? She was feeling this way more and more lately. When Dylan was in kindergarten, she was deeply engrossed in the water coalition. She'd been its communications director, and the group had accomplished its colossal task—levying bonds to buy Cielo Vista's water rights and its infrastructure. The community's water would belong to its residents in perpetuity. She and the other volunteers became local heroes when the deal went through; it had been enormously gratifying.

But with the coalition's mission accomplished, she was no longer needed. The district had hired a web designer who could write newsletters and email blasts, along with an accountant and a general manager, and it had retained a hydrologist—a real hydrologist with more than two letters after her name. The water district was fine, thanks much, and if she wanted to continue volunteering, it could probably find something for her.

Next she threw her energy into streamlining Ellis Landscaping to make it as profitable and efficient as possible. Liam was grateful for her help, and business was booming. He wanted her to work full time for the business, but, truth be told, at thirty-four, she did not relish returning to landscaping. Most of their clients were in Cielo Vista, and she knew the area's class attitudes all too well. She'd discovered that if she drove her Subaru to the grocery wearing capris, Birkenstocks, and a cute summer blouse, she would be smiled at and given good service. But if she drove the battered company pickup to the same store wearing old jeans and a T-shirt, with her three Hispanic crew members, she would barely be seen. Some of their clients, women whose yards she worked in, wouldn't even recognize Rosemary if they saw her at the pool or the coffee shop.

So she was at a loss. When she mentioned this to Liam, he said, "I guess this is when women have another baby." But they didn't want another kid. Dylan was exhausting, and she didn't want to jeopardize their financial stability. Finally, they could pay their bills and even afford a few luxuries. They'd bought a swing set for Dylan and their furniture actually matched—standard issue in every other home in Cielo Vista but new to them. And their Jeep—they bought it new even before the old Subaru fell apart. And she couldn't bear to get so fat again. So no, no more babies.

She could go back to school, but it sounded like drudgery, driving seventy miles down to UNM several times a week, writing papers late into the night. She wanted something new. There had to be something more for her.

"Boo!" Dylan leaped down from a rock ledge above, landing in a dusty scramble at her feet. She screamed in fright.

"You stinker!" she shouted, laughing.

"Whatcha doing, pretty lady?" Liam asked, also leaping down several feet.

"Waiting for my boys."

"Well the boys are back in town. God, it's great to be back here. It's been too long. I talked to a ranger about some trails that would be good for junior here. I'd like to set out later for a hike, if you're up for it."

"Sure.

"I found some good sticks for marshmallows," Dylan said, holding out his treasure. "And we saw a horned toad and nineteen ravens and three piles of coyote scat."

"Well, all right!" she said. "Very cool."

"We saw some other bird, too. I'm gonna see if I can figure out what it was." He found his book on desert dwellers and became quickly absorbed.

"He really is very observant," Liam said to her quietly. "It's sort of mind-blowing. Does the paperwork say anything about that?"

Rosemary thought back to the evaluation report on Dylan they'd received a few weeks ago that said his IQ was a hundred forty-eight. "Well, unusual curiosity, a long attention span, and excellent memory are part of the characteristics in general."

"He about talked my ear off the whole time, too. Is there anything about that?"

"Above average verbal ability, yes. But you can read up on this too, you know."

"Why should I when I have you?" he asked, flashing her a smile. "He boulders really well, too. He's so flexible. I'm feeling like an old man next to him."

"You are an old man."

"Thanks for that."

"You know I'm really starting to wonder about his school. Will they be able to keep challenging him?"

"Who knows? It seems like a crapshoot."

"We might have to go private."

"I forgot that we're rich."

"We could do it if we had to."

They paused to watch Dylan. He was still crouching in the sun, reading.

"Just imagine," Liam said. "He could be a big deal someday, a major dude who invents something, or a guy in a think tank who creates a whole new paradigm of how we all see the world."

Ah yes, Rosemary thought. The longing for the Christ child. Maybe this golden child could turn it all around. . . .

"He says he wants to invent a car that can run on garbage," Liam said.

"Like a moving incinerator?"

"And the exhaust will also become fuel for it. It'll consume its own pollution."

"A self-contained system. I'd invest in it."

After lunch they embarked on a hike, and for nearly two miles Dylan told Rosemary a story about a world in which fire was an animal, or many animals, really. The fire animals would move through the landscape grazing on plants and trees when they were hungry, and devouring buildings when they were angry. Sometimes when they swarmed like that, they were given names like hurricanes. Now one day, there was a fire named Emily. . . .

His voice, so light and lilting at first, soon drowned out the birds and the wind and every other sound. She imagined they were tiny figures in a comic strip, and Dylan's speech bubble filled the sky. He did this often, but she was usually doing something else, like driving or cooking, and she only half-listened. But here, it wore her down.

"Why don't you tell Dad this story?" she asked, noting how Liam had pulled ahead.

"Dad doesn't like my stories."

"OK," she said, taking a deep breath. "What happens next?"

After Emily passed through the town of Brog, scorching the landscape and causing thousands of half-melted Broggians to lose their homes, the townspeople were forced to placate her by offering up their entire winter store of food. To survive, they were forced to gather boogerberries that grew high in the mountains. But there weren't enough for everyone, so a war broke out.

When Dylan paused to observe a stinkbug, Rosemary scooted ahead to catch up with Liam.

"Enjoying your hike?" she asked snidely.

"Of course. It's great out here. Why do you ask?"

"Because Dylan has diarrhea of the mouth, and you look way too relaxed."

"Then tell him you need him to quiet down for a while."

A familiar wave of anger washed over her. "He wants to make up stories and share them!" she said, louder than she'd expected. "And I'm quite sure he would also like you in his audience."

"And sometimes I do listen, but I don't want to right now."

"So where does that leave me?"

"Wherever you choose to be."

"Oh, please—more like where *you* choose me to be," she said, squaring her shoulders.

"Hey, we've been through this. I parent by choice, remember? And you can too, if you want to."

"I'm not sure there's enough room for my choices in your parenting world."

"There could be. You should try it some time. You'd be happier."

She lowered her voice as Dylan approached. "I'd be happier if you gave him more attention."

"I give him plenty of attention," Liam replied coolly. "It's just not your kind of attention. I'm his dad, not his mom."

"What are you guys fighting about?" Dylan asked, searching their faces as he walked toward them.

"We're not fighting," Rosemary replied.

"It looks like you're fighting."

"It's not your concern," Liam said. "Let's check out this little canyon here."

∽ ∽ ∽

That night, after Dylan was asleep in the tent—the tent he'd had absolutely no interest in putting up—Rosemary said to Liam, "We need to figure out how to parent him."

"We're doing a fine job of parenting him," Liam countered, rearranging the wood in the fire pit. "He's doing great. Why do you worry so much?"

"He needs a lot of stimulation and I don't know if I have what it takes."

"He would find his own stimulation if he were forced to. If you would just stop trying so hard, he'd find his own way."

"You always say that!" she huffed. "But it doesn't work that way! When I'm not there either to listen to him talk or play with him or suggest things to him, he's—I don't know—lost or something. He seems to require constant attention."

"But he's in school all day."

"And as soon as he comes home it starts up again."

"He needs more friends."

"I agree, but I can't make those friends for him."

Liam sighed. "Of course you can't make his friends for him, Ro." He paused as if he wanted to say something more, but reconsidered. "Look, some of the kids on the soccer team seem to really like him. They think he's funny. Maybe you can arrange a play date or something with one of their moms."

"OK, I'll do that."

After Liam had gone to bed, Rosemary sat huddled in a sweatshirt, trying to extend the life of the fire in the chill night. As she fed the flames scavenged twigs and bits of garbage and newspaper, she felt the familiar, heavy feeling of being alone in her perception of Dylan. She and Liam had had so many fights about their son over the years, about what he needed and why and who should do more of this and less of that, but it seemed there was no winning these arguments. She'd always believed she understood Dylan in a way that no one else could—she was his mother, after all—and if she could just find the right words, then eventually Liam would see things her way. But it occurred to her now that that would never happen because Liam no doubt held the same conviction—he was his father, after all. And Dylan's girlfriends and wife would feel the same way, and on and on.

She looked up at the rock that ringed the campsite, the quiet stars above, and exhaled slowly, as if she were in a yoga class. The notion quickly became a certainty: Liam would never see Dylan as she did, no matter what she said—and the reverse was true as well.

Now what was she supposed to do with that?

Liam had asked her once, "Why is it always your goal to change my mind?"

She'd paused for a moment before asking candidly, "Isn't that what everybody does? With everyone?"

"No," he'd said. "It isn't."

She tried to imagine that he was right, just like she tried to imagine things from his point of view: Everything was fine. You make the best decisions you can based on the information you have at the time, and then you live your life. If there are hard times, you adapt. You don't second-guess, and you don't blame yourself for lacking the powers of prescience. You just do your best.

But she couldn't shake the conviction that that wasn't good enough when it came to parenting. The stakes were too high. It was her responsibility to get it right.

It was nearly ten o'clock. She needed to sleep so she could be in good shape for a family day tomorrow. She took three Melatonin tablets and waited to become drowsy.

It was Lou who'd introduced her to Melatonin as a sleep aid. He took a ton of it when he was sick, along with every other herb, vitamin, and supplement he hoped could fight the cancer. All those pills, tinctures, teas, poultices, and shots were supposed to strengthen his immune system, shrink the tumors, cleanse the blood, calm his mind, and do a million other things, but he still ended up on a hospice morphine drip, with a ragtag circle of acquaintances wandering through the house, wondering what to do next.

Lou had been their next-door neighbor, a transplant from New York in his late sixties. He used to sit in a lawn chair at the end of his driveway, reading a newspaper in the shade of a juniper tree as if it were his front stoop in Bay Ridge. It was clear he hadn't chosen his retirement home too well—spacious, scattered Cielo Vista was not the place to live if you hoped to casually converse with passersby. She enjoyed his conversation when she was out for a walk. But she'd wondered how he would cope in winter, when he couldn't sit in his lawn chair. Who would he talk to?

A week before Christmas last year, she found out when he showed up at their door unannounced on a Saturday morning. She was helping Dylan make a gift for his teacher, and was expecting to spend the day doing the last of her Christmas shopping and a thousand other errands. But there was Lou, with a Pannetone cake under his arm, clearly expecting a visit. So she made coffee and they ate the dry fruited cake and chatted, with her pointedly saying, "Well. . . ." and mentioning how it was such a busy time of year and what a crazy day she had ahead of her, and there he sat. She learned that he was an odd mix of Brooklyn Italian turned hippie turned lonely old man.

"Is Lou your new project?" Liam asked that night as she stayed up late wrapping gifts.

"Don't be mean."

"Are we inviting him for Christmas dinner?"

"No."

"OK, just so I know what to expect."

The next time he came by, bearing a sack of tangerines, he told her he'd be getting a third of his left lung removed the following week.

"I never smoked cigarettes in my life, but I did smoke my share of doobies," he said with a wink. "And lung cancer—it seems to run in my family."

"Oh no!" she was aghast. "I'm so sorry!"

"It'll be OK."

After a while, she said, "You know, living at seven thousand feet here complicates things, don't you think? You might want to move back to New York."

"No," he said, shaking his head dismissively. "The key is to harmonize with it."

After the surgery, and after the home healthcare aide became too expensive, they tried to help, but it was all very awkward. Rosemary picked up his medicines at the pharmacy, and Liam installed grab bars in the shower, but they had no idea how he managed the rest of his daily needs. When she learned he had grown children in Seattle and Tampa, she asked when they would be visiting.

"I don't know," Lou replied, no longer jovial. "Maybe never. I didn't do too good as a dad. You could say we're estranged."

Lou recovered, and for several months Liam and Rosemary remained The Helpful Neighbors. But the following fall, the morning before Halloween, there was a desperate phone call.

"Rosemary," Lou breathed heavily into the phone. "Please, I need your help. Can you come over?"

She rushed to his house, expecting to call 911. The front door was locked, so she found the key under the fake rock and let herself in. As she closed the door behind her, she heard Lou whimpering, "Careful, careful."

He was lying on the edge of a large Navajo rug in the living room, moaning, wearing nothing but black sweat pants. The coffee table that usually sat on the rug had been cleared away.

"Come around," he said, gesturing to the brick floor behind him. "Don't try to cross."

"I shouldn't step on the rug?"

"Don't fall in!" he shouted, and then repeated with a breathless moan, "Don't fall in. Please, be careful."

"What?"

"I'm on the edge of the abyss!" he said louder, beginning to weep. "I'm so frightened."

"What abyss?" Rosemary asked, looking around in a panic.

"This here," he said, pointing to his right, to the hand-woven rug. "The hole opened up hours ago." He began to sob loudly, shouting, "I can't take it anymore! I can't take it anymore!"

She walked around the rug and crouched down next to him. A purple scar gleamed across his back, grinning like a lurid smile. She had never touched him before beyond an air kiss or two, but now she put her hand on his shoulder and said soothingly, "It will be OK. Tell me what's going on." His skin was damp, and he smelled like acrid, fear-driven sweat.

He didn't answer, but his body relaxed a little under her touch. She sat down next to him, cross-legged. "I don't understand," she said.

But when she saw the jar nearby, half full of what looked like dried dog turds, she thought she did understand. Removing the lid released a fungal perfume in the air.

"Lou, you ate mushrooms?" she asked.

He opened his eyes and looked at her quizzically.

"You ate some of these?" she asked, shaking the jar in front of his face.

He looked at the jar and at her face and back to the jar again. Slowly, and with great wonder in his eyes, he said, "I did eat some of those."

"When?"

"When." He closed his eyes for over a minute. "At dawn."

"Do you realize that any abyss you believe you're lying next to is a hallucination?"

Lou stared up at the ceiling for another minute, then closed his eyes. Her watch said 10:20, which meant he'd taken the mushrooms nearly four hours ago.

"I'm so frightened," he said, rolling onto his side, turning his back to the rug's abyss. He stared at her knee without seeing. "So frightened."

Rosemary managed to place a pillow under his head before he fell asleep. She watched him for a while, and when she was satisfied he wasn't about to start seizing or stop breathing, she stood up and stretched her legs. She recalled the stories she'd heard about bad trips—the characters in those cautionary tales, the dorky "Just Say No" young adult novels and made-for-TV movies, were always crazed teen-agers who thought they could fly, not decrepit old men fighting cancer.

She sat down on the couch and stared at Lou. His gray comb-over fell the wrong way across his balding head like a luggage flap that wouldn't stay snapped. His gnarled feet showed unkempt toenails and a prodigious amount of hair—hobbit feet, really. The flaccid belly, slipping toward the floor, was riddled with birthmarks and jiggly things she didn't want to know about. She covered him with a throw blanket and stared glumly around the room, wondering what to do next.

Lou had assembled the same assortment of Santa Fe kitsch that every newcomer to New Mexico seemed to assemble—the wooden howling coyote with a tiny bandana, the dancing Hopi kachina doll, the Georgia O'Keeffe print framed in steel. The wall area above his fireplace was empty, but she felt confident there would be a cow skull there soon.

She looked back to Lou, relieved to find him still asleep. Was this what it would be like when her parents grew old or ill? Wondering whether to leave them alone or not? Hoping they would take long naps so she could get a few things done? Would she have to change their diapers? Ugh. What a thought.

Leaving didn't seem right, so she wandered around for a

while, attempting to tidy up a little. It was hard to put a cheerful touch on it, but she tried, opening blinds, wiping down dusty surfaces, making the bed. There was precious little food in the house—a few withered avocadoes, a half box of fiber cereal, a collection of Styrofoam restaurant containers. She made herself a cup of instant coffee.

Psilocybin mushrooms—at his age! Where could he have gotten them? Was there a drug trade in Cielo Vista she didn't know about? Did someone mail them to him from Brooklyn? What had he hoped for when he ate them alone, at dawn. A revelation of some kind? A healing miracle?

It was while she was straightening stacks of junk mail that she found the notebook. A cheap spiral notebook, open to a page with its margins full of intricate line drawings. The middle of the page had writing—pointed, right-slanted, cursive writing. It appeared to be a journal of some kind. Private. She would set it aside and not look at it. She would just close the cover and place it near the stack of old newspapers.

But maybe she'd just glance at the drawings first. They were intriguing; the lines appeared to have images embedded in them, though it was hard to discern what was what. Was that a bird? A tree? An eye? Words were embedded as well: One said, "WELL." Another might have said "MINE." Hard to tell.

OK, time to stop. After all, this was Lou's intimate stuff, and—well, maybe she'd just look at the one page that was showing. After all, the book was open, and she was here because he'd asked her to come over. It wasn't like she'd broken in. Just one page.

"You are not welcome," it read. "You have already stayed too long. I have learned what I needed to learn from you. You have fulfilled your role, and now it is time for you to leave."

Who had stayed too long? The guy seemed to be alone all the time. Just one more page.

"What do you want from me? I've given you my flesh. I've shared myself with you, yet you still spread and eat me up. How much is enough? Why must I work so hard to rid myself of you?"

The next page: "I do not choose you. Out! Out, you mother fucker! You are a goddamned mother fucking scum sucking pile of shit! You are a predator, a trespasser, an interloper, an evil, greedy parasite! You have no right to claim me!"

For one hundred college-ruled sheets, Lou talked to his cancer. He questioned it, challenged it, reasoned with it, wondered at it, negotiated with it, and then began pleading with it. "Just go, please, just go," he wrote, and the line drawings grew more blunt and black.

On one page with various drawings of necklaces, he wrote, "We all hope for a life like a beautiful string of pearls—long and shimmering, with each smooth, lustrous pearl a milestone or wonderful event. But some of us get just a few pearls, or we get bumpy, lumpy beads instead, or rocks, or we have long empty gaps between our pearls—too much string. And some of us get short strings."

It took nearly an hour to read the whole thing. When she reached the end, she stared out the window at her own house, feeling sick with shame and grief. How could she have done that? What kind of horrible person reads a dying man's journal without permission? And how could Lou stand it every day, living alone with this disease?

"Oh!" Lou shouted from the living room rug, as if on cue. "Help me, please."

She scrambled toward him and sat in the same place she sat earlier, as if she'd never left. "I'm here," she said. "It's your neighbor, Rosemary. You're not alone."

"I'm so frightened," he said, grabbing her hand.

He fell asleep again and the pattern continued into the afternoon: a cry, a reassuring hand, some soothing words, and sleep again. Rosemary longed to leave, to get out of this house and erase everything she now knew about loneliness, old age, illness, and despair.

At 2:30, she pulled away to call Liam.

"You're where?" he asked.

"With Lou," she whispered into the phone. "He's having a bad mushroom trip."

"A bad mushroom trip!"

"Sshhh!"

"Lou, from next door, is on mushrooms."

"Yes."

"Is this a joke?"

"No, it's not a joke, and he can't be alone. I know it's weird, and I'm not having a bit of fun over here, if that makes you feel any better."

"No, that does not make me feel any better."

"Can you get Dylan from school?"

He sighed. "Yes, Saint Rosemary, I can get Dylan from school."

"Please don't say that. This is a really heartbreaking scene."

"OK, OK. I'll get Dylan while you save the sad man next door from his terrible fate."

Of course she was angry at Liam's attitude, and of course when Lou came down later that day he was grateful and thankful and whateverful, and of course Dylan was resentful that they had to rush the making of his Halloween costume, and of course she and Liam argued about it that night, and of course she felt justified in her actions and misunderstood by her selfish family.

But she began to see it all differently a few weeks later. She was at the grocery, picking up her Thanksgiving turkey, when she ran into Lou.

"Rosemary!" he called to her in a voice that seemed to grow gruffer all the time. "I'd like to introduce you to someone." Lou was holding the hand of a woman whose small lined face was dwarfed by a huge turquoise scarf. Her suede jacket glimmered with silver studs. She appeared to have a tan, and her silver hair was cut bluntly at the jaw line.

"Rosemary, this is Pearl, my new love. And this lady," he said, gesturing toward Rosemary, "is the woman who saved my life."

Pearl's face brightened in expectation. "Well!" she said.

"I did nothing of the kind," Rosemary insisted, instantly wishing she could escape. She shifted the turkey under her left arm to shake Pearl's outstretched hand. "Nice to meet you."

"You did so save my life," Lou nearly shouted. "Who knows where I'd be right now if it weren't for you?"

"What in the world happened?" Pearl asked.

"It's a long story," Rosemary said, recalling the notebook and its desperate content. She winced at the memory.

"Well, I'd love to hear it." Pearl looked directly into Rosemary's eyes.

"I'll let Lou tell you," Rosemary said, averting her eyes. Garnet Yams were fifty-nine cents a pound. She suddenly felt nauseous. "I need to run."

In the checkout line, she breathed deeply and evenly, trying to settle her nerves. She had told no one about Lou's journal. On Halloween, when she was out trick-or-treating with Dylan, Lou had left a poinsettia on their doorstep along with a heartfelt note thanking her for her help. But she hadn't seen him since that day, and the memory of his vulnerability and despair, so absolute and untouchable, and his trust in her, so misplaced and undeserved, rattled her now.

Later that night, sitting alone with a glass of wine, she wondered about the encounter at the grocery. It should have pumped her up, all that praise and recognition, but it had done the opposite. Looking around her kitchen at the pumpkin and apples that would soon become Thanksgiving pies, the yams and the sparkling cider, the olives and other delicacies that would make a beautiful appetizer tray, she suddenly realized that the person Liam unkindly called "Saint Rosemary" was really quite ridiculous. There it was—the truth—as clear as a Pyrex pie plate: The daily sacrifices necessary to keep a family functioning, whether it be caring for a newborn or mopping a floor, brought with them *no* glory. Zip. Yes, there was some satisfaction and approval, and oftentimes fulfillment, but just as often there was fatigue, boredom, and resentment.

But the sacrifices made for others—the grand, public gestures that exceeded the expectations of all involved—those offered a crap-ton of glory. Boatloads of glory. One enjoyed thank you cards, gifts, and a kind of fame that could last for years.

Sure, nice people did nice things for others, but there was something else going on for Saint Rosemary. She saw now that her motivation for being selfless was actually. . .selfish.

She looked out the kitchen window into the dark night and snickered. "Get over yourself," she said aloud, gulping the last sip of wine.

❦ ❦ ❦

Rosemary watched the campfire die out on this April evening with no remorse. She knew that that part of her life was over, and good riddance. Lou died in February. His kids showed up in the end. She brought a casserole. It was a sad few days, and that was that.

Now what? She had pulled in her tendrils these past few months. She had volunteered for no PTA committees, cooked no birthday dinners for friends, begun no major projects in the house. It felt strange, but OK, to reserve her energy. She had the feeling that something new was coming.

She stretched her legs, crawled into the tent, and settled in to the sleeping bag between Liam and Dylan. "Thank you for helping me find my path," she whispered aloud, as she had more times that day than she tried to count.

❦ ❦ ❦

"Mom!" Dylan shook Rosemary awake. "Mom!"

"What, what?" she replied, dazed with sleep.

"There's a bird out here."

"What?"

"A Gambel's quail. Come see it. And I wrote a poem. . .well, just the beginning so far. Listen—"

"Dylan!" Liam shouted. "This is inconsiderate behavior. Leave the tent now and don't disturb us until we wake up on our own."

Dylan left without a word and Liam went back to sleep. A few minutes later, though, Rosemary poked her head through the zippered opening. Dylan was dragging a stick through the embers of last night's fire, talking quietly to himself, which meant he was working on his poem.

She climbed out of the tent. "Hey, buddy," she said, closing the zipper behind her.

"You're up!" he called brightly, scrambling to his feet to give her a big hug around the waist.

"Sshhh!" she said, running her fingers through his hair. "Did you sleep well?" She briskly massaged his head, feeling the familiar shape of his skull beneath her fingertips.

"Yeah. I love sleeping next to you."

"Yeah," she agreed. What a joy the kid could be. They stood embracing in the morning light for a while, absorbing each other.

"Do you want to hear my poem?"

"Sure." She pulled away to look into his face—the clear eyes, the rosy cheeks. His face was like a cup of light.

"When I was one, I had a dream, a magic mountain, and a stream. I lived alone for many days."

"Wow," she said, meaning it. "That's beautiful. Do you know what will happen next?"

"No. I heard a Northern Mockingbird this morning."

"Really?"

"Yeah, but I don't know which call it was imitating."

"How long have you been up?"

"I don't know. It was just getting light. I've also been working on a song. Wanna hear it?"

"Of course!"

"Rothstein, Donatelli, Hughes, Dahlstrom, Schoenburg, fa, la, la, la, la, la, la, la, la," he sang to the tune of "Deck the Halls."

"Huh? Why are you singing about a law firm?"

"It's my favorite ad on KUNM. Here's another one: National Native News, a project of Koahnic Broadcast," he sang to the tune of "Let It Be."

"Jeez, Dylan. I didn't expect to hear radio ads out here at Joshua Tree."

"What do they flavor bird food with?"

"I have no idea," she yawned.

"They should make it bug-flavored."

"Bug-flavored bird food?"

"Or worm-flavored."

"Good one, Dylan."

"And they should make bird-flavored cat food."

She laughed and added, "Mouse-flavored, too."

"There could be chunks of fur in the box, like marshmallows."

"Yum," she said laughing.

"Good morning, family," Liam said, appearing suddenly.

"Oh!" they shouted, startled.

"Allow me to introduce myself," he announced, repeating a stock joke. "I'm Liam. I'll be your husband—and your father—this lifetime."

"Sorry," she said, catching her breath. "We didn't hear you."

He gave Dylan a brief bear hug and Rosemary a kiss on the cheek.

"Big day today," he said. "Grandma and Grandpa are coming out for dinner."

"Yes, better start scrubbing the rocks," she replied.

"Oh, it will be fine."

"Yes, it will be fine. Let's get the coffee going."

❧ ❧ ❧

The day was full of surprises—bird sightings, new places to climb, and then the big shocker: Deet. When Rosemary's brother stepped out of her parents' car at four o'clock, she danced with joy. They hadn't seen him for over a year. After greeting Rosemary and Liam, Deet turned to Dylan.

"And here's the big guy!" he shouted, scooping Dylan up over his shoulder. "Okay, so where did you want this package?" he asked. "In the trash can, you say?"

"No!" Dylan shouted with a squeal.

"You sure?" he asked, carting Dylan away. "Oh, all right."

He set the boy down and stood with his hands on his hips, surveying his nephew as if he were considering buying him.

"You're getting so big, buddy!"

"Why does everyone always say that?"

" 'Cause it's true, I guess."

"Hey," Rosemary said, giving her brother a shove. "How come we didn't know you'd be here?"

"I wasn't sure I could make it, so Mom didn't want to say anything."

"Oh, Mom," Rosemary said, rolling her eyes. "You didn't think I could handle the disappointment if this goober didn't show up?"

Her mother smiled shyly.

"Well, how about a glass of brine?" Liam offered.

"Wine? Yes, I brought some!" Deet announced, retrieving a bottle from the car, along with a corkscrew.

"And I brought a cake," Martina said proudly, handing over her Pineapple Upside Down Cake.

"Another cause for celebration!" Liam said. "Thanks, Mom!"

The pinot noir was rich and smooth, far better than the twelve-dollar bottle they'd splurged for. Deet said he'd just bought a case of it, and would leave them a few bottles.

He was living temporarily in Flagstaff, Arizona, working as a consultant for a resort developer. They were negotiating with several Arizona tribes at the moment, looking for the right fit for a new casino.

"Indian gaming?" Rosemary asked. "Since when do you work with gambling?"

"I don't. I work on the land acquisition side, and I sometimes help with executive staffing."

"Don't the Indians run their own casinos?" Martina asked.

"They usually partner with a hotel company, like Hilton," Deet explained. "It takes a lot of expertise to run a resort casino. You just don't wing it."

As the conversation continued and more bottles were opened, Martina looked relieved when Dylan led her away from the picnic table and toward his books. Rosemary stole glances at them as she pressed avocadoes for guacamole. She could tell by the way her mother looked at Dylan—that ardent, penetrating gaze—that she couldn't care less about the plants and animals he'd seen this week, or about anything else in Dylan's stash of books. She was just taking in her grandson in big gulps, filling up on him as if she'd just survived a drought.

While Liam and Deet discussed the merits of marinades over rubs, Rosemary got an update on her dad's new life. He'd be taking the bar exam in six weeks and felt confident he would pass it.

"There's an opening in the district attorney's office," he said. "I'm hoping to get a position there."

"Wow, Dad, I thought you'd be a cop till the day you died."

He nodded and smiled. "I'm just as surprised as you are, honey," he said, refilling his glass. He looked around the campsite with pride. "Would you look at this wonderful group? Now all we need is for David to meet someone and settle down."

"I heard that!" Deet shouted.

"Yeah," Rosemary chided. "What are you, a monk or something?"

"No, he's a playboy," Liam said.

"Or are you too embarrassed to introduce your girlfriends to us?" she continued. "To your small town, down home folks?"

"Aah," Deet said, dismissing their comments with a wave of his hand. "The day will come."

When it was time to grill the meat, Liam invited Martina to see how clean they'd scrubbed the grate. "I'm quite sure this is the cleanest grill in any national park, anywhere, in the entire universe," he said with his arm around his mother-in-law. She thanked him for the effort, looking embarrassed, and accepted a glass of wine.

As they ate and talked and built up the fire against the evening's chill, Rosemary felt a combined sense of awe and ease. This was her family, all in one place, enjoying each other's company. At Joshua Tree even. She never thought this would be possible, yet here they were. Later, she knew, she and Liam would give this night one of their special labels: "PFI"—Pretty Fucking Idyllic.

She was reminded of the time she'd come to Joshua Tree alone, back when Dylan was around two, and she'd met those two families. They'd spent the day together and sung songs around the campfire. And Wade! Oh yes, there was Wade, too. But the point was, she'd felt this same sense of wellbeing that night as well. What did it take, really? Food, people, conversation, a fire. Maybe some music, maybe a little alcohol. Couldn't she create this on her own? And couldn't she create it more often, even for people she didn't know?

CHAPTER 12 | NOVEMBER, 2005

State Road 62, San Gorgonio Pass, California

P AYROLL FOR THE CAFÉ WAS DUE TOMORROW. HOPEFULLY Liam could write those few checks. She had sixty pounds of coffee being delivered, but accepting that shipment would be no problem for Breanne. The firewood would last the week, but Breanne would need to shop for a few things: milk and cream, cheese, produce, fresh bread. Rosemary was worried about the musicians lined up for tomorrow evening, though. If they took too long a break halfway through the show, they'd lose the audience; Breanne would have to be assertive to get them back on stage. But after the show, would she remember to set the alarm at closing?

"Mom," Dylan called. "Mo-om." He tapped her arm.

"Huh?" she replied, blinking.

"You're so unpayattentionative!"

"What?"

"You're doing it again, that trance where you don't hear anything."

"I'm not in a trance, Dylan, I'm driving."

"And thinking."

"Of course I'm thinking."

"About what?"

"Fire Ring."

"That's all you ever think about."

"Well, it takes a lot of energy."

"Sometimes I wish you'd never started that business."

"But you love it, too," she said with a yawn. "All that music, the people. And the coffee you're always sneaking."

He looked at her wide-eyed.

"It's OK, Dylan, relax. Just stick to the decaf, OK? And get your feet off the dashboard."

"But it's a rental car!"

"So what! Feet down."

He exhaled loudly, looking straight ahead, and lowered his feet to the floor. A moment later he said, "I wish Dad came with us."

"Me too, but it's hard to get away now with the two businesses."

"Can we get a wind turbine like that?" He pointed to the wind farm dominating the view near the I-10 interchange. Rosemary loved this stretch of highway, just north of the Palm Springs Airport where they'd landed a half-hour earlier.

"No, but we'll probably be getting solar panels soon."

"Cool!"

"Yes, very cool."

"What exactly is wrong with Grandpa, anyway?"

"I told you, he suffered a mild heart attack."

"Is he going to die?"

"Of course not! He just needs to rest for a few weeks, and Grandma thought a visit from us would cheer him up."

"How are we supposed to cheer him up?"

"We just need to be there with him. We don't have to do anything special."

"Is he going to have tubes and stuff sticking out of him?"

"No, he'll just be a little tired." She fought back tears as she imagined her strong, capable dad being tired and weak. It was hard to imagine that Assistant District Attorney Mark Sabin was at home recovering from a heart attack. Her mom said he seemed quieter lately, preoccupied.

"Will Deet be there?"

"I think so, and remember—he's Uncle David to you."

"Is he flying too?"

"Probably."

"Why didn't we drive? I like the drive here."

"You complain about the drive every time, and now you say you like it? Anyway, I can't get away for that much time."

He sighed and returned to reading *Harry Potter and the Half-Blood Prince* and she returned to thinking about Fire Ring, the café she and Liam had opened about a year earlier. Fire Ring featured a large fireplace and a tiny stage in a spacious, open room, with a collection of couches, pillows, and comfortable chairs arranged around them. Last summer, when it was too warm for a fire, Rosemary moved in a large cage of tropical birds, which Dylan mostly cared for. She brewed the best coffee for miles around and paid Breanne, her top employee, good money to bake Fire Ring's cookies fresh on the premises, so the place smelled like coffee and chocolate pretty much all the time. A fountain burbled in a corner, and cell phone conversations were prohibited. They served soups, salads, and sandwiches, and were waiting on their wine and beer license.

When Rosemary had conceived of the idea of Fire Ring, she figured it would take years to become a reality. But a building became available that she couldn't pass up—a failed restaurant on the highway frontage road about halfway between Cielo Vista and Santa Fe. It was close enough to pull in both Cielo Vista people for morning coffee and lunch, and folks from town on the weekends. It could even be seen from Interstate 25. And the landlord had let them install the fireplace. She wasn't making money yet, but she was at least breaking even most months. It had been a scary undertaking, taking out a business loan, but the economy was strong and the future looked bright. Liam helped out with the café, but Fire Ring was mostly her deal, like Ellis Landscaping was mostly his. She was astounded to see that their family was becoming a mini-dynasty in Cielo Vista.

"Mo-om—"

"Dylan, Mom is a one-syllable word. What?"

"My stupid teacher thinks that a light year is a measure of time."

"She's not stupid."

"She is too."

"And what do you hope to gain from believing she's stupid?"

"I'm just saying the truth."

"No, you're choosing a story that will make you feel superior to her, and which will make you feel more unhappy and alone in school." They'd been through this type of conversation countless times. She had come to believe that her son provoked them just to hear her say certain things, the way people fish for compliments.

"She just lacks knowledge, right?" Dylan asked.

"Yes, people are not stupid because they lack specialized knowledge. We all lack knowledge of certain things."

He paused for a while, but she knew what was coming.

"How do you know if people are truly stupid?"

"If they are unable to reason logically, or unable to learn new things." She'd come up with that definition the year before, when Dylan complained that his third grade teacher was stupid because she didn't know that bald eagles only reared one chick a year.

"Well then I think Ms. Garcia might truly be stupid."

"Stop it, Dylan. I don't want to get into this. It's ugly and it just makes us both miserable."

They drove in silence for some time.

"Why do all the annoying instruments start with a B?" he asked.

"What?"

"Bagpipes, banjos, and bongos. They're all so annoying."

"Huh."

"Do you know what we did in music last week?"

"Isn't there still a sub in there?"

"Yes, Mr. Jiggle."

"Mr. Jiggle?"

"That's what we call him 'cause his throat jiggles when he yells."

"I think that's called a wattle."

"Well, he showed that same stupid movie again, *Fluffy the Magic Tuba* or something. But that's still not as bad as last year, with Mrs. Bionda, when we banged rhythm sticks together for weeks and weeks. When she left the room we'd all try to start a fire with those sticks."

She couldn't help but laugh, but she knew she had about thirty seconds to steer the conversation elsewhere, or it would spiral into a negative cascade of complaints about school and everything else in Dylan's world.

"Look," she said, pointing at the car in front of her whose license plate read 177LHR. "In January of 1977, Larry halted rain."

"No," Dylan said. "In the seventeenth hour of the seventh day, Legos had radiation."

"No, there are one hundred seventy-seven little hot rods."

"No, there are one hundred seventy-seven little hairy radios."

"Hah!" Rosemary shouted. "You repeated a word."

"I did?"

"Little."

"OK, you win," he said. "Let's play the story game."

"God, not that."

"Please? We can do heads and tails to make it harder."

"Whatever."

In this game, they made up a story one word each, but the last letter from his word had to become the first letter of her word, and so on.

"The," she said.

"Eagle," Dylan said.

"Eased."

"Doughnuts."

"Stupefied."

"Down."

"Nottinghamway."

"Yolanda."

"Annoyed."

"Doug."

"Gently."

"Yet."

"Troubled."

"Doris."

"Slept. Oh God, this is a dreadful story."

"It's over already?"

"Yeah, how about geography?"

"Fine, but only the United States," he demanded.

"No, North America, but no bodies of water."

"OK. . .Michigan."

"Nebraska."

"Atlanta."

"Arlington."

"North Dakota."

"Arkansas."

"Santa Fe."

They played geography until they reached her parents' house about an hour later, in the early afternoon. Her mom was out and her dad was asleep.

"I could use a nap," Rosemary said quietly to Dylan.

"You never used to nap."

"Let's see what's on TV." She found the remote, hit the power button on the old, boxy television, and heard the theme song of "Star Trek, The Next Generation."

"Yes!" Dylan exclaimed.

"Sshhh!"

She lay down on the couch, her head on one of its arms, while Dylan sat at the opposite end with both pairs of legs in the center, their usual TV-watching arrangement.

"Awesome! The Borg," he whispered.

They knew the episode well: The *Enterprise* crew would try to poison the mind of a single Borg, the hive-mind collection of humanoids, to subtly teach it the principles of individuality, hoping to infect the whole hive with this thought virus.

"Great," she said, instantly feeling sleepy. "Star Trek" was like Valium to her, a fact she explained by noting that the scripts were all composed of about the same two hundred words and phrases, slightly rearranged and then peppered with names and places somewhat unique to each episode. "On screen," Captain Picard said repeatedly, along with "on my way," "report," "subspace transmission," "engage," "slow to impulse," "energize," and many other stock phrases that wooed her with their pleasing familiarity.

"Dylan," Rosemary said thickly, her eyes closed. "Wake me up when Grandpa gets up or when Grandma comes home, OK?"

"Sure," he whispered, and she drifted off into the Borg, wondering how she would behave in the twenty-fourth century if her life were threatened by an imperialistic race with a collective consciousness and superior weaponry. "You will be assimilated," they said repeatedly. "Resistance is futile." Kind of like life with Dylan.

"Mom!"

A commercial for a car dealer promised easy financing.

"Mom!"

Bad credit, no credit, no problem.

"Mo-om!"

"Let your mother sleep, Dylan," she heard her dad say.

She opened her eyes, saw her dad standing over her, and burst into tears.

"Oh don't be silly, honey," he soothed, patting her back. "I'm fine."

She wiped her face with the back of her hand and sat up. "It's really good to see you, Dad."

"Thanks, Rosie. You too." He kissed the top of Dylan's head and held his grandson's chin in his hand. "Just look at this handsome young man!"

"Where's Mom?" Rosemary asked.

"Running a few errands. David will be here in a little while and he's threatening to bring his new girlfriend."

"Really. Are they staying here?"

"No, at the Best Western."

"Well, this should be interesting. But if she's a freak like all the others and gives you another heart attack, I'll kill her."

"Now, now," he chuckled.

The last girlfriend she'd met was Tiffany, the twenty-six-year-old with the fake boobs. She and Deet had spent the night with Rosemary and Liam on their way to Denver, and all the woman did while she was there was steal glances of herself in shiny surfaces and repeatedly say, "I can't believe you live here." The one before Tiffany was a regal Senegalese woman who spoke little and was so strikingly beautiful that Rosemary was dumbstruck. The one before the African queen was Samantha, a blonde from Seattle who said she worked with "collateralized debt obligations," which Rosemary could not understand no matter how many times she and Deet tried to explain it. And of course there had been Isabelle, but all he would ever say about their fleeting, meteoric relationship was, "That was a mistake."

"Her name is Lizbeth," Mark continued, "and they've been together for six months, David tells me."

"Six months! Could be real."

"Yes, maybe."

She and her dad watched wordlessly as Dylan, singing softly to himself, looked at the books his grandmother had borrowed from the library for his visit. Rosemary could tell they were too easy for him, but it was sweet of her nonetheless.

She found a beer in the back of the fridge—a lonely Michelob Light—and a bag of unsalted rice crisps to snack on. As if Martina's no-fat obsession were not gastronomically disastrous enough, she had now also eradicated salt from the household since Mark's heart attack. Also in the fridge was the meal she had prepared for that evening: cut-up vegetables, already in a steamer pot, and what looked like boneless chicken breast under sheets of waxed paper, marinating in some vinegar thing. On the counter was a box of brown rice. Ugh. What a sorry showing of food and drink she was in for this weekend. Hopefully Deet would bring some good wine.

"Hey," Mark said to her, helping himself to some rice crisps. "Let's play a little game of Boggle."

Boggle, their old standby. How long had it been?

"Sounds great, Dad, but Dylan will give you a run for your money, you know."

"Oh yeah?" Mark said, giving Dylan a playful push. "I'll take that challenge."

Rosemary won the best of five rounds and was still gloating over it when her mother and Deet and Lizbeth all arrived at the same time.

Martina's paper shopping bags crunched loudly while Deet yelled a cheery "Hey!" and Dylan bolted to his uncle with arms wide. "Whoa!" Deet shouted, exaggerating the force of the body check. "Look at this guy!"

Lizbeth stepped through the door then, looking as if she'd stumbled onto the wrong movie set. At about five-foot-eight and an easy size four, she stood in her perfectly tailored ensemble—cream silk blouse tucked into gray slacks, a light jacket, strappy black heels, and a Coach bag—and stared impassively at the room and its occupants. While Deet set down some packages, greeted his parents and kissed Rosemary, Lizbeth stood at the door like a silent sentinel with precision-cut hair.

Rosemary smoothed her own hair and longed for lipstick. Then she lunged forward with her hand outstretched.

"Hi, I'm Rosemary, Deet's sister," she said. "Welcome."

Lizbeth shook Rosemary's hand, her brow furrowed. "Deet?" she asked. "I beg your pardon?"

"Ro," Deet scolded, taking Lizbeth by the hand. "No one in my real life calls me that."

"Long story," Rosemary offered, smiling big enough for the both of them. "I guess I'm David's sister, then."

She looked past Lizbeth to the BMW parked at the curb. "Is that a rental?" she asked.

"Yeah right," Deet said. "We rented a Beemer, a 328i convertible, at the airport. Please. That's mine, Ro. We drove here."

"You drove? I'm shocked."

"I just got the car last month. I wanted to try it out on the open road, and there's nothing like I-10 for driving a hundred miles an hour."

"David!" Martina scolded.

"It only took us three hours from Phoenix!" Deet exclaimed with a wink.

"Times like this I'm glad I'm not a cop anymore," Mark said, shaking Lizbeth's hand with a nod and a warm smile.

"Oh yes, much better to be a fancy lawyer, huh Dad?"

"Oh no, the fancy lawyers are the ones you take to lunch. I'm just a public servant, and you know it."

"Yes, I know it, Dad," Deet said, smiling at his father.

They settled themselves around the coffee table as Deet unpacked a box of wineglasses and uncorked one of the three bottles of Cabernet he'd brought.

"We own wineglasses, David," Martina said.

"Yes, but you only own white-wine glasses. Do you see how these have a rounder, wider bowl? The shape increases the rate of oxidation—it enhances the flavor."

"Oh," Martina said.

"These are for you," said Lizbeth, which turned out to be the only sentence she directed at Martina during their whole visit.

"Oh, well, thank you," Martina said, beginning to stand up. "Let me wash those out."

"Aw, let's rough it, Mom," Deet cajoled, pouring the first glass like a Crate & Barrel Santa Claus. Martina's lips pursed as she sat back down.

"Here you go, Dad," Deet said, handing the glass to Mark.

"It's a little early, isn't it, son?" Mark asked.

"You know red wine is good for your heart, Dad. Consider it medicine."

"Well," Mark said after taking a tiny sip. "It's very tasty."

Deet passed the next glass to Martina, who waved it off. "No, thank you."

"Oh, Mom," Deet said in halfhearted protest. He handed that glass to Rosemary and continued pouring for himself and Lizbeth.

"To die for," Rosemary said after a sip.

"Wine is gross," Dylan said with a scowl.

"Oh, I almost forgot!" Deet exclaimed, withdrawing a can

of Arizona tea from the bag. "This is for you, Buddy. I would have gotten you a Coke, but I know what a killjoy your mom is, but I figured she'd allow you some sweetened green tea."

"Thanks!" Dylan beamed while Rosemary made a show of kicking Deet. He poured the tea into the fine glass.

"A toast!" Deet said with a grand gesture. Four glasses were raised while Martina awkwardly raised her empty hand.

"To Dad!"

"Oh, come on now," Mark said.

"To health and long life!" Rosemary proclaimed with a hearty gulp.

"I need to get dinner started," Martina said, standing abruptly.

"Can I help, Mom?" Rosemary asked, knowing the answer.

"Oh no, it's practically done already."

"So," Mark said. "Lizbeth, tell us about yourself."

Lizbeth turned her flawless head to Deet. "I don't know how much there is to tell," she said.

Maybe, Rosemary thought, you could tell us how long it takes you to style your hair, or how much those shoes cost.

"I'm an investment banker in Phoenix," she said.

"Oh? What's your area of specialty?"

"I work with commercial land acquisitions."

"That's how we met," Deet explained. "I've been looking at land for the developer I work for, and this lovely lady has been very helpful."

"What kind of developer?" Rosemary asked.

"Golf courses," Deet said with a touch of defiance. "More wine?" As he refilled Rosemary's glass he looked at her pointedly as if to say, Don't start. She turned up her nose slightly at him, and he smiled. OK, Rosemary thought. She'd skip the appropriate-land-use lecture this time.

"Where are you from?" Rosemary asked.

"Santa Barbara."

"Oh, what part?" Mark asked, fueling a conversation about his hometown that went on for a long while. Rosemary found the crossword puzzle from the daily paper and set it in front of

Dylan with a pencil. He began working away with only an occasional poke at Rosemary's elbow when he needed help. As he completed the puzzle without a word, Rosemary joined in the conversation and sipped the best cabernet she had ever tasted.

When the conversation turned to the best coffee in Santa Barbara—a point that was about to become ridiculous as Mark brought up the names of diners while Lizbeth talked about which Starbucks had the friendliest baristas—Rosemary broke in.

"Speaking of cafés," she said. "Fire Ring is going well."

"So I hear," Deet said. "Good for you, Ro."

"Our second business—it's been open for nearly a year," Rosemary said, looking at Lizbeth. "We haven't bought a Beemer yet, but you know, we're on our way," she said with a laugh. She explained the café: the food, the music, the fire, the Fair Trade coffee beans, the organic food, the graywater system that reclaimed the dishwater, and what inspired the whole concept—that night of singing around a fire at Joshua Tree nearly seven years earlier with Wade and the others.

"It's a lot of work, but it feels good, too. Both businesses really capture our value systems," she said with the secret thrill she always felt when recalling that night—and that kiss.

She paused to refill her wine glass and the room fell silent. At that moment Rosemary wanted someone to ask her about her value system. She wanted someone to remark at her ingenuity, and to say that she and Liam were brave to take these sorts of risks in a world that seemed to be all about technology and greed and addiction and the destruction of families. She wanted someone to say, "Wow, and you do all that while being a mom? That's amazing." She wanted someone to say something, for God's sake.

"Cool, Ro," Deet said.

Well, that would have to do.

She was realizing that Lizbeth had not asked one question—about her, their businesses, Liam, Dylan, Santa Fe. This polished thing from the world of high finance wasn't the least bit curious about Rosemary.

"So how long will you folks be in town?" Mark asked Deet. "Till tomorrow afternoon."

"That's a fast visit," Rosemary remarked, staring at her wine as she swirled it in its round, wide bowl. Oh, that oxidation really was something else.

"It's all the time we could really get," Deet said with a shrug of his shoulders.

Rosemary suddenly realized she was starving. What had she eaten that day? A yogurt and a few rice crisps. Dylan was probably hungry too, but he was too distracted by the Sudoku to notice. Some cheese and crackers would be great right then, but she knew nothing like that existed in the house. Actually, she was more than just hungry—she was feeling a little drunk.

But the topic of trips was on the table, and Rosemary saw an opening. "You know," she said, "Liam and I just took a trip back east in August."

"Right," Deet said, uncorking another bottle. "Where to exactly?"

"New York. You know his dad died."

"Huh?"

"Nate, his dad. He died nearly three years ago, but no one had ever done anything with his ashes. Gwen, my sister-in-law, finally decided what she wanted to do with them, so we flew out to join her."

"And they didn't let me come," Dylan interjected.

"Yes, we left the kid home," she said, smiling at Dylan. "It was our first vacation without him."

"A vacation to scatter a man's ashes," Deet said with an exaggerated nod. "You two sure know how to have fun."

"It was a great trip!" she replied. Actually, it had cost a small fortune, which she'd bitterly resented. But, knowing that Deet did not know New York and presuming that Lizbeth didn't either, she let the tale just spin itself out, with as many proper nouns dropped as possible.

"We flew into LaGuardia and spent the night in the Gramercy Park Hotel. We spent the next morning at South Street Seaport and had lunch on Mulberry Street, in Little Italy. Then we took a train—well, a few trains—to the Upper West Side and walked around the park. Then we hopped a train out of Grand Central Station up to Chappaqua, near where Gwen lives. The next day we went to Kykuit, the old Rockefeller estate? And also to this amazing chapel nearby that has stained glass windows designed by Matisse and Chagall. They're just stunning! And the next day we all drove up to Cooperstown, where the Baseball Hall of Fame is."

"Cooperstown?" Deet asked.

"Yeah. Nate was a sports nut, and that's where Gwen wanted to spread his ashes."

"It's usually illegal to spread ashes without a permit, you know," Mark said.

"Well we learned that later," Rosemary said, sneaking in a gulp of wine. "But what was really strange is that I was reading this Tony Hillerman novel at the time, *The Dark Wind.*"

"I know that one!" Lizbeth chimed in. "I've read them all!"

"Really!" Rosemary exclaimed. "Then you remember the part of the book that has to do with superstitions around dealing with corpses? How they're bad juju?"

"I don't remember that."

"Well it's in there somewhere. Anyway, so Gwen thought we should all go to Doubleday Field and run the bases, spreading Nate's ashes like we were frolicking in some meadow or something. So we get there, and Gwen has some prayer thing prepared and a bottle of chilled champagne, but there's a Little League tournament going on. There are kids everywhere, games scheduled all day, all weekend in fact, and parents and coaches and hot dogs, and here we are with this five-pound box of corpse powder to deal with."

"You never told me all this," Mark said.

"Well it's a long story, and you hate to talk on the phone."

"OK, so what did you do?" Deet asked.

"So we go over and talk to this guy. He looked like he was in charge, but it turns out he was just one of the coaches. Anyway, we tell him what we have planned, and he tells us that it's not only illegal to spread the ashes but that you're not even allowed to spit gum or sunflower shells on that field. Anyway, he tells us there's a little break in the games between 1 and 1:30 and if we come back then, he'll help us out."

"He'd help you out how?" Mark asked.

"We didn't really know, but he was a nice guy, and he loved that we were honoring Nate in this way. So anyway, he told us to come back later. So we go walking around town for a while, looking at the shops. All the while Liam's lugging around the ashes because we'd had to park so far away. So we finally sit down at the Doubleday Café for an early lunch, and Liam sets the box of ashes on a chair. There's just the three of us, but the waitress comes and sets the table for four, and we're just blown away."

"Oh no," Mark said with a chuckle.

"Yes! So anyway, even though it's hardly noon, Gwen and Liam decide we have to have a beer because Nate loved beer. So we order beers."

"Did you order three or four?" Deet asked.

"Three, doofus."

"Just checking."

"Well we ordered six, eventually. We had a fair amount of time to kill, and Liam and Gwen started to get all weepy about their dad, telling stories and whatnot. So by the time we get back to the field, we're a bit tipsy. I find the coach and he tells me that he'll guard the gate in the fence around the field, and if we're quick about it, it should work out. So we hop the wall to the field and frantically open up this bag. But like, who wants to touch this stuff? Gwen hadn't thought of that. So we go over to a trash can and find some discarded plastic cups, and we use them to scoop out the ashes. Then we start running the bases, but it's so damned hot, and you can see a clear line where we've scattered the ashes."

"For Christ's sake, Rosemary!" Deet shouted.

"You never told me this part," Dylan remarked.

"Oh, well, I guess I didn't want you to know!" she said with a laugh.

"What were you expecting?" Deet asked. "That they'd just magically blend in with the environment? The gray ashes with the red infield dirt?"

"Gwen hadn't figured on all this," Rosemary shot back, exasperated.

"OK, then what?" Mark asked.

"So we get rid of a few cupfuls of ashes along the baselines, but there's still a ton left. So we head out to the outfield and scatter some there, but the coach starts waving his hands, shouting at us to hurry up, so we hop the wall and get off the field. Then we don't know what to do. So we climb up the bleachers and drop some beneath them, figuring that Nate was more of a spectator anyway, not an athlete, so that seemed sort of appropriate. But there was trash and stuff on the grass below the bleachers, and it seemed so tacky. So we left, still with more than half the ashes left."

"Oh, God," Deet said.

"So we figure, OK, how about the Hall of Fame? That would work. So we walk down there, and out front are all these benches and flowers and happy, shiny people eating ice cream, and there we are, like a bunch of ghouls with our corpse powder."

"A bunch of drunk ghouls," Deet added.

"Tipsy ghouls! We try to surreptitiously dump some ashes in the flowers, but that's not going too well. They're falling on the sidewalk and people are looking at us."

"Oh for heaven's sake," Martina said, leaning in from the kitchen. "You never told me all these details."

"I figured it would upset you," Rosemary said.

"It's upsetting me," Mark said. "That's for sure."

"This is so gross, Mom," Dylan said.

"Oh, you can take it," Rosemary said. "So we leave the Hall of Fame and we go back to the car to regroup. There's still half left, and we're out of ideas. So we decide that maybe a body of water is the way to go. After all, Nate liked boats too. So we drive out toward Otsego Lake, and we stop at this wooded area by the side of the road. We can see the lake through the trees, so we figure we'll just take a little walk through the forest, say a few words, and empty the ashes into the lake."

"And kill how many fish?" Deet asked. "I thought you two were environmentalists."

"Shut *up!*" Rosemary said with another playful kick. "We were under duress! So we set out to walk through the trees, but the leaves are so deep we sink to our waists."

"Ugh," Lizbeth said. "That sounds creepy."

"It was, but that's what happens, I guess, when no one rakes up the leaves of a billion maple trees."

"The fungal life of that forest must have been messed up," Dylan said thoughtfully. "The mycelium should have broken the leaves down."

"You're right, buddy," Rosemary said.

"Thank you, Mr. PBS Voiceover," Deet teased.

"Oh, very nice, Uncle Deet," Rosemary said.

"It's David, remember?"

"Now, now," Mark said soothingly.

"Anyway, so we wade through these ridiculous leaves. It's hard to stand upright, they're so deep, and we get to the lake all sweaty and gross, but there's not much of a shoreline. There's just about a foot of sand before the water begins. Across the lake we can see people swimming and playing in the sun and here we are with our corpse powder, in this shady, moldy place."

"With beer headaches," added Deet.

"How did you know? Yes, with beer headaches, waist-deep in all these musty, old leaves. So Gwen and Liam crouch down on this little bit of sand—there wasn't enough room for me—and Gwen says this prayer-slash-thank-you-slash-parting-wish thing, and they dump the rest of the ashes into the lake. But it creates this puff cloud, and they freak out because they don't want to breathe in the ashes of their father."

"Oh!" Mark and Deet shouted together.

"Oh, no," Lizbeth added.

"And then this gray pall spreads out, like, like. . . ."

"Like a swath of death for all the happy swimmers to bathe in," Deet supplied.

"Oh, will you put a cork in it!" Rosemary scolded.

"Just sayin'."

"So," she said, exhaling loudly and draining her glass. "It was done. They rinsed out the plastic box in the lake and we trudged back to the car through the leaves. Then we got an overpriced motel room and ate greasy take-out and drank the champagne."

"Mom!" Dylan exclaimed. "Is that really what happened?"

"Well, yes," Rosemary said, her face growing hot. She looked at all the stricken faces and thought, What was the problem? She'd just told a great story.

"Sounds like a real romantic getaway," Deet broke in. "Golly, Lizbeth, maybe for *our* next vacation *we* should spend it scattering the ashes of some old geezer. Forget Cabo, forget Bermuda, forget the Maldives. Let's go to Cooperstown and snort some corpse powder!"

"Please," Lizbeth said, shaking her head as if to remove the image.

"Oh, come on," Rosemary said. "We did our best under the circumstances."

"I'm sure you did, honey," Mark said. "I guess it's just not what any of us expected to hear."

"No, it certainly wasn't," Lizbeth agreed.

"Drinking and Dumping, by Rosemary Sabin Ellis." Deet said. "A cautionary tale—though I don't know what it's cautioning me against. But that's nothing, Lizbeth. Watch out or my sister might tell you all about dams and how evil they are, and reservoirs, and silt deprivation, and abatements, and. . . ."

"And Katrina bore all that out a hundred percent, dear brother. If the Mississippi wasn't dammed and leveed up the wazoo, there wouldn't have been that catastrophic flooding in New Orleans."

"I sent money to the Red Cross, Ro. I know what happened in New Orleans."

"Yeah, and we sent money too. But even without global warming contributing to more and more extreme weather, the way the river is managed is creating another disaster down there. If the river were allowed to be a real river, and deposit silt in the delta, then a football field of land wouldn't disappear from southern Louisiana every forty-five minutes. In a few decades, you know, New Orleans is going to be on the open ocean, with no wetlands to protect it, or filter the polluted Mississippi water—"

"Dinner's ready!" Martina called.

"Oh, thank God," Deet said, jumping to his feet. "I'm starved, and I've had enough reality."

"Wimp," Rosemary said, slapping him and stumbling in the process.

"You wonder why I don't spend more time with my family, Dad," Deet said, grabbing Rosemary's wrists and twisting her arms behind her back. "When all I get is abuse and ghoulish tales from this one."

"That's enough, you two," Mark scolded.

⊰ ⊰ ⊰

Dinner was dreadful, as expected, and not just because of the bland food. Dylan was obsessed with explaining the difference between white meat and dark meat chicken, and how the human body had analogous muscles, a topic that either bored or nauseated everyone.

"Let's change the subject, Dylan," Martina said.

"So!" Mark said with forced joviality. "What do you all think about the World Series? Will it be the Sox or the Astros?"

But Rosemary was too despondent to care. She watched Lizbeth in fascinated wonder. She was so polished, yet so dull. What did men see in women like that? Was her thinness that appealing? Her style? Her money? Her urbanity? No, Rosemary thought, none of that mattered so much. What mattered, she theorized, was her contained nature. This woman was quiet, reserved; she was, most definitely, not a pain in the ass. She was a refined porcelain statuette, ready to be placed on some lustrous table, while Rosemary was a loud piece of folk art, a coarse weaving in primary colors.

How did this happen? Rosemary had a college degree, she read books and magazines, she owned a house, she was an activist, she was an entrepreneur. She knew that Georgia O'Keeffe had two Fs in her name, she knew the difference between "infer" and "imply." Yet she was a peasant in the face of this pallid aristocrat. It was so unfair.

After dinner, while the decaf was brewing and the guests were nibbling on a fruit plate, Rosemary fell asleep on the couch. She woke an hour later as Deet and Lizbeth were getting ready to leave for the hotel. She was so ashamed she nearly cried.

"Oh, honey, don't give it another thought," Mark said, locking the door and switching off the outside lights. "You work hard and you're tired. It's not a crime to doze off."

"Lizbeth thinks I'm a drunk."

"Don't be silly. No one thinks you're a drunk."

Mark waited with her while she drank a huge glass of water in the kitchen and swallowed some Tylenol. "So did you like Lizbeth?" she asked.

"Oh, she's a nice girl, I suppose."

"Uh-huh."

"She didn't have much to say, did she? I found her kind of uninteresting."

"You think?" Rosemary said with a snort. "And she wore those heels all night."

"Yes, she was quite formal."

"Why is Deet so weird?"

"Weird?"

"He has never once dated anyone I would want to spend any time with."

"Well, you're very different people. Just look at that car. It couldn't have cost him less than fifty thousand dollars."

"He's crazy."

"I just hope he can truly afford it. I hope he isn't overextending himself."

"Me too."

"That's something I've always admired about you and Liam," Mark said. "How you too are so practical. You seem to live within your means—you have your priorities straight."

Rosemary's eyes filled with tears. Her dad—he saw what she so wanted him to see in her.

"And you're doing a great job with Dylan. I'm sure he's not an easy child to raise."

Those words were like a soaking rain on parched soil. Through newly sprung tears she asked, "Would you like me to tell you the difference between white meat and dark meat?"

"Oh no you don't," Mark said with a laugh.

"Well, thanks, Dad," she said, wiping her eyes with her sleeve. "You don't know how much it means to me to hear you say these things."

"Well I should say them more often. I shouldn't have to have a heart attack before I tell you I'm proud of you."

Her eyes welled up again.

"Now don't get too nutty here," he said. "I'll be fine, and so will you. Good night, honey."

"Good night, Dad," she said, giving him a quick hug. "Thank you."

"Thank you—for coming to visit, and for being my sweet daughter. Sleep tight."

CHAPTER 13 | MARCH, 2007

Interstate 40, California

FIRST THERE WAS THE CALL IN THE PRE-DAWN HOURS. CHEST pains, sweating, and dizziness. Another heart attack. But he was stable, her mother said, and this was her dad after all, so of course he would be OK. She and Liam spent the next two hours extricating themselves from their lives—from the businesses, the house, the cats. They packed, brewed a thermos of coffee, got cash from the ATM, filled up the tank.

And then there was the second call: He was gone. Another heart attack, and this one massive. Gone.

Next came the hyperventilating and the panic, the screaming and the running into the street as if to escape the words. Then the pressure of trying to be sensible in front of Dylan, which was hopeless. Then the desolation, which was absolute.

They drove in near silence, aware without voicing it that these were the last hours in which his absence was not yet real. They existed in a nebula of distress and shock, but the loss—the reality of the loss—was still theory. Somewhere south and west was Martina, a grief-stricken widow. Somewhere south and west was a funeral to be planned, a closet full of clothes that smelled like him, and decades stretching out before them without Mark Sabin. But for now it was just the three of them enveloped in a dazed sorrow, in feelings that morphed into and bridged each other's, a ten-hour drive that was not nearly long enough.

When they arrived and parked in front of the house, they dawdled. They stretched, gathered their bags, looked at each other in silence, and finally trudged to the door, where the nebula dissipated. Martina lay on the living room couch, staring blankly at the ceiling. She began to rise, but Rosemary fell quickly to her knees beside her mother and laid her head next to hers.

"Oh, Mom," she moaned, and began to sob. Martina reached for her daughter's hand, clasping it tightly as tears streamed down her face.

"He was here just last night," Martina whispered. "Just last night."

Dylan turned toward Liam, buried his head in his chest and began to wail. Liam stroked his son's head, uttering soothing sounds as tears ran down his own face.

It took Rosemary some time to realize that the voice coming from the guest bedroom was her grandfather, Ira.

"Grandma and Grandpa are here?" she asked, pulling away from her mother.

"Yes, they got in a few hours ago," Martina said, pushing herself into a sitting position. The bedroom door opened and her grandmother, Ruth, emerged.

"Rosemary!" Ruth called, her arms open before her. Rosemary felt the familiar recoiling she always felt around Ruth, but as they embraced she lingered for a moment in her grandmother's arms. Ruth's signature scent—Burberry London perfume and Lancôme lipstick—unleashed a nostalgic tenderness that renewed her tears. Poor woman, Rosemary thought: She's lost a child.

"I'm so sad for you, Grandma," she said, pulling away to look into Ruth's face. Her skin was taut and suntanned, her makeup perfectly applied. Was this woman ever going to look old?

"It is a dark day," Ruth said, moving toward Dylan. She held his head in her hands, looked into his eyes and said, "Your grandfather loved you very much. He was so proud of you."

Dylan looked up at the woman he hardly knew and said, "OK."

"Liam," Ruth said with a brief hug. "You're our rock."

Liam nodded, looking bewildered.

Rosemary realized then that what they were hearing from the bedroom was Ira on the phone, making funeral arrangements. At the word "casket," she buried her face in Liam's shoulder.

"This is a dark day," Ruth repeated. "I never thought I'd see this."

After a moment Rosemary wiped her face and asked, "Where's Deet?" They'd talked by phone during the drive, and she knew he'd been due to arrive first.

"He's out buying some things," Ruth replied. "Food and drinks. He was so helpful today. He called a lot of people to tell them the news." She was seized with a sob. "People will probably start coming by soon."

Martina leaned back on the couch, her arm shielding her eyes.

"You must be exhausted, driving all this way," Ruth said to Rosemary.

"We're fine," she replied absently, looking around at the familiar room. The life she had known here was now over. It was disorienting to recognize that. The house felt at once both empty and crowded.

"—the arrangements," Ruth said, looking at Rosemary for a reply.

"What?" Rosemary asked.

"We need to talk about the arrangements. Grandpa and I need to know your wishes."

"Huh?"

"Ruth!" Ira called from the bedroom. "I need you!"

"Excuse me," Ruth said, rushing away. Rosemary sighed audibly and returned to her mother's side. Liam and Dylan sat on the other side of Martina.

"It was an ordinary evening," Martina said. "We had dinner and watched the news and went to bed. And then he woke in pain. It was 3:37. He told me to call an ambulance, so I did. They gave him oxygen and some type of medication in the ambulance, and he seemed fine. He spent the whole time reassuring *me*. At the hospital they admitted him into the cardiac care unit, and he fell asleep there. That's when I called you, and David, and Ira and Ruth. It seemed like he was going to be just fine, and I dozed off too. But suddenly the room was full of nurses and doctors and people shouting." She covered her face with her hands and wept. "He had another attack in his sleep. He never woke up. They shocked him and did CPR, but he never came back. I watched them try and try, and then I watched them give up!" She quickly became racked with sobs. "And then they covered him with a sheet! Oh, oh," she moaned. "Someone said 'I'm sorry' and they all started to leave the room, and that was it. He was gone. And that was just this morning," she wept. "A few hours ago. How could this happen?"

"Oh, Mom," Rosemary said through tears, rubbing her mother's back as her shoulders shuddered with sobs.

The kitchen door opened with a grunt. They could hear the crackling of paper bags.

"That must be David," Martina said. As Rosemary and Liam rose, she circled her arms around Dylan and began to sob again.

"Hey," Deet said as Rosemary and Liam came into the kitchen. "How you doing?" He embraced them both briefly. "Does this suck or what?"

"Unbelievable," Rosemary replied.

"Hey, can you help me unload the car? This place is going to start filling up with cops and lawyers any minute. We need to get things ready."

"Wow, Deet." Liam said, poking through the bags. "You took care of all this?"

"I needed something to do. It was a relief to get out of here for a little while."

"Well, let us help with the expense," Liam said.

"Yes," Rosemary said. "Let us help."

"I don't really care either way," Deet replied. "Just help me unpack and get all this going. Come on."

They unloaded vegetable trays and bags of cheese cubes and cases of juices and sparkling water and dumped ice into coolers and warmed up taquitos and mini-quiches and set out plastic cups and plates and arranged boxed cookie assortments onto serving plates. They set out wine glasses, uncorked a white and a red, and lined up the beer choices in the fridge. And then they encountered Ira.

"Hello, kids," he said stiffly, stepping into the kitchen as if he were entering the home of a stranger. He delivered perfunctory hugs and stepped back to take in the spread. "Thanks for doing all this," he said.

He had lost weight and was shorter than he used to be, but he still took up so much space. He was eighty-four, she believed, but he, too, looked suntanned and fit.

He popped the top off a Grolsch and filled his meaty hand with cheese cubes. "This is something else, huh?" he asked, taking a long pull from the beer. "No one should outlive their children."

"No, they shouldn't," Liam agreed. They all fell silent, but soon the murmuring of Dylan and Martina could be heard from the living room.

"Thank God for the little ones," Ira said. "They keep you going." They all fell silent again as Ira sipped his beer. "I'm going to miss him," he said, and began to weep in a blustery, snorfley way. Liam, Rosemary, and Deet looked away, embarrassed. After a moment he composed himself and said, "We need to talk about the service. Certain prayers, whether we want flowers or music. He'll be buried tomorrow in Forest Lawn, near Palm Springs."

"Huh?" Deet said, voicing their collective surprise. "Why there?"

"I bought plots for all of us years ago," Ira replied. "I've even bought yours and Rosemary's."

"What?" Rosemary yelped.

"If you don't want it, that's OK. I understand you and Liam don't follow Jewish tradition, but they're there if you want them. When the time comes."

"I had no idea," Rosemary said. "But why Palm Springs?"

"Years ago they were a bargain," Ira stated. "A much better deal than Santa Barbara. Regardless, you know that delaying burial is unacceptable, so the service will be tomorrow at 2 p.m."

The words hung heavily in the air until Dylan walked into the kitchen.

"What are you all talking about?" he asked. At ten, he stood as tall as Liam's shoulder. He would likely have Mark's height. The adults all gazed at him intently, as if he were a zoo exhibit.

"What?" he asked.

"Hey, buddy," Liam said. "Unfortunately, we're talking about Grandpa's funeral."

Dylan leaned his body against the counter, folded his arms over his chest, and stared at the floor.

"Well, first things first," Deet said and uncorked a bottle of wine. "This is for us. The guests get something, shall we say, a bit more modest."

He poured the heavenly pinot noir and a Coke for Dylan, and they all raised their glasses.

"To Dad," he declared, and they toasted Mark in tears.

Martina and Ruth were suddenly at the kitchen doorway, watching in silence. Martina gazed around at the food trays and the coolers of drinks. "My, this is something," she said. "It looks like a party." She choked on a sob as they heard the front door push open.

"Hello?" a man's voice called. "Martina?" They all moved into the living room to greet Hugh, who had worked with Mark at the sheriff's office. He looked aggrieved and bewildered. "Oh, Martina," his wife, Nell, said, hugging her while balancing a casserole in her hand. "We're so sorry."

Next came more cops and their wives, and paralegals arriving straight from the office in cheap suits, bearing flowers. And lawyers in better suits, bearing better flowers. They ate and they drank and they offered their condolences and they whispered about how exactly it happened and they asked Dylan how old he was, and one actually uttered that pathetic platitude that the

Lord works in mysterious ways and another emptied the trash when it filled with paper plates and they all said, "If there's anything we can do. . . ."

And finally it was quiet again. Dylan fell asleep on the couch, Martina lay on her bed alone, Ira and Ruth went to the Best Western, and Rosemary, Deet, and Liam sat around the kitchen table and cried.

"Unfuckingbelievable," Deet said, pouring them all more wine. "He was only sixty-two. What a ripoff."

"He should have had another twenty good years," Rosemary agreed.

Liam rubbed his own chest in a sleepy daze.

"Don't tell me you're having a heart attack now," Deet said.

"Nah," Liam said. "I just feel so tight, like someone knocked the wind out of me."

"And you lost your own dad not long ago," Deet noted.

"This is so much worse," Liam said as Rosemary rubbed his shoulders. "I don't know how I'm ever going to get used to this."

"And my God, what about Mom?" Rosemary asked. "How is she going to live alone? She doesn't even know how to balance her own checkbook, let alone keep a house up and everything else. How is she going to fill her days?"

"Crap, who knows?" Deet replied. "I guess we're going to have to visit her more."

"Maybe she should start going to church or something," Liam suggested.

"No, no!" Rosemary and Deet shouted together, raising their hands in defense.

"We don't need her doing her 'Hail' or 'Father' thing," Deet explained.

"Yeah, no power praying for days and weeks on end," Rosemary added.

"All right, all right," Liam said. "I'm just saying she needs some friends, some company of some sort."

"Maybe she'll move closer to one of us," Deet offered. "Probably to you, since you have Dylan."

"What a thought," Liam said. "I really can't imagine her leaving this place."

"Whatever happened to Lizbeth, by the way?" Rosemary asked.

"Oh," Deet said with a wave of his hand. "That ended months ago."

"Are you seeing anyone else?"

"Not really."

"But you're still in Phoenix. That's a record."

"Yeah, nearly four years. You know, Liam, I need to go to Albany in a few weeks. I thought I might look your sister up."

"She's married, you know."

"Yeah, thanks, asswipe," he said as Rosemary and Liam laughed. "It would be nice to visit her while I'm out there. Maybe I'll call on your mom, too."

"They'd like that."

With the wine bottle empty, stupefied, they found their way to bed.

Sleep came quickly, but at 3:30 Rosemary woke, stirred by a howling wind. She eased the bedroom door open and slipped into the living room. The house was silent except for the refrigerator's hum and the wind buffeting the house from the west. Knickknacks on the front windowsill stood in garish silhouette against the moonlit night. She unlatched the front door and crept outside, instinctively closing her eyes against the windborne grit.

The desert night was cold. She huddled on the front steps and brooded over the idea that this sinister wind had come to take her dad away. The phone call from her mother, not even twenty-four hours ago, played over and over in her mind, Martina's words resounding like a shrill alarm that destroyed her charming dream—that she would have her dad forever. She was just thirty-eight and he was gone, and it was all wrong. Would she ever believe someday that this was part of some divine plan? No, she would not. It was wrong. It was broken. It was a rip-off.

She went back into the house to warm up, sneaking a fleece throw out from beneath Dylan, who was curled up in his sleeping bag. With the blanket wrapped around her in the moonlit room she watched her son sleep, aware that the time when she could do such a thing was fleeting. His face was becoming more defined, less round, and his jaw thrust forward now from under his mop of hair. Swaddled in his Gore-Tex and down chrysalis, he was a pupa ready to transform. He would indeed be a man soon, and her dad would not be there to see it.

She recalled Mark's voice then, its rich, bassoon-like timbre, and how he emphasized the o's when he said "Hello Rosie" so that her name sounded like a polished wooden sphere. She would never hear that voice again, and tomorrow she would see his coffin lowered into the ground. She sat down heavily on the carpet, leaned against the couch and wept, and fell into a numbing sleep as the sky lightened.

When Liam woke her at eight, she was stiff and disoriented. Dylan had already cleared away his sleeping bag, and she felt like a forgotten husk. A wine headache throbbed on her forehead like low-lying clouds before a storm. At the bathroom door she heard Dylan singing in the shower, grunting out that same infernal Green Day song he'd been singing for months.

"Hurry up, Dylan!" she shouted.

"I just got in, Mom!" he whined.

"There's only one shower in this house. And it's a desert, you know!" she shouted back.

There were too many people to deal with in the kitchen, and no decent coffee. Deet kept taking phone calls on his Blackberry, and Martina was impossible to motivate. "Mom," Rosemary harped, "it's your turn to shower. Mom, eat something. Mom, Grandma says they'll be here by ten. Mom, find your good black purse. Mom, let's go."

By noon they were in a limousine on the way to Palm Springs, with Rosemary quietly seething. Any tenderness she had felt toward her grandparents the day before had vanished. She was furious that she had to sit in this ridiculous vehicle and be driven to a place that had nothing to do with her dad. He had lived his life in Twentynine Palms, not in Palm Springs.

How many local folks would make this trip today? She guessed none. This was bullshit.

After a brief service, Mark was to be buried in the Jewish section of Forest Lawn Memorial even though the last Jewish ritual he had observed was his bar mitzvah. When Ira and Ruth said they'd wanted to incorporate everyone's wishes into the service, they only asked about the superficial crap. What a crock. The damned place was too far for Martina to make the trip on her own. But Ira had told her early on that this was a done deal, and she did not fight him. Now she sat next to Rosemary like a pouting child, staring out the tinted windows in silence.

The chilling wind continued throughout the graveyard service, and the rabbi couldn't give a rat's ass about her dad or the mourners. Of course he didn't know Mark at all—he had to check his notes to make sure he said the right name at the right times—so the service turned out to be a combination of incomprehensible Hebrew and generic admonitions to be grateful for Mark's life and now to let him go. A couple from Santa Barbara sitting behind Rosemary erupted in chatting over and over, no matter how ruthlessly she sneered at them, and some fatass man she didn't even recognize sat next to Deet in the front row, in the row reserved for family, and coughed continually. It took a lot of restraint for Rosemary to remain quiet throughout the service, to resist hurling dirt clods at the rabbi, or pushing her grandfather into the hole.

After a while she stopped listening to the words and focused her anger on the grass. What body of water, she wondered, and what native landscape were being destroyed to water these acres of monocropped turf? Did the water come from Mono Lake, or the Colorado River, or was it sucking dry some underground aquifer instead? Why didn't this seem to bother anyone else?

When it was finally over, she was exhausted and her headache had become crushing. Then the mourners followed Ira and Ruth to a restaurant, where a row of uniformed servers dished out chicken florentine, baby potatoes, and carrots with thyme. But this was just more bullshit—if Ira cared about true Jewish tradition, the community was supposed to provide this food, she'd learned on Wikipedia the day before. And why hadn't he torn his clothing? Obviously it was OK to pick and choose among customs and traditions to suit his needs. He had hijacked her dad's funeral, and she believed she would hate him for it forever.

Getting the food down was impossible for Rosemary. Forty-eight hours earlier, her dad had been alive. He'd gone to work that day. He was investigating allegations of fraud in a municipality near Barstow. He was fit. He was well. He loved his job, and he loved her. And now he was in the ground.

"Rosemary? Is that you?" A scrawny woman in a lime green dress interrupted her sullen trance. Rosemary had no idea who she was. "This must be your family," the woman said, shaking Liam's hand. "Pamela Pratt."

"Liam Ellis," Liam replied, shaking her hand. "And this is our son, Dylan."

Pamela Pratt? Miss Pratt? Her fourth-grade teacher?

"Oh my, so grown up," she said to Dylan. "It seems like just yesterday your grandma told me you were a newborn.

"Your father was a good man," she said to Rosemary. "I'm sorry for your loss."

"Thank you," Rosemary managed.

"And I hadn't seen your brother since his high school graduation. My goodness, but he's a hotshot."

"Yeah," Rosemary said blankly.

"He told me about his job in Arizona. Now I'd like to know how a boy who never went to college finds himself negotiating water rights contracts for a golf course developer. Now that is something."

Rosemary and Liam shot each other confused looks.

"Water rights?" Rosemary asked Miss Pratt. "Deet buys water rights?"

"Well, that's what he told me," Miss Pratt replied, her brow furrowing. "Is something wrong?"

"No, no," Rosemary forced a smile. "It's nice to see you too."

"Well you take care," Miss Pratt said, shaking their hands again.

"Can we leave? I hate this place," Dylan whined. "I don't know any of these people and the chicken tastes like shoes."

"Not yet," Rosemary replied, and turned to see Deet walking toward them with three glasses of wine in his hands.

"Can you believe this thing?" he asked, nodding his head toward the crowd. "Who are these people? I tried to get Mom out of there, but Grandma is parading her around like some little doll on display. Here, I got us some wine. I think it might be Manischevitz, God help us."

"Thanks," Liam said gratefully, taking his glass.

"You buy water rights for a living?" Rosemary demanded.

"Huh?" Deet replied.

"You buy water rights for a living? For a golf course developer?" Rosemary repeated.

"Ro," Liam cautioned. "Not now."

"It's part of my job to buy water rights, yes. Do you want this?" Rosemary took the glass he offered and set it roughly on the table, splattering red wine onto the white linen.

"You buy ancestral water rights from families so some dickhead developer can water miles of turf for rich people?" She'd read about this happening in Northern New Mexico. People whose families had lived on the same land for generations would sometimes sell their water rights for $5,000, a tiny sum for people living in a high desert often stricken with drought. For the cost of a used car or a semester at UNM, they would sell forever their right to draw water from the Rio Grande—or from their own wells. It was an everyday tragedy.

"What the fuck is your problem?" Deet hissed.

"Ro, you can talk about this another time," Liam said, reaching for his wife's hand, but she lurched away from him.

"You're acting like this doesn't matter," she said to Liam.

"People own water rights and they don't even know it," Deet continued. "It's an unused resource for them, like money in a mattress, so I take it off their hands. They get some cash and the golf course gets its water. Everybody's happy."

"Everybody's happy," Rosemary mocked. "In New Mexico, families who've owned water rights to their land since the Treaty of Guadalupe Hidalgo are hoodwinked into selling to people like you."

"Hoodwinked? Don't you dare insult me like that."

"Ro!" Liam shouted.

"So you tell yourself that you're not exploiting the poor," she persisted. Her head pounded now, and she brought her hands to her forehead, trying to soothe herself amid her peculiar fury. She knew Liam was right, but she couldn't stop.

"I'm not holding a gun to anyone's head," Deet said through clenched teeth. "I place an ad and they respond. We consult the Water Planning Division. I make an offer, they make a decision. I'm not exploiting anyone."

"And the Colorado River continues to be drained for bullshit like fountains in the desert and swimming pools in every backyard." Her head seemed to explode now, and she pressed all ten fingers to her face.

"And that's all my fault," Deet said, raising his voice. "I forgot that I'm powerful enough to single-handedly destroy the mighty Colorado."

Guests at nearby tables were beginning to take notice of the quarrel, some scurrying away, some observing intently.

"Please, you guys, stop," Liam pleaded.

"You're full of shit," Rosemary spat.

"Why are you being so mean, Mom?" Dylan cut in.

"You know what, Ro?" Deet continued, lowering his voice to a pointed hiss. "You're full of shit. It's not *your* river. It's not even your goddamned state! I've been listening to your lectures for years, ever since you smoked your first joint and got all groovy with Pete. Remember him? Pete the dealer? Pete the human trafficker? And let me ask you—have I ever lectured you on what you should or shouldn't do? How about living in that suburb of yours? I don't see you walking to work. How about all the wood you burn at the café? How about having a kid, for that matter? What about overpopulation? I've been listening to your sanctimonious bullshit forever, and you know what? It ends now."

He stomped away, down the carpeted steps and out of the restaurant as the Ellis family looked on. Despite the noise of the place and the relentless smooth jazz, it suddenly seemed so quiet. Rosemary turned to Liam, hoping to find comfort, but he was furious.

"You just had to do that, huh, Ro?" he fumed. "You just had to trash your brother at your father's funeral. You just couldn't set it aside for one day."

"He deserved it," she said, instantly aware of how stupid she sounded.

"No, he didn't," Liam argued, lowering his voice to lose the attention of the onlookers nearby. "He didn't deserve any of it. He's been nothing but a gentleman since we arrived. Ever since I met him, actually, he's been nothing but a gentleman."

"Well I'm sorry," Rosemary said, sitting down heavily. Her chest was pounding now and she felt nauseous. Suddenly awash in regret and sorrow, she let her head drop onto her folded arms on the table and began to sob loudly. Liam sat down next to her and stared blankly at the gathering of well-dressed people who had driven down from Santa Barbara to pay their respects to the Sabin boy. Then he began to cry too, and Dylan joined in.

"So," Dylan asked through his racking sobs. "Can we go now?"

CHAPTER 14 | NOVEMBER, 2008

Twentynine Palms, California

THE COFFEE WAS GOOD AND HOT. PROBABLY A BLUE MOUN-
tain varietal, though roasted a bit light for her taste. The
breakfast burrito was lame, full of salsa instead of chile, but that
was California for you. But the sun was perfect, warm and full,
helping her breathe. It was always there, the sun, something
you could count on, with its big constant face.

Talk about lame. Gee, maybe she should write a poem about
that. Certainly she was the first person ever to notice that the
sun came up every day no matter how fucked up your life was.
No, wait—it was hot, too. She'd have to include that unique
perspective in her groundbreaking poem. No, not a poem, a
collection—maybe "a slim volume of contemporary verse," in
which she would also note that although the moon looked different every day, it was still the same moon. Oh my, such a par-
adox. Huh. Maybe writing the worst book of poems ever
should be her next project. At least she wouldn't have to get a
bank loan for that venture.

"Ro," Deet asked, shoving her gently. "You with us?" He
took a huge bite of his burrito and reached into his briefcase,
retrieving several file folders. He rested his laptop on the stack
to protect them from the light wind.

"I'm here," she replied heavily.

"What does 'no tomatoes' mean?" Liam groused, unrolling his burrito to pick out the chunks of tomato that had stowed away in the salsa.

"OK," Deet said with a sigh. "Let's figure out some stuff here."

They sat around a table at Bucklin Park Downtown Plaza, one of Rosemary's favorite places in Twentynine Palms. With its old palm trees and one of the city's trademark murals, it was a place she hoped would make this meeting easier. They'd left Martina and Dylan home to eat scrambled egg whites and watch "My Three Sons."

"So these old TV shows," Rosemary interrupted. "What's with that?"

"Mom?" Deet asked.

"Yeah, she just watches old TV shows all day?"

"No, just when I'm here and she can use my laptop. Other times she watches old movies on Netflix."

"You actually got Mom to use Netflix?"

"I know, it's weird," Deet replied, responding to an alert from his iPhone. "She says the old movies calm her nerves. I maintain her queue online and she mails back the DVDs."

Rosemary stared blankly at an incomprehensible steel sculpture as she absorbed the latest example of how Deet had suddenly stepped in to take care of Martina. It had been eighteen months since her dad died, a period of sadness and disorientation for the whole family, but it had not played out as she'd expected. She'd thought she'd speak to Martina every day, to visit frequently, and, frankly, to be overwhelmed by her mother's needs. But instead Deet had taken on most of the burden, and he tended to communicate through Liam. Ever since her blowup at Mark's funeral, he'd been cool toward her.

A gust of wind fluttered the wrappers and napkins on the table and they all rushed to secure them with phones and coffee cups.

"Sorry," Rosemary said, knowing that Deet was doing her a favor by meeting here. He'd suggested his hotel room, but she implored him to meet her and Liam at Bucklin. Being indoors to talk about selling their parents' house—something she had protested vehemently for months—was something that would feel utterly oppressive inside a hotel room. She was getting better at knowing her limits.

"Real estate values have really started to slip here," Deet said, pulling a market analysis report from one of his folders. "We need to move quickly. She's still in a good position, since she owns the house outright. If credit is too tight for a potential buyer, we can offer to owner-finance it."

Martina was just sixty-one years old and remarkably healthy. She did not need to sell her home and move into a goddamned retirement community. So there had been a break-in at her home. Of course it had been traumatic, but she was unhurt, and nothing of great value had been stolen: the TV, her purse and—why?—the George Foreman grill. She could have a security system installed, Rosemary argued, with high-tech locks on the doors and windows. She could join a neighborhood watch group. She could get a dog. There were any number of solutions better than waiting to die in some old people's ghetto.

But Martina was unmoveable. In the five months since the break-in she had done little else than prepare to move, relentlessly organizing and categorizing the family's possessions and shipping much of it off to Rosemary and Deet. Envelopes arrived at random, labeled, "Report cards and other school papers" or "Letters from college." A large box had arrived just last week labeled, "Birthday dresses." Rosemary had no idea that Martina had saved every dress that she'd worn on her birthday until she was ten. And there they were, like ghosts from a forgotten land: A strawberry-festooned shift with matching panties; a white sailor dress with pinstripes and a red bow; a skirt with loud daisies against a hot pink bodice. Some she recalled only from photos, but a few unleashed memories so visceral that she was overwhelmed with nostalgia.

After a while Martina also began meting out memorabilia of her husband's life. "Photos of Dad," one envelope read, and another said, "Mark – Certificates." Was she keeping anything for herself? Rosemary stopped opening most of the packages, leaving them stacked in her bedroom closet. They were too much.

But at least this was slightly less unnerving than Martina's obsession with organizing and categorizing her own feelings. She'd picked up a brochure on the Five Stages of Grief at the funeral home after Mark's service, and it became her new gauge of, well, everything.

"I believe I have moved through Denial and am in the Anger Stage," she said to Rosemary about six weeks after Mark passed. "It is just not fair that your father passed on so young. He ate well and exercised and had a manageable stress level."

This shocked Rosemary, who had simply asked, "So how are you doing, Mom?" But it soon became the norm.

"I've found myself thinking strange thoughts lately," she told Rosemary a few months later. "Last night I woke up and forgot your father was gone. I went to use the rest room and wondered why he wasn't in bed. It was strange. But then when I realized that he died four months ago, I found myself telling God—out loud even!—that if he would just bring Dad back, I wouldn't tell anyone that he died once. I wouldn't tell a soul; it would be our little secret and he could trust me."

"Oh, Mom," Rosemary replied, beginning to cry. She had had similar thoughts, and was relieved to think she could share them with her mother, but the door quickly closed.

"I think this means I have moved on to the Bargaining Stage of grief," Martina said.

The Depression Stage, according to Martina, lasted the longest, approximately eight months, but it abruptly ended when "that monster" broke into the house while she slept and defiled her home. That was in June, just a few days before Father's Day, which added to Martina's outrage.

"I must move out of this house," Martina told her children. "I will never feel safe here again."

"But Mom," Rosemary whined in a fit of nostalgic sorrow. "It's our home! It's full of memories! It's still Dad's place."

"Your father is gone," Martina insisted. "I am now in the Acceptance Stage, and you should be too."

But Rosemary was also grieving another loss: She had lost the café. What had been promising and profitable just a year earlier had quickly crashed and burned. It's a funny thing, but when the economy tanks and people go broke, they find it in themselves to brew their own coffee and make their own sandwiches. And when gas costs $4.40 a gallon, they question whether they need to drive to Fire Ring to sip a $5 glass of "everyday" wine and listen to some dude sing when they could stay home, drink a whole bottle of wine, and watch movies on their TiVo.

So the café died—but the bank note lived on. Somehow she and Liam were supposed to pay off the $32,000 business loan although Ellis Landscaping had all but crashed, and Liam ran it further into the ground by keeping his crew on for weeks after the work had dried up. That was another thing people could do for themselves when they were unemployed: pull their own damn weeds and water their own stupid flowers.

So she was looking for a job. Liam had already found one and seemed to have settled in to his new routine. She had some prospects, but the pay was a joke. To be earning ten or twelve dollars an hour at age forty was just pathetic. She was pathetic. And the house? The house with the beautiful kitchen and the water catchment system and the solar panels and the stone fountain? The house wasn't worth shit. If they sold it now, after paying off their debts, they'd have nothing left. And to think they'd hoped to send Dylan to private school by seventh grade. Right, like that was going to happen.

But it would have been a colossal waste of money anyway because Dylan hated school, and had been nurturing that hatred since. . .was it fifth grade? Yes, fifth grade. Suddenly Rosemary thought she could pinpoint the time. It was around Thanksgiving when the class was a few weeks into a money management project. The kids were supposed to decide on an imaginary career, research the salary for a particular job, and gather information on the expenses of daily life. Then they were to devise a budget. Dylan had researched being an architect—he'd recently begun noticing how he felt good or bad in particular buildings—and was happy with his project. But he came home from school one day scowling.

"This girl Jennifer," he said, "do you know what career she chose? She decided to be a waitress. A waitress, Mom. She could pretend to be anything, and that's all she could come up with. So in her budget she could only afford a tiny apartment. What is wrong with her? Why would anybody do that?"

"What did other people choose?" Rosemary asked.

"One girl was a ballet dancer, one was a doctor. Blake was also a doctor too, and this other kid was a rodeo rider. One kid was a lawyer. Oh, and a bunch of them—like half the class—said they wanted to be photographers, but that's only because this girl Mariah said it first. But then Jennifer says, 'waitress.' I wanted to puke. And then you know what? We had to write this stupid thing: 'If you could have one wish that would change your life for the better, what would it be?' First of all, who can come up with a good answer to that in like five minutes? Anyway, so it's time to *share*," he said with a pronounced sneer. "And all the girls say 'world peace' or 'everyone would be nice to each other' or something and someone says there would be no pollution, but do you know what this one kid said? He said he would make the price of gas lower so it wouldn't be so hard to visit your family when they're in prison far away. His uncle is in prison in Texas, and visiting him costs too much. I mean, why wouldn't he just wish that his uncle wasn't in prison? Or that there would be no prisons? Or that gas is free? No, all he can think of is to make gas cheaper. How can people think that way?"

An uncle in prison. Ugh. Wasn't his school supposed to be all cozy and middle class? She took a deep breath then, gathering courage to ask the next question.

"And what did you wish for?" she asked.

"That I would never have to go to school again and pretend to be friends with so many idiots and listen to so many dumb teachers."

But there he was watching "My Three Sons" with her mother, evidence of a bond that Rosemary could scarcely understand. They were family, of course they loved each other, but they couldn't be more different, her son and her mother. Yet he seemed to find his grandmother's presence soothing, and lately he played a unique role in her life that even Liam had noticed—he was the only one who could push her out of her routine responses to the world. Like last night. Martina had bought chicken breasts for dinner—piccata cut, about a quarter-inch thick—and had marinated them in lemon juice and black pepper. But somehow Dylan convinced her to let him bake them. After he shuffled the women out of the kitchen, he proceeded to arrange the cutlets into the shapes of continents. On a large cookie sheet, he laid out a map of the world in chicken. He even remembered to cut away some of the largest bodies of water and use those pieces for major islands. When he set the pan down on the table, alongside the baked yams and salad, he matter-of-factly explained that he'd had to leave out most of the Pacific islands because they were too small, he'd forgotten Baja California completely, and he was sorry that Panama had burned. The adults were speechless.

As to the old TV shows, he said he liked "seeing how other people think." But then why did he have so little interest in the living, breathing people in his life? He did have one good friend, Kristopher, who spent a fair amount of time at their house. For a while they were obsessed with building a fort out of straw bales. They had quite a little shantytown going on the side of the house, with furniture made out of scrap wood and old blankets for doors, but eventually Liam needed the bales for a landscaping job. Next it was inventing trampoline games. There was "Mummy" and "Crack the Egg" among others, including one that Rosemary eventually banned, called "Punch." Then they spent about a month on "The List of Surprising Truths," trolling the Internet and competing to see who could unearth the strangest factoids.

Next they invented their own language code. Since so much of human interaction was pointless drivel, they reasoned, they would streamline it by assigning numbers to the most common questions and responses. One through ten were greetings. Instead of wasting time saying, "How's it going?" a person could just ask, "One?" Then, rather than bother with "OK. You?" the other could simply reply, "Two." Or, if he were feeling poorly, he could say, "Three" to indicate a bad mood or "Four" to mean he was sick, and so on. Eleven through twenty were the what-do-you-want-to-do type questions, and twenty-one through thirty were common complaints. They were working on thirty through thirty-nine, which would be about Legos, when they quit, saying it was too hard to remember it all.

As odd as it was, she had found herself wanting to apply the Dylan-Kris language to her own life back when she was running the café. People would ask the same questions over and over, even though signs everywhere answered the questions. She might be standing beneath a sign that read "All of our dairy products are organic," and someone would ask, "Is the half-and-half organic?" It happened just as often with questions about whether she accepted credit cards or allowed dogs on the patio and a hundred other things. Rosemary wished she could just point to a sign or toss out a one-syllable response rather than smile and answer cheerfully, over and over again.

God, she missed the café. It was lonely being unemployed. Sure, some of her interactions there were tedious or annoying, but listening to people talk about their lives was altogether fascinating. She had taken to writing down a lot of what she heard, and had even begun an experimental project on the inside of a large window on the north side of the building. She typed up all sorts of things she overheard people say—sometimes single quotes and sometimes dialogue—and printed them out. Then she taped the sheets to the window and listened again as people remarked on them. Although she worried that they would think she was a creeper, and that the whole idea was an invasion of privacy, the customers loved it. If they recognized their own words and objected, she never heard about it; the window seemed to offer a blend of voyeurism and confirmation of who they were. They snickered at political tidbits ("Did you hear that when John McCain was asked how many houses he owned, he said he didn't know?"). They raised their eyebrows at relationship talk. ("I don't know how much longer I can stay with someone who's so fat and so depressed!") They were chilled by other people's parenting worries. ("It's not the first time he was picked up by the cops.") They commented on world events. ("There's no way Iran's nuclear power is for peaceful purposes.") They were disturbed by admonitions. ("Watch what you 'Like' on Facebook, Corporations use it to gather information about you.") They paused at the philosophical musings. ("If we all just stuck with one idea and saw it through—if we were all total libertarians or total communists, either would work. But all we do is compromise, so nothing ever works.") They laughed at the many non sequiturs. ("It was while we were playing Pictionary that I realized I needed a new dog.") And they marveled at the weird advice. ("Whenever you get a new car, you should give the fender a good whack with a ball peen hammer. That way you don't have to worry about maintaining perfection.")

But in the end, when the text began to reflect the worsening economy, people seemed to derive genuine comfort from the window, and Rosemary realized it was because no one wanted to admit to their friends how scared they were. The first quote about the economy was, "I'm trying to sell my RV, but if I drop the price any more, I won't even be able to pay off the loan." Next was, "What if I lose my retirement savings? I'm already sixty-two." Then, "My broker told me, 'Don't sink your inheritance into paying off your mortgage. Let me make it work for you.' Well, it's gone now."

Then Rosemary figured out something better: She placed several markers on the windowsill and hung a sign that said "Express yourself here." Soon the "overheard" window became a sort of public conversation window. The statement "I just lost $300,000 and I'm sick about it" brought the reply, "I wish I had $300,000 to lose." It didn't take long after "I can see why people threw themselves out the window back in 1929," before "A human life is sacred. Get help" appeared. When someone wrote, "I've been thinking positive for all these years, believing I would receive what I needed. What went wrong?" another replied, "God doesn't care about money." Eventually the window was covered, but soon the café grew quieter and quieter. After operating at a loss for three months, and with Ellis Landscaping becoming less and less able to support the family let alone the café, Rosemary closed the doors.

When the business started to slip, Liam suggested she ask Deet if he wanted to invest or lend her money, but she refused. She looked at Deet now, in his fitted button-down shirt and Rolex, and wondered if she'd made the right decision. He probably would have said yes, but it would have just galled her. It would be like having a local organic farm bankrolled by Monsanto.

There was one overheard conversation, though, that she wrote down but never put on the window. She told herself she held it back because it was too recognizable, but she secretly knew there was more to it.

Five friends, in their forties and fifties gathered around a table drinking beer and snacking on salsa and chips. From what she could gather, they had run into each other after a show downtown at the Lensic, and agreed to meet up at Fire Ring since they all lived nearby. They were the last table of the night, so it was easy to hear their conversation, which had first been about the show and then about their kids' schools and college plans. But sometime during their third round of beers, after one of the women talked about how awful it was to care for her stepfather as he died a long, slow death from leukemia, the tall, blonde woman said, "Well, I've been taking steps to make sure that never happens to me."

"How's that?" someone asked.

"Every time I have a medical issue that is even a little bit painful, I ask for pain meds. You know how I had tendinitis once really bad, and I've had back problems, and I had all that work done on my teeth? So I get the script and I fill it, but I put the pills in the freezer. I never use them; I just save them. If I ever decide it's time to go, I can go."

"Whoa!" said one of the men. "Are you serious?"

"I've been tempted to do exactly that," said another, "but I figure I'd probably just barf it all up and end up in a psych ward, which would be worse than dying from cancer or whatever."

"That's why you need suppositories," said the third woman, who was wearing flowered cowboy boots. "I do the same thing Kim does, but I tell the doctor that I have a very sensitive stomach, and I get suppositories. You can't barf them up."

"Oh, for Christ's sake, Darlene, are you for real?" one of the men shouted.

"Of course!" the woman exclaimed. "I'm a nurse. I got this."

"Well, shit," said the man with the grizzled beard. "I figure that's what trains are for. Thank God for the Rail Runner. Now I can just lay down on the tracks whenever I've had enough. Sounds simpler than drugs."

"Sounds messy," someone said.

"But it's outdoors," the bearded one said in defense. "They can just hose me off and let the ravens take care of the rest."

"You're all whacked," said the skinny guy in the vest, and the others erupted in protest.

"You want to sit there with your living will and wither away forever? asked the nurse. "Hoping your loved ones obey your DNR, or wait for some hospital doc to mercifully take too long to respond until you finally croak?"

"I don't know," the skinny guy said. "This is all just so morbid."

"Wait till you spend months with someone who's terminally ill," the first woman said. "You sit there with hospice pumping in the morphine, waiting for the right time to call the rest of the family, worrying you'll call them too early and everyone will sit around wondering what to do with themselves—too guilty to say they wish it would just end—or you'll wait too long and everyone will arrive after dear old Dad has departed and they'll feel like they wasted the plane fare. Then there's the hospital bed in the living room, the IV, the machines. Shit, I'm with Kim and Darlene. As a matter of fact, I nabbed as much of my stepdad's opiods as I could after he passed. I've got them stashed away."

They sat in silence for a few moments until the tall man finally said, "Ice floes."

"Huh?" someone asked.

"Ice floes," he repeated. "I figure the Eskimos have it down. Grandpa can't chew his meat anymore? Grandma can't hardly walk? Send them out to sea on an ice floe. It's quiet, it's simple, and it costs nothing." He drew his hand away from his body in a straight, sweeping motion. "Gone."

They all chuckled. Then the nurse said, "You'd have to move to Alaska."

"No problem," the man said. "It's gonna be my new business: For a coupla thousand bucks, I'll fly you up to the Yukon, say a prayer for you, and shove you off."

Kim said, "The health insurance companies would love it."

"Hell, they'd invest in it!" shouted the skinny guy, and they all started to stand up and make their goodbyes.

The conversation played again and again in Rosemary's mind until it began to worry her. Did she secretly want to die? She searched her mind for a hidden death wish, but no, it wasn't there. What was there was a need to rest. Just for a while. She wanted to feel safe. The adventure of the business was great while it lasted, but now she was terrified that she and Liam were becoming poor people. Poor people! How could they become poor people?

And she just felt so stupid. Stupid from the moment she woke up to the moment she fell asleep. Stupid for letting this happen. They should have saved more during the good times, lived more frugally, not added on to their house. If they'd been super careful even when money was good, they wouldn't be in this mess now. But hindsight was 20/20, as everybody seemed to be muttering these days, and life was for learning. She thought she knew plenty—how to run a home and a business, how to parent a kid, how to stay married, how to tread lightly on the earth—but all the rules had changed. Or maybe there were so many lessons to learn in life that you just couldn't learn them all. Maybe it was like the common cold—after you got over one, you would be forever immune to that virus, but there were so many viruses in the world that you could never be immune to all of them. And evidently there was an endless supply of mistakes to be made. She'd always thought she was above it all, only to find out that she *was* "it." Just an ordinary turd in the shitpile of life.

Truth be told, she felt like she had been rejected *by* life. It was like that old Starkist tuna commercial: "But Charlie, Starkist doesn't want tunas with good taste; Starkist wants tunas that taste good!" Who cared how smart she was, or how strong her principles? When push came to shove, the world just wanted what it could get out of her, and she suddenly had nothing more to give.

Another gust of wind forced her out of her sad reverie. Deet and Liam were hunched over Deet's phone, viewing recently sold properties in Twentynine Palms. She gathered up the cups and wrappers from their breakfast and dropped them in a trash can across the plaza, then leaned over to stretch her back. When she straightened back up, a short, stocky guy was standing in front of her.

"Oh!" Rosemary sputtered. The man said nothing. He looked at her without curiosity from under the brim of a cap that read, "Video Kingdom." He looked like he had Down Syndrome. Where did he come from? Where were his people?

"I'm Frankie," he said.

"I'm Rosemary."

The two stared at each other for a few moments, and then Frankie moved on

Rosemary stared after him for several seconds and was startled when a group of teen-age boys approached. She stumbled a bit to make way for them, and tried to establish eye contact, expecting an apology. But they seemed not to have seen her at all.

"Dude!" one of them shouted to his friend. "Those bitches were so fucked up!" The others laughed and continued loping away in their sagging pants, leaving Rosemary stunned. No, they hadn't seen her at all.

She was used to not being looked at by men anymore. A friend had once told her—and she was right—that the only people who look at forty-year-old women were old men and other forty-year-old women who hope you're fatter than they are—but to be utterly invisible was another thing altogether.

It had happened once last summer as well, at the beach in San Diego. Liam and Dylan had gone for ice cream, and Rosemary sat in a beach chair, reading, when a group of teen-age girls plunked themselves down a few feet away. They talked loudly about the boys they would be meeting there, tossed their shorts and sandals just inches from her feet, and spread their sheets and blankets so close that Rosemary really did begin to wonder if she were invisible. So she moved her chair in a huff and settled back into her book. Then she sensed someone in front of her and looked up, expecting to find Liam, but instead saw some guy's butt. He was standing so close that he cast a shadow across her, close enough for her to read the label on his shorts. They were O.P., size large. She cleared her throat loudly but he didn't notice. After another minute or so—she was so flabbergasted she couldn't imagine what to do—he took off at a run and dove into the ocean, spraying sand on her as he went but never noticing she was there.

Rosemary returned to the table, stunned, but neither Liam nor Deet had noticed Frankie or the teen-age boys.

"So let's start at $120,000, OK?" Deet said.

"$120,000!" Rosemary exclaimed, quickly changing gears. "Two years ago her house was worth $175,000!"

"Welcome to 2008, Ro," Deet said. "I suggested that she just wait for the market to rebound. She could hire a property manager and rent it, but she's adamant—she wants to sell."

"Well, how could she possibly afford to live in a retirement community without selling?" Rosemary asked.

"She has money," Deet said plainly.

"Yeah, but you've seen the prices of these places. The least expensive is over $3,000 a month."

"I know, but she can swing it. I promise I've researched this fully."

Again, with her brother taking over her mother's affairs. Probably her grandparents were helping out. She let it drop.

A homeless man shuffled by and asked for a dollar. He smelled like a dirty crotch, and Rosemary was tempted to give him something just to get rid of him, but Deet did it faster.

"Thanks, brother," the man said.

"Yeah," Deet said. "Take it easy."

When he was out of earshot, Deet said, "They're a lot tamer out here, the homeless, that's for sure. I've been in San Diego a lot lately on business, and man, out there they're outrageous. I've never seen such aggressive people. I wouldn't know whether I should give them money, or call a social worker or punch them in the face."

"Punch them in the face?" Rosemary remarked.

"I was tempted. OK, what were we saying?"

"$120,000," Rosemary reminded him.

"Right."

"One-twenty it is, then!" Liam announced with finality.

Of course Liam was not above wishing that a portion of that cash could fall into his lap. It would certainly make a big difference. He'd never weathered such a hard time before, but you read about times like this, about recessions and bubbles and bad luck, and people survived, right? He didn't enjoy watching the value of his business or his house slide like mad, but what upset him most was how his wife reacted to it all. She wasn't just bummed; she was devastated. It was impossible to know where the grief from her dad's death ended and the anguish over the café began, but the fact was that she was becoming someone else entirely. She was brooding, distracted, angry, and overcome with—well, it seemed to be shame. Yes, she was ashamed that they were having a hard time financially. "We should be done with this sort of thing," she would whine, as if being affected by a worldwide economic downturn was a personal failing. She would listen to the same CDs over and over like a lovesick teen, and it got to the point that he could predict her mood by the music he heard. Grateful Dead? Nostalgic for her youth. Carole King? Missing her dad. Joni Mitchell? Angry at Liam. Greg Brown? Trying to come to terms with it all.

He'd had to let most of his crew go, which really bothered him, but the men would be able to collect unemployment through the winter, and he would hire them back as soon as possible, maybe even by spring. Surely, things would be looking up by then.

Meanwhile, he'd picked up a gig as an escort driver for oversized and wide loads. Trailer homes mostly. It brought in some money while giving him enough flexibility to keep Ellis Landscaping limping along. All he'd had to do was get a license, install lights on top of his pickup's cab, and carry some extra insurance. He worked for a local couple who made a living moving these loads. Two or three runs a week helped pay the bills and got him out of the house, away from Rosemary's seemingly endless funk.

He'd been patient with her depression for a long while, sublimating his own sadness at his father-in-law's death to be "the rock" for her and Dylan. And at first she was grateful for the support, but after a time she seemed to grow resentful. Accusatory actually, as if his ability to function in the day to day meant he had never really cared about her dad, or the cafe, or Dylan, or whatever else she felt like raging about that day. Or he was being dishonest about his feelings, or was in denial. She never considered that he was keeping it together for her, or that he had faith in the future, or that he was simply a strong person. Somehow she managed to twist his ability to cope into something negative, and that's when he realized he needed to get away from her, if only for a few days a week. It seemed that as long as he kept her at arm's length, they could at least get along as civil housemates.

But he remembered a day a few months earlier when he'd questioned even that. Although he usually did local escorts, this time he'd escorted a double-wide from Santa Fe to Tucumcari, near the eastern border of New Mexico. Once the job was done and he'd made his way back to I-40, he found himself idling at the entrance ramp. He was supposed to turn right, to head west toward home. But he kept staring at the "East" sign, overcome with the realization that he could simply cross the overpass and make a left. It would be so easy to just head east. To take off. Blast some music and speed across the crisp-dry panhandle of Texas. Spend the next day in gleaming Oklahoma City. Pass through swampy, lackluster Arkansas and finally cross the stunning Mississippi into Memphis. He had a full tank of gas and a credit card. He could get a job in Memphis, get an apartment. Meet new people. Make a whole new life. People did those things. Men said things like, "My son lives in Santa Fe with his mom." They said things like, "After my ex and I split up, I just needed a fresh start." They did things like that, and the world kept turning. Kids got used to it. Ex-wives got used to it. He could do that.

He turned around and went back into Tucumcari, stopped at the Sonic and ate a burger. People did that, too, when they weren't constantly being harangued by their holier-than-thou wives. They sat in their trucks and ate burgers, and they did not drop dead or feel responsible for the utter destruction of the earth.

He remembered when he and Rosemary were first together. About six months in, he realized the best way to get her in a good mood was to bring her food—certain foods, like mangos, dark chocolate, sharp cheese, giant prawns, tomatoes still warm from the sun. She would smell them deeply and he'd watch as her pupils dilated and her whole body revved up. It was amazing, and lots of times would even lead to sex. But it seemed that as the years went by there was always something to worry about, some new cause or threat: The perfectly ripe peach wasn't organically grown, shrimp farming was killing the mangroves, cacao was rife with slave labor—it was always something—and he just quit thinking about food as a way to approach her. What had been an avenue for sensual pleasure turned into something to fret over, like another child. She wasn't much different from his mother-in-law, really. As much as she made fun of Martina, his wife was just as rigid and dogmatic as her mother.

"It's a damn shame," he said aloud.

He turned off his phone and found a cheap movie house and sat through a silly movie and laughed. He was touched by the families on the screen and felt stupid for being touched by the families on the screen. Then he walked out into the night, lay down on the hood of his truck, and looked up at the stars. Yes, he could drive east. But he was suddenly certain that, ultimately, he would enjoy that life even less than he was enjoying his current life. He was reminded of a conversation he'd had with Rosemary years earlier, after a fight. He'd hated some idea of hers, and she was taking it way too personally. Finally she asked, "Why did you even marry me?" And he'd replied, "Because I thought my life would be better with you than without you."

The statement hadn't gone over too well. Evidently she'd expected something different, something more romantic or spiritual, but to his mind, he had paid her a high compliment. It felt that way now, too. Ultimately, it would be worse to make that left turn.

And there had been that glimmer of hope earlier in the summer. They were in the kitchen. She was cooking dinner and he was going through the mail when something happened to make them both laugh. They laughed long and hard and then before he knew it, he had her up against the pantry and they were tearing at each other's clothes. They sank to the floor and had weird, loud, awesome sex. Afterward they looked at each other for a long time and touched each other's faces, and it gave him faith. Within a day or so, Rosemary's funk descended again, but he felt less hopeless about it. And it was with that faith that he drove back to the Interstate and headed west.

Rosemary. Of course he loved her. He just couldn't stand her.

∽ ∽ ∽

"So do you care which realtor we use?" Deet asked, gathering up the file folders.

"Huh?" Liam asked.

"Do you care which realtor we use?"

"Oh. No, whatever."

"Well I know a guy out here I'd like to use."

"Fine."

"So there's just no talking her out of this, is there?" Rosemary asked half-heartedly. But then her stomach started to tighten, and a clenching fear gripped her. Oh no, not here! She couldn't be having a panic attack with Liam and Deet so close by. She could stop it if she tried. She'd done it before. She began to massage her stomach with the heel of her hand, fixed her gaze on a coffee ring on the table, and concentrated on her breath. Her heart started to pound and she suddenly felt hot, but she stared at the coffee ring and breathed slowly. In, out. In, out.

"You know?" Deet asked.

In, out, in, out. It's all good. Life is good. Life is good. Life is good.

"It's true," Liam said, standing up.

OK, they're standing up, so it must be time to stand up. In, out, in, out. Buy some time—pretend to look at your phone. Straighten your clothes. Just keep staring at the coffee ring. In, out. In, out.

"Ro, you coming?"

"Yeah," she said mechanically. The sun is warm. The breeze is soft. Life is good.

"It'll be good, Ro," Liam said, rubbing her back.

What would be good? He smiled at her. He hadn't noticed anything!

Her heart was calming down. What would be good? Had she agreed to something?

"You think?" she asked, hoping the question might elicit some information.

"Definitely," Deet said. "Mom's lonely. Once she's in the retirement place, she'll meet people. Sometimes I think she's just using the break-in as an excuse to quit living alone."

Oh, Rosemary thought. OK, Martina was lonely. That was sort of a given.

"Yeah," Liam agreed. "It might be a good thing after all."

"One tricky thing, though, is that these places don't really allow kids," Deet said. "If you stay there with her when you visit, Dylan is only allowed to spend like two days there at a time."

"That's ridiculous," Liam fumed. "I saw that no-kid rule on the website, and it made me sick."

"I guess we'll have to start staying in hotels, like you do when you visit," Rosemary said. She was trying to stay cool, but she was still struggling to bring her heart rate down. At the same time, she felt triumphant that she was able to head off the panic attack. She was in control after all. When the attacks had started a few months ago, she felt powerless and didn't know how to handle them. Now she was coming back to herself. She could do this.

"Well, Dylan will have to get his "I Love Lucy" fix some other way," Liam said.

"You know," Deet said when they reached the car. "I've been wanting to talk to you two about this. What's with him lately? Is he OK?"

Liam and Rosemary locked eyes but said nothing.

"What do you mean?" Rosemary finally responded.

"I don't know," Deet replied. "It just seems like he used to be so much more fun, so much—happier."

"Well, I don't know," she said. "I think it's just the age. How happy were you when you were twelve?"

"Me?" Deet said. "I was happy. At least I think I was. I don't recall any major traumas."

"Well most tweens today have some angst," she stammered.

"Look, I'm sorry." Now it was Deet's turn to stammer. "I don't mean to pry. He just doesn't seem like himself."

❧ ❧ ❧

Unbelievable. His brother-in-law had said it. Aloud. Something he was completely unable to talk to his wife about. May God bless Deet.

"No problem, man," Liam said. He reached to shake Deet's hand but gave him a quick hug instead. "Be good. We'll see you later, right?"

"Yeah, dinner at Mom's, huh?"

"It might be the last time we're all together in that house," Rosemary added.

"Wow, all those years of caring for the place, and boom, it's over," Liam said with a shake of his head.

"Come now," Deet said, his voice rising in falsetto. "Aren't we in the Acceptance Stage yet?"

"Right," Liam said with a chuckle and unlocked the car. He got into the driver's seat as Deet and Rosemary chatted at the curb.

But it really was sad. Liam missed his father-in-law deeply, and he didn't like this house sale any more than Rosemary did. Mark had kept the house up so well that it was like a work of art—bland art, but art just the same—with the wood window frames smoothly sanded and stained, the gutters clear, the bushes properly cut back each fall. You had to love a guy who kept things up.

He worried too about how Dylan would handle the change, and felt the profound heaviness that was always there when he thought about his son in any serious way. Dylan, the ever-present conundrum. At every age, no matter what was going on, the kid somehow confounded him. From the beginning, parenting Dylan had not been what he'd expected, and as time went on it didn't get any more normal or predictable—the weirdness just changed. As an infant he cried half the night, then he wanted to swing constantly, then he wanted to have the same book read to him over and over—some godforsaken picture book about the animals of North America—and then there was playing the same game forever—Dylan was a cat on a houseboat, and he and Rosemary had to keep coming up with new adventures for Flames the cat.

Then Rosemary decided he needed friends, and that seemed to become her full-time job for way too long. The boys down the street were OK until their dad blew his brains out, and then there were some playmates from soccer and school, but they didn't last long. Then there was Legos, an eternity of Legos, and then there was Kris, the kid who smelled vaguely of lunchmeat. The only constant for the first eleven years of Dylan's life had been his endless need for attention, but over the past year, he had gone one hundred eighty degrees to being mostly sullen and withdrawn, which scared the hell out of Liam. He'd even stopped singing under his breath, a habit Liam thought would be with the kid till he was old and gray. Now even Deet had noticed it, and though he was relieved that he had broached the topic, he worried that if it was obvious to Deet, then maybe there really was a problem with his son.

Liam had been worried about Dylan for some time, but he had no idea where to go with those concerns. Rosemary got defensive whenever he brought up the subject, as if he were personally insulting her, like saying her meatloaf was dry. And she had a different explanation every time. "It's just developmental," she'd say, or, "He just steps to the beat of his own drummer," or, "Why does he have to measure up to your idea of normal? Why isn't he good enough as he is?"

Good enough? She so didn't get it.

Something that Dylan's second-grade teacher said in an offhand way years ago still haunted him. Liam and Rosemary were waiting for a routine conference to begin when the teacher came in breathless from a conversation with another parent in the hall. "It's always a shame to hear one of your former students has gone wrong in middle school," she said as she shuffled through a stack of folders.

"Wrong?" Rosemary asked.

"That woman—I had her son in second grade, but she says he's always in trouble these days. And he was such a sweet little boy back then. I'll tell you, sometimes I think kids go bad when they get older because parents just get tired of parenting. They all want to clock out after twelve or thirteen years, but the job only gets harder, don't you think?"

"Well, we wouldn't know."

"Oh, of course! Dylan is an only. And isn't he a great kid!"

Lately Liam found himself wondering: Had they given up? Were they just sick of parenting Dylan, or was there something truly awry?

A few months ago, without Rosemary's knowledge, he went to the school counselor and asked him to check in on Dylan, just to see if he thought there was a problem, but that quickly blew up in his face. According to Dylan, he was branded as a freak forever because the counselor dude had come into the classroom and pulled him out for "a little visit," and Rosemary was furious. After the counselor said he didn't see a problem, the whole thing now seemed even more impossible to deal with.

Liam's thoughts turned to the Wooster kids—how were they doing, he wondered, growing up without a dad? Probably Colleen had remarried; she didn't seem the type to raise two boys on her own. But if Matthew had lived to raise his sons, how would that have turned out? Would their situation have gotten better, or would his drinking and obsessive behavior have come to a different, inevitably sad end? What parenting worries would have kept him up nights? What advice would he have given Christopher and little Matthew? Suddenly Liam had a vision of himself as a coach, trying to send Dylan out onto the field but unable to think of anything to say. It's halftime and the team is down, and somehow he has to motivate his boy to get back out there, but he's at an utter loss.

But the world was full of dads in locker rooms coaching their sons. Millions of locker rooms with millions of dads giving their sons millions of sermons, tips, and warnings on how to get through the game. Be careful of the Blacks, son; never trust the Jews, boy. Watch out for the fascists, the Pakis, the skinheads, the gangsters, the socialists, the Baptists, the townies, the gays, the Brits, the bureaucrats, the Republicans, the junkies, the mothers-in-law, the neighbors, the Democrats, the auditors, the Muslims, the hippies, the surgeons, the jocks, the critics, the Marines, the priests, the drunkards, the artists. Watch out, watch out, watch out. And knock 'em dead, too.

At times like this he needed someone to tell him the things he always told Rosemary: "Everything will be fine," or "We've been knocked down by a big wave, but we'll come up soon." It was easy to say, and he believed it whenever Rosemary was freaking out about bills they couldn't pay, but with his son, he worried they might all run out of air before the big wave played itself out.

They were virtually silent on the drive back from meeting with Deet When he and Rosemary entered the house, Dylan and Martina were looking through old photo albums.

"Mom, you look like Grandpa," Dylan said. "I never noticed it before, but you look like a girl version of him."

"You think?" she asked, sinking next to him on the couch. It was nice to see him interested in something other than bad TV reruns. Liam picked up another album and idly thumbed through it. They'd seen these many times before.

"Your father loved that you resembled him," Martina added. "When David turned out to look more like me, I think Dad was a little disappointed. Being adopted, it was important to him that at least someone in the world looked like him."

"Huh," Rosemary muttered, turning the familiar pages.

"Grandpa was adopted?" Dylan asked.

"I was thinking that we should go through these albums and

split them up, so you and David have some photos too," Martina said.

"No, Mom, please don't," Rosemary said decisively. "You keep them. They should stay together. We can always make copies."

"Well, I don't know."

"I mean it, Mom. And I'm sure Deet feels the same way."

"Grandpa was adopted?" Dylan repeated.

"Yes, you knew that," Rosemary replied.

"No I didn't."

"Yes, you did."

"What I can't believe," Martina interjected. "Is that no one ever noticed how much your father looked like Aunt Ellen."

"Huh?" Rosemary asked.

"Your Great Aunt Ellen, Grandfather Ira's sister."

"Aunt Ellen? What about her?" Rosemary had only seen her great aunt a handful of times. She lived in Oregon and attended few family gatherings, but she'd been at her father's funeral, and Rosemary remembered she seemed pretty broken up. "What are you saying?"

"Oh, Ruth finally told me, a few days after Dad died, that his biological mother was Aunt Ellen."

"What?" Rosemary asked.

"All those years of your father wondering who his real mother was and they knew all along."

"What?" Rosemary repeated, scrambling to her feet. "They never told him but they told you just like that?"

"Yes," Martina said, exhaling loudly. "Ruth said that after your dad died, Ellen was overcome with remorse for never having told him."

"What the hell?"

"Don't use that language in front of Dylan," Martina scolded.

"Mom, what the hell? All these years?"

"I know, Rosemary," she said. "I feel the same way."

Rosemary looked at Liam in shock, and he mirrored her reaction.

"But Mom, Ruth told you days after Dad's funeral, and you haven't told me for all this time?" A sudden thought made her heart race. "Have you told Deet?"

"David? No, I haven't told him. I guess I was waiting for the right time, and this seemed to be it." She set the photo album down and watched Rosemary as she paced the living room.

"My God, I hate that woman!" Rosemary fumed.

"Grandma Ruth?" Dylan asked. "Why?"

"Because Grandpa always wanted to know who his real mom was. It always bothered him that it was a closed adoption."

"I know," Martina said. "It was Ellen's choice and Ruth respected it. It's not her fault."

"Why didn't Aunt Ellen at least tell you herself?" Rosemary asked.

"Oh, I certainly don't know," Martina said wearily. "She just didn't. She had him when she was eighteen. She'd gotten into trouble, and by then Ruth and Ira had been married eight years with no children, so it seemed the right thing to do, and no one ever talked about it again. Ellen went on to have her own family and I guess they all moved past it."

"What selfish bitches," Rosemary spat.

"Rosemary!" Martina shouted.

"Come on, Ro," Liam warned. "Don't get like that. People make the best decisions they know how to make. They weren't trying to hurt anyone."

Rosemary sank into a chair in defeat. "It would have made such a difference to Dad," she said, her eyes filling with tears.

"Yes," Martina added, running her hand lovingly though Dylan's hair. "It would have."

"Well I never even knew Grandpa was adopted," he said.

"I'm sure we told you," Rosemary said halfheartedly. After a few moments of silence she said, "Gee, Mom, you got any more bombs you want to drop today?"

"No, I don't think so."

"You know, maybe we should all go for a walk or something," Liam suggested, standing up.

"It's all so unfair," Rosemary said, covering her face with her arm.

"How about a walk?" Liam repeated.

"I wanted to get a little more packing done," Martina said.

"Packing?" Liam asked incredulously. "What's left? You've been packing for months!"

"I was hoping you could go through Mark's tools, in the garage," she replied. "I'm sure he'd love for you to have them."

"OK, Mom," Liam sighed. "Let's do that."

"I'll come too," Dylan said.

Liam was happy to load Mark's belt sander and jigsaw into the car. The Japanese saw was a great find as well, with its blade that cut both ways. He took the hand tools too because Martina insisted, figuring he'd set those aside for Dylan. The tangible connections to Mark were something he was happy to have. Truth be told, Liam had imagined asking his father-in-law for advice many times over the past year or so, and the answer he always seemed to get was, "Just keep on keeping on." So he had.

After they'd gathered up a surprising number of paint cans and other things Liam didn't want, Dylan noticed two boxes on a high shelf.

"What about that stuff?" he asked Martina.

"Oh, I don't know what to do with that."

"What is it?"

"Pictures."

"Pictures? Of what?"

"Well, there's a lot of stuff in there I don't know what to do with. It doesn't seem right to throw it away, but I don't know."

"Can we see it, Grandma?" Dylan asked.

Martina sighed and her eyes welled up.

"Mom?" Liam asked. "What is it?"

"I'll get them," said Dylan, dragging a stepladder over to the shelves. He set the smaller box down on the garage floor and unfolded the cardboard flaps. In it were several dozen disposable cameras, some with their packaging intact but most of them used.

"Grandma, what are all these cameras?"

Martina suddenly began to sob, and Liam had no idea what to do.

But Dylan did. "It's OK, Grandma," he said, rubbing her back. "It's OK."

Liam stepped outside into the driveway as Martina cried and Dylan soothed her. After several awkward minutes, Martina called him back in.

"I'm sorry," she said. "These cameras, well—they have a lot of happy memories and a lot of sad ones, too. Did you know I started taking pictures?"

"No," Liam answered.

"It was back when Betsy was here. It was her garden that made me start. It was so beautiful, and I was so taken with it. I would go outside at certain hours because I liked the way the light looked against the plants, against their shapes. I loved the colors, I loved the shadows, and I wanted to capture it. I wished I could paint it, but I don't know how to paint, so I would take pictures. And that," she said, pointing toward the much larger second box, "is what I would do with them."

Liam set the heavy, unwieldy box on the floor and again Dylan unfolded the flaps.

In the box were canvases, 10x13 combinations of photos and other objects affixed to brightly painted backgrounds. There were cut-out photos of flowers studded with tiny stones, photos of cactus with feathers glued to them, pieces of cloth shaped into blossoms, pull-tabs linked together to form storm clouds, bullet casings filled with dried petals, and more.

"Grandma! You did this stuff?"

"Wow, Mom," Liam said. "This is your work? And you've kept it hidden out here?"

"Well at first I put the photos in albums, but that didn't seem right. So I started putting them together, and then I started cutting them up. And I would find things when Betsy and I walked to the school, back when we read with the kids. Sometimes we'd walk out in the desert too. That's where I found those old pull-tabs and the bullets. People go out there to drink and shoot things, which sounds just crazy to me, but—"

"Mom, they're beautiful. Why didn't you ever show anybody before?"

"Well, Mark liked them, and I had started these others, as well." She unwrapped several more canvases that featured photos of the family in addition to nature images. "I was making this one for Dylan," she said. In one, she had cut out the center of a sunflower and replaced it with Dylan's infant face, and there was a series of images from when he was four or so and clearly had been telling a story, each print capturing a different sweet expression.

"Is that me?" Dylan squeaked.

"No, it's Santa Claus," Martina smiled.

"Mom," Liam said. "I'm just stunned. These are so beautiful."

"Thank you. It's been so long since I've looked at them. Let's spread them out."

They set the canvases against the wall of the nearly empty garage and then stood in silence, taking them in. Liam was shocked to find one with pictures of him cut up and artfully arranged along with a logo from his business, a Yankees emblem, and even some text cut from a magazine that read "son." It wasn't quite finished, though, and neither were ones for Rosemary and Deet.

"I had planned to make one for each of you for Christmas a few years ago, but. . .I didn't finish."

"Mom, they're amazing."

"They really are quite nice, aren't they?" she agreed.

"You know, people get thousands of dollars for things like this in Santa Fe."

"Well, I made them for love, not money. Maybe I should hang some in my new place." Martina started to tear up again. "I never got around to making one for Mark."

"Don't cry, Grandma," Dylan said. "You can still make one for him."

"Yes, I can, but I miss him. And this other box makes me sad, too." She gestured toward the box of cameras.

"Why don't we develop them?" Liam asked.

Martina looked from Liam's face to Dylan's and back again to Liam's.

"What, Mom?"

"Well." Tears streamed down her face. "I haven't told you the whole reason why I stopped volunteering at the school."

"Are you OK?"

"That principal, Mrs. Teag. She was a terrible person."

"I remember she didn't appreciate you."

"Oh, it was worse than that. I loved those kids. I had this little group of four boys who became like my own children. I worked with them for two years—I watched them grow up. Well, after Betsy moved back to Minnesota, I missed her so much. I made one of these collages for her, and she loved it. So I got the idea to make one for each of the boys. I thought they could be gifts for their parents. So I began taking pictures of the boys. Well, Mrs. Teag heard about it and became furious. She said I didn't have permission to take those pictures, that it was against the law, and if I wanted to keep working at the school, I would have to get fingerprinted, and get a background check. She made me give her the cameras and said I couldn't be alone with the kids anymore!"

"Oh, Mom," Liam said.

Martina wiped her face roughly with her sleeve. "She made me feel like a criminal! Like some kind of pervert!"

"That's so mean!" Dylan shouted.

"Yes, Dylan, it was mean." Martina exhaled loudly. "There was something wrong with that woman. She was so hateful. I don't think she's there anymore; I think she retired. But that's how that whole thing ended. Mark was so upset. He wanted to step in and defend me, but I wouldn't let him. I just left. I don't think I've taken a picture since."

They were all quiet as she sifted through the cameras. "Why don't you take these unopened ones?" Martina said, handing several packages to Dylan. "You might enjoy taking some pictures."

"Sure, thanks."

"Oh look," she said. "Several of these are labeled. Here's one from the vacation Mark and I took to Mexico. And this is when Rosemary opened the cafe, and this is from Mark's graduation from law school." She smiled. "Yes, let's get these all developed."

⤙ ⤙ ⤙

After a strained family dinner, over a dessert of sorbet and fruit, Deet asked Rosemary about the details of Fire Ring's decline.

"You know, I could have helped you," he said.

"Thanks, but we couldn't have handled any more debt," she replied.

"There are always options," he continued. "I could have become a silent partner, or I could have invested some of your cash flow. I could have gotten you steady gains with some careful stock purchases."

"Right, we could have sent you the tip jar, and you could have invested it for us. Why didn't I think of that?" Rosemary said, stabbing a slice of mango. "And hasn't the market just crashed? Isn't that what all the hoopla is about?"

"Some parts of the market have crashed, but not all," Deet explained. "How do you think Mom can afford to move into a retirement home? Because I've been handling her investments."

"You've been handling Mom's investments?" Rosemary asked, looking from one face to another. Martina began to fidget.

"Yes, Ro, I've been handling her investments. We started years ago with the $5,000 life insurance money left from Grandma Deedee's death. Dad said it was hers to do with as she pleased, and I tripled it in just a few years. Then when Dad died, she gave me more to work with. He would never let me invest his money before, but Mom said she wanted to make sure she was safe as she got old, so I've been maximizing his retirement savings."

"So you're not getting help from Grandma and Grandpa?" Rosemary asked Martina.

"Heaven forbid," Martina retorted. "I wouldn't ask them for help if my life depended on it."

"You're able to afford these fancy places because Deet has been investing your money? Without Dad's blessing?"

"Well, yes," Martina replied.

"So," Liam broke in, clearing his throat. "What's the magic portfolio in these hard times?"

"I thought you'd never ask!" Deet said, smiling broadly. "The magic formula, dear brother, is natural gas. Drilling for those rich shale deposits in Pennsylvania and beyond. That's your stock tip of the day."

"Fracking?" Rosemary shrieked. "You own stock in fracking?"

"Yes I do, and so does Mom."

"Fracking? Are you kidding me?"

"I thought fracking was bad," Dylan said.

"Only if you're fear-based and close-minded," Deet said.

"Deet, how could you?"

"And self-righteous," he said pointedly to Dylan.

"You took Dad's savings and pension, which he earned from a career in public service—from living an honorable life—and sank it into the worst environmental disaster ever perpetrated on the public?"

"You're overreacting. Yes, there have been missteps, but the technology is improving."

"Missteps. Like the little matters of dead livestock, poisoned crops, and flammable tapwater?"

"Rosemary, must you get so angry?" Martina asked.

"Mom, do you know what hydraulic fracturing does to groundwater? To the earth?"

"Well no, I—"

"They drill seven or eight thousand feet into the earth, down to ancient shale deposits, and inject tens of thousands of gallons of fluid at high pressure to fracture the shale. Then the shale releases its gas."

"OK—"

"But the fluid is toxic. It has benzene and methanol and formaldehyde and tons of other chemicals—no one really knows what's in it—and only some of the fluid gets removed from the well. The rest stays in the ground, where it contaminates groundwater! It spreads and destroys the water! People can set their tapwater on fire!"

"Oh, dear."

"And the fluid they do draw out evaporates in volatile open pits, which pollutes the air and results in more global warming. And the whole thing is unregulated! It's exempted from the Safe Drinking Water Act!"

"Mom," said Deet in a controlled tone. "It is American fuel. We don't need to fight wars for it. And it's clean-burning—cleaner than the coal plants that power your house, Ro—and it's affordable."

Martina covered her face with her hands.

"Ro, let's give it a rest," said Liam. "Your mom's had enough."

"Oh, Deet, how could you?" Rosemary's voice, which began with fire, trailed off to a whisper. "How could you?"

"I did what was best for Mom."

"By giving more power to corporations that poison the earth."

"Well I don't actually know what kinds of shares I own," Martina said.

"You're diversified, Mom," Deet assured her.

Rosemary looked into the faces of her family. Dylan looked from one adult to the next, like a bird trying to judge the wind's direction. Liam was studying the tablecloth. Martina looked pale and exhausted. And Deet was triumphant.

"And now Mom is independent," Deet said. "She can live where she wants and how she wants."

"Well, I'm not rich," Martina corrected.

"But you're comfortable," Deet said. "We've made a series of sound investments."

"I feel safe, that's the main thing," she continued. "I'm alone now, Rosemary. You've got to understand that. I didn't want to go against Dad's wishes, but I don't want to be a burden on my children. You read about old people eating cat food, getting victimized by gypsies and what-not. I don't want a life like that."

"You don't need to explain yourself, Mom," Liam said. "It's your life—you get to do what you want. And we hope you're happy in the new place."

"Of course we do," Rosemary said mechanically.

Martina sighed deeply. After a few moments, she picked up the photo album she'd been leafing through earlier and began tracing its embossed Kodak logo with her fingertips. They all watched as if she were doing a magic trick. Then she smoothed her palm over the words on the cover, where *Do you remember the times of your life?* was printed in ornate cursive font. Just seeing those familiar words set the song from the old commercial playing through Rosemary's head. Those Kodak commercials always made her cry—everyone looked so happy. But the happiness was always fleeting.

"Come on, buddy, let's get you to bed," Liam said to Dylan.

"Dad, I'm twelve. You don't need to put me to bed."

"Well maybe we can catch an episode of "Green Acres" or something on Hulu before we turn in," Liam said with false enthusiasm.

"That's a stupid show," Dylan replied glumly through listless good-night kisses. "It's as bad as 'Mister Ed.'"

"Fine then, we'll just go to sleep," Liam grumbled. "Good night, everyone."

Rosemary watched her gangly boy leave the room behind her husband. In a few years Dylan would be grown and gone, and what would she have to show for her life? A minimum-wage job? A mountain of debt? A strained marriage?

She felt utterly alone as she watched them leave. After a few moments, she gathered up the courage to look squarely at Deet, expecting to find reconciliation. But instead she saw smug self-satisfaction.

"I'd better turn in as well," Martina said, gathering up the fruit plates. "Somehow this day has wiped me out."

Rosemary began to panic. "So early?" she said, sitting up straight. "Maybe we can play a game of Boggle or something."

"Boggle? Oh, goodness, no thank you." Martina carried the plates into the kitchen, returned to the living room, kissed her forefingers and pressed them to her children's foreheads. "Please remember to turn off the lights before you go to bed, and don't stay up too late. Good night, kids."

"I guess I'll turn in, too," Rosemary said, springing to her feet.

"Wait, Ro!" Deet exclaimed. "I'll play Boggle with you!"

"Well, there you go, honey," Martina said with a smile as she padded off down the hall.

"Let's see," Deet said, reaching for the orange box in the side table. "Maybe I'll win this time. You usually beat me, but I'm feeling lucky tonight." He pulled out the hard plastic case and loudly shook the letter dice inside. "Maybe we'll get some really good letters, like F, R, A, C, K. Or maybe we'll get F-U, or—"

"Enough already, what do you want from me?"

"S-O-R-R-Y would be nice."

"For exactly what?"

"For being the bitch of the century. Tonight, at Dad's funeral, and plenty of other times when I just let it roll off my back."

"And you've been a perfect gentleman every day of your life, I forgot."

"I've never insulted your integrity."

"I'm sorry, Deet. I'm sorry about Dad's funeral."

"That's why you've said nothing about it for the last year and a half?"

"We've fought before and sometimes we never apologize. Why is this so different?"

"Because you insulted me!" He shook the Boggle case violently. "You said that I took advantage of people!" He shook the case again. "Like I was some force of evil in the world. That's a big deal, you know? It's not like saying you don't like my tie."

"I'm sorry, Deet."

He shook the Boggle case again.

"Stop that, it's so loud," Rosemary scolded. "People are in bed."

He slammed the case on the table, removed the lid, and looked at the letters. "Aw, shucks," he said. "I was hoping there might be a T-H-A-N-K-S!" He looked at her with eyes narrowed, his lips in a hard, fixed line.

"Now what?"

"How about thanks for dealing with Mom? How about thanks for handling the house appraisal and the listing and the move? How about thanks for making it so she can have a new life in a place where she can meet people her own age, instead of moving in with you? How about that?"

"OK, thank you, thank you!" Rosemary paused for a moment, knowing she shouldn't say more, but she did anyway. "But I still can't believe there was no other way to do it than investing Dad's money in natural gas."

"In these times? No! And what's the problem with it anyway? You're not above any of this, Ro. You use just as much fossil fuel as the next person. Don't start that self-righteous crap—no one's listening. Look at you, all noble and defeated, like—shit, you're like some Polish soldier on horseback going up against Hitler's tanks. With a lance. You know what? I was watching you tonight, and suddenly I thought I could read your mind. You know who you remind me of? Mary Bailey. You know, George and Mary Bailey, Jimmy Stewart and what's her face, from *It's a Wonderful Life.* I watched that movie with Mom last Christmas, and that's who you remind me of. You think someone's going to come along and reward you for being such a fine, upright person."

"Fuck you, Deet," Rosemary said quietly. "You don't know me."

His voice became a falsetto: "Oh, George, look! Everyone will come to our rescue if we just live a good, honest life. If we just eat our natural food and catch our rainwater and put up solar panels, our guardian angel will step in and reward us for a life well-lived!"

"Shut the fuck up, Deet, OK? You got your apology and you got your thank you, now just shut up."

"No, I've been listening to your 'right livelihood' crap for years. Just remember that it's my evil ways, my careful investing and risk-taking that's allowed me to live as comfortably as I do and made Mom financially secure. Just remember that when you go home to your life with your Green Party and your Prius payments and your ski swaps and your whatever the hell. Just remember how Mom's doing and who made that happen."

A strangled laugh erupted from Rosemary's throat, followed by a plume of self-loathing that surprised even her. "Hey, Deet. Thanks for the newsflash. Thanks for the blinding flash of the obvious: Rosemary is a loser. You think I don't know that? You think I don't know it's my own fault that I'm broke? That I'm fat? That my marriage is in trouble? That my kid's as weird as the day is long? You've got nothing to tell me that I don't already know. So now you really can shut the fuck up. You win, OK? Congratulations, Deet, you win. At everything."

Her words rang in the sudden silence. Deet sat back heavily in his chair. Finally he said, "Oh, for Christ's sake, Ro." Tears filled his eyes.

"There is nothing I want more at this moment than to disappear," she said. "To just beam up to some spaceship, to walk through a magic tunnel and come out in a different life, or just . . .granulate and blow away on the wind. To cease to be Rosemary Sabin Ellis. You know, if this was a job, I'd really enjoy quitting it." She began to snap her fingers and sing, "You can take this life and shove it, I ain't living here no more."

She laughed for a moment and the room suddenly felt oppressively small.

"So what now?" she asked. "You want my blood? Get me a knife—you can have that too."

"Ro," Deet said. "I don't want to win. I don't—look, I'm sorry."

"Yeah, me too," she said, breathing deeply, deeper than she had for a long time. Her eyes fell on the TV's blank screen. She recalled that night from long ago, nearly twenty-five years ago, when she watched "The Carol Burnett Show" with her mother in this very room, and how she suddenly saw how silly and fake it was. How she decided that night that TV and so many other things were bullshit, and how she was going to do things differently in her life. Do things the right way. And how when she had that reaction to the paint remover and went into the coma, it all crystallized for her: natural good, manmade bad. She had applied that dogma to so many everyday decisions: Organic good, conventional bad; breastfeeding good, formula bad; herbals good, pharmaceuticals bad.

But as she looked deeper, she saw that her rigid dogma had spread to every area of her life. Where else could she have gotten her relentless judgments? Savings accounts good, hedge funds bad; small business good, corporations bad; conservation good, extraction bad.

Rosemary good, Deet bad.

She felt the old surge of confusion and jealousy she'd felt as a kid when Deet and her dad did things together, without her. How could Mark love them both when they were so different from each other? Wasn't that like saying cherry and orange were both your favorite flavors?

God in heaven, had it gone that far? Yes, it had.

People often praised her for her firm convictions, but what was a moral compass, and what was a snap judgment? What was believing you knew right from wrong, and what was simply close-mindedness? She thought of her mom, her tender-hearted mom, and knew instantly that she had done the same thing with her parents: Dad good, Mom bad. Well, not really bad, more like Dad a fount of wisdom, Mom a dud. Dad a person to seek out, Mom someone to tolerate. How terrible! And she also knew just as clearly that she had been choosing sides between Dylan and Liam from the start, and between herself and Liam, as if there were no way for everyone to be happy. She was as simple-minded as anyone she had ever known, as hidebound as some paste-eating redneck. She'd been choosing sides her whole life, like a lab rat conditioned to receive food or an electric shock when it pulled a lever. Only she had set up the levers herself. Did everyone set up their own levers? Did people really create their own reality? Her wheatgrass-drinking-organic-cotton-wearing-affirming-the-positive Santa Fe friends would say yes, but how about that amputee living on the streets of Mumbai—what would he say? Who knew, ultimately, who set up the levers?

But suddenly she realized she could fix this. Suddenly she knew that the life she saw only as a hopeless tangle, a Gordian knot of fuckups—she knew with an unexpected and ineffable calm that it didn't really matter at all. Somewhere just this side of the morass was an exit. She could let all of it go. She *would* let all of it go. It was time.

She looked at Deet. "Is there anything more you want to say?" she asked gently.

"No."

"You sure?"

"Yeah. Except that I do love you, Ro."

"Even though I'm such a pain in the ass."

"And you're a good person."

"So are you," she said, and meant it. "And I love you too."

"You just try so damned hard all the time. It's OK to just be, you know? You don't have to have a—a position on every-thing. You can just be."

"Yeah," she said, feeling a curious mix of shame and libera-tion, like a great gush of clean water was washing something ugly down the drain. "I'm gonna step outside for a moment."

Deet rose from his chair and looked her in the eye for a long moment. "You OK?"

"Yes."

"Then good night."

"Good night."

Outdoors, it was blissfully still. Cold, black, and still. It took several minutes for her to find Orion, but he was still there. And so was she.

CHAPTER 15 | OCTOBER, 2009

Joshua Tree National Park, California

Rosemary inched the Prius toward Campsite 38. Cool darkness filled the car as the headlights illuminated the site—picnic table, fire ring, rock walls, just as they had been all these years.

She cut the engine but left the headlights on. They had pulled her through the darkness for hours, a pale comfort at the end of the seven-hundred-mile push from Santa Fe. Breathing deeply to slow her pounding heart, she dropped her head to the steering wheel. Moments later she was asleep, floating, rising with a jerky motion like a needle on a skipping record. She saw the blueprints for a backyard gazebo, heard the sounds of a Yankees game, knew her mother-in-law was coming up the walk, and then jolted awake, her head jerking into the seatback with a grunt.

Crickets throbbed. Rosemary took a few more deep breaths, opened the car door, shifted her body to the side, and swung her feet to the ground. Her heart raced as she began to hyperventilate, breathing with short, shrieky yelps. Suddenly terrified, she clutched the car door, wishing like a child that Liam were there.

The door lurched open as she leaned into it, and she fell to her knees, still clutching the handle. Her eyes widened with pain as the sharp gravel pressed into her knees. She fell back against the car, feeling the last of its heat. Was she there ten minutes, thirty, sixty? Shivering in the desert night. The sky blazed a brilliant black. She stared at the stars, scattered in their changing patterns, and her breathing slowed.

Eventually she rose, unfolding herself clumsily. A strange sensation drove her backward against the car again. Panic spiked through her. What was this? She couldn't feel her body? Was she having a stroke? Then she felt the dull tingling. Oh. Her butt had fallen asleep. Pounding the cheeks with her fists, she stepped over the chain that kept cars off the campsite. Her eyes, now adjusted to the darkness, searched for her favorite ledge, the one they called the breakfast nook—flat as a table, cool and shady in the mornings.

Rosemary felt her way along the rock face in the moonlight and found its familiar inset. Running her hands over the smooth granite, she climbed onto the ledge and instinctively brushed away dirt and dry leaves. She caressed the stone, recalling the hours and days she had spent there, and the loved ones she had shared those hours and days with. Then she began to cry, a high-pitched moan that soon morphed into a whimper and ended in deep, guttural sounds that silenced the crickets. She rocked back and forth, weeping in the night, unaware of anything but the anguish that emptied from her. Eventually she collapsed onto her side and surrendered to sleep.

At dawn Rosemary was still there, curled in the nook, chilled and stiff. She stretched her limbs slowly, trying to recall the dream that was quickly slipping away. She'd been driving. Driving up one side of a tree and down the other. Driving a car that jumped from one street to another with just a tap on the gas pedal. Driving a car she couldn't control.

She sat up and rubbed her face. Her eyes were swollen, her breath vile. She suddenly became aware of how deeply cold she was.

She made her way to the car and extracted a Thermos and a sleeping bag. Moments later, wrapped in a down cocoon and sipping the warm coffee, she became fascinated by its cylinder of dull green metal that looked like something out of Herman Munster's lunch box. This morning it seemed more like a giant syringe. Once its contents were flowing through her veins, she might feel a little better. Just then a warbler sounded. Yes, she would feel better.

It had been a week since the accident, five days since she agreed that Liam was right, four days since Dylan had been moved to the long-term care unit, and one day since she realized she had to come to Joshua Tree. She didn't know how long she'd be there—a day? A week? Long enough to sift through boatloads of fear, remorse, and recrimination. Long enough to trace it all back to the beginning. Long enough to form some sort of plan of how they would get through the next few months.

Or would it take years?

A week ago, at this hour of the morning, life was normal, or normal enough. It was Saturday. Rosemary was putting a load of laundry in the washer as Liam and Dylan prepared for a bike ride to town. They were going to follow the railroad tracks, about a nine-mile ride, so that Dylan could get the route down and start biking to Kristopher's house on his own.

Rosemary welcomed the quiet morning alone after a busy week of work. She had a job now at the Green Pueblo Fund, a private foundation in Santa Fe that supported community projects in Latin America. A former customer from the cafe had called and offered it to her just before Christmas, which Rosemary regarded as a godsend of seismic proportions. She'd begun as an administrative assistant but was now evaluating grant proposals. The pay was decent, the job had benefits, and she was learning a lot about spending other people's money.

She and Liam had sold the house, a wrenching decision that left her sobbing for weeks. It netted a profit just large enough to pay off their credit cards and the loan from the cafe, and now they were renting another house in Cielo Vista. But as long as she didn't drive by their old house or think about it too much, the new one was fine. They were the same people they'd always been, with the same voices and the same furniture and the same food cooking on the stove regardless of their address or whether they paid mortgage or rent. Little by little, life had become OK again.

Well, most of it. Dylan continued to worry her. Connecting with him was like trying to get a cell signal in an underground parking garage, virtually impossible except at some seemingly random moment in some seemingly random location. They might have a meaningful conversation on the way to the grocery, in the dentist's waiting room, or as they passed each other in the hall to the bathroom. But he was largely silent at the dinner table, impossible to motivate about his schoolwork, and prone to spending entire days in his dark, cluttered room.

Sometimes she tried to force her way in to him, driven by concern and longing for his company. "Let's go to the pool!" she'd say brightly on some summer afternoon. "How about a movie?" or "What do you say we go get an obscenely expensive latte?" But usually he declined, and left her feeling hurt. Hurt and foolish, actually, considering that, like most moms, she had spent most of his childhood plotting to get time away from him—manipulating the day's events to maximize nap time, engineering play dates and screen time to string together the largest swaths of time possible so she could do what—cook dinner? Balance the checkbook? Paint a wall? It was all so ridiculous, the seeker becoming the sought and the sought becoming the seeker, round and round in a sorrowful dance like binary stars with misaligned centers of gravity.

According to her mom friends, it was perfectly normal. According to the self-help books, she might have a problem with intimacy. According to Liam, even thinking about it was a waste of time. "We humans want balance," he'd say. "When we have a lot of salty food, we crave something sweet. When we've been in a room with loud music, we want quiet. Dylan was a demanding child, so we often wanted a break. It's not a crime, Ro. You missed nothing of his childhood—you were always there for him."

But she didn't tell Liam how the push-pull dance was still in effect, how she sometimes still indulged in the fantasy of backing down the driveway and never returning, especially when Dylan displayed his remarkable new talent for scrutinizing seemingly all her words and actions:

"Why do you buy organic grapes, but not organic cheese? You seem to be saying that just because something is expensive, it's OK to selectively uphold your morals."

"Your rule limiting my 'screened entertainment' is completely unreasonable. You watch as much TV as you want after I go to bed, and don't try to tell me it's just the news. I can hear the 'Star Trek' theme, and those cop shows. You two are just hypocrites."

"You tell me I should think for myself, but whenever I do, you say I don't know my place and you get mad at me."

His friend Kristopher was still around. They played Wii games and ate giant snacks and the kid slept over for days at a time, but they really didn't seem to have all that much fun together. It was as if they were two passengers on their own little ark of misery—wearing wool beanies all summer long, ignoring the basics of hygiene, scoffing at her suggestions of how they might spend a day.

But then there was what she later called the Third Cup of Coffee Address. Around noon on a Sunday, the day after she and her book group had drank far too much Shiraz as they discussed *Out Stealing Horses,* Dylan noted that she was brewing a third cup of coffee.

"Usually you and Dad share the one pot, which equals two cups for each of you. Why do you want a third today?"

"I'm a little more tired today, I guess," she said, reaching for some Tylenol.

"You have a headache and you're tired because you stayed up late and had a lot of wine," he stated.

"Yes, that is most certainly true," she replied, trying to head off her annoyance with the consolation that at least he was talking to her.

"I've noticed this before, and to me it's like the way you swim laps."

"What?"

"Like how you only use your arms for one length, and then you only use your legs on your back going the other way."

"Pulls and kicks," she explained. "It gives the arms and legs a better workout."

"It creates more of an extreme, like the wine and the coffee. People seem to like extremes."

"Yeah, I guess you're right," she agreed, swallowing the pills.

"But sometimes you have to pay a price for them, like with roller coasters. The extremes are fun, but sometimes they're too scary, or you puke."

"Yeah."

"Even lemon meringue pie is like that, you know?"

"Huh?"

"I've watched you make it a million times: You put the egg yolks in the pie part so it's really rich and creamy, and then you beat the egg whites so the top is fluffy. It's just like your laps—it creates extremes."

"Well I guess you're right about that, buddy," she said, feeling her old pride in his intelligence.

Over the following weeks, Dylan's voice changed—an unqualified mindblower—and he began emerging from his room more and more. He and Kristopher, who had moved from Cielo Vista into town, spent a lot of time riding their bikes at the "stunt place," a washed out arroyo in the greenbelt not far from the house, and she and Liam began to relax a bit. He was still an abysmal student, but at least he was getting exercise and seemed to be enjoying life more. According to Kristopher, he was quite a daredevil on his bike, but as long as he was wearing his helmet, Rosemary tried not to interfere with his new passion. It seemed that maybe they were out of the woods with their son. Maybe it was all just a tough time he had to get through, what with her dad's death, their financial stress, his hormones—maybe it would all work itself out.

But soon there were calls from his school. He'd insulted his science teacher, claiming the man understood nothing about anything that mattered. "You just list facts, like that's all there is," Dylan complained. "You want us to remember all this boring stuff, as if that's what life is all about."

"This is a life sciences class, not a philosophy class," said Mr. Franks, who was muddling through his first year of teaching.

"Yeah, life science, *life*—I could learn more about life by watching the birds outside my window or boiling water. You're stupid and boring, and I shouldn't have to be in your class."

Well, there was no fixing that. Dylan was assigned to in-school suspension and had his schedule changed to get him out of Mr. Franks' class. Rosemary and Liam punished him by taking his computer away for two weeks.

"No problem," he said with arms crossed. "I'll be fine without it. All of humanity's problems stem from man's inability to sit quietly in a room alone."

"What?" they shot back.

"Grandma always says that."

"Grandma says that?" Rosemary asked.

"Yes, she likes to quote Blaise Pascal."

"Who is Blaise Pascal?"

"A French mathematician and philosopher from the 1600s. She found it in a book about meditation."

"Of course," Liam said, throwing up his hands. "Who else would she quote?"

But Liam had really started worrying about him after the Lowest Note Freak-out Incident, when Dylan had come to them with a fun fact and was furious when it did not impact them as much as he'd expected.

"You guys," he began as they sat at their computers after dinner. "Do you know that the lowest note in the universe is the sound of a dying galaxy? And that they even know what note it is? It's a B-flat, fifty-seven octaves below Middle C. Can you believe that? It's too low for a human to hear, and they say it's been playing for two and a half billion years."

"Wow," she replied. "No, I didn't know that."

"Huh," Liam grunted, reading the day's headlines.

"There's a super-massive black hole at the center of a cluster of galaxies that generates acoustic waves. It's two hundred and fifty million light years away."

"That's amazing," Rosemary said, turning to face him.

"I can't believe there's something like that that we can't hear, like they say there are colors we can't see because they're off the visible light spectrum. It's terrible, don't you think? How can there be all this stuff we can't see and hear? How can we go along living our stupid lives when there's all this stuff we can't see and hear?" He was beginning to get agitated, wiping his nose with the back of his hand.

"Our lives are stupid because our ears can't detect these sounds?" she asked.

"We see stuff and hear stuff and we think that's all there is, but that's obviously not true."

As Dylan's voice grew louder, Liam said, "But we never see everything. We can't know everything."

"But why not?" Dylan pleaded. "Don't you feel stupid only knowing a fraction of what there is to know, hearing only a tiny bit of the sounds being made?"

"No," Liam replied. "If we heard and saw and knew everything, there would be nothing left to learn. It might actually be boring."

"Boring?" Dylan shrieked. "Boring to know everything?"

"We would have no ambitions," Liam said, defending himself. "We wouldn't strive for anything."

But just when Rosemary thought Dylan would blow, his head tipped sharply to the left and he looked up toward the ceiling. "Actually," he said, "maybe we really are hearing it without realizing it, and if it stopped, we would suddenly feel empty, like something was missing."

"Yes, maybe that's so," Liam said, visibly relieved.

"OK," Dylan said, and abruptly walked away.

Although that exchange was a red flag for Liam, Rosemary

was more troubled by Dylan's reaction later that week to a sight at a parade. The pet parade, a pageant of animals and kids along with marching bands, community groups, and all manner of homegrown good will, was every kid's favorite part of Santa Fe's annual Fiesta celebration.

Rosemary and Dylan had arrived downtown an hour before the parade started to claim their usual place ar the curb on Palace Avenue, in front of High Desert Healthcare and Massage and across the street from where La Residencia Nursing Center used to be. Even though the nursing home had moved, attendants still brought a handful of old folks in wheelchairs to the shady sidewalk along the side of the building, in a cordoned off area. Seeing them, Rosemary ran through her usual train of thought when confronted with the elderly and infirm: Were they glad to still be alive, or were they sick of it all?

But a sound interrupted her thoughts, a sound that carried over the crowd of people who lined the streets in lawn chairs, sipping their Big Gulps and Ventis, laughing together and scolding their children to stay out of the street. An intermittent sound that had pitch but no melody, and Dylan heard it too. Soon they spotted its source: An ancient man in an old, ratty wheelchair was playing a clarinet. He was propelling himself west along Palace Avenue with his feet, digging his heels into the pavement just enough for the downward slope of the street to give him forward momentum. On the back of his wheelchair, in lettering made of reflective tape, were the words "2B or not 2B." Every few seconds, he played a note on his clarinet as he made his way down the street, progressing in his halting way past the area where La Residencia's elders were kept within their bounds.

Somehow he was ignored by the police motorcycles that patrolled the street, just as, somehow, he had seemingly dodged the fate of his confined contemporaries. Alone and disheveled, wildly vulnerable, the old man played on. At Cathedral Park on the next corner, he stowed his clarinet in a side bag, slowly got out of his wheelchair, and laboriously pushed it back up

Palace. When he got to the corner of Paseo de Peralta, he would turn the chair around, sit back down, and resume his playing. After the third pass, Rosemary realized the notes he played were not random—he was playing "As Time Goes By." The whole scene was astonishing, a feat that made her want to get the parade-goers up on their feet to cheer, but as far as she could tell, the onlookers regarded him only as an oddity to point at.

Once the parade started, the old man disappeared, but the memory of him preoccupied Dylan. He looked right through the dogs dressed as Harry Potter-style wizards, the turtle tanks pulled in Radio Flyer wagons, the Capital High volleyball team, the Santa Fe High ROTC, the Fiesta Court on horseback and elaborate floats in full period regalia. After a while, he stood up and said he wanted to walk around on his own, and Rosemary agreed. When they met up later on the Plaza, to wait in an endless line for breakfast burritos, Dylan's mood was unsettled.

"Why do you think that man was all alone?" he asked.

"I was wondering that too, if he has a son or daughter who's always begging him to stop going out there on the streets. Or maybe they live far away and have no idea how he spends his time. Maybe they don't ask or maybe he lies. Or maybe he really has no one."

"Would you ever have let Grandpa do that?"

"I don't know, Dylan. That man is an adult, and frankly, he seemed to really be enjoying himself. I don't know what the best thing for him would be."

"I looked everywhere for him."

"I figured that."

"But I couldn't find him."

"What would you have done if you found him?"

"I don't know. Maybe see if he needed any help."

"You're a good guy, Dylan, she said, hugging him to her. He pulled away quickly.

"What was with that '2B or not 2B' thing on his chair?"

"It's from Shakespeare, *Hamlet*. It's from a part in the play when the main character is considering suicide."

"So that old man might kill himself?"

"I doubt it, but who knows what goes through his mind?"

Dylan folded his arms over his chest and stared resolutely at the food booth's menu sign. Subject closed.

∽ ∽ ∽

A warbler sounded again and Rosemary was suddenly aware of how badly she needed to pee. She stood up, wriggled out of the sleeping bag, and walked down to the pit toilet. She'd forgotten to bring Purell. Gross. Afterward, she was still cold, so she maneuvered back into the sleeping bag and resumed her place at the picnic table. The sun would be over the rise soon.

From the outside, the accident had looked so simple and straightforward: a boy, a bike, a train, a few moments of confusion. But nothing about Dylan was simple and straightforward. She accepted that now.

Looking back, that day at Fiesta probably mattered more than she knew, but what had kept her up nights through the fall was the Black-Man-White-Lady-Scene.

Later in September, she, Liam, and Dylan were out for a bike ride in their neighborhood, taking part in what seemed to be another PFI moment: Pretty Fucking Idyllic.

As they passed a house, a white woman, probably in her fifties, was standing in her front yard, hands on hips, as a black man raked up weeds and plant debris. She was wearing a light-colored dress and a broad-brimmed hat; he was bare-headed and bare-chested, his broad back gleaming in the morning sun. He worked; she watched.

At the end of the block, Dylan skidded to a stop and said to them breathlessly, "Can you believe that? It looks like slavery was never abolished."

"Oh, you can't say that," she soothed. "We don't know the story behind that."

"What are you talking about? That was obviously racist."

"Actually—" Rosemary began, but he rode away in a huff

before she could finish. When she and Liam arrived home ten minutes later, his bike lay on the porch, and he was in his room with the shades drawn.

The topic came up again at dinner.

"Maybe the woman pays the guy well and he's glad for the work," Liam said dismissively.

"Right," Dylan sneered. "So she stands there like an overseer."

"Maybe she loves to garden, but she has a bad back, so she needs help," Rosemary offered. "She watches because she wants to feel a part of it."

"You know that's not what it seemed like, Mom."

"Maybe she was doing just as much work as him, but when we rode by she was taking a little break," Liam said. "Or maybe he owns the house and she's a landscape designer, giving him advice. Maybe she's working for him."

"I know what I saw," Dylan said darkly.

"Or they're married," Rosemary broke in brightly. "He takes care of the outside and she takes care of the inside. She'd been cleaning the oven and came outside for some fresh air."

"He looked a lot younger than her," Dylan argued. "There's no way they were married."

"Well, we were pretty far away. Who really knows?" she said.

"I know what I saw!"

"Actually, you don't," Liam pressed. "You saw two people, the black guy working and the white woman not working, and that's it. You didn't see the whole story. You saw a moment in time with your own subjective point of view."

Dylan dropped his eyes to his plate, glumly shoveling lasagna into his mouth as Rosemary and Liam had fun trading ideas on the story behind the scene.

"Maybe he's volunteering from some church or something," Liam said.

"Or they're best friends. He helps her with yard work and she does his sewing."

"He lost a bet, and this is the payment."

"He's her adopted son—he's just helping out his ma."

"He's a dowser, and he discovered a freshwater spring, right there on that spot."

"No, they discovered oil."

"It's all a hologram. Really there's nothing there."

"Just a wrinkle in the time-space continuum."

"A wormhole, actually, to another dimension."

"He's Doctor Who."

"And she's Rose Tyler."

"Or they're explorers. They found a treasure map under a floorboard, and there's a sack of Spanish eight buried under her tulips."

"The Ouija board led them to it."

"No, they murdered the dowager countess, stole her jewels, and were taking turns digging her shallow grave."

"No, they were practicing for their new improv tour. Minutes later, the scene changed. . . ."

"To an elevator, and they were ad execs competing for the same job."

"Actually, raking is the new workout craze. It was all R & D."

"Yes, forget the Nordic track. . . ."

"And the rowing machines. . . ."

"They were out there measuring ergs."

"And joules, because it's not just a crossword word anymore!"

"It's the new Rakeover Makeover Machine!"

As they laughed and high-fived each other, Dylan slammed down his fork in tears. "You have no idea how horrible you two sound!" he shouted. "A black man was being treated like an animal, and you make jokes about it!"

"Dylan," Rosemary began.

Liam looked out the window, sighing loudly.

"Dylan, this is 2009, in Santa Fe, New Mexico. No black people are being treated like animals."

"You just don't want to face the ugly truth!" he shouted, pushing his hair back roughly.

"And you don't want to face the beautiful truth that whatever we saw there had about a thousand possibilities," she said.

"I know what I saw!" he shouted and stomped off to his room.

After a moment, in the ringing silence, Rosemary said, "Someone has a rather fixed point of view, does he not?"

"I think we're in some deep shit with this guy."

"And I really thought it was getting better."

A few weeks after the dinner explosion came the second phone call from school, this one scaring her so much that she had her first panic attack in nearly a year.

"Mrs. Ellis?" asked the voice, just as she was about to step out to lunch.

"This is she."

"Mrs. Ellis, this is Principal Jaston, and I need to inform you that your son, Dylan, defied school personnel a few minutes ago and left the premises."

"He left?"

"Yes, Mrs. Ellis. When a lunch duty supervisor informed him that he did not have permission to lounge on the grass, which is outside the perimeter of the outdoor recreational area, he hopped the fence and walked away."

"He walked away?"

"Yes, Mrs. Ellis, and when the lunch duty supervisor called after him, he took off at a run. I'm afraid I have no idea where he's gone."

She called Liam and they sped over to the school's neighborhood and drove the streets for over an hour, looking for Dylan. He would not answer his cell, and they were frantic. Finally Rosemary got the idea to check at home, so they raced back to Cielo Vista and there was the kid, slumped in a bean bag chair, watching Simpsons reruns on his laptop. After fleeing from school, he'd run to Kristopher's house, taken a bike out of the garage, and ridden home to Cielo Vista on the shoulder of I-25.

"What the hell are you doing?" Liam shouted. He shoved Dylan's computer aside, yanked him to his feet, and shook him violently. "Do you have any idea how worried we've been? Do you have any idea how badly you screwed up today?"

"I had to leave!" Dylan whined, his body lurching forward and back in Liam's grasp. "I just had to get out of that hellhole!"

"It is not a hellhole, it is a school! And you are a spoiled brat who needs to get a grip on reality!" Liam shoved the boy backward onto the bed, then yanked him to his feet again. "You need to go to school! This is not negotiable!"

"I hate that school!"

"Tough! Deal with it!"

"Let go of me!"

He released Dylan, who fell to the bed again.

"If you hate it that much, then apply your superhuman intelligence and go somewhere better!" Liam barked. He grabbed Dylan's laptop and slammed the door behind him as he left.

Rosemary watched the exchange from the hallway, oddly detached. It was the first time she'd ever seen Liam be at all violent with Dylan, but she had no objection. He deserved their anger, and he did need to get a grip on reality.

Dylan was home for the next week on out-of-school suspension, a "consequence" that was truly laughable. "Make no mistake, Mrs. Ellis, the kids hate to be isolated," Mr. Jaston declared. "They might enjoy being home for a holiday or a weekend, but they don't like missing the action when all their friends are at school."

Right, Mr. Jaston. Thanks.

Liam stayed home to monitor Dylan that week, working only in the afternoons after Rosemary got home. She offered to take some sick time or to see if she could work from home, but Liam insisted on the arrangement with a simple explanation: "This is best."

She didn't argue. She certainly had no bright ideas about how to proceed with their son, and frankly, some days she was happy to put the whole issue out of her mind. Liam had told her for years that she needed to learn to compartmentalize, that her obsessing didn't help anything.

"It's all about the serenity prayer," he was fond of saying.

"But that doesn't work for me!" she'd insisted, popping a handful of melatonin as he quickly drifted off to sleep. "I wasn't given the wisdom to tell the difference!"

And while Rosemary still believed she lacked that wisdom, she was indeed getting better at compartmentalizing, at no longer trying to control everything. She began to utter a new mantra in the evenings: "I did all I could for the good of my family today, and now it's time to rest." She said that aloud, around 9 p.m. each day, and then she relaxed. Chatted with her boys, watched a movie, read a book. She did not worry about money, or about Dylan, or about her mom, or her quarrels with Deet, or her weight, or forest fires, or her marriage . . .and the world kept turning.

Plus, things had happened lately that served to further divorce her from her monkey-mind habits. Her friend Caroline got cancer—mad cancer, as Caroline's twenty-something son had put it, shaking his head sadly next to a watermelon bin at the farmers' market. And seven months after she was diagnosed, she died.

Of course, other people in Rosemary's life had died; that wasn't the strange part. What was strange is that Caroline's best friend, Rose, had pulled together a huge fundraiser to help defray Caroline's medical expenses and to pay for alternative treatments. Inside of a month, Rose and several other of Caroline's closest friends got bazillions of donations and conjured up a huge auction and dinner that raised $30,000. But Caroline still died. For a few loving friends to find that much money in a month, in a city as small as Santa Fe, seemed nothing short of magical. But that it did not ultimately contribute to Caroline's survival—what did that mean? What was money, anyway?

Rosemary used to imagine money as a foundation of bricks upon which to build a safe life, a bulwark against the floods of potential disaster. But now it seemed that the water itself was the money, an amorphous river of energy that people spent their lives trying to direct their own way, and her new job only confirmed that suspicion. The foundation she worked for owned a watershed of assets, which formed tributaries of income, which fed a river of money, and her job was to direct that flow into certain irrigation ditches. The grant applicants—the "gardeners"—had to strike a balance of appearing neither too parched nor too saturated to qualify for a portion of that water. Their projects—the incipient children's theaters, the micro-credit loan centers, the community wells that would stop the spread of typhus—needed to appear wonderfully rich in potential, requiring only that she open the sluice for their many seeds to burst into flower.

Of course not every watershed was vast. There was Canada, and then there was the Sahara. The water was still uneven and confusing, but it all flowed along. And it changed. Some people's reservoirs drained and others were formed, seemingly overnight. But those who were used to playing in the river seemed to know how to create and recreate their own reservoirs. Rosemary was watching the projects and the funders, and learning.

Seeds bursting into flower. Actually, this was how she had always viewed Dylan, as a small mass of soil holding an innumerable variety of seeds. Books, outings, sports, art, nature, her endless attention—these were the fertilizer with which she enriched the soil of his young self. She'd always believed it was up to her to make sure that Dylan's talents came into fruition, but that was changing now. He was thirteen—it was getting on time for him to start watering his own seeds, or at least it was time for Liam to do the tending for a while. Some days she missed her role as the center of her son's life, but most days—zooming off to work with a cup of coffee in her hand, planning the agenda for a board meeting, wording an email to a grant recipient in her head—she was pleased with the change. How many times when Dylan was little did she envy Liam's role in going off to work every day? She would make his lunch and kiss him goodbye and watch his truck back out of the driveway. Even after he was out of sight, she and Dylan would keep watching through the living room window at a certain thicket of trees, across the greenbelt, where they would see his pickup again as he sped along.

Liam made sure the out-of-school suspension was productive, keeping Dylan on track with the assignments Rosemary ferried from and to school. He got his son up at 7 a.m. every day, cooked him fried eggs and toast, and had him sit at the dining room table until all his school work was done. Although they barely spoke on Monday, by midweek they had softened to each other. Wednesday afternoon, Dylan helped Liam sand new bookshelves for the den, and on Thursday, they built frames for the beehives Liam had always wanted. On Friday, they dropped off the last of Dylan's school work, rented a raft, and drove up to the little town of Pilar, where they began paddling down the Rio Grande to Española.

"Now there's a tough punishment," Rosemary sniped.

"It's supposed to be about rehabilitation, right?"

"Whatever you say."

By Saturday they were an unstoppable duo, like an infatuated couple who couldn't get enough of each other.

"I don't know what's going on here, but I'm enjoying it," Liam said as he pumped up their bike tires. He had extracted a promise from Dylan that he would never bike along the Interstate again, never, ever, ever, and in exchange promised to show him a better bike route to town.

"Go Dad," she said.

"The guy is actually a lot of fun to be with."

Like she didn't know that.

Dylan helped Liam insert a healthy dose of sealant into the tires to keep them from going flat from the billions of poky things they'd encounter on the trail, which ran along the railroad tracks. Kristopher's dad would drop him off at Dylan's house so the three could ride up the trail together.

"The trail is sandy and hilly in places, but most of it's level and firm, and it goes through some really pretty areas," Liam explained. "And Kristopher lives pretty close to Santa Fe High School, where the tracks run. I'll show you two how to get to his house. It's easy."

"Sounds great, Dad!"

So they took off, and Rosemary headed out to deadhead her day lilies.

An hour later, she answered the phone to hear Liam scream, "Meet me at the hospital!

CHAPTER 16 | OCTOBER, 2009

Joshua Tree National Park, California

HOW IS IT THAT THERE WERE NO CARS ON THE ROAD THAT morning? No bargain hunters looking for garage sales, no octogenarian on his way to the post office, no teen-ager learning to drive a stick. Open roads out of Cielo Vista, I-25 virtually empty, and all green lights down St. Michael's Drive.

Rosemary parked in the first space she saw and tore into the Emergency Room, but neither Dylan nor Liam was there.

"My son has been injured!" she shrieked at the triage nurse, who was helping a hugely fat woman complete a form. "His name is Dylan Ellis! Where is he?" she shouted over the mountain of flesh.

"Ma'am, please. I'll be with you in a moment."

"But it's my son, where is he?"

"Ma'am!" the nurse scolded.

The mountain of flesh turned toward Rosemary, and the women locked eyes.

"Your son is here?" the mountain asked.

"Somewhere, yes. My husband called me and told me to meet them here."

"Oh!" the woman gasped, clasping a hand over the hillocks of her bosom. "Take her first."

"No children have been brought in this morning," the nurse announced, looking at her computer screen.

"What? How can that be?"

"I don't know, Ma'am. I just know that I've been here since 6 a.m. and no children have been brought into the E.R."

What did that mean? Had he been brought to the morgue instead? No, stop that, Rosemary. Stop that!

"He's thirteen. Is that still considered a child?" she asked.

"Name again?"

"Dylan Ellis."

"There's no one here by that name, Ma'am."

"How could that be?" she asked, growing desperate.

"An ambulance is en route. An accident at the train tracks. Could that be your son?"

"At the train tracks?" Her chest heaved, and the room began to whirl.

The flesh mountain stood up, took Rosemary's hands in hers, and maneuvered her into the chair. "Breathe," she said. "Breathe."

"That's all I know," the nurse stated.

The woman locked eyes with Rosemary. "Breathe with me," she said soothingly. "Breathe in?" Her voice rose like a question. She inhaled with her eyes locked on Rosemary's. And then she exhaled, announcing as if she'd answered her own question, "and out."

Pause.

"In?" Again an inhalation. "And out." The exhalation.

"You're doing great," the mountain-angel said, her eyes trained on Rosemary like a birthing coach. "One more time."

After another round of angel-led breathing, Liam burst into the waiting area, his shirt bloody, his face pale and stricken.

"Ro!" he shouted.

"Thank you," Rosemary said, squeezing the angel's hand as she leaped out of the chair and turned to Liam. "What happened? Where is he?"

"He'll be OK!"

"What happened?"

Liam grabbed her by the shoulders and clung to her. "He'll be OK," he said and began to weep. "He'll be OK."

Liam wiped his eyes and explained that Dylan had tumbled down an embankment and flipped over his handlebars. He'd landed flat on his back, unconscious. But although he came to just a minute or two later, he quickly went into shock, probably from the pain. His leg was most likely broken, and possibly some ribs—he'd fallen into a clump of rocks and cactus. He'd also gotten a gash in his left arm from the cactus he fell on. Liam had tied up the wound with his sweatshirt.

"He's going to be OK, right?"

"To see him lying there so hurt!"

"It's OK. . . ."

He continued to sob loudly, his face buried in her neck, but finally pulled away to wipe his face with the back of his hand. He looked around the waiting room, at the clumps of forlorn people unabashedly staring at them, and paused. He ran his hands through his hair, took her elbow, and led her to the automatic doors to the treatment rooms just as a nurse was coming out and let them in.

"So the ambulance finally found us," Liam continued, his voice lower. "But there was no way for it to maneuver all the way to the tracks, so they had to carry him about a quarter-mile on a stretcher, which is why you got here before we did."

"Oh my God, where is he?"

"Down this hall."

"Is he conscious?"

"Sort of, but the EMTs stabilized him and gave him something, so he's calm now."

"Oh my God, Liam, I can't believe this is happening," she said, her step quickening. "Where's Kris?"

"His parents were in the parking lot when I got here, and they took him home. They said they would go get the bikes. But wait, listen to me a minute." He pulled her aside into an empty patient area, with its glaring lights and expectant whiteness.

"What are you doing? We need to go to him."

"Yeah, we do, but I need to tell you something first. Look, the reason he tumbled down the embankment is because a train was coming, the old Lamy train. I heard it coming, but we were all on the trail, like twenty yards from the tracks. He and Kris were a ways ahead of me. They kept daring each other, racing down the hills, jumping over clumps of rock or whatever, and it was fine. But then Dylan went up onto the tracks. On purpose, Ro. He rode up the embankment. First I thought he just wanted to push himself a little, to get up the slope, or get a better look at something, but he got up there on purpose and stopped on the tracks!" Liam's voice started to rise again. "The train blew its horn at him, Kris was yelling at him, and I could see the whole thing. I was yelling at him to get off the tracks and trying to catch up to him and the train was blowing the horn and he just stood there on his bike! He just stood there!" Liam began to cry again. "I dropped my bike and ran up the hill, but at the last minute he rode down the other side. I couldn't get to him because the train was passing. I heard him yell as he lost control and then I heard him hit, but I couldn't get to him because the fucking train was passing! The fucking train! I'm screaming at him, and I can see him a little between the cars, and I can hear the tourists in the open car yelling, but I can't get to him! Finally the train passes and I run down and there he is, unconscious. I thought he was dead!"

He began to sob anew, but when she reached out to comfort him he pushed her gently away.

"I'm fine," he said, exhaling loudly. "I didn't tell the EMTs all that, but we need to face this, what he did. When he's stable and whatever, we need to face this."

Rosemary felt as if a deadening cloud enveloped her, muffling her senses, filling her eyes and ears with a great inchoate fog. She leaned back into the wall and slowly slumped down to a sitting position on the floor.

"Come on, not now," Liam said, grabbing her hand and trying to pull her up. "We need to get in there."

She looked at him from far away in her new insensate condition. What did he want, and why was he pulling on her?

"Ro!"

It was not pleasant to have him pulling on her.

Liam shouted something again, locked his hands under her arms, and pulled her to her feet like a stubborn child.

"Now!" he shouted, and began gently slapping her face, first the left cheek, then the right, the left, the right, back and forth until she got so annoyed she slapped him back. They stood there dazed, looking at each other in confusion.

"OK," she said. "Let's go."

Dylan lay on a bed in the treatment room with an oxygen mask on his face, an IV in his arm, and a mob of scrubs-clad people around him. Rosemary couldn't tell who was in charge; everyone seemed to be on his or her own personal mission. Eventually a man approached them.

"I'm Doctor Evans," he said. "We need to get—Dylan, is it?—to Radiology, to look at that leg, and the ribs, but the EKG is good and I see no signs of internal bleeding. It's a good thing he was wearing a helmet, because even with that, he has a concussion. We can't be sure of anything until we see the x-rays, but I believe he'll be fine."

Both Rosemary and Liam exhaled deeply.

"He's quite torn up from those cactus—he's already swelling up quite a bit—but it's nothing that won't heal. I do want to watch him, though, since you say he lost consciousness. We'll definitely need to admit him."

"OK," they said in unison.

"You'll need to go to Admitting and do the paperwork. I suggest one of you stay with your son while the other deals with the insurance and whatnot."

"OK," they said again.

Rosemary stared at the doctor blankly, unclear what to do next.

"I'll stay with him," Liam spoke up. "They might need information about the accident."

"Good. Please excuse me," Dr. Evans said, walking away.

"OK," she said, still staring in his direction.

"Go back to that desk, Ro, and I'm sure they'll tell you what to do next," Liam said.

She looked over toward Dylan, trying to find his face through the small mob around him.

Dylan, my Dylan!

"Ro, go," Liam said, guiding her gently toward the door.

She retraced her steps to the triage nurse, hoping to see her angel, but the woman was gone. She handed over the insurance cards, filled out a raft of forms, used the restroom, and then found her way back to the trauma room, but it was empty.

"Your son is in Radiology, Ma'am," someone in scrubs said. "I suggest you go to the waiting room on the lower level. When he's done in Radiology, they'll wheel him by there, and you'll be able to catch up with him."

Rosemary found the waiting room and sat heavily in a fake leather chair, still feeling that anesthetizing fog. Busy people whisked here and there, pushing beds and chairs and carts, saying things to each other, buzzing through doors. What a strange place to be on a Saturday morning.

She was in a hospital. Because Dylan had been hurt. But according to Liam, there was more going on than some broken bones and a concussion. Could he be right? Did Dylan really go up onto those tracks on purpose? Maybe his wheel got stuck. Maybe he was just trying to get a better glimpse of a bird—a hawk, probably—and his wheel got stuck.

Dylan had seemed so happy lately. He had finally emerged from his room, was getting exercise out in the sun, spending time with his dad. He was even caught up on his school work. Why—especially now—would he pull a stunt like this? A suicidal stunt?

The word "suicidal" made her stomach lurch, and a sting of bile rose in her throat. She fixed her eyes on a blue wispy circle within an abstract painting on the wall and breathed. She wished her fat angel were there to help. Breathe, Rosemary. Your son is alive; he'll be fine. There had to be an explanation for this. When he was fully conscious, they would talk and she would understand and everything would be fine.

All right, panic attack averted. Fog dissipating, for now.

So her son was in the hospital. This was new. He'd never been seriously sick or injured before. Neither had anyone else in the family, really, except for her freak coma so many years ago.

Right, the family. She should call Martina and Deet, let them know what was going on, and Liam's mom, Jean, and his sister, Gwen. What a weird thing to have to do. She wished her dad were there to take charge, to assure everyone that everything would be all right. Oh, Dad.

Just then an electric door swung open and Liam entered the hallway, walking next to Dylan's bed wheeled by a woman in scrubs. Rosemary hurried toward them.

"Hey," Liam said, squeezing her hand. "They're taking him to his room, Room 333, and in a little while, we'll know the results from his x-rays."

"Hi, buddy," she said, tears springing to her eyes. Dylan's eyes fluttered and he managed a little smile. She clasped his hand in hers as the bed was whisked along the corridor. "It's so good to see you." Oh, this kid! Her chest ached with love and worry. "You're going to be OK, you know. You know that, right?"

He nodded slightly and then winced. "Everything hurts," he said thickly.

"I understand. You don't have to talk."

"He's been through quite a lot today, haven't you, Dylan?" the scrub-clad woman said loudly.

Dylan grunted.

They got into an elevator along with another woman in scrubs who was pushing a cart with some machine on it.

"Hola, chica!" the cart scrub said. "What time you here till?"

"Off at two. You?"

"Six."

"Well all right," the cart scrub said, pushing the 2 button. "All right."

They rode in silence to the second floor, where the cart clattered over the gap.

"You have a good one!" both scrub women said simultaneously, and the door closed again.

Scrub girls actually, hardly women, Rosemary thought. She was older than both of them. In fact, she was probably older than Dr. Evans, too. Shit, to be escorting your teen-age son through a hospital was such a grim, grown-up thing to do. She looked over at Liam. He'd aged ten years since that morning.

Another doctor, Dr. Alvarez, gave them the test results: a broken right femur and two broken ribs. They would set the leg within the hour.

Dylan slept fitfully, kicking off the sheets. Although welts and abrasions dotted his arms and legs, his face had emerged unscathed. Rosemary watched in silence as he drifted in and out of sleep, his undamaged face presiding over his wounded body like a shiny bell tower on a bombed-out church. He could have died in that accident. If his helmet had been too loose, if an artery had been cut, if he hadn't gotten his wheel unstuck from the train tracks at the last instant. Dead! Her son!

Liam drifted off, slumped in a chair, as soon as the doctor left. He looked like a shooting victim in his bloody sweatshirt. What an ordeal the man had been through! Just the thought of seeing Dylan on the tracks with that train approaching, watching through the gaps as he fell to the ground, waiting to get to him, calling 911, tying up the wound—good Lord, that was too much for anyone. Yet he had done all the right things. He had saved their son's life. A flood of gratitude almost knocked her off her feet. Dylan's bike wheel came unstuck in time, and Liam had done the right things. Their son was alive!

ॐ   ॐ   ॐ

Rosemary felt the sun on her back and realized she was sweating. For how long had she been sitting at this picnic table wrapped in a sleeping bag? The coffee was cold and her legs were stiff. It had been a common problem lately, losing great swaths of time that could not be accounted for. She peeled off the bag and her fleece jacket, splashed water on her face, and turned her phone on. Nearly twenty texts instantly downloaded and there were six voicemails from Liam asking if she had arrived safely. The messages grew steadily more frantic through the night. Shit, she was supposed to text him when she arrived. How could she have forgotten? "Sorry to worry you," she messaged. "I'm here. Got Jumbo Rocks #38. You OK?" When he did not respond she set the phone aside.

She had a maximum of nine days to be away, including one to drive back, but she should probably return sooner. Liam needed some time alone too, but not that much. And she would be bringing her mother back to Santa Fe with her. Martina had called nearly constantly since the accident. She was a wreck. She and Dylan would be good for each other once he was back home.

Fourteen days in a pediatric psych ward for suicidal behavior. No contact with the outside world. No sharp objects.

And no bicycles.

She and Liam had fought bitterly the day after the accident over whether to tell the doctors about his actions that day on the railroad tracks, his behavior in the months before. She thought that they, his parents, should take care of him, that only they could reach him. She didn't want him on drugs, didn't want him in the "system." She'd tried to get to the bottom of it, to get Dylan to say once and for all what happened out there, but he was evasive, claimed he couldn't remember. She was convinced he was lying, convinced that Liam wanted to believe the worst, convinced the doctors weren't seeing her son for who he truly was. He wasn't some list of symptoms; he wasn't a "case." He was a highly intelligent boy who saw the world differently from the norm, who felt the world differently. Sure, he was disengaged at school. How many seventh-graders were eager young scholars? Sure, he was disaffected much of the time. Who wasn't? The world was a discordant mess, and he just felt that fact too deeply. Maybe he was healthier than all of them because he wasn't willing to push aside all the bullshit that the well-adjusted masses casually accepted.

"But he's a danger to himself," Liam argued.

"His tire got stuck," she insisted.

"Then why didn't he call for help?"

"Maybe he did. How could you hear him over the noise of an oncoming train?"

"Why didn't he get off the bike and yank at the tire?"

"He's a kid. He wasn't thinking clearly."

"Why didn't he just leave the bike and step off the tracks?"

"He loves that bike. It was a birthday present."

"He loves the bike more than his life?"

"It was a scary, confusing moment for him."

"He's a depressed adolescent who's a danger to himself. He needs medical treatment, professional help."

"You're selling him out! You're caving into the world of Western medicine. We just need to get him outdoors, go camping in the mountains. Let him hear the river instead of the TV, feel the earth beneath his feet, see the stars at night."

"You're in denial!"

"You're a bastard!"

Liam told Dr. Alvarez everything on Sunday afternoon, without her consent, and Rosemary was sure she would never forgive him, could never trust him again. She would certainly file for divorce, but first she had to fight for her son, to protect him from the doctor who sought to turn his brilliance and sensitivity into a bland compliance. Then Alvarez brought in a psychiatrist, Dr. Woodson, and she presented her arguments to him too, but he was unimpressed. When he couldn't be reached on Sunday night, she left him several long, ranting voicemails. They met again briefly on Monday morning.

"Mrs. Ellis, with all due respect, I must say you are overreacting," Dr. Woodson asserted. "We need to keep Dylan safe as we learn what's troubling him. There is no shame in this."

"But he's my son; he's not your patient!" she shouted, knowing she was losing the fight.

"He'll still be your son at the end of fourteen days."

Ultimately, it was a conversation with a nurse that convinced her that Liam and Alvarez and the shrink were right, that her son had slipped into terra incognita, that he needed something his parents could not provide.

The nurse, Kim, said she had been chatting with Dylan as she changed his bandages, remarking at the many welts the cactus spines had caused.

"He said they were no big deal," Kim told Rosemary and Liam. "He said they were a small price to pay for a little meringue, and he couldn't wait to get out of the hospital to find some more meringue because it was so damned cool."

Rosemary was stricken, Liam confused.

"I didn't know what he meant by that," Kim continued. "But when I asked him, he just laughed."

Meringue! The little fucker was going for extremes. He had done this on purpose! All that bike riding wasn't about exercise, his gutsy moves at the stunt place weren't about the risks that all adolescents take believing they are immortal, and his wheel had not gotten stuck on the railroad tracks. This was something else. Liam was right. She was wrong. She was way out of her league with this boy whom she thought she knew so well.

They signed the papers on Monday afternoon to commit their son to a psychiatric facility.

When they told Dylan, he was furious. He hauled himself out of the hospital bed like a drunken bear cub and tried to punch things, but was easily subdued. Throughout the rage and screaming that followed, Rosemary stayed unentangled in his protestations, did not apologize for their decision. They kissed him goodbye. They were crying, but they did it.

The next morning, the question "How could he do this to me?" hovered overhead, ready to steal her resolve, but she shoved it aside. This was not about her. This was not about betrayal. This was not about failure. She had been a good mother. They had been good parents and would continue to be, though they would have to accept the help of a few professionals for a while. Life was just hard sometimes. And it certainly wasn't fair.

As they sat stiffly over coffee in their unnaturally quiet house, Liam ventured, "You know what your main man Greg Brown would say about this, don't you?"

"No, what would Greg say?"

"'Life is a thump-ripe melon, so sweet and such a mess.'"

"Yeah," she agreed with a half-hearted chuckle. "Good one." A few moments later she said, "I've had different lyrics of his in my head the past few days."

"Oh yeah? Which?"

"Sometimes in this world I'm wondering that we ain't grateful for every breath, sometimes in this world I'm wondering that we all don't just drink ourselves to death."

"Yeah," Liam said with his own half-hearted chuckle. "Good one."

⤦ ⤦ ⤦

Rosemary unpacked the rest of her gear. As she snapped the hatchback closed, she stopped to look at her car, the terribly expensive hybrid that she had maintained in pristine condition for two years. What it needed was a good whack with a ball peen hammer.

The day was lovely—warm and with a light breeze that whispered of better days. She changed her clothes, found some food, and settled back into the breakfast nook to survey the campsite, this place that had been her spiritual home base for so many years. It was just what she needed—quiet and spare, like a monk's chamber, only outdoors. Here she would be on terra firma again. Here was a foundation like the one Thoreau spoke of. She needed to go deep, "below freshet and frost and fire," to understand the truth of her life and plan her next steps. There she would be able to breathe, to find comfort and clarity.

But instead her chest began to pound. Something was off, something was wrong. Yes, this was her place, but suddenly, somehow, it was not where she belonged. Suddenly, it was time to go. No, she would not spend the night here, nor the coming days. It was time to go.

Rosemary stood up and marveled at the shift that had swept over her. Standing felt good. Maybe she would go for a walk. Yes, moving her body would be good. And then she would visit her mom, in her new condo. They would drive back to Santa Fe together, maybe even tomorrow, and she and Liam and Martina would be together in the days ahead. She would call Deet and invite him to visit. Maybe Liam's mom or sister would fly out. She might return to work sooner than she'd planned, or she might not. She didn't need to know right now. She would feel it out, take it as it came. But she would not be alone.

Rosemary scrambled up the rock face, pleased with the strength and responsiveness of her limbs. As she pulled herself over the rim, feeling suddenly light and calm, she saw a cloud of dust boiling up from a speeding car in the distance. It was just 8:30—who would be speeding into Joshua Tree at this hour?

As the car reeled along the snaking park road, Rosemary thought with amusement that if she were fifteen years old, or even twenty, she would imagine the car was coming for her, that she was special enough and singular enough to warrant some mysterious envoy—from where?—to seek her out in this remote place. But that time of her life was over. She wasn't special, she wasn't blessed, and she wasn't destined for greatness. She knew that now. When she was younger, the specter of being fallible and unremarkable would terrify her, like being buried alive in an unmarked grave. But now it looked welcoming, like a calm, flat plane. Like a good place for a long walk.

The car's engine grew louder. It seemed to be headed her way. She watched in disbelief as it stopped at her site and Liam tore out of the driver's seat.

"Ro!" he shouted. "Ro!"

"Liam? Liam! What are you doing here?" She scrambled back down the boulders and ran to him.

"Ro, oh God, I was so worried." He hugged her tightly to him.

"What? What's wrong?"

"All last night you wouldn't answer your phone! Oh God, I'm so relieved." He hugged her tightly again in a deep, grateful embrace.

Then he pulled roughly away and began shaking her by the shoulders. "I was afraid you were dead! Why didn't you answer your phone?"

"I'm so sorry, Liam, I'm so sorry. How did you get here?"

"I flew into Palm Springs and rented a car. I couldn't take it. I was afraid you were, I don't know, gonna commit suicide or something. Goddamn it, Ro! Why didn't you answer your phone?"

"I'm sorry, Liam, I'm so sorry."

"You drive seven hundred miles alone, you're an emotional wreck, and you don't communicate!"

"Oh God, Liam. I turned my phone off. People kept calling and I wanted to be alone. But I texted you this morning."

"Well I didn't get it. I was on a plane, I guess, or driving ninety miles an hour."

"I can't believe you're here."

"Yeah," he said, rubbing his eyes. "I'm here. And I'm exhausted. That was a hellish night. Goddamn it, Ro!"

"I don't know what to say, except that I screwed up. I'm so sorry."

"Yeah, it's OK."

"Liam, you came all this way."

"I was freaking out."

"I can't believe you did this."

"Well, I did it."

"Thank you," she said, looking into his bloodshot eyes.

"You're welcome, I guess." He exhaled deeply and looked around the campsite. "Well if it isn't the old homestead."

"Yeah, it doesn't change much, does it."

"No, but we change."

"Yes, we do."

"Where's the tent?"

"I slept out last night."

"You're kidding! In October?"

"I was pretty cold when I woke up."

"Are you OK?"

"I think so. How are you?"

"I'll feel better when I sleep. I feel so foolish being here. I guess I panicked."

"It seems so—unlike you."

"Well these are strange times."

"They are. But you know? I'm really glad to see you."

"Thanks," he smiled. "But I'm intruding."

"Nah."

"No, I am."

"We're going to be OK, you know."

"I hope you're right."

"Things feel better today."

"How long are you going to be here?"

"I was going to take a walk and head out."

"Out where?"

"Leave. This isn't where I need to be right now. I was wrong. We need to be together, and my mom needs us. We can spend the night at her place."

"You're kidding."

"No, I'm not. Suddenly, it just feels like time to go."

Liam's face relaxed, and he reached for her hand.

"That sounds really good to me."

Rosemary looked around to take in the place she loved so well. Sunlight shone like gilt on the desert brush, and long shadows filled the empty spaces between countless outcroppings of rock. It was so expansive, so beautiful. Facing east, she squinted into the low sun and was glad to be alive. She was a survivor now, like one of those people she'd see on television after a natural disaster. A tornado rips through a neighborhood, and a woman stands in front of what used to be her home. Unshowered, unscripted, unflinching, she stands amid the splintered door frames, the shards of sheetrock, the piles of brick that were a chimney only yesterday, and tells a reporter, "We'll just have to rebuild."

Rosemary had always marveled at those people, the ones she sent old blankets and canned food to in the drives that always followed those tragedies. How were they so resolute, so positive, so tough? Why weren't they kicking around the smashed kitchen cabinets, yelling, "Why me?" Why weren't they crying over the destroyed dining room set that they hadn't even paid off yet? Why weren't they stricken, aggrieved, furious that ill fortune had found them like a heat-seeking missile, trashed their security and all they had worked for, and left them to pick up the pieces? But there they stood amid the exposed wreckage of their unexceptional lives, in ill-fitting clothes from the emergency shelter, with kids on their hips and elderly parents slumped on cinder blocks, calmly stating that they would just rebuild, that the community would rebuild. And presumably, they did.

They were that family now. Together she and Liam would sift through the huge pile of debris—figure out what to keep, what to chuck, what to have hauled away. And then they would rebuild.

Barbara Gerber

B arbara Gerber has had a love affair with words since she learned to read. In her work as a writer, teacher, editor, coach, and presenter, the power of "the story" has been paramount in her life. In addition to placing her own journalistic work in local and national publications, Gerber enjoys working with students, friends, and clients as they craft their own writing, helping to elucidate their messages and bring forth the stories that need to be told.

It was during a 2007 vacation with her husband and two children at Joshua Tree National Park that this book began to take shape. At times since that idyllic week of hiking and camping, it seemed as the story developed that Rosemary and her family were living in Gerber's own home. A sequel to *Love and Death in a Perfect World* is already in the works.

Originally from Seaford, New York, Gerber earned a degree in English literature from San Francisco State University and has lived in Santa Fe, New Mexico, since 1987. After working in management and marketing in the natural foods industry, she shifted into freelance writing and then became a teacher in 2004. This is her first novel.